The Rogue Who Rescued Her

THE BRETHREN
THE SERIES

USA TODAY BESTSELLER

CHRISTI CALDWELL

The Rogue Who Rescued Her
The Brethren Series

Copyright © 2018 by Christi Caldwell

For more information about the author:
www.christicaldwellauthor.com
christicaldwellauthor@gmail.com
Twitter: @ChristiCaldwell
Or on Facebook at: Christi Caldwell Author

For first glimpse at covers, excerpts, and free bonus material, be sure to sign up for my monthly newsletter!

Printed in the USA.

Cover Design and Interior Format

Other Titles by
Christi Caldwell

HEART OF A DUKE
In Need of a Duke—Prequel Novella
For Love of the Duke
More than a Duke
The Love of a Rogue
Loved by a Duke
To Love a Lord
The Heart of a Scoundrel
To Wed His Christmas Lady
To Trust a Rogue
The Lure of a Rake
To Woo a Widow
To Redeem a Rake
One Winter with a Baron
To Enchant a Wicked Duke
Beguiled by a Baron
To Tempt a Scoundrel

THE HEART OF A SCANDAL
In Need of a Knight—Prequel Novella
Schooling the Duke

LORDS OF HONOR
Seduced by a Lady's Heart
Captivated by a Lady's Charm
Rescued by a Lady's Love
Tempted by a Lady's Smile

SCANDALOUS SEASONS
Forever Betrothed, Never the Bride
Never Courted, Suddenly Wed

Always Proper, Suddenly Scandalous
Always a Rogue, Forever Her Love
A Marquess for Christmas
Once a Wallflower, at Last His Love

SINFUL BRIDES
The Rogue's Wager
The Scoundrel's Honor
The Lady's Guard
The Heiress's Deception
The Wicked Wallflowers
The Hellion
The Vixen
The Governess
The Bluestocking

THE THEODOSIA SWORD
Only For His Lady
Only For Her Honor
Only For Their Love

DANBY
A Season of Hope
Winning a Lady's Heart

THE BRETHREN
The Spy Who Seduced Her
The Lady Who Loved Him

BRETHREN OF THE LORDS
My Lady of Deception
Her Duke of Secrets
A Regency Duet
Rogues Rush In
Memoir: Non-Fiction
Uninterrupted Joy

CHAPTER 1

Winter, 1821
Kent

THE WORLD HAD NEVER THOUGHT much of Lord Sheldon Graham Malin Whitworth.

When he was a boy, there'd been no shortage of opportunities for the world—father and brothers included—to remind Graham of his numerous failings: too short, not clever enough, not the best at riding or fencing.

By the time he'd grown to be several inches taller than both his brothers and had become a more skilled rider, fencer, and boxer, those accomplishments had ceased to matter to his father, the Duke of Sutton.

Until Graham had ceased to try and instead learned to live for only his own pleasures.

In what could only be the most clichéd of directions a duke's second or third son could travel, Graham had contentedly wandered the path of rogue, uncaring about paternal disapproval.

Neither was he one who particularly cared for those all-too-frequent ducal lectures. The latest of which Graham now subjected himself to.

And had been subjecting himself to since he'd entered his father's office twenty-five minutes earlier.

"Are you even listening to me?" the Duke of Sutton called. The affected shout boomed off the thirty-foot-high ceilings. Of course,

Graham's illustrious father was too distinguished and refined to ever do something so gauche as to actually bellow.

"Indeed," Graham drawled. From where he stood at the duke's floor-to-ceiling windows overlooking the Kent countryside, Graham glanced at his father in the crystal panes and caught the manner in which his father drew his thick gray brows together. And because Graham knew it would raise the sterling-haired patriarch's ire, he tossed back a long swallow from the snifter in his hand.

The duke *wanted* to bellow. It was there in the bulging vein at the right corner of his eye. In Graham's youth, his father's slight, uncontrollable twitches had represented a triumph. Now, they meant nothing. They changed nothing.

As always, his father collected himself. "Your mother is having a house party."

As if to punctuate that statement, a pink carriage rolled down the long graveled drive. "Yes, I see that." Graham followed it with his gaze until the garish conveyance came to a stop. Liveried servants immediately poured from the front door, scurrying off to greet the just-arrived guests, like mice sprinting along the bowels of the naval ships he'd served on seven years earlier.

"She wanted you here."

Graham could not fathom why. "Did she?" Oh, it was not that he doubted his mother's love. In the way of devoted parents, she had bestowed equal affection and regard on each of her three—now two—sons. Even when she had every reason to hate him for the loss of one of her sons, she hadn't. But taking the grousing from her husband because Graham was around hardly seemed worth the bother.

"She did," his father said coolly, in tones that betrayed a like confusion.

Graham swirled the remaining contents of his glass.

"I wanted you here, too."

The amber spirits splashed over the rim of his glass, staining Graham's fingers and falling upon the hardwood floor. For the first time since he'd been summoned to the duke's offices, Graham faced him. His mother had wanted him about through the years as much as the Duke of Sutton hadn't wanted the spare to his heir underfoot.

"Wipe that surprised look off your face." There was a faint plead-ing there so at odds with the Duke of Sutton who commanded all. "That is no doubt the reason both the king and I together couldn't convince the Home Office to put you to some use."

"This again?" he drawled, tension snapping through him, and he resisted it. *People, all people, will attempt to use your weakness as a weapon against you. Do not...*

This time, with that lesson reverberating around his brain, he dispelled the old hurts. This time, he refused to give his father the satisfaction of his fury, nor did he allow himself that show of weakness. It was enough that Graham knew the truth: That he, the unlikeliest of rogues, had been tapped as an agent for the Crown, trained, and set to serve.

His father thumped the surface of his desk. "Your mind is wan-dering again."

What is wrong with you that you cannot—?

"Focus."

"Or what? You'll drag out one of my esteemed former tutors to apply the rod?" The pain, indignity, and shame—of both the act and his pathetic self for failing to put an end to it—stung sharper than the wood instrument had all those years ago. As a child, he'd been unable to maintain any sense of self-control. His father, a ducal master of all emotion, had railed at Graham, ultimately hir-ing the sternest tutors.

"They did it to clear your head of cobwebs and clouds," his father shot back, his cheeks flushed red. Was it guilt? Regret?

How utterly ridiculous to believe his father had any compunc-tion about how he'd treated his youngest son. Ultimately, it had been Graham's mother who'd put the humiliating punishments to an end.

"It did not work," he said with a lazy grin, toasting his father. In the end, he had developed mechanisms on his own to help cope with an inability to attend his studies or... anything.

"Mayhap if your mother hadn't coddled you, you would have been strong enough to merit a role with the Home Office."

He curled his fingers. *Let it be enough. You know the truth.* At the end of the day, his father believed he'd been rejected, but Graham had been selected to the illustrious organization. Nonetheless, as the duke launched into his familiar tirade, Graham clung to every lesson doled out by his mentor within the Brethren and every strategy he employed to retain a grip on his self-control.

"I sent you to the Home Office with every opportunity," his father was saying, "and it was just one more failing." One more failing… among a countless number of them. Oh, how Graham would love to hurl the truth in his face. But the other man's pompous—incorrect—assumption where Graham was concerned was perversely satisfying, too. "Wipe that smug smile from your face, Sheldon Whitworth." He winced at having that hated first name tossed his way. "You went to them with connections, letters from me and His Majesty, and you blundered it at your first meeting."

Graham's entire body went taut. "You spoke to someone after my… rejection?"

"Of course I did." His father bristled. "Do you think I didn't have words with my connections and demand an answer as to why they passed you over for any post?"

Of course, there was that eternal concern for the Duke of Sutton about how he was viewed by his peers. Graham made his lips move up in a coolly mocking grin and again toasted his father with his drink. "How very loving you've become in your old age."

The duke's cheeks went red. "It had nothing to do with… with…"

"Love?" Graham supplied. His father had turned tail and ran whenever discourse moved into the emotional territory.

"That or any other puling sentiments."

"I was being facetious, Father. Of course it didn't."

His father slashed a hand Graham's way. "It had to do with the fact that you are approaching thirty, and you're still the same rakish person you were ten years ago."

Ah, but now Graham was more. "I have always been able to rely on you to provide a detailed enumeration of my failings."

"Either way, that isn't why you are here."

"And here I thought I was invited for the annual Whitworth winter house party."

"Don't be a fool. You stopped coming to your mother's festivities years ago. Can't bother to tear yourself away from whatever whore you're bedding or whatever wager you're making."

That had been the case, though it had been more about not wanting to. He had been the failure of a student his father accused him of being, but he'd not been such a fool that he'd have willingly put himself through any more of his father's lambasting diatribes. This year, however, was different. His purposes for being here, for trying to meld more with Polite Society, at whom he'd otherwise spent his life turning up a middle finger, were quite different.

Graham downed the remainder of his drink. Strolling with long, lazy strides to his father's desk, he set the empty glass at the edge of the perfect, gleaming mahogany desktop and sat. "Why don't we move past all the dancing about, then, and have out with whatever it is I'm doing here?"

The duke's hard lips moved, but no sound slipped forward. Of course, His Grace wasn't accustomed to anyone compelling him to do anything. No one short of the king himself. It was why he'd taken such affront at the denials of his requests for a post at the Home Office for his reprobate son. It had stung his ducal pride. Something flashed in his steel-gray eyes, something that looked very much like pride. It was gone as quick as it had come and likely had been an imagined hope that the foolish part of Graham still carried for the man's acceptance.

"You've been a disappointment in many ways…" *Schooling.* "Your schooling."—Because, for his father, that was where Graham's failings had all begun.—"Your reputation. Your—"

"Yes, yes, I think we're all well familiar with the impressive list you've compiled," he said dryly, looping an ankle across his opposite knee.

"I'm trying to *help* you, Sheldon."

"How very…kind of you."

His father went on over that droll interruption. "There is something you can do."

"And here I thought there was nothing I could—"

"The Duke and Duchess of Gayle are expected any day."

Oh, bloody hell.

"Along with their daughter, Lady Emilia."

A joining of ducal families is what the Duke of Sutton craved then. "No," Graham said flatly.

His father flared his nostrils. "I didn't say anything."

Yet. "We both know where this is headed." And it would end nowhere.

"Your mother was friendly with her mother and feels badly

about the girl's circumstances."

"Then send her a puppy and French chocolates. But sending the failure of a son?" He chuckled. "That hardly seems like an act of charity for any of the aforementioned parties."

A knock sounded at the door.

"Enter," His Grace called out.

A servant entered bearing a silver tray. "This arrived a short while ago—"

"Hand it over, then," the duke said impatiently, snapping his fingers.

"It is not for you, Your Grace." The young man glanced to Graham. "But rather, Lord Whitworth."

At any other time, there would have been jubilation at seeing the duke effectively silenced. For it would be a bruising to his massive pride to have a letter arrive mid-meeting for his scapegrace son. Not this time. Graham stood straighter. Feeling his father's stare boring a hole into his every action, Graham forced himself to accept the note with his usual boredom. After sliding a finger under the familiar wax seal, he unfolded the missive and scanned the handful of lines. Then, curving his lips into the usual lazy grin, he tucked the page into his jacket. "We are finished here."

"Are we finished? We've only just started—"

"It was not a question," he said dryly, climbing to his feet. "I've had matters come up."

"An irate husband, no doubt."

"Hardly." Graham waggled his brows. "All the respectable ones who'd care that I'm bedding their wives are away from London until the Season begins." Whistling a bawdy tavern ditty, he clicked the heels of his boots together and started for the door.

The duke's chair scraped the floor. "You would simply run off," his father thundered after him, his patience giving way, as it invariably did.

Graham paused with his fingers on the door handle and shot a glance back. "Oh, I'm not running off. I'm leaving. They are two very different things, you know. Who the hell cares either way?"

With his father sputtering and cursing after him, Graham let himself out.

"Of course, the one task I charge you with, you cannot even see through. You are a fail—"

The remainder of the accusation was lost to the heavy oak panel he closed in the duke's face. Now he faced the man who might as well have been a mirror image of him, save for the blond hair.

Ignoring him, Graham started off in the opposite direction. "Withington?" he called after the servant stationed at the end of the hall. "Have my bags packed and my mount readied, please." He didn't have time for lectures, and there was no doubting that was precisely what had brought his brother to listening outside the duke's offices.

Heath, however, was not to be deterred. "It's really not well done of you. Upsetting him."

"Withington?" Graham scoffed. "He's more than capable of gathering my bags without—"

"Don't be an obnoxious arse," his brother muttered, joining him. "You know I'm referring to Father."

"Yes, but it is a good deal more fun baiting you." They hadn't always been at each other's throats. Graham and his two elder brothers had once delighted in making mischief *together*. Until the duke had taken Heath, the heir, under his proverbial wing, and the empty-headed rapscallion, as Graham had been called, had been cut out. Lawrence when he'd been living had retreated to his books. And just like that, the easy bond between Graham and both his brothers had been destroyed by the duke.

"It's shameful that you'd take such pleasure in upsetting your own father, Sheldon," his last living brother was saying.

Why can't you be more like your brothers, Sheldon? Why…?

Graham flexed his fingers. *Will your greatest weakness aside and let self-control triumph.* That lesson, imprinted into his mind, brought his hands open, as he was in command of himself once more. "I've long moved beyond parental or fraternal lectures," he drawled, lengthening his strides.

His brother adjusted his steps, easily matching Graham's. "He wants what is best for you. He always has. You cannot fault him for that, Sheldon."

"Actually, I can," he said with a go-to-hell grin. And he did fault his father. The expectations he'd placed had always been too great, and Graham was never one who'd be able to meet them. Not with his many deficiencies.

Graham reached the end of the corridor and stopped. His brother skidded to a stop beside him, and the hopeful glimmer in his eyes suggested he thought Graham might turn back, make peace, and remain on for the interminable week-long festivities. Instead, Graham took his brother by the shoulder and lightly squeezed. "If you're worried about the duke's wishes being appeased, then *you* can wed Lady Emilia."

Heath sputtered. "Don't be ridiculous." He bucked Graham's grip from his shoulder. "Furthermore, this isn't about Lady Emilia's marital state."

Graham folded his arms. "The hell it isn't."

His cheeks flushed. "Well, mayhap a small part of it has to do with Mother's wish that the girl could be settled. But this goes beyond that. He's getting on in years and wants to know that his remaining sons—" Heath's features contorted.

And despite his bid not to give a single damn about what his brother or father had to say, pain lanced through him. It was, however, fleeting. "If you think His Grace gives two goddamns about me, then you're a damned fool." His father had never cared. Graham had long been the disappointment. One who very rarely served a purpose.

"You're wrong," Heath called after him, and this time, his elder brother allowed Graham to continue on, uninterrupted.

Until he reached the foyer.

His mother had positioned herself at the doorway, with the same height and carriage as the late Boney himself and, by the glint in her eyes, no less determined. "I believe this is a new record for you, Sheldon Graham Malin Whitworth."

Several servants came forward with Graham's belongings. With a word of thanks, he accepted his cloak from one of the footmen. Tossing the article around his shoulders, he adjusted the clasp. "Mother," he murmured, with a bow for the graciously aging woman. "Using all four of my names? That never bodes well."

She held a finger up, commanding the room with nothing more than that slightest of gestures. Just like that, the servants dispersed, fading into the shadows and quitting the rooms. Her hair still a pale blonde and her skin not marred by even so much as a wrinkle, she bore the same youthful aura she had as a mother chasing about her three wayward boys.

And she said nothing. The silence, however, struck a place of guilt deeper than any insult or word she could have leveled.

"I have to go."

"You just arrived, Sheldon," she said, her voice faintly imploring. Sailing over, rustling her satin skirts as she glided to a stop before him, she stared expectantly back. "You always leave, but never this quickly." She did not attempt to make excuses for her husband. She'd always been a better mother than Graham had ever deserved.

"This time it is different." And it was. He couldn't say more than that. Wouldn't say more.

"Is it because of Lady Emilia?"

"It has nothing to do with Lady Emilia," he said simply, from a place of truth.

Her doubt was reflected in her eyes.

Always look a person squarely in the eyes for the answers you seek. A person's gaze is a window into what they see or feel.

It was a lesson that he wished he hadn't remembered at this moment, because then he wouldn't see the disappointment in her eyes, too. She was the one person who'd given him far more credit than he'd deserved. "I have to leave," he said again, adjusting the clasp at his throat.

She reached up and moved his hands out of the way to complete the task for him, much the way she had when he'd been a small boy. "Are you in trouble?"

Oddly, no. He winked. "Not this time."

Mother pinched his cheek.

Graham winced. "I'm not," he muttered. Or, at least not the trouble they expected him to find himself in. The urgency to quit this hall that had filled him when the note had been placed in his hand intensified.

His mother proved as resilient as always. She placed herself between him and the door. "Promise you'll return for the holidays."

Lie without compunction.

"I promise," he said automatically, that lesson pulling the promise from him.

She sighed and slid out of his path. "I'm not sure if I believe you."

Graham turned to go, and this time, he stopped himself. Leaning down, he bussed his mother on the cheek. "To the moon and back," he said, repeating the vow of love she had made each night when she'd put him and his brothers to bed.

Her lower lip quivered. "And back again."

A short while later, Graham left.

Sixteen hours later

As GRAHAM DISMOUNTED AND LOOPED the reins of his mount around a nearby tree, he surveyed the heavily wooded grounds.

A tall figure stepped out from behind a barren oak tree, its trunk and limbs gnarled from age and weather. "You made good time," the gentleman noted as Graham approached, his words a statement more than praise. "I feared you would be delayed with the slight snow."

"I'm here," he said evenly, adding nothing more for his superior. Though recently returned to the Brethren from his previous retirement, Lord Edward Helling, with his ink-black hair and unwrinkled face, might have been a man twenty years younger and new to the organization himself.

"I have your first assignment," his superior said, handing over a file.

And there it was.

At last.

Graham's fingers fairly twitched with the need to yank that coveted folio from the older man's fingers. With unhurried movements, Graham accepted the file, flipped it open, and read.

~Location
Luton
High Town, England
~Duration
Fortnight
~Role…
Stable master—

Graham stopped and blinked slowly. He reread the words, but

the detail there remained the same. "What is this?" he demanded.

"Your assignment." Lord Edward gave him a long look that contained a warning—that Graham promptly ignored.

"You know what I meant," he snapped. "A damned stable master." This was what he'd waited for? "After months spent training in the damned English countryside and then additional months spent being mentored in London, this"—he held the file aloft—"is what I'm asked to do?"

Lord Edward rubbed his gloved palms together quickly. "You've a reputation for being skilled with horses, having trained with them as a young man."

He growled, "I hardly think that makes me a damned expert. I cared for the horses in my father's stables."

"And mucked stalls and groomed and fed those horses. Why, you even took part in the birthings of five foals." A smile ghosted his superior's lips. "Yes, we know all."

Graham studied the file once more, reading the details, and as he did, the greatest of ironies was not lost on him. With this, his first assignment, the task he'd so loved that his father had berated him for enjoying, and eventually had forbidden him from doing, should now see Graham trapped in a bloody thankless post.

"Every assignment is important," Helling murmured.

He ignored that empty assurance. Frustration broiled in his gut. "I'm to be a servant, then, for…" He searched for that important detail on the first page. "A widow?" Graham laughed, the expression coated in cynicism. "Oh, this is rich." He'd countless dealings and experience with widows, always sexual in nature. There'd been servant role-playing, but with the widows as naughty maids.

"Because you've a reputation for bedding widows?" Lord Edward put forward. "If I may point out at this time, your… reputation was one of the reasons you were initially overlooked by the Brethren. Furthermore, it is not simply the young woman you are reporting on. There's a boy, too."

Oh, bloody, bloody hell. His assignment had gone from a joke to a farce. "A boy," he said flatly.

"A ten-year-old. Frederick Donaldson. He lives with his mother, Martha Donaldson. She is known as Marti to her family."

"Charming." He didn't give a bloody damn if the woman went by the name of Virgin Mary. Graham's first damned assignment would be to play stable master in a small country cottage removed from all society? "So I'm clear…" As if the inked words hadn't spelled it out in very specific black letters. "I'm to spend *fourteen days* as a servant and report back on the woman—"

"And her son," Lord Edward interrupted with a nod. "Precisely. This is an assignment that was abandoned by the recent leadership. I've taken the liberty of reinstating it."

For the first time since the folder had been placed in his fingers, Graham felt his interest stir. The lesson, of course, was that people of all ages and genders were capable of treachery. "Is she a threat to the Crown?"

"Not at all." The immediacy of the response confirmed the older man's confidence.

Reining in his annoyance, Graham flipped to the next page. "Well, it must have been determined that this woman and her child offer *something* of value to the Crown."

"Actually, no. On the contrary. The lady and her son offer *nothing* of specific value to the Brethren."

Martha Donaldson was neither a threat, nor of any meaningful value to the Brethren, and yet, she was important enough that the moment he'd come out of retirement, Edward Helling had reopened her file. "I… see." This… Martina… Martha… He searched the page again for her damned name. Martha Donaldson was Lord Edward's mistress, then. Perhaps the boy, Frederick, was his bastard son.

His superior narrowed his eyes. "Careful," he said warningly, having followed the unspoken supposition. "A former member feels a sense of responsibility to the young woman and asked that I have an agent assigned to her."

"Why?" Being a member of the Brethren did not mean a man blindly accepted an assignment without questioning the ins and outs of every possible angle.

"Not quite two years ago, the Brethren agreed to see the woman was cared for. With the transition at the Home Office, the previous command deemed any oversight of Miss Donaldson supercilious. She'd fallen by the wayside. Until I… came upon the young woman's file." Out of retirement for an interim post, Lord Edward was also responsible for Graham's hiring after the previous members had rejected him. "We're trying to make contact with her once more and secure any information about her and her son's current state of affairs."

"What of the dead husband?" he asked, perusing his folder once more. "Who was he?"

"It doesn't matter."

"It always matters," Graham shot back, one of many mantras of the Brethren.

The branches stirred overhead. That rustling let a shaft of moonlight through and briefly illuminated his superior's face. An unanticipated approval glinted in the other man's gaze. "In this case, it does not. It isn't your need to know. The details surrounding her marriage are irrelevant," Lord Edward said bluntly. "This isn't a case that needs solving. She represents no threat, and there is no one at risk because of her. She is simply a woman a certain member of the Brethren is concerned after."

Graham leveled a probing stare on the other man. Lord Edward might be Graham's superior, and Graham new to his role, but he was astute enough to gather a key detail: The other man... nay, the organization was withholding details about Martha Donaldson for reasons Graham didn't know and that they likely wouldn't tell him. His suspicions deepened and put forward another probing question. "Is there reason to suspect she's in any danger, then?"

"We do not believe so." Another gust of wind whipped through the copse, sending their cloaks snapping loudly in the breeze. "It is our hope you locate the woman and confirm she and her son are well."

"And that requires a whole fortnight?" Graham pressed. They'd have him play nursemaid for some widow and her son for fourteen damned days?

"The organization wants assurances about her well-being. You aren't going to have that in a day or even two," he said with a finality that indicated that argument was at an end. "After you're finished, you'll have another assignment. In the meantime, while you are there, remain unobtrusive. Make yourself as invisible as possible."

A near impossible feat for a stranger to—Graham consulted the pages again—High Town, a tiny town on the northeastern crest of Luton.

"It's your role to determine how to make yourself invisible."

The other man had correctly followed his ponderings. "Uninteresting people, regardless of how long they visit a place, lose notice quickly."

Graham shook his head. He'd awaited his first assignment, and this was the role he'd been given. That of a minion put to work on a nothing case because some former member had called in a favor. He gritted his teeth. Oh, the amusement his father would have had with all of this.

Lord Edward rubbed his gloved palms together quickly. "I trust there are no problems, Whitworth."

"No," Graham replied automatically, which wasn't a lie… There were any *number* of problems he had with the assignment. This assignment was no different than the years he'd served in the navy, a duke's youngest son coddled by the men in command and kept from any truly purposeful work.

The other man slapped his shoulder. "I was you once."

"You were never me," he said curtly.

The faintest smile ghosted Lord Edward's lips. "I was. New to the role, frustrated over the speed with which I was put into the field. Resenting the slowness of the process." He held Graham's stare. "Being the second son and, for that ordering of my birthright, always falling behind another."

Yes, mayhap there was something they shared, then. For surely it was the way of all lords to have little use, appreciation, or regard for those youngest sons.

"There will be other assignments, Whitworth," the other man said. "I promise you that." He turned to go, but then stopped. "Oh, and Whitworth? I was ordered to give you one more instruction about your assignment."

Graham stared back expectantly.

"Do not go seducing the young woman."

Another spy for the Brethren might have been insulted by that directive. With Graham's well-established reputation as a rogue, however, Helling's was a fair order. "You've no worries there," he drawled. The women he kept company had reputations as scandalous as his own. Wicked ladies with inventive skills in bed and morally bankrupt, like Graham himself. Not decent, young women tucked away in the English countryside.

Lord Edward touched a fingertip to his nose and then pointed in Graham's direction. "Let us hope not."

This time, with that veiled warning hanging in the copse, his superior left, and Graham was saddled with his first assignment.

CHAPTER 2

High Town
Luton, England

IN TERMS OF SURVIVAL, WOMEN had few options available to them.

Two, if one wished to be *truly* precise.

One might marry.

Or one might whore oneself.

Martha, however, was determined to never suffer either fate. Never again, that was.

Having finished the morning chores, Martha stood at her easel. Just as she'd been for the hour since she'd sent her son, Frederick, off to tend the livestock. All her muscles screamed in protest, and still she worked through the pain. Desperately needed funds awaited her and Frederick when she completed the commissioned piece.

Art, which had long been cathartic and joyous, had now taken on new purpose and meaning: work.

It was a foreign concept that something that brought such joy should now carry with it an element of pressure. For it was one thing to find solace on the blank canvas that was now a luxury to purchase, and it was an altogether different thing to know other people had expectations of that artwork and visions of what they wished from her craft. Shoving the self-doubts to the furthest corners of her mind, Martha settled into the long familiar comfort of her sketches. She let her fingers fly over the page, capturing the stills with the worn-down nub of charcoal. A curl slipped from her perfunctory chignon that had long since protested its constraints and joined the other loose curls falling around her shoulders.

Martha paused and assessed the landscape upon the page. For a moment, panic set in. It knocked around inside her chest, robbing her of her earlier focus. There was too much to be done. It was the never-ending artwork that would never be completed. A piece that she'd been forced to start and stop and then restart again.

Martha briefly closed her eyes. There should only be gratitude that she possessed a skill that allowed her to earn desperately needed funds to care for her son, because the pittances the commissioned pieces earned were a gift. How many other women would have already lifted their skirts or accepted the first formal offer of marriage?

She opened her eyes and stared blankly at the High Town countryside.

But then, there were no offers of marriage. There were few offers of… anything respectable. Such was the fate of a woman who'd committed bigamy and whose father had murdered the man who'd made her a bigamist.

It didn't matter that Martha hadn't known the truth of her husband's circumstances. It hadn't mattered that Viscount Waters had offered her marriage on a lie. For the world, guilt lay only with a woman. They were all Eve, responsible for every sin and derided and mocked for it.

And in a way, she was guilty. For she had allowed herself to be swayed into that match, had believed there would be a life of respectability, away from High Town.

Nay, you convinced yourself that a nobleman who rarely left London would take you there, and you could have explored the museums and taken art classes and had the life you dreamed of outside this place.

Martha's throat convulsed.

Mayhap the world was right about her after all. Mayhap she was the whore they all professed her to be, just not for the reasons they believed. She'd sold her soul, freedom, and happiness with the hopes of leaving this place and exploring the world away.

Only to find nothing had been worth the hell she'd endured. His piteously poor ability to converse on anything. His fetid, brandy-scented breath. His touch.

Martha's gaze caught in the lead windowpane over the top of her canvas. Her sad, bitter smile reflected back, an empty echo of the one that had once come so easily.

Do not think of him… Do not…

Her stomach churned, and her entire body went clammy.

You are my wife, and I am permitted these liberties. Now part your legs. Unless you'd like to fight me again…?

Martha focused on breathing, counting the seconds for each inhalation and exhalation. Even with the year and a half that had passed since she'd suffered that special hell, the horror of it still lingered.

His ghost haunted her in this cottage she'd been born to and resided in for the whole of her twenty-eight years.

If she let him, he'd rob her of what remained. Martha firmed her jaw, and her resolve strengthened. Viscount Waters had taken her virtue, good name, pride, and happiness. She'd be damned if she ceded anything else to that demon rotting in hell alongside his master, Satan.

"Enough," she said into the quiet, the sound of her own voice dislodging the useless self-pitying. Bending down, she resumed her work and swiped the tiny portion of her broken charcoal across the canvas. For there was something he'd left her. Something good. The only thing good and wonderful that had ever happened to her—her son.

Frederick was the joy that had come from great darkness, and he was the reason she hadn't crumpled under the hell of her existence.

Focusing on the focal point of the sketch, the one that served as the greatest contention between her and the commissioner of the art piece, Martha rubbed the tip of her index finger over the front façade of Oxley Manor. She blended the charcoal, softening the shadows, creating a more realistic, subtle gradation.

The past was the past, and every lesson a young woman could learn had been learned. A person couldn't control the past. They could only look toward controlling their own future. Rejuvenated, Martha lost herself in her work, that great equalizer of pain and heartache.

Martha sketched until the gray charcoal crumpled to dust in

her fingers, and she moved on to the color spectrum of greens. Until Surrey's most prominent household in all its age-old splendor stared back, a perfect replica of that focal point of her smallest corner of the world. All the world receded, so that only her artwork remained.

A lone knock sounded at the door.

Martha gasped, and her green charcoal skidded over the page. Who…? She stared at the door a moment and waited. For another knock? For someone to announce themselves? For something to happen.

She gave her head a shake. "Hearing things," she muttered into the quiet. Martha gathered another piece of charcoal. Dusting off the pad of her thumb along her skirts, she smeared a mistake into the page until it was perfectly faded and part of the sketch.

Rap-rap-rap.

Her gaze went to the doorway. No…she'd not imagined it. There it was again. Who in blazes…? *No one* visited her.

That was, none who were honorable. Numerous men from the village had come with indecent propositions to make. Stalking over to the door, Martha lingered at the window overlooking her gardens and squinted, trying to make out the shape of the murky shadow lingering there.

The fancily attired gentleman consulted his timepiece, all the while tapping his other hand against his leg.

Martha puzzled her brow. *Squire Chernow?* Her father's closest friend, the squire was also the only person in High Town who'd commissioned work from Martha. The older gentleman turned, as if to leave. Martha rushed for the handle and drew the door open. "Squire Chernow," she greeted. "How do you do?"

"Martha, my girl," he said cheerfully, his gaunt cheeks florid with their usual crimson color. "I've come… about the sketch." He peered past her shoulder, and she followed his stare. "Mrs. Chernow is growing impatient."

Mrs. Chernow, the village gossip who wasn't content unless everyone was discontent. Her stomach dropped. "I've not quite finished. I believe we said I have until tomorrow to complete the final rendering."

He reached out a gloved hand and patted away those ramblings. "No. No. I've not come to collect. Rather, I've come to finalize several details about the arrangement."

With just one patron, and still seeking employment from the posts she responded to in London, she couldn't afford to offend him, and yet, life had taught her to be wary of all men. She drew the door panel closer, shielding her modest residence from his stare. "Perhaps we should speak tomorrow regarding the piece." When her son was about. "Frederick is due to return inside," she lied, tacking that on as a reminder of not only her status as a mother, but also that she was not alone.

Squire Chernow widened his grin. "But he's not returned yet, and with him otherwise occupied, this should prove the ideal time to discuss, no?"

He persisted with the same dogged determination he'd had in the late-night debates he'd engaged in with her father.

The memory of the bond they'd once shared weakened her defenses. Reluctantly, she drew the panel open.

Squire Chernow sailed past her, removing his gloves as he walked. Uninvited, he made his way to her small workstation and assessed the page clipped in place at the top of the easel. "Hmm," he murmured, slapping his gloves together as he contemplated the sketch.

Hmm. It was the noncommittal utterance she'd come to find from all his past visits indicated displeasure.

Panic knocked away at her chest. His payment would not come until he approved the piece, and every day she spent attempting to create the rendering of his property was time… lost.

"You don't like it," she said flatly.

"No. No. It isn't that, my girl," he said and reached back to give her shoulder an awkward pat. "It's simply… the front façade. It's not quite right."

She frowned. The front façade remained the area in question they'd now debated for the past two, now three, sketches. "I've not quite finished, but the ivy"—she gestured to the green charcoal, nearly perfect in its shading—"does reflect the hues of your manor."

"In the summer."

"The summer," she repeated dumbly.

He wagged a finger under her nose. "This is a seasonal piece."

Martha called forth every shred of patience she'd mastered through the years. "We agreed that, given Mrs. Chernow's favorite time in High Town is, in fact, the summer when her gardens are most vibrant, she wished the piece to reflect that."

All jovial warmth dissipated. "I changed my mind."

He'd changed his mind? That was… it? There was no consideration for the time she'd put into a project she'd not yet received any recompense for? And would not receive payment until he offered his final approval. But then, that was the way of the world for a woman: at the mercy and whim of a capricious man who'd toy with her time and efforts. Still, regardless of how she felt in this moment about this particular man, she needed his coin. And she hated the desperation that had held her captive since her world had been upended. With purposeful strides, Martha stalked over to the leather trunk at the corner of her makeshift workstation. "I've the earliest rendering," she explained, lifting the lid and drawing out the first attempt she'd made. "I can resume my work on—"

"I don't want that one," he said like a petulant child. How had she ever failed to note that incessant whine? "I want… a new one," he went on, stuffing his gloves into his jacket front in a clear display of one who had no intention of leaving. "But then, mayhap this is simply a waste of both our time, Marti."

At both the insult and the familiar use of her Christian name, her back went up. "Squire Chernow?"

"Your father sang your praises, but you've never been that talented." The barb, so casually tossed, found its unwanted mark upon the part of her that took pride in her sketches.

Her art represented the one accomplishment she'd felt capable in. Even as devoted a mother as she'd tried to be, she saw all the ways she'd failed her son. Everything that she'd been unable to provide or do. As such, her need for funds be damned, she'd not be disparaged by him… not in her own home. "I believe we are finished here," she said evenly. "I'm afraid I've been unable to adequately capture that which you'd hoped for."

She took a step toward the door, but with a startling speed for one of his age, the wiry gentleman hurried into her path, blocking her. The warning bells chiming at the back of her mind blared wildly. "I've offended you," he said quickly. "That was not my intention. I only sought to speak the truth." He slid closer, and she retreated. "I am worried after you, Marti."

Aside from her son, no one worried about her or her future. Her life was nothing more than fodder for gossips. "You needn't worry. I am doing fine," she lied.

"But you're not," he persisted, continuing his approach. "Surely you see that with your father gone and your *prospects* what they are, you'll not survive, Marti." At last, the squire stopped.

"I don't see that," she said crisply. Moving away from him, she began cleaning up her workstation, putting distance between them. She saw how perilously close she was to faltering, to being crushed by what life had become for her and her son. And mayhap if it weren't for Frederick, she would have given in to that despair, but as long as there was her son, there was hope. "I'm sorry we were unable to come to a consensus in terms of your piece. Now, if you'll excuse me?"

He gave her a pitying look. "It doesn't have to be this way, Marti. You toiling during the day with running this"—he glanced around the cottage and curled his lip in a sneer that said louder than words his ill opinion of the only home she'd known—"place. You can enjoy the material *comforts* you once knew," he murmured, walking the same path she'd just traveled. "And security. Surely you want that once more? Hmm?" Her skin crawled. "If not for you, then for your son." He stretched a hand toward her, and she slapped his palm away.

Of course that had been the only reason he'd commissioned a piece. Hadn't she learned firsthand that all men were self-serving bastards with an eye on nothing more than their pleasures?

"You've overstayed your welcome, Squire Chernow," she said coolly. "If you would?" She pointed past him to the arched doorway.

"You've not even heard my proposal, Marti," he chided.

"I don't need to." She'd heard the undertones, and that had been enough.

"No man will marry you," he went on anyway. "Your work will not sustain you, but you can enjoy a comfortable existence… as my mistress." A pleased smile formed on his thin lips as he smoothed his lapels and stared expectantly at her.

Rage stung her veins. Why, he expected she should be grateful at receiving his indecent proposal? And why shouldn't he? The world took her for a whore anyway. "I'll be no man's mistress, Squire Chernow. Now, I really must insist you leave." She stalked past him, a gasp escaping her as he caught the back of her dress.

Her heart pounded hard in her chest as she pulled out of his reach, but he retained his hold, drawing her closer.

"If you'd rather put on a show of offended sensibilities," he whispered against her ear, "I will play the game, kitten." He roved a hand along her hip, just as another man had before.

And yet, that man she'd foolishly given a legal right to that act. Panic and loathing roiled in her gut. She'd never allow any other man that right.

Fight him. Fight him. "Release me," she ordered in shockingly steady tones.

"You do know the village hasn't already run you off because of the kindness I've insisted the villagers show you. That can all change."

Her throat worked.

"After all, you are a bigamist, Marti. Scandalous stuff." He clucked like a chicken. "I expect it could be a good deal worse for that boy of yours."

Frederick. Frederick, who had remained when his sisters had been sent away to escape and, because of it, who had not been spared the shame that went with being a bigamist's by-blow.

"Ultimately, I possess everything of value in this village, and you are the prettiest of the lasses, aren't you?" He placed his mouth near her right lobe.

She squeezed her lashes shut. The biting scent of basil from whatever meal he'd consumed flooded her nostrils. *I am going to be ill...* Through the nausea, she wrestled for control of her panic. "I'll not be any man's whore."

"Ah, but you already have been, no?" he asked, almost jovial. "We will be very good together, and you will be very grateful. This is the right decision, Marti," he lauded, like a proud papa over a daughter's cleverness.

In the end, salvation came in the unlikeliest of forms.

The door burst open. "Mother, it's starting to—" Frederick's words trailed off, and his suspicious gaze moved from his mother to the man with an inappropriate hold upon her. His little brow furrowed. "—snow," he finished. "What are you doing?"

The squire removed his grip. "Master Frederick," he greeted with the same jovial tones he'd used when he'd once visited Martha's father and ruffled the top of her son's head.

Where a warm greeting had once fallen easily from Frederick's lips, now he took a step closer to his mother and said nothing. "I asked what you were doing?" he asked with a bluntness only a child could manage.

She positioned herself behind her son and rested a hand on his shoulder. "We were just discussing the squire's sketch." Over the top of Frederick's head, she leveled a hard stare on the squire. "The squire was just leaving, however."

The older man drew out his gloves. "Of course. Until our next meeting." He sketched a bow and then, tugging on those fine leather articles, he left.

"I don't like him," Frederick said before the door had even clicked shut behind the squire, drawing away from her. "I don't like how he looks at you."

His gaze, more jaded when before there had only ever been innocence, ripped a fresh hole inside her heart. She gave him a light squeeze. "We still must respect him." After all, he had influence enough in Surrey to see that the village was even more hostile to them.

"I don't have to respect anyone. He's nothing to me or you."

He was, though. He was the one who owned their cottage and could turn them out. For that was coming. She knew it. He'd grown bolder, and she'd learned enough to know that no man was truly capable of charity. They ultimately wanted something and would take it. And if it was not freely given, they'd secure a woman's capitulation in any manner they saw fit, propriety and the law be damned.

Frederick stared accusatorily back with so much concern—too much concern in his ten-year-old eyes. Concern that no child should be made to feel for his mother.

Martha gestured for him to come close.

Where he once would have rushed to her side and with a kiss for her cheek, this time he stood planted where he was, his arms folded angrily at his chest, his eyes snapping with defiance.

"Frederick," she began, going over to him. She sank to a knee. "He owns this property." She wiped a bit of dirt from his cheek.

He swatted at her hand. "We'll go somewhere else. I don't like it much here anymore." He'd only ever loved this Surrey countryside. Her throat moved. Hope transformed her son's previously troubled gaze. "And then Iris and Creda can come with us."

Martha froze as those names ripped through her heart like an arrow.

Iris and Creda. Always joyous, always mischievous, her firstborn girls had been the first light to come from the darkest of marriages. "Oh, sweet," she said, her voice choked with emotion. "Your sisters are in a better place." Anywhere that Martha was not was a better place. "And this is where we'll remain." Forever. Because she wasn't so foolish as to believe an unmarried woman and her young son with limited funds and no prospects could start afresh somewhere else.

"I didn't like how close he was to you," Frederick stated flatly, and mortified heat scorched her from the tips of her toes to the roots of her hair.

"He was simply looking at the sketch I'd been working on for him," she hurried to assure, brushing his unkempt locks back behind his ear. "Which… he did not like." She tacked on that belated lie.

"He didn't like your sketch?"

Warmth filled her breast. For the layers of cynicism and maturity Martha's scandal had added to her child, his devotion to her artistic abilities had not wavered. "He didn't." The squire's opinion on her art was far safer to discuss with Frederick than the lecherous gentleman's dishonorable intentions.

Fire flashed in Frederick's eyes. "Then he's a fool. You are the best at sketching."

She lightly cuffed him under the chin. "You are only partial because I'm your mama."

"I'm not," he said, color splotching his cheeks. "I just know that you're the best."

Martha tossed her arms around him and squeezed.

"Mother, stop," he mumbled.

And that had been just one more way in which he'd been changed: Where he'd once been unabashed in his affections, now he rejected all maternal shows of warmth.

Coming to her feet, Martha resisted the urge to wipe another smudge of dirt from his cheek. "Go. Get yourself washed and changed for the evening."

He'd turned to go when she registered that which had previously failed to escape her.

Muddy tracks marred the floor, left by the soles of his boots.

"What have you done to your shoes?" she chided, dropping to a knee.

"I was playing at the river." Frederick folded one leg behind the other in a bid to escape her questing fingers. "It is *just* mud."

"Sit," she urged, giving him a light tug.

He hesitated.

Most everything had changed, but Martha was still and would always be a mother. "I said sit, Frederick," she said with a look that sent him promptly down to a seated position in the middle of the floor. Martha wrested off one sopping boot. She went to set it down.

Her heart sank.

"Oh, I… got a hole in one." Frederick ducked his head with uncharacteristic sheepishness. Martha relieved him of the other. "And mayhap the other, too," he mumbled under his breath.

Oh, blast… There had been a time when they'd worried not at all about the cost of shoes and shirts and trousers. But… everything had changed. Everything. There weren't funds for… anything, let alone a new pair of boots.

"You're angry."

"I'm not." He should be free to run the countryside as she once had, chasing rainbows and running after tomorrows. "I do want you to have a greater care, though."

He leaped up. "I will," he promised and started to dart off before abruptly stopping. "You aren't working anymore for the day, are you?"

"Just a bit." He worried after her when he shouldn't have to. When he should know only a child's pleasures and joys. "But only because I enjoy it."

"You need someone to help here so you can work on your sketches. No one ever responded to your notices?"

And no one would. They no longer had the funds for that. "I'll add another post to the next mail," she lied. Her weekly trek that represented the fledgling hope she had for a future of respectability with her son wouldn't include a post for employment, but rather, a request herself for work.

He lingered. "We will find someone."

With that, he darted off. As soon as he'd gone, her shoulders slumped. The struggle to be everything, when life had given them nothing, was drowning her, the waves battering at her, sucking her under, and leaving behind an empty panic.

The walls of their circumstances were closing in all around. Should there be no funds, Martha well knew what future awaited them…

She shivered.

For Martha knew all too well the evil that drove men's souls… and how easily that evil could, and would, destroy a woman's life.

And she'd be damned if she would erroneously place her trust in any one man again.

CHAPTER 3

THERE HAD BEEN A TIME when Martha had enjoyed nothing more than the long, silent walk to the White Stag Inn. The two-mile journey represented some of her favorite times. The birch-lined path, quiet and untraveled, had offered her stolen moments where she lived solely in her head. During those times, there were no responsibilities or obligations. There was no livestock to feed and care for. There were not four people alternately asking questions or ordering her about.

And most of all, there'd been no thoughts of the husband who'd periodically come to High Town, exercised his husbandly rights, and then, thankfully, left. Or the regrets at how life had turned out.

For along with those sentiments had also come a mother's guilt… for both stealing that time away from her three children and, worse, for having wanted that time for herself.

And yet, just as her existence had changed, so too had those simplest aspects of her life.

Now, her journeys to town were made with reluctance and born of necessity. Those visits invariably resulted in stares and whispers and, even worse, the shouts of *harlot*.

"You folded the page correctly?" her son was asking as Martha latched the fraying wool cloak that had seen better days two years ago.

"I did." The folded sheets would eventually be wrinkled in the mail. The hope was that the creases had been made in such a way that they at least minimized the damage and allowed those who'd eventually view them to see the potential there.

"And you are certain it was dried enough?" he persisted with his dogged determination.

"I finished it before I went to bed," she assured him. Which had only been two and a half hours prior to the completion of that sample piece.

Her son frowned. "You went to bed late. I heard you enter your rooms—"

Martha laid a fingertip against his lips. "I'm sure it is dried," she promised, hating that Frederick had come to worry after her... and their future. Dark circles marred his face, heightening the anxiety in his expressive eyes.

"It is going to be fine."

Did he seek to reassure her or himself with that? The thought of either caused a rending in her heart. "Do you know what?"

"What?"

She leaned down and bussed his cheek. "It is going to be better than fine."

Wrinkling his little nose in boyish distaste, Frederick made a swipe at the place her lips had landed.

"While I'm gone, you need to tend the—"

"Stables. I know, I know," he muttered.

The problem with that chore, however, was it wasn't a task suited for a child alone. It required the work of a grown man, with the height and weight to heft bags of feed. Martha started to leave, but with a finger lifted, she quickly turned back. "And don't—"

"Get my boots wet again. I have it," he groused. He gave her a little push. "Now, go, or you're going to miss the post."

Mayhap that was even now why she procrastinated, going over daily instructions for tasks Frederick had undertaken long before his grandfather had been sent to prison. Because each post she sought, and then was subsequently rejected, represented the slow death of hope and options for the both of them. Drawing her hood up, Martha accepted her father's leather satchel that Frederick held out.

A short while later, she found herself walking the now barren path to the White Stag Inn. The tiniest snowflakes fell around her. Martha shivered. Had she really loved the snow? It was cold and wet and required more wood to burn. She huddled deep within the folds of her tattered cloak and forced her feet along the snow-dusted path. The gravel crunched loudly under her heels, the moisture coating the ground penetrating the thin soles of her boots.

Martha stopped, and resting her hand on a narrow tree trunk, she lifted her foot. Her heart promptly sank.

"No," she whispered. Mayhap it was a stain. Mayhap it was merely mud stuck to the bottom. Except, even as she prodded that small spot, she knew. She sighed. In fairness, they owed her nothing. They were the same boots she'd worn the day Lord Exeter had escorted her father off, leaving Martha behind with a new future to sort through.

Knowing that she'd had several years of use from those boots, however, did nothing for her in this moment. She let her foot fall and resumed her walk.

This was what her life had become.

She'd gone from the life of a viscountess—granted a viscountess tucked away in the country with her three children and an absentee husband, but a viscountess nonetheless—to this, the village bigamist with holes in her boots, making a two-mile trek each week in the hope that this might finally be the day when she'd receive word from London about her artwork.

Her teeth chattered, and she rubbed her gloved palms together in a bid to bring warmth to the chilled digits.

Her father had always wanted more for her. The best. And she'd so unfailingly trusted his judgment that she'd let herself believe marriage to Lord Waters represented her best option. That, however, was a mistake she could not lay at her father's feet. Just sixteen, she'd been a young woman who'd ultimately agreed to the proposed match.

Marching down the middle of the barren path lined by an endless row of birch trees, Martha kept her gaze forward. She did not allow herself to look directly at those proudly erect trees devoid of greenery.

Do not look… Do not look…

Except, unbidden, her gaze locked on one of the towering white trees, its thick trunk split into a perfect horseshoe shape.

Martha slowed to a stop, keeping ten paces between her and that one birch.

It's called a merrythought bone, poppet. The English got it from the Romans, who got it from the Etruscans. It will predict your future…

Of her own volition, her legs carried her forward, and then she stopped before the tree. She stared vacantly at the tiny row of slash marks carved upon the trunk. Wishes were for children. She'd once deluded herself into believing wishes could come true, that she would have a life outside of Luton. That she would have a happy home, with a devoted husband and an even happier child. A bitter smile formed on her lips, and Martha trailed the tip of a gloved finger along the last notch that had been made.

A fool. She'd been a fool in so many ways.

Nay, for all the times she'd been upset with her father, the guilt belonged only to Martha.

From the moment she'd met the paunchy, balding lord, she'd ignored every instinct that had urged her to reject any of the gentleman's interest in her.

Never again. Never again would she ignore those instincts that would save a person, if one let them.

A strong wind whipped down the narrow path. The gust parted the fabric of her cloak and sent snow slapping at her face. Martha let her arm fall to her side and drew her wool garment close. With her resolve strengthened, she made the remainder of the long trek.

Over the top of the birch trees, white smoke spiraled up to the gray, cloud-filled sky, signaling a lone establishment in the distance. At the end of the path, Martha quickened her steps until she reached the White Stag Inn.

As she approached the inn, a woman pressed her forehead to the dusty windowpane. The shadowy figure rubbed a circle, clearing a space. Mrs. Lowery. The innkeeper's mother stared back at Martha. Then with a pinched mouth, the older woman ducked from sight.

Martha slowed to a stop as her courage faltered.

Yes, everything had changed. Even the people who'd been warm and friendly to her father and late mother. She briefly contemplated the path over her shoulder. But then fury roiled in her stomach. To hell with them. To hell with all of them. Aside from believing a nobleman's intentions to wed her were real, she'd done nothing wrong.

Forcing herself to walk the remaining way to the inn, Martha stamped her boots to dislodge the mud caked in the soles. Before her courage deserted her, she entered the tavern.

Plastering a smile on her lips, Martha reached back and drew the door shut. As she pushed her hood back, she did a quick, visual sweep of the establishment.

When the village people had discovered the circumstances surrounding her '*marriage*', of all the things that changed from that point on, Martha had marveled at one peculiar detail: how her entrance had the power to fill a room with a tense energy, much like an empty field right before a lightning strike.

She, a woman whose life had previously been so mundane as to attract barely a look, found herself, of a sudden the town's obsession. Of course, in this forgotten corner of Luton, a scandalous tidbit such as a bigamist living amongst them—a woman whose children were therefore illegitimate and whose father had arranged the murder of her late husband—would only ever attract the rabid curiosity.

Martha loosened the fastenings at her throat and looked around. Nearly all the tables were filled with local villagers.

Not even the warmth cast from the fire could chase off the chill that spilled off the occupants in the inn. *You have nothing to be ashamed of. Get your business done and be gone.*

Reflexively, she curled her fingers. Her gaze briefly collided with an unfamiliar patron. Dressed in the same coarse garments as the other men present, he was of a like station, and yet, there was a directness to his clear, ice-blue eyes that cut through her.

She braced for the familiar lascivious stare that inevitably met her arrival.

But the stranger merely met her gaze with a bored disinterest.

Bored disinterest. Who could have imagined the sentiment should be so… glorious, and so very welcome? It was, of course, because the man was a stranger. He didn't know the details of her past, the shameful seeds of her story scattered by some unknown villain. Because, invariably, when a person discovered her scandalous past, the bored disinterest always faded. The stranger forgotten, Martha hurriedly sought out the old innkeeper. "Good morn, Mrs. Lowery. I trust you are well this fine winter's day?"

The old woman attended a table the way she might a lecture from the Lord himself.

"Mrs. Lowery," she repeated, drifting over. The older woman had begun to lose her hearing two years ago. Martha knew, because she'd sat through numerous visits where she'd assured the old gossip that all would be right.

"Miss Donaldson," the other woman said tightly, not bothering to look up. "I heard you."

That brought her up short. "Oh." Collecting herself, Martha drew the missives from inside her father's old satchel. "I have mail to post."

"Mail has gone out for the day."

No! "What?" Her heart sank. "But... that isn't possible."

"Can't help you." Mrs. Lowery tightened her mouth. "Now, you should go. I've work to see to." The older woman made to step around Martha.

Martha's jaw went slack. Why... why... the mail *hadn't* gone out. The old busybody was simply refusing to collect her notes. She hurried over, placing herself in Mrs. Lowery's way and blocking the next table she'd been about to clean. "The mail is *never* picked up at this hour," she said, proud of her steady voice.

"Well, this time it is." The innkeeper glowered at her. "Now, go." She flicked her sopping cloth at Martha, splattering the front of her cloak with dirtied water. "I've my grandson here, and I'll not have him around the likes of you."

As Mrs. Lowery hurried off, Martha stared numbly down at her skirts, damp from the remnants used to clean the tavern tables.

Noisy whispers filled the White Stag.

This was what her life had become. Through no fault of her own, she'd been both shamed and made a whore. She'd unwittingly lived a lie perpetuated by a nobleman, and she should pay the price for it. Turned into an outcast. Both she and her son. Nay, not just them. Martha's heart spasmed. Her daughters. Forced away, so they'd be spared from this, when all the while, no other possible future awaited them... but this. One where the Donaldsons were reviled. Taunted and mocked at every turn, and now... she could not even post mail.

A loud humming filled her ears. It blurred and blended with the whispers of the High Town villagers. They clinked their tankards together. Their laughter blared in her mind, distorted and twisted, the warped expressions of amusement at odds with the tumult of her existence.

Martha snapped. "The mail has not been picked up," she said softly. When the room went quiet, she shouted it. "The mail has not been picked up." A gape-mouthed Mrs. Lowery turned back. Fury, frustration, and hurt propelled Martha forward. "I have lived here for the whole of my life, all twenty-eight years. I know when the post is taken. I know who picks up the mail and delivers it. I know Mr. Browbridge enjoys his spirits too much to ever do something as unlikely as to take the damned mail early."

Gasps went up, and chairs scraped the floor as patrons leaned forward, riveted. "How dare you?" Mr. Lowery shouted from across the tavern.

"You can let yourself out now, Miss Donaldson," Mrs. Lowery said, and then the older woman launched into a scathing diatribe.

Martha's chest rose hard and fast, a tightness making it difficult to draw breath or words. The world was caving in on her. *I should leave.* She should stuff her notes back into her bag, turn on her heel, and march off, asking nothing from this woman… or anyone. Each time she raised her voice or defied the nasty innkeeper, Martha fed every last ill opinion the world had of her.

"Now, I said, *go,*" the other woman said, emphasizing the last word with another flick of her cloth.

Go. Leave. Flee.

And yet, that had been the pattern of her life since her secret had been found out by the villagers of High Town. Since that moment, she'd been defeated in nearly every way. If she left now, it would be just one more failing. One more time they had won, and she'd been ground down by the truth of her circumstances.

Martha shook her head slowly. *I will not.* "I will not," she said, the last vestige of pride pulling the curt rejoinder from her. Letters outstretched, she stalked forward and waved them in the other woman's face. "Now, I've asked you to post my mail, and I'll not ask again." She flattened her lips into a hard line. "In fact, I'm not leaving until you do." Someone grabbed her forearm, wringing a gasp from her.

"You were asked to leave," Mrs. Lowery's son barked. Near to her own height, and painfully thin, the slight man gripped her hard.

Martha, however, had been subject to another man's punishing touch, and she'd never suffer in silence through it. "Do not touch me," she spat, trying to wrest her arm away. He squeezed her tightly, and tears blurred her vision from the pain. Martha blinked back the crystalline expressions of weakness. She'd not allow him or anyone that triumph.

"We don't need your sort darkening our establishment. You want your mail sent? Then you can walk to some other v—"

"Unless you care to have your hand separated from your person," a cool voice intoned, "I suggest you release the young woman."

As one, Martha and the younger Mr. Lowery looked to the tall figure towering over them both, making the most unexpected of interventions. *Him*. The stranger she'd seen earlier. Mr. Lowery jerked his hand back and stumbled away from her.

Martha's heart hammered. Dark-haired, with aquiline features that could have been chiseled from stone, he had the look of that disloyal angel forever cast from the gates of heaven. The frost in his gaze sent a chill through her, and she took a step back in a reflexive attempt at self-preservation.

Those sapphire eyes, so dark they were nearly black, homed in on her, freezing her retreat. Her mouth went dry.

"I believe apologies are in order," he said in a low, smooth baritone that contained an edge of heat and ice all at the same time, contradictory, and yet, perfectly suited to the dark stranger before her.

Her heart resumed a slightly normal cadence. So he sought to play the role of peacemaker and end the scene that she'd caused. Well, he could go to hell with the rest of them.

Martha tipped her chin up at a defiant angle. "I'll not apologize," she said when she trusted herself to speak. "To him, her, you." She turned a harsh stare on the other patrons watching in riveted silence. "Or any of you," she spat. When she again faced the towering stranger, she saw that the faintest smile ghosted his lips.

"You misunderstood, ma'am. Our"—he peeled his lip back in a sneer—"fine proprietors are who I'll have an apology from."

Shock chased off her earlier fear, outrage, and befuddlement. *For me.*

"Indeed, for you," he drawled, and her cheeks went hot at the realization she'd spoken aloud. That brief façade of warmth lifted as the stranger leveled a flinty look at Mr. Lowery.

With this stranger in command, for the first time since her scandal had shaken the village of High Town, Martha was not the figure on display… but rather, another person, this man, was. And as she watched Mr. Lowery and his mother swallow loudly and sputter, questions swirled in Martha's mind, and she could settle on only one with any real clarity.

Who *was* he?

CHAPTER 4

IT TOOK THE UNEXPECTED, YET fortuitous, arrival of Miss Martha Donaldson for Graham to determine two very significant details about his first assignment with the Brethren: One, the young woman whom he was to report on was no insipid, downtrodden widow. And two, the crimson-haired siren, with her flashing eyes and undaunted spirit, possessed a beauty to tempt both sinner and saint.

And Graham had only ever fit firmly in the former column.

The earlier intrigue that had swept through him the moment she'd stepped inside the White Stag, however, receded under the biting sting of fury at the small innkeeper who'd dared put his hand upon Martha Donaldson. While he was guilty of any number of sins, harming a woman was not among the black marks on Graham's soul. Nor would he tolerate any such treatment by another.

When no apology was forthcoming, Graham wrenched the innkeeper's arm back.

The small man squealed. "Please," he implored.

"The apology."

The proprietor proved himself either more foolish or brave than Graham had credited. "She doesn't need an apology."

"Oh," Graham countered, stretching out that syllable, "I disagree. Perhaps we should let the young woman decide, though I doubt if any words from your lips would be worth her even hearing out."

Miss Donaldson glanced around, as if there was another "young woman" in question who'd be the ultimate arbiter of the innkeeper's apology. When she glanced back, her eyes formed round saucers.

"Well, what will it be Mrs.…?" Graham stared expectantly at her.

From somewhere within the tavern, a patron piped in. "She ain't no—"

Graham turned a hard glare on the crowd that effectively silenced the remainder of that utterance, along with what any of the other pathetic men might say. There'd be time enough later to consider the not-so-small scene he'd caused, a direct violation of Lord Edward's commands. Graham looked once more to the young woman who'd set the whole tavern upside down with her presence alone.

Martha Donaldson darted the tip of her tongue out, dampening a plump mouth he really had no place noticing, either in that moment or, with the orders laid forth by his superior, ever. Nonetheless, he was a rogue. And he would remain a rogue until he took his last devilish breath, at last freeing the world of his wickedness.

"Miss Donaldson," she finally said, uttering her first words to Graham in tones that were slightly husky, sultry, without the shrill edge that had marred her exchange with the villagers of High Town. "My name is Miss Donaldson." It was, however, not the temptress pull of her voice that gave him pause.

Miss Donaldson.

Not… *Mrs.*

At his hesitation, the young woman's red brows drew together, bringing Graham back to the task at hand. "The apology," Graham ordered tightly.

Mr. Lowery's fleshy lips moved. His throat bobbed. "I'm—"

The old shrew with her wet rag came racing over. "My son is not apologizing to that woman."

Graham turned his gaze on the harpy, leveling her with a stare that his emotionally deadened father himself couldn't have managed.

The woman recoiled. "Be done with it, Jameson," she commanded.

"I'm… sorry," Mr. Lowery squeezed out.

"I'm sorry, Miss…?" Graham gave the spindly arm another squeeze and took perverse pleasure in the cry he rang from the proprietor. Good. The craven bastard had thought nothing of handling Miss Martha Donaldson in the same way.

"Miss Donaldson," he whined. "I'm sorry, Miss Donaldson."

Graham retained his hold. "Will that suffice, Miss Donaldson?"

Wordlessly, she nodded, and her long crimson plait flopped over her shoulder.

"What do you want now?" Mr. Lowery pleaded when Graham maintained his grip.

"The young woman has some letters she'd like posted."

Silence met his pronouncement, and then with a growl of fury, Mrs. Lowery stalked over and ripped the notes from Martha Donaldson's gloved fingers.

Graham touched a fingertip to the corner of his right eye. "See that nothing happens to it, or I'll return."

With that, the entire room picked up motion once more. Tankards clanged, dilapidated wood chairs scraped the hardwood floor as the show was... forgotten.

Dismissing the miserable lot of High Town villagers, Graham looked toward the young woman whom he'd been tasked with watching after... and caught the flash of her brown wool cloak just as it disappeared through the door. The noise of the room drowned out the click of the panel.

Disbelief swept through him.

Why... why... she'd simply... left. That was hardly what he'd expected. Not that he'd intervened because he'd sought anything from her. He had, however, anticipated his intervention would have been beneficial to his securing an audience with the woman.

Muttering under his breath, Graham hurried over to the table he'd abandoned at the back of the tavern. He gathered up his worn leather satchel and set out after the spirited minx. As soon as he let himself outside, Graham did a quick survey of the grounds to find her.

The young woman moved quickly. Her long-legged steps sent her cloak whipping about her ankles. She'd already built a sizable lead between them. As he closed the door behind him, Miss Donaldson cast a glance over her shoulder... and continued walking.

Swinging his bag onto his arm, Graham hurried after her. "Miss Donaldson?"

The spitfire didn't spare him another look. "I am uninterested."

"I did not offer you anything," he countered, lengthening his stride, and this time, the minx broke into a near run.

"You were going to," she tossed back, quickening her steps to outdistance him.

He'd dallied with any number of women, of all stations and backgrounds, and this humbling moment was the first time his mere presence had set a woman running off.

Of course, given the manner of miserable bastards she shared a village with, it was hardly a wonder, and had she been any other woman, and had the circumstances been unrelated to his business on behalf of the Crown, he'd have stalked off in the opposite direction and left her to her solitude.

But she was his business.

"I want to speak with you."

This time, she did stop. She spun back in a beautiful display of spirit. The quickened pace she'd set, together with the winter wind, had left her cheeks red. "Oh, do you?" she countered in crisp tones. In the cold, her breath stirred little puffs of white. "Never tell me." She folded her arms. "You expect some form of thanks for your rescue."

He bristled. "Actually, I do not." He'd been a selfish bastard plenty of times in his life, but when he'd intervened a short while ago, he'd done so without the expectation of anything in return. "Though, one might argue it certainly is called for."

The young woman eyed him for a long moment. Never had he known a single woman more jaded and world-weary than this spirited beauty before him. And in that instant, she, who'd previously existed only as an unwanted assignment, became something more—a person. It was a dangerous allowance to make, one that presented an agent's assignment as... human. That added layers and emotions that muddied the proverbial waters and could only complicate one's mission.

Finally, she cleared her throat. "Forgive me for seeming ungrateful. I'm not. I'm simply accustomed to—" She abruptly stopped.

"Crass, cruel villagers?" he supplied, jamming the old John Bull hat on his head.

Her lips turned at the corners in a smile, dimpling her left cheek, and for the briefest of moments, she was utterly transformed from the jaded creature who'd taken on the lot of High Town into the bright-eyed innocent she'd surely been at one time. Her grin faded. "You are correct on that score." She held his gaze with a directness most men of his acquaintance couldn't manage, when the ladies he kept company with, as a rule, averted their eyes in masterful acts of coquetry. "Again, I thank you for your earlier assistance." Strangely, he found himself preferring Martha Donaldson's directness. "There is nothing you want in return?"

With that, she gave him an avenue of entrance, and he took it. "I'm looking for employment. I—"

Her expression grew shuttered. "I cannot help you."

He'd made a misstep—he'd moved too quickly. "I understand you are searching for a stable master."

"How do you know that?" she asked sharply.

Bloody hell. Mayhap the Brethren had been wise to ease him into damned missions. Graham curled his lips into the half grin that had charmed Lady Jersey and her disapproving fellow-leading hostesses. "You do not deny you are in need of a stable master," he cajoled.

For the first time in the whole of his rogue's existence, he'd come up empty in his ability to charm. "You heard wrong," she said flatly. "I wish you the best." With finality, she hurried on.

Graham rocked on his heels. "That is it?"

"There is nothing else to say," she called out, not deigning to glance back.

Graham stared after her retreating frame and the back-and-forth sway of her generously curved hips as she marched off with all the regal bearing of a military commander. Any other time, he'd have given the proper rogue's attention to those hips, molded by the threadbare wool cloak dancing wildly about her ankles as she moved.

Why… why… she hadn't given him the time of day.

His assignment was to have been simple: Seek out a young widow in need of a servant, offer his services, and gain access to her, her family, and household. Get in. Get out. And wait for a real assignment. The simplicity of that task had also, ironically, been the reason he'd chafed at his role.

As her figure grew smaller and smaller upon the horizon, Graham confronted the mess he'd made of his first meeting with not only Martha Donaldson but the whole of the High Town village.

He'd put on a spectacular display defending the woman—of which he'd do nothing differently—when his role here demanded he be invisible.

And by the speed with which she'd dashed off, and the guardedness in her gaze, there could be no doubting one truth about the woman he'd been charged with looking after: She didn't trust him.

Now, he was left trying to sort out just how he was to remain close to the spitfire, so he could get on with his assignment and then be done with this place.

MARTHA HADN'T TRUSTED HIM AT sight—Mr. Mystery Stranger, who flawlessly spoke the King's English.

In fact, warning bells had gone off at the back of her mind the moment she'd spied the nameless stranger at the White Stag. Strangers didn't have a place here. There was nothing to attract anyone to this remote corner of Luton. Nor had it mattered that the darkly handsome man had come to her rescue, like some kind of avenging angel. Experience had taught her that men weren't angels. Ultimately, they were all devils of some degree who'd not be content until they had what they wished from a person.

Martha paused at the edge of the Birch Path, and slipping behind one of the thicker trunks, she peeked out. Even with the distance she'd placed between them, the mystery stranger stood out. At six inches past five feet, she'd never been considered short, and yet, with his impressive height, one such as the nameless man across the way would only have earned notice.

Mr. Lowery's son, a slip of a child who'd once been friends with Frederick, approached the man, carrying the reins of a dark mount. She squinted in a bid to bring more clarity to the exchange unfolding. Whatever the stranger said earned a laugh from the boy, and he caught a coin tossed to him by the patron.

A coin…

Martha puzzled her brow.

The stranger's coarse garments and ancient hat stood in direct contradiction to everything else about him: the quality of his horseflesh, his speech, seeking work but handing out coin.

She chewed at her lower lip. No, not everything was as it seemed with that *avenging angel*, and though she'd been besieged by guilt at her failure to properly thank him for his role at the White Stag, she had reason enough to add him firmly to the "not to be trusted" column.

Of course, she didn't trust any men, and with deserved reasons. Life had given Martha countless causes to be suspicious of all men.

There had been: the husband who'd married her under the greatest pretense, and then beat her and bedded her as was his pleasure. The father who, in a twisted bid at obtaining justice for Martha, had seen that bounder murdered. And then, of course, there was Lord Exeter, the man who'd carted her father off but vowed to leave the Donaldson "fortunes" intact. For a brief time, Lord Exeter had restored her faith in men: he'd helped settled her affairs, he'd arranged for Martha's daughters to attend a respectable finishing school.

Until the earl had ceased to visit and another gentleman had come months later to relieve Martha of her funds. That was the last she'd heard or seen the Earl of Exeter.

No, there were no *honorable* men. They thought only of them-selves. After all, how many of the men in High Town had offered her their *assistance*, all the while wanting more? Expecting more from the High Town Whore, as she'd come to be called.

Even coarsely attired as he was, a man with crisp tones to rival the king's speech was hardly the one to be traipsing through the forgotten corner of High Town. Her mouth hardened. The last such man who'd journeyed to her residence, seemingly friendly—his tones, however, giving away his more lofty station—had come to clear her cottage of all the valuables there, at the Crown's doing, of course.

And only after he'd sought to strike a barter system: her body for those baubles.

Well, now nothing remained.

Not even the silver and porcelain; cherished baubles that had belonged to a mother Martha no longer remembered.

There was nothing.

Martha had been stripped bare of everything, and nearly every-one, so that all that remained was her son.

Martha curled her fingers into the tree trunk, and closing her eyes, she allowed the agony and sorrow and desperation, all of it, to wash over her. She let all the sentiments swirl together and batter her with those she'd lost. *Creda. Iris.*

She took each lash of the heartache those beloved names now earned, welcoming them upon her soul.

The daughters who should be with her, but who were better off away from her. At a place where they could flourish. Where they were not constantly reminded of their origins and declared whores at the tender age of eleven, or their fates sealed by men and women who'd never be worthy to kiss the tattered soles of the girls' shoes.

Martha pressed her forehead into the jagged trunk, inviting that pain, too.

Something hard struck her back and brought her eyes flying open. She wheeled around, and another stone found its mark at the center of her chest before falling onto the tip of her boot. Martha glanced down, just as her unknown assailant launched another projectile, this one sailing just past her ear. Her heart climbed into her throat, and she cursed the weakness, hated the fear that always followed her, when her life before had only ever been safe. And because of that previous innocence, she'd been left to try to navigate her way through a world she'd never before known.

She dropped to all fours and crawled. The cold of the frozen ground penetrated her gloves, and she ignored it. The distant rumble of laughter came from five or so paces ahead.

Bastards. All of them. And that included her father for consigning them all to their current fate.

To hell with them all. She'd be damned if they had her crawling about like a kicked pup. Scrambling to her feet, she darted off, weaving between the birch trees. Her pulse pounded loudly in her ears in time to the frantic beat of her footfalls.

Several stones bounced off the nearby trunks, and Martha panted from the pace she'd set for herself, damning her skirts for slowing her flight.

Chase us, Mama. Be the monster… Be the monster…

Her vision blurred as her daughters' pleas and then peals of laughter pinged around memories of happier times.

I will get you… I will—

Martha's hem tangled on a low branch. The fabric caught and then gave with a rending tear. With a cry, she pitched forward and shot her hands out—too late. She came down hard on her stomach. All the air went flying from her lungs, sucking the breath from her, stealing even her scream. The force of her fall sent little flecks of light dancing behind her eyes.

An eerie silence fell over the Birch Path, the quiet honored by all but the gusting winter wind that sent flakes falling around her. On her. And she lay there, absolutely motionless, with her face buried in a slick patch of mud. She dimly registered a jagged rock ripping a hole through her glove and shredding her flesh.

Numb, Martha turned her head and stared beyond the nearest tree, unable to move.

This is what I've become. Her gaze locked on the faintest dusting of snow that lingered under a low-hanging branch, the white patch sullied by a smattering of dirt and brush. Stains upon what had once been pure. How did that hidden spot of snow come to be so marred? How, when it was tucked away, so neatly hidden under the protective cover of the High Town trees?

She felt something damp trickle down her cheek, and her heart stirred. She'd lost. Those drops had filled her eyes and, each time, had gone unshed. Until now.

She reached a quivering finger up and caught the bit of moisture, needing to see the stain upon her glove. To remember that she was capable of crying after all and that she'd not become the dead-inside figure that she so oftentimes felt.

Martha drew her hand back and didn't blink.

Mud clung to the tips of her gloves.

Not tears. But grime and dirt that dripped from her ear and even now soaked her garments through.

With a half sob, Martha rolled onto her back and stared blankly overhead. *I cannot even cry.* She'd not managed that simplest of acts since her father had been carted off.

The wind continued to gust around the countryside. It sent the branches dancing overhead, parting and swaying to reveal the gray, heavily clouded sky.

Snow hung in the air. This time of year had once been her favorite as a girl, and then as a young mother who'd chased not one but three children through the snow-covered hillside.

Martha sucked in a shuddery sigh, and with the snow falling around her, she at last conceded the truth she'd kept from even herself.

I need help.

CHAPTER 5

ᴇARLY ON, GRAHAM HAD PERFECTED the art of silent footfalls.

That skill had come long before his training with the Brethren. As a boy in eternal competition with two older, and more accomplished in every way, brothers, he'd pushed himself in foot races until he'd proven the most fleet of foot.

As such, the reins of his mount loosely tied to a nearby birch, Graham ventured down the path Martha Donaldson had traveled a short while ago with those same measured steps, his gaze taking in everything as he went.

Everything with the Brethren, each assignment's success, hung upon the art of timing: how long to wait before setting out in pursuit of one's quarry, what pace one should set. All of it was more an art that ultimately decided one's success. It was a lesson his mentor had delivered, and in those discussions, they'd always come back to one's quarry being the enemy.

Martha Donaldson, however, was no enemy of the Crown. She was no threat to the country's peace or wealth.

And yet, this search for her was no different.

Graham might resent the post he'd been given and crave the more worthwhile pursuits of other members of the Brethren. However, this was his mission, and he'd be damned if he'd fail at it. Particularly when everything about the task indicated it should be easy. He should complete it successfully, and then be on to the more meaningful work he craved.

Graham sidestepped fallen branches lightly dusted with snow and brush that would alert anyone of his presence. While he walked, he examined the narrow pathway, touching his gaze on everything, including broken twigs and footprints.

Three sets.

Two larger…

Graham stopped. And one smaller. He sharpened his stare on the delicate-sized imprint, the faintest fleck of white beginning to conceal the mark. Dropping to his haunches, he measured the indent with his palm.

Too large to be a child and too small to belong to most men.

Unease prickled at his nape, that innate sense that urged a person to flee or perish. It was that instinct that was to guide an agent of the Crown. A sentiment that wasn't to be ignored.

She'd been followed. Set after by someone. Two someones.

With slow, measured movements, Graham straightened. He resumed his earlier march along the lightly snow-covered ground, registering a detail he'd failed to note before—the utter silence.

There was no distant echo of footfalls. There was… nothing but the forlorn whistle of the wind.

Cursing, Graham quickened his pace, weaving among the birch trees as he walked.

Then he heard it.

A tortured half sob echoed in the winter quiet, carried by the wind, made all the more explosive for the silence ushered in by the snow.

He took off at a dead run, measuring the distance in his mind between him and the owner of that expression of misery. His pulse pounded in his ears as he leaped over a log. Landing on his feet, Graham took off running again and then skidded to a stop.

Out on the main path, a slender figure lay sprawled, arms and legs outstretched, her wool cloak spread about her.

Martha Donaldson.

Panic knocked around his chest. By God, he'd not fail her or the damned mission. At last, Graham reached her.

The young woman opened her eyes. Those aquamarine pools went wide as terror filled their depths. A scream tore from her throat. She shot a foot up, nearly catching him in the groin.

Cursing, he stepped out of her reach.

For what the minx missed in efficacy, she made up for in determination. She rolled out of reach and then came at him from behind, launching herself at him, briefly upsetting his balance.

Graham came sprawling down hard on the earth. "Oomph."

She made to deliver another attack, but he caught her by the ankle, toppling her. He rolled swiftly, bracing her fall so that she landed atop his chest.

"What are you doing?" she rasped, bucking against him. Her frantic breath stirred the winter air. She managed to wedge a knee between his legs, but again, he anticipated that strike, and her blow landed ineffectually.

Lessons. The young woman was going to require lessons in how to defend herself. Graham mentally filed that detail away. "I was saving you," he gritted out. God, she was feisty. Spirited, and yet, unskilled in the fight. She expended more energy than her body could sustain.

Her teeth chattered in the cold. "I do *n-not* need saving." She thrashed against him, and her frenzied movements twisted her cloak with his, hampering her efforts to dislodge him.

He'd known her less than an hour but would wager his coveted post with the Brethren that she needed precisely that—saving. He was also wise enough not to counter the avowal, particularly from a spitfire with fire glimmering in her eyes.

"I d–don't," she gritted, having followed his unspoken statement. She drew her boot back and kicked him hard in the shin, an impressive deliverance given the awkward angle of her body.

Graham allowed the young widow her fury, and when she showed no sign of quitting, he rolled her under him, effectively trapping her. "Enough," he growled, catching her wrists, securing them with his left hand.

Her eyes bled fear. It spilled from every delicate plane of her expressive features.

His gut clenched, and damn if he didn't feel like a bloody monster. When he spoke, he gentled his tones. "I'm not going to hurt you," he assured. He made to reach for his cloak, but the young woman recoiled, and he abruptly stopped.

The terror only deepened in eyes that were neither blue, nor green, but a shade in between that conjured those mystical finned sirens his shipmates had told tales of.

"Get off me," she panted, and despite the faintest tremble to that last syllable, there was a splendid display of resolve and strength. Not for the first time since she'd entered the White Stag, admiration stirred for the young widow.

When Graham had been a young man just entering university, his father had purchased, Scoundrel, a prized thoroughbred from another nobleman. The previous owner had attempted to beat the spirited thoroughbred into submission. Not a single stable master Graham's father had brought in to train the mount had succeeded. Only Graham had. Martha Donaldson put Graham in mind of that now loyal, affectionate mount.

Those lessons at the forefront of his mind, Graham came to his feet slowly and then backed away. "My name is Graham Malin." He stretched out a hand.

And waited.

And waited.

Martha Donaldson eyed his fingers like they were the forbidden fruit that would doom all mankind to eternal sin if she touched them.

Everything, however, came back to the matter of timing, of knowing when to push and when to wait, and this woman, skittish like a wounded beast, required time.

And a good deal of it.

At last, she reached tentative fingers out and allowed him to help her stand. The moment she was on her feet, she took several quick steps away from him.

Graham noted the details that had escaped him during their earlier tussle. Crimson curls had come free of her long plait, with muddied strands plastered to her face and cloak. Dirt caked her cheeks and garments.

Again, Graham reached inside his cloak, and Martha Donaldson tripped over herself in her haste to put more space between them. "What are you—?" Her words cut off abruptly as he withdrew a white kerchief and held it out, a silent offering.

She hesitated before rushing over. She ripped the article from his fingers and hurried back to her respective spot. As she cleaned the mud from her face, she studied him over the top of the fabric.

Every woman of his acquaintance, his own mother included, filled voids of silence. As a rule, people were uncomfortable with them and prattled on in a bid to have something, rather than nothing, said. In those instances, agents for the Crown were instructed to gather every last revelation and later sort out what incriminating piece a person had shared.

Martha Donaldson, however, proved different once more. She owned the silence with a pride that not even the queen could command.

At last, she finished wiping off her face and tossed the kerchief back to him. A gust of wind caught the stained fabric and carried it closer. Graham shot a hand out to catch it.

A glob of mud remained at her temple. "You've missed some. May I?" he murmured. Taking her silence as a concession, he gently wiped away the last remnant of her fall. He should be singularly focused on the task, as pragmatic as tying a cravat, and yet, even as he reminded himself of that, his gaze took in details he had no place noting: the cream-white hue of her skin, dusted with the lightest swath of freckles. The delicate shells of her ears, the right lobe graced with a heart-shaped birthmark. Wide, crimson lips. Lips that were made for kissing.

I am going to hell…

Of course, that had been determined long ago… on the fields of Kent, to be precise, when he'd challenged his brother to that last, and fatal, race. His focus should be entirely reserved for how the woman he'd been tasked with looking after had come to be in such a state. "What happened?" he asked quietly after he'd finished cleaning away the mud.

She eyed him suspiciously. "What does it matter to you, Mr.…?"

"Malin. Graham Malin." The two names had been decided by his mother, and he left off his first name, the hated one selected by his father.

"What does it matter to you, then, Mr. Graham Malin?" she asked, stepping around him, and for a moment, he thought she intended to march off and leave, as she'd done twice before. This time, however, she ambled around in a small circle, searching the ground as she went. There was no biting inflection to the question, but rather, a tiredness, the first hint of flagging from this woman.

"Because it does," he said as she continued to walk about. And it did. She was his assignment, and it was his role to determine the state of her existence and report his findings to his superior.

Martha Donaldson muttered something under her breath as she wandered around in a little circle. "Where is it? Where is it?"

Graham did a sweep and swiftly located the leather satchel she'd been carrying. He jogged ahead, registering Martha Donaldson's stare as he moved past her. "Here," he called over, gathering the bag by its strap. Returning, he tossed it over.

The young widow caught it in her arms and clutched it close to her chest in a protective manner. "Thank you," she said carefully.

He lifted his head.

"What do you want, Mr. Malin?"

"I told you—"

"No, really," she said flatly. "You're a stranger to High Town. No one comes to High Town." And with good reason. The people were bloody horrid and the ale rot. Yes, there was little to recommend this corner of Luton. "You've come to my assistance now twice. Three times, if one considers your now dirtied kerchief." She shook her head. "People don't do that without reason."

She was correct. Men and women of all stations were driven by ulterior motives. "Some do." His, however, must remain cloaked in secrecy.

"Mmm-mmm," she countered. "That is not my experience. Your horse." She jerked her chin toward the end of the path. "Where is your mount?"

He furrowed his brow.

"I saw you," she went on. "I watched you leave the inn. Your garments are coarse, your boots old. But your speech and the quality of your horseflesh don't belong to a… man in search of employment," she said in a flawless echo of the lie he'd given her at the White Stag Inn.

Bloody hell. The minx missed nothing. With her astuteness and clever attention to detail, the Brethren would be best served with her among their ranks. And he knew in that moment, if he didn't offer her some truths, she'd stalk off one more time, and that would be the end of his efforts at employment in her household. "I spent a large part of my life in a nobleman's stables." Truth. "I was skilled with the mounts." Also true. That skill, however, had only earned him his father's ducal disapproval. "I aspired for more and believed the King's Navy was my path to a greater opportunity." The King's Navy, that most glorified of all the navies in the world, had represented his hopes for leaving a mark upon the world for being something more than a duke's third, and least clever, son.

Her features softened, but her eyes remained wary. "And it wasn't?" she ventured quietly.

"It wasn't." He'd been searching years after and only just found it. "I returned home and sought employment. To no avail." Which was *also* true. He'd been initially rejected from the ranks of the Brethren.

And Graham, who'd believed himself long jaded by life to cease feeling anything, felt his heart pull at the wariness from a woman just twenty-eight years old. What struggle had she known that she'd come to view the world with the same suspicions he himself carried? "I served in the Royal Navy, and after my service, when I returned to England…" He glanced beyond her shoulder. *I was thrust once more into the mindless pursuits that existed for members of the peerage, an empty, purposeless existence.*

Her soft, husky contralto called him back. "H–how did you come to be here?" she asked, rubbing her gloved hands together, her long digits close to her mouth, as if she sought to breathe warmth into them through the fabric.

He noted the fraying at her fingertips.

The lady was in dire straits. Whichever member of the Brethren had sought to see her looked after had failed in several regards.

She followed his focus and swiftly tucked her hands behind her back.

Wordlessly, Graham reached inside his jacket.

Martha Donaldson hesitated, but some of the tension left her when he handed over the advert.

With the snow falling around them, she accepted the page and read. "I sent this nearly three months ago," she murmured, lifting the neatly clipped piece. The wind toyed with its edges. "No one responded. Why should you do so now?"

God, the young woman was clever. And not for the first time since she'd arrived at the inn, he acknowledged that he had dangerously underestimated both her and this assignment.

"Because my hopes for other work proved unfruitful." He offered another truth there. "Have you filled the post?" Graham asked when she continued to study the words on the advert.

She shook her head. "I've… not."

It was that moment, with those two words and a slight pause, when Graham knew. He knew, despite her earlier resistance, that she wanted to hire if not him… then someone. That, for her reservations and suspicions—both of which had proven correct—she wished to ignore her instincts and offer him the post.

In the end, her misgivings won out.

"I did seek an all-purpose servant. I haven't since I sent that out. I stopped… I…" Martha trained all her focus on the advert. "I am… no longer looking for anyone." The color deepened on her cheeks.

She didn't have the funds.

Her eyes sparked in a fiery defiance that dared him to voice that understanding.

What had happened to Miss Martha Donaldson to see her both wary and impoverished? And why, when his work required neither of those details, should it matter? Aside from his case, why did he feel that familiar stirring of regret for what her life was and a need to know those answers?

It isn't your need to know.

His superior and the Brethren could all go to hell with that directive. He served, but not blindly. He'd carry out his mission, but he'd not be content until he found out the secrets that this woman carried.

Sensing her weakening, Graham pounced. "I require a bed, food, and a roof over my head until I can secure other work. If you can provide those, I'll oversee your livestock and tend your horses and serve in whatever capacity you require."

Martha Donaldson warred with herself, the battle reflected in her expressive eyes. "I…cannot. Even if I wished to help you, I've other people who rely upon me, and I can't afford to have strangers about."

There was a finality to that rejection that indicated it would be the last she gave. Her mind wouldn't be altered.

She was desperate for help, but not so desperate that she'd take it wherever it was proffered. Martha Donaldson resumed walking.

"Miss Donaldson, someone followed you here," he called after her.

She missed a step, steadied herself, and turned back. "Mr. Malin?"

"Whoever it was sent you running. That is how you fell. You

were attacked."

The young woman hugged her arms close about her chest and then, catching his stare on that protective gesture, swiftly dropped those long limbs to her sides. "It was just nasty village boys," she said, her lips trembling in the cold. Only, this time, there was uncertainty in her gaze.

"You are wrong," he said flatly. Nor was his merely a ploy to secure her trust or the post. "I saw the tracks, I measured the steps. Those weren't the footprints of young boys."

The blood drained from her cheeks, leaving crimson splotches of cold stark circles upon the cream-white flesh. "Wh-why would anyone seek to harm me?" Her slender body quaked. Was it the cold? Fear? Mayhap both.

"I don't know the answer to that," he admitted, beating his hat against his leg. He had an entire file with the limited details he was expected to know. Everything else about her and her past, present, and future was, and would remain, a mystery. "I only know what I observed. And the local villagers hardly seem the friendliest lot toward you. Now, I'd ask you to permit me to escort you home."

A heavy wind gusted down the path, whipping up a whorl of snowflakes.

"And why should I trust you?" Martha Donaldson jutted her chin up. "You're nothing but a stranger to these parts."

"I trust those villagers you've known… what? The whole of your life?"

Martha Donaldson cocked her head.

Graham took a step toward her. The snow, increasing in intensity, swirled between them. "You were likely born here, grew up here, never left."

A muscle jumped at the corner of her eye.

"Based on that, it hardly seems the length of a relationship means much in terms of reliability, Miss Donaldson," he explained.

The young widow twisted her fingers in her cloak. He saw it. She wanted to send him on his way. She wanted to tell him to take his suppositions and head to the devil. "They were… not children's footsteps, then?"

He shook his head.

There was a rustle ahead, deep in the brush, the tread of someone moving quickly away from them.

Martha Donaldson automatically took a step toward him. "If you accompany me home, there is no work for you there," she said, her lips trembling.

He inclined his head in acknowledgment.

With that, she nodded, urging him on, and together they first gathered his mount and then started on for her cottage.

She'd not sent him away.

Now, how to go about convincing the stubborn minx that she not only wanted him in her employment but she also needed him.

CHAPTER 6

IT WAS UNDOUBTEDLY A MISTAKE.

Having made countless of them in her life, everything about her decision this day had the makings, trappings, and indications of an error on Martha's part.

I shouldn't have allowed him to return with me...

And yet, he'd come to her rescue twice. He'd wiped the grime from her face with a tenderness not even the man she'd married had managed in any exchange during that false union.

Fool. You've always been and will always be a fool.

"Who is that?" Frederick asked spiritedly, darting from window to window and following the stranger inspecting his mount in front of their cottage.

"Drop the curtain, Freddie," she whispered, setting her satchel down.

The excited little boy pressed his forehead to the frosted windowpane, and Martha sighed.

There'd been a time when Frederick had listened, when he'd been dutiful and hung on every word or request made by his mother.

"Did you find someone?" he asked, finally glancing at her.

"No." He'd found her. She did not, however, no matter how desperate she was, intend to allow Mr. Graham Malin to remain on.

"Then what is he doing here?"

It was a fair question from the befuddled boy.

"He... helped me home."

The curtain fell from Frederick's fingers. "Did someone hurt you?" he demanded, his hands making fists at his sides.

"No," she said quickly.

Except, her son now saw too much. "Your gloves are ripped." Martha curled her hands reflexively. "They weren't before." He lifted accusatory eyes. "You and your cloak are covered in mud."

"I fell," she soothed. "That is all."

Frederick stomped over. "You are lying. I know, because you're a rotten liar. You get all quiet and talk in that fake voice."

"I'm not lying," she returned, taking his hands in hers. "I was rushing to avoid the storm and fell along the Birch Path. Mr. Malin came upon me and offered to accompany me home." Which he had. While she'd braced for him to assail her about the position of servant, he'd asked not once. In fact, he'd not offered another word along the whole journey back. He'd merely requested to feed his horse before returning.

Frederick eyed her for a long while. "Who is Mr. Malin?"

"He's… a stranger. New to High Town."

"What is he doing here?" As if overnight, her son had gone from a ten-year-old to a twenty-year-old, challenging her at every turn.

And blast if her son, a mere boy, wasn't correct—she was a rotten liar. Making a show of removing her gloves, Martha stalked over to the hearth and set them down to dry. "I couldn't say. He's passing through and asked that we allow him to feed his mount, and given his earlier assistance, I thought it would be fair." Fair, even as the funds were so limited that it would strain their monthly allotment for feed. Unfastening her muddied cloak, she removed it. The sopping garment littered the floor with mud and remnants of the snowstorm.

"He helped you when you fell," her son repeated, following her as she walked past.

"He did."

"And accompanied you back?"

He peppered her with more questions than Lord Exeter had when he'd taken her father away. "Yes, and he'll be on his way soon," she assured him.

Except, it seemed she'd misread the reason for her son's concern. "He helped you, and you are going to turn him out in a snowstorm for it?" Frederick scoffed. "That hardly seems properly appreciative to me."

So this was what his questions were about. He wanted Mr. Malin to remain on. "He's a stranger, Frederick," she said, the matter at an end. Martha stalked over to the kitchens. Entering the small quarters off the main living area, she went through the rote movements of boiling a kettle of water for tea.

Undeterred, Frederick followed her. "He is a stranger who helped you," he pointed out tenaciously.

"You know what I've told you about strangers."

He lifted his shoulders in an insolent little shrug. "You've told me a lot of things. Given the way the villagers we've known all our lives have treated us, I hardly think it's fair to judge a stranger."

Martha frowned as her son echoed Mr. Malin's earlier opinion.

"Mayhap he wants to remain on here and assist us," he suggested, just as she reached for a teacup from the top shelf.

The delicate porcelain, one of the remaining pieces left from her mother, toppled to the floor and exploded, spraying the floral-painted remnants around the room.

Her son widened his eyes. "It's what he wanted, isn't it? The post? It's why he's here in High Town?" he asked before she had a chance to answer his first question.

Blast and damn. When had her son become so bloody perceptive? Her hesitation was enough to answer his question.

"That is it! He's come for the post, and you've turned him down," he cried.

"We don't have the funds, Frederick." Martha picked a careful path over the shattered porcelain and fetched the dustbin and broom.

"He's the first person who's expressed an interest," her son shot back as she returned and began tidying the mess. "The stables are falling apart, Mama."

"They're not *falling* apart," she said defensively as she dropped to a knee and began collecting the larger fragments and dropping them into the dustpan. "They are in a bit of disrepair. But they aren't as bad as all that."

He stomped over, and hovering over her, he dropped his hands on his little hips. "Aren't they? The stalls are a mess. The livestock needs looking after. We cannot keep up with the digging in." With every word fired back, his voice pitched higher. "You don't have the time to care for the house and your artwork and the stables." Each accurately leveled charge struck, more painful because it came from her son. While children were supposed to see their mothers or fathers as invincible, capable of anything and everything, as she had her own father, her son saw only her failings.

Martha stared vacantly at the crimson flower upon the shard in her hand. Mayhap Frederick was better off. Mayhap seeing the failure she was as a woman and mother would cure him of unrealistic expectations. That way, he'd never be so blindly loyal, as she had been when she'd trusted her father and his decisions about the viscount.

"Are you even listening to me?" he cried.

She forced herself to look at him, this tiny person who'd once only ever been smiling, but was now riddled with suspicion and fear. "I am listening to you, Frederick," she said softly. Both to the words he'd said and, just as important, the ones he hadn't—he was afraid for the both of them. "We don't have the funds to afford Mr. Malin's services." *I require a bed, food, and a roof over my head.* Frederick's gaze bore into her, and for a horrifying moment, she feared her far-too-insightful son had gathered that she'd lied to him—again. "But we'll be fine," she rushed to assure him. Quitting her task, Martha came to her feet and took a step toward him.

Eyes flashing, Frederick took a hasty step away from her.

Since the state of her marriage had come to light, rejection was to be Martha's fate.

It was, however, the first time that rejection had come from her son. It had been inevitable. She'd braced for it. Known it was coming. Dreaded the moment.

Nothing could have properly prepared her for how much it cut. "We're doing fine, though, aren't we?" she whispered, her voice cracking in a show of weakness that turned the query into an entreaty. "We aren't doing so very terribly."

"We are not fine."

Her fingers automatically curved around the shard in her palm. Had Frederick shouted those four words, it would have been easier to take than the somber pragmatism from a boy who'd once had a joyous smile on his lips.

Frederick stepped around her, and coward that she was, Martha couldn't look at him. She couldn't follow his retreat. Suddenly, he stopped. "Do you know what I think, Mother?"

She winced. *Mother*.

Not the beloved *Mama* she'd always been. Her eyes stung. "What do you think?" she brought herself to ask when.

"I don't think you fell. I think you were running from someone, and Mr. Malin saved you."

Her mind stalled. How could he know that? How could a child whose greatest challenge one year ago had been finding the best hiding spot in games of hide-and-go-seek with Billy Lowery now suspect darker truths that she herself had, a short while ago, denied.

"And for that help, you'd turn him out in the middle of a snow-storm?"

"It's hardly a storm." Her voice emerged pathetically weak to her own ears.

A sound of disgust left her son. "I'm going to see if Mr. Malin requires any help with his mount."

Martha dimly registered his quiet tread, the click of the door, and then silence as he went off.

Martha held herself absolutely still, afraid to move, afraid to breathe. Afraid that if she did, she'd splinter apart like the broken teacup and remain as useless as that beloved piece.

They were falling apart—in every way.

Despite Lord Exeter's vow to see that their fortunes would remain intact and her future secure, all of it had been ripped asunder. What reason did her son have to trust in Martha's ability to care for him? Why, when the extent of her caring for his sisters had been to send them away?

I don't want to go, Mama. Please… Let us stay with you.

A sticky warmth wound its way down her wrist, and she looked at the crimson stain dripping on the floor.

Giving her head a hard shake, Martha released the jagged cup fragment, and it landed with a little clink atop another larger piece of porcelain.

She'd been wrong many, many times. Too many to count. Those errors had taught her to move through life more cautiously and to be suspicious of everyone. She was not wrong. Not in this.

Even as she told herself that, and believed it with each fiber of her cynical soul, her son's charges against her echoed in her mind.

For Mr. Malin had come to her defense and escorted her home, asking for nothing in return but to care for his mount. And along the way, he'd been perfectly respectful.

And for that help, you'd turn him out in the middle of a snowstorm?
She groaned. Blast and damn.

She'd allow him to remain the night, and then he was gone.

Except, as she wrapped a kitchen rag about her hand and finished cleaning the mess, Martha could not rid herself of the worry that nothing good could come from Graham Malin being here—even for just a night.

THE FIRST THING THAT HIT Graham as he entered the stables was the odor. More specifically, the stench of urine. It stung his nostrils and lingered. He briefly pressed his forearm against his nose to dull the strength of the pungent smell.

Letting the stable door hang open, he let some of the winter air spill into the previously closed-up space.

Doffing his hat, Graham scanned the darkened stables to assess this particular state of Martha Donaldson's affairs. Row after row of stalls that were empty. Floors were littered with hay that was dusty and moldy from age. Rusted equipment, an ancient muck fork and rake, hung from one wall. A broom lay in the middle of the floor, as if it had been hastily abandoned by a worker who'd quit and never returned.

As a boy, as a young man, and then as a man, Graham had long thought of stables as his sanctuary. They had been the one place he'd escaped to and found joy. For there, he'd not been riddled with reminders of everything he couldn't do. Instead, everything made sense.

Horses he understood. He'd long preferred their company to all—his mother's company the only one excluded. Horses understood a person's mood, what they were feeling, and they sought nothing that a person could not give.

He stopped and did a small circle, inspecting Martha's stables. To see one in such a state of disrepair filled him with a restlessness.

He'd protested his assignment, chafed at being made a servant, and yet, Lord Edward had been correct—horses were his strength. The sole one he possessed. This was something he could set to rights… if the spitfire allowed it.

From the far back stall, a lone whinny split the quiet, forlorn and lonely in this empty place. As Graham approached, a white mare ducked her head over the top. "Hello, love," he cooed.

The beautiful creature stomped nervously at the floor.

"You're as wary as your mistress, I see."

Big brown eyes stared back.

Fishing a piece of peppermint from inside his cloak, Graham held it out. The horse consumed the sugary offering in one bite.

"You're short of company, I see."

She stamped her foot in equine acknowledgment.

Stroking her between the eyes, Graham sighed and added another mental note to the report he'd construct that evening.

With just one horse to five empty stalls, the young widow had been forced to sell off her mounts.

He'd known Martha Donaldson less than two hours, and in that time, he'd surmised the lady was in dire straits: financial, emotional, and by the state of her stables… structural. Whichever member of the Brethren had sought to see her cared for had failed miserably on every score.

The mare's ears pricked up, and Graham stilled, alerted to the presence of another before he even heard the approach.

"Hullo," a little voice piped in from the front of the stables.

Graham found the owner of that child's voice.

There's a boy, too. A ten-year-old.

This was the son, then.

Painfully small, slender, and pale, he put Graham in mind of himself all those years ago. Back when he'd sought his father's ducal approval. Back when Lawrence had been alive, and the Whitworth boys had been friendly to one another, children who'd delighted in making mischief together. "Hullo," he called out in return.

The child hesitated a moment before drifting forward.

Graham followed the boy's careful approach. The extent of Graham's experience with children was consigned to… this moment and this moment only. Women—the boy's mother excluded—Graham was utterly at ease around. Children… With their innocence and tiny sizes, they might as well have been creatures born to another planet.

The boy stopped several paces away. "My name is Frederick

Donaldson. You may call me Frederick."

Graham adjusted his collar. So this was how the nameless White Mount felt, then. Uncertain. "Uh… hullo," he repeated, because, really, what else was one supposed to say to a ten-year-old boy? What would you do if he was a grown man? *Names. Introductions.* "I'm—"

"Graham Malin. I know," the child said flatly, folding his arms at his chest. "My mother told me."

They stared at each other for a long while, neither speaking.

In the end, the child proved far more capable of striking up discourse than a twenty-eight year old Graham. "I understand you found my mother."

Just how much had the young mother divulged to her son? "Uhh…" *Stuttering.* This was what the Donaldson family had reduced him to.

"I'd like to thank you," Frederick said, puffing out his chest. "For helping my mother." He stretched his hand out. "I appreciate your coming to her assistance."

Graham placed his gloved hand in the boy's, closing his fingers for a formal shake, but not before noting the coarse, dry skin dusted with blood. He narrowed his eyes, sharpening his gaze on the boy's bruised knuckles. "Don't thank me," he murmured. "That is merely what a man should do. Help where one is able."

Frederick nodded his ascent. "Yes." His eyes darkened. "But that isn't always the way people are, though."

In that moment, he who'd been hopelessly uncertain around the boy found a kindred connection. "You are right on that score."

"Were you talking to her?" Frederick cleared his throat. "That is… I heard you speaking to her. The horse."

Graham followed the boy's gaze to the white horse. "Indeed." He rewarded the mare with another caress. "What is her name?"

"Guda."

"That is quite an interesting name for a beautiful girl," Graham murmured to the horse, continuing to stroke that sensitive place between her ears. "Guda." Feeling Frederick's eyes on him, Graham looked down at his small companion.

"It is kind of silly, talking to horses, no?" Frederick asked. "I mean, they are just animals. I used to speak to them…" The boy stole a peek up at Graham. "My mother insisted I stop speaking to them."

Graham frowned. "Did she?" It fit with the serious young woman, cool at every turn.

Frederick nodded.

Graham retrieved another piece of peppermint and offered it to the mount.

They are just animals, Sheldon. I'll not have you visiting them and speaking to them as such anymore.

Graham rested his arms along the top of the doors leading into the stall. "They are just animals," he concurred, warming to his and Frederick's discussion. For all his earlier discomfort, this was a topic on which he could speak with any person. "Horses are *just* animals who are responsible for helping us travel. Or plowing fields." He grinned wryly. "I'd say better than most men. Our mail is delivered because of them. They'll charge into battle, with nothing more than a command, and give their lives without so much as faltering in the face of cannon fire." Opening the stall door, Graham slipped inside to better inspect the horse's condition. As he evaluated the Donaldsons' remaining mare, Graham made a show of stroking Guda's withers.

"Did you know"—he glanced back to the boy lingering at the threshold of the stall—"the ancient Greeks would use horses for those people with incurable diseases?"

Wide-eyed, Frederick sidled closer. "For what purpose?" Unabashed curiosity coated his question.

"Hippocrates—"

"The Greek physician!" Frederick interrupted, his eyes glowing with excitement.

"You've heard of him?"

The child nodded frantically. "My grandfather…" His words died, and the light went out. And just as that brief moment of pleasure had emanated from Martha Donaldson outside the inn, and then died moments later, so too was Frederick's joy extinguished.

What secrets and sadness plagued this family? Graham knew not to prod, instead allowing the boy to finish his thought.

"My grandfather told me of him," Frederick finally said, offering nothing more.

"Hippocrates discovered and wrote about the therapeutic value of riding. Since then, there have been writings all hailing the benefits of equine riding for gout, neurological disorders, and people…" *Suffering from low morale.* He looked to the boy and found the child's eyes on him.

"And people…?"

Graham returned his attention to Guda. "And people of a vast many other needs."

"Hmm. I never heard any of that," the boy marveled. Going up on tiptoe, he mimicked Graham's gentle caress and stared on with a new appreciation in his expressive eyes.

Outside, the increasing tempest pummeled the stables, sending the aged wood creaking and groaning.

Guda tossed her head back and bared her teeth.

"Easy," Graham soothed. "Do you know the most wonderful thing about horses, Frederick?" he asked when the fierce wind had died down.

Frederick shook his head.

"They ask for nothing in return. They only give."

CHAPTER 7

THE MYSTERIOUS STRANGER, MR. GRAHAM Malin, spoke to horses… and children.

Martha remained rooted to the entrance of the stables. Even with the chill cutting through her and snow slapping at her face, she was unable to enter. Because in this moment, she would be an interloper. Because of the intensity of that exchange. And because of the foreignness of it.

They ask for nothing in return. They only give.

Those nine words, just two sentences, stirred equal parts guilt and wonder in Martha.

At every moment, she'd questioned Graham Malin's motives, even the story he'd given her about his work with horses.

Only to find herself humbled by her own cynicism.

Through her tumult, Frederick and Mr. Malin continued their easy discourse about horses, their exchange as natural as two who'd known each other a lifetime rather than a handful of minutes.

"…a horse can run just hours after their birth."

"Truly?" her son asked with an enthusiasm she'd not heard from him… mayhap ever. Oh, he'd always been an excitable child, easy to smile, and easier to laugh. But he hadn't been untouched by life's cruelty. Having an absent father, one he forever asked after, Frederick spent too many hours wondering about a man who'd never deserved him.

Emotion clogged her throat as a mere stranger proved that mayhap there were men who listened to and spoke to children.

"And look here," Mr. Malin was saying. "Do you see how her eyes are on the sides of her head? Because of that positioning, they are able to see nearly three hundred and sixty degrees at one time."

"Mayhap my mom has horse eyes," Frederick muttered. "Because she's always able to see what I'm doing."

Mr. Malin laughed. That unrestrained mirth, joined with her son's, suffused her chest, filling her. With a lightness. With a joy, she herself had also not known… in more years than she could remember. Such warmth went through her that she ceased to feel the cold ravaging her through her garments. She closed her eyes, allowing the two distinctly different and wonderful expressions wash over her.

A heavy wind yanked the stable doors open, and the loud creak slashed through the quiet.

"Hello," Mr. Malin called out, rushing forward. He held a staying hand up behind him, warding Frederick off.

Oh, God. That protective gesture on her son's behalf sent her heart flipping over itself.

As he caught Martha standing there, Graham Malin stopped abruptly.

Frederick crashed into him. "Mother?" her son asked in high-pitched confusion, like old Mrs. Blackwood had when she'd caught a thirteen-year-old Martha sneaking through her properties in the dead of night to sketch a star shower.

She forced herself to move. Avoiding the older, more mature of the gazes trained on her, the probing one, Martha hurried inside, closing the door behind her. "You should be inside."

Frederick stepped out from behind the stranger he'd been speaking so freely with moments ago. "I said I was going to help Mr. Malin before you *send him away.*"

She winced at those slightly emphasized words delivered as an accusation. "Run inside so I might speak to Mr. Malin."

Her son opened his mouth to protest, but Martha fixed a look on him. For now, the potency of that "mother's look" still possessed some power.

With a sigh, Frederick kicked at the hay. Except, instead of rushing off, he turned to Mr. Malin. "Thank you for the lessons."

Mr. Malin inclined his head. "A pleasure, Frederick."

By the ease with which that assurance slipped from the dark

stranger, Martha believed it, when she still wanted to distrust him and his motives. It would have been easier to face him, to send him away, to doubt him… had he been coolly aloof or unkind to her son. But he hadn't. He'd proven himself a man who not only tolerated a child about, but treated him with the same respect he would a man. She waited as her son took his leave and closed the door, leaving her and Mr. Malin… alone.

"I did not properly thank you before," she said, beginning her prepared speech.

He made to speak, but she held a hand up, silently begging for him to allow her to finish her thoughts. Exhaling, her breath stirred a little cloud of white, and she continued her rehearsed words. "I know you did not intervene because you sought my gratitude or… or…" She recoiled. *My body.* That favor that so many had come here asking for, demanding, and expecting. "Anything," she finished lamely. There had been a time when she'd been an honorable lady, respected by all, a young woman who honored and adhered to all propriety. All that had been lost the moment she'd committed bigamy. Giving this man a proper thanks restored one piece of normality to her upended existence. "It is important to me that I express a deserved gratitude for not only what you did earlier at the White Stag, but also on the walk here."

This time, he offered no protestations. He simply lifted his head in silent acknowledgment.

Martha twisted her fingers in her damp cloak. "I also wanted to thank you for your patience with my son."

"He's a clever boy. As I said, I enjoyed conversing with him," he murmured. Returning to Guda's stall, Mr. Malin favored the old mare with a pat on her withers and then brought the door closed.

Her heart stirred. Frederick's own father had not recognized Frederick's worth. Hadn't cared to recognize Frederick's skills or strengths. Nor had he even noted his daughters.

He's pathetically weak. How can I ever be expected to bring him to London? How could I be expected to bring any of you to London?

Hatred spiraled through her, that dangerously powerful emotion still as potent more than a year after her husband's murder. Her soul was surely as dark as her father's for being unable to muster anything but relief that her life was no longer haunted by Lord Waters.

She was so mired in those ugliest memories that she belatedly registered Mr. Malin walking past and drawing open the stable doors.

Wind tore through the entryway, snowflakes whipping inside, covering the old hay.

"Wait…" she called out after him, but he was already leaving. It was better that he went. There was nothing more to say… and yet, there was. Her pulse racing at the insanity of her own idea, Martha rushed after him.

And yet…

She caught the edge of the wood doorjamb and stared out as Graham Malin gathered the reins of his horse and drew the tall, regal creature forward.

Martha stepped out of the way, allowing master and horse entry, and then closed the door behind them. "I thought you were leaving," she blurted out. She promptly curled numb toes into the soles of her boots.

"You've my word, I'll leave shortly," he said crisply, guiding the mount into the stall next to Guda's.

And why should he think otherwise? You've done nothing but order him gone since he first approached you at the White Stag.

Moving with the ease of one who owned these stables, Mr. Malin proceeded to gather up tools scattered about the untidy space: the brush, combs, a shovel. His arms full, he carried the items over to the stall and set them down.

"You misunderstood," she called after him and then winced.

Do not. Do not… Trust your instincts. Trust your instincts when you've not before. It is not too late this time.

Mr. Malin turned back.

There was a question in his dark blue gaze, the shade an entrancing hue of the summer sky early on in the day, when her family had slept on while she'd sat and sketched its wonder. Now, that color called to her for different reasons. With his square jaw and noble features, he fair begged to be captured on canvas.

Say something… You are staring like a lackwit. "I wasn't turning you out."

He angled his head, an endearing half tilt that tumbled a dark curl over his eye and softened him, giving him a boyish look.

"That is, I wasn't turning you out *now*. Before, I was," she clarified, rambling once more. "At the White Stag, and then again—" *Stop talking.* Martha pressed her lips into a silencing line.

She'd forgotten how to be around people. Martha tried again. "I don't have funds with which to pay you," she said before she could call back that humiliating admission. And then the words came slipping out and rolling unto one another. "It is why I am... was... no longer hiring someone." Martha gestured to the disorderly stables. "As you can see, we're in need." They'd been in need since her secret had somehow come to light, and all of High Town learned the truth. And that had only been after her family's funds were lost. "I simply cannot hire you." She grimaced. "Pay you," she corrected. "I cannot pay you."

He set down Guda's brush. "And that is why you turned me away?"

Tell him yes and leave it at that. There'd been so many lies, however, mistruths that had gotten her tripped up over herself. "No," she said quietly, drifting over. "That isn't why. I don't trust many people. I've had strangers come through here. Men who've promised to help. Men who've offered to help." She bit at her lower lip and shook her head once. "And they didn't."

MARTHA DONALDSON DID NOT SPECIFICALLY articulate what offers of help had been made, but as a rogue with little opinion of most men, Graham knew precisely what those men had sought.

Men, who've promised to help. Men, who've offered to help... And they didn't.

And with that, she'd revealed another detail about her life. Rage threaded through him. It knotted his gut, a seething sentiment that defied the cool pragmatism with which he was to approach each case.

That fury within him was a dangerous response, a careless one born of emotion that could end a mission and, on most any other assignment, a man's life. He struggled to rein in the burning rage, to file it away and focus on nothing more than securing details to report back to his superiors.

"I thought you lied," she confessed, toeing a piece of hay the way her son had earlier. "About working with horses, but I heard you with Frederick. You're very knowledgeable of them."

And with that, an encounter she'd secretly observed between him and her son, Graham had managed that which he'd previously failed to do—secure her trust.

There should be only a thrill of triumph and relief. The sooner he was able to acquire the requested information on Martha Donaldson and her circumstances, the sooner he'd return and be granted a meaningful mission.

So why did guilt shred his conscience? Why did he feel like the biggest bastard for that undeserved faith?

Stop. You're a damned member of the Home Office. She is your assignment and nothing more. "Given your experience with previous… men, you are entitled to your suspicions," he conceded. His efforts here were different. His were true. Telling himself that did not alleviate the slow-creeping guilt.

"Perhaps. But neither was it fair to judge you for the crimes of others." Sweeping over, Martha retrieved the stiff brush and began to disentangle Scoundrel's mane, which had become knotted from the wind. She moved the bristled comb deftly, a woman clearly accustomed to working in these stables, but also with a gentleness that displayed her regard for the animals. Yes, Martha Donaldson cared about animals. She simply didn't have the funds to care for her own.

"What is his name?" she asked. Holding a hand out for the softer brush in Graham's hand, she traded him for the one she had.

At his silence, she looked over. His neck went hot. "Scoundrel."

Martha paused briefly. Her lips twitched, a smile ghosting her full mouth and transforming her delicate features. "They say a man chooses the name of his horse as a reflection of his own character."

Bloody hell. He deserved to be sacked from the Home Office. And when they did turn him out on his arse, they'd be wise to hire this minx in his stead. "Do they?" he asked, keeping his voice even. "Who, exactly, are 'they'?"

"I read it in a book on the history of horseflesh."

Of course she had. Clever. Cautious. And well-read. The woman was triply dangerous. "Is that how your son came to learn about Hippocrates?" The question was unfair. The child had revealed just where he'd learned that bit of knowledge.

Martha stopped mid-brush. The blood drained from her knuckles, indicating the death grip she had on it. Dancing back and forth, Scoundrel tossed his head. "He spoke to you about that?" she whispered.

"He did," he said carefully, studying her reaction. "He mentioned his grandfather."

"I… see."

What did she see? Graham studied the top of her bent crimson head, trying to gather anything from that non-admission. The gentleness of her touch as she cared for Scoundrel belied the image of a woman who forbade her son from speaking to animals. And yet, according to Frederick, that was precisely what she'd done.

Abandoning her brush, Martha rushed off. She returned a moment later with a small knife. Dropping to a knee beside Scoundrel, Martha placed her near hand on the horse's shoulder and slid her outside hand down the horse's leg, near the fetlock. Sliding her other hand down the rear cannon, she lifted the foot and proceeded to pick out debris.

Graham had long had an appreciation for a voluptuous beauty draped in dampened silk. He'd come to admire the flirts skilled in the art of the wicked gaze.

Never, in his life, however, could he have imagined just how enticing it was seeing a woman skilled with horseflesh expertly tend a mount. Martha moved with a quiet ease and efficiency to rival the Duke of Sutton's finest stable master. "You've some skill with horses."

She briefly looked up from her exertions. A curl the color of sunset fell over her eye, and she blew it back. "A young woman on a farm comes to have many skills."

Graham rested a shoulder against the wall. "Yes, but this is one you enjoy."

Martha didn't blink for several moments. He expected a curt dismissal at his bold supposition. "I do," she conceded, surprising him at every turn. "Or I did." She added that last part more as an afterthought.

Graham was not long for this place. How she lived her life or raised her child was not his concern, in any way. And yet, in Frederick, he saw so much of himself. Graham couldn't leave without attempting to make it better where he could for the small child. "You discouraged Frederick from speaking to Guda."

Martha's upper body went whipcord straight. She stood slowly. "Is that a question?" she asked, a warning there.

He'd be a fool to fail to hear it. Nay, to ignore it. *Hold your words. What directives she gives to her child aren't your business.* That the Donaldsons were safe, looked after, and accounted for was to be the extent of his dealings with them. In the end, he ignored those warnings. "He's a boy, and there's no harm in his speaking to his horse."

Just like that, the barrier went up between them. Martha stepped away from Scoundrel and handed Graham the knife. "You'll need to clean the stables. When the weather warms, portions of the roof will need to be replaced. We need the livestock cared for." With that detailed enumeration, she studied him intently. Did she expect him to balk at that list? All the displeasure at his current state he'd already reserved for his superior. "And…" She wavered, troubling at her lower lip as she was wont to do, a telltale mark of uncertainty in an otherwise undaunted woman. "I'd ask that you instruct Frederick on the proper care of the stables." She held his gaze. "We've servant's quarters off the kitchens. You'll stay there as long as you remain. If at any time I ask you to leave, I want your belongings packed and you gone. If you can honor those requests, then you may remain. Does that all sound… agreeable?"

In terms of his assignment, it sounded convenient. "It does."

She nodded and then turned to leave. "Oh, and Mr. Malin?"

He inclined his head.

"If you intend to remain, then I'd advise you to not presume to speak on what you cannot possibly know."

With that, she stalked off.

Graham waited until the stable doors slammed shut behind her before grinning.

He'd gained entry.

CHAPTER 8

LATER THAT EVENING, WITH FREDERICK abed, Martha stood at her easel.

Her hand ached from both her fall on the Birch Path and the porcelain she'd crushed in her palm.

But, if she were being truly honest with herself, her inability to sketch had nothing to do with her throbbing, bandaged hand. Her mind, just as it had been since earlier that morn, remained firmly entrenched in her and Frederick's exchanges with Graham Malin.

Graham Malin, who'd proven to be an expert stable master, who knew not only how to care for horses, but also knew equine history. "He also speaks to animals," she whispered, her voice barely meeting her own ears.

You can always tell about a man's character by the way he treats his animals, Marti. Never, ever trust a man who is cruel to even one.

Martha stared emptily at the canvas. She'd first received that lesson from her father as a girl of five or six, sitting raptly at his feet, while he spoke about the care they ought to show for their livestock. He'd given her that lesson and, then twelve years later, with dreams of a title for his daughter, had forgotten it. Or perhaps he hadn't forgotten. Perhaps, he'd seen just what Lord Waters had been, and his desire for a noble husband for Martha had proved greater than… all else.

"Your boy is strange. He was speaking to my mount. See that it stops."

"He is not strange, and he is your boy, too. He'll speak to whatever or whomever—"

The crack of Lord Waters' meaty palm striking her cheek, ending her defiant words, reverberated around her mind, and she recoiled.

She forcibly thrust the memory back into the darkest chambers where Lord Waters and all his evil would forever dwell, trapped there, let out only when she allowed it. Or when she was not strong enough to keep thoughts of her marriage at bay. *Do not think of him. Do not think of any of it.*

Through the mire came another memory, this one recent, of her son with another man and another horse. In a moment that had been born of tenderness.

Of its own volition, her hand went to the page on the easel.

Some of the tension eased from her, and she surrendered to the calm that always came from her art. She let the charcoal fly over the previously empty sheet, covering the composition. Martha stopped periodically to smooth the gray-black into the background and then added layers to the shading as she went. At last, the lines and shading began to take the shape of familiar forms.

She continued her strokes until three figures dominated the page. Martha paused to study the trio: a boy, a man, and a horse.

Her fingers stained black, Martha traced a jagged nail around that proud, noble creature.

With icy flakes pinging the windowpanes, she angled her head, staring at Mr. Malin's horse.

You can always tell about a man's character by the way he treats his animals, Marti. And never, ever trust a man who is cruel to even one.

Her father's booming tones continued to echo in her head, nearly deafening.

And yet, her father, who'd sworn by those very words, hadn't given thought to the viscount he'd found at the White Stag whose mount had come up lame. The moment the pair of them had arrived, walking the viscount's gelding, everything she'd needed to learn about the *nobleman* had been there. Rather, it had been—the ears.

Lord Waters' horse had continued to flick his ears back and forth, rapidly swiveling them. Those restless movements had spoken to the sweated creature's fear. Having cared for the livestock as she had, she'd become expert at reading the nuances of each animal's habits and behaviors. As such, she'd seen the horse's unease at first glance, and instead of recognizing it for the telltale marker it was, instead of trusting that adage her father had told Martha as a young girl, she'd allowed herself to believe that the foreignness of the situation and surroundings had been the reason for the horse's anxiety.

And while she'd cared for the mount, rubbing him down, feeding him, her father had ushered the gentleman into their modest cottage. So had begun the start of the rest of her life.

Only, all these years later, she acknowledged every other detail she'd failed to heed: the elevation of the horse's head. As if he'd sought to flee. As if he'd wanted in that moment, with his master otherwise occupied, to be set free.

Martha pressed her eyes closed.

She'd ignored every last instinct that would have ensured her preservation. She'd ignored every last lesson she knew to be true about horses and the subtleties of their body movements.

With that chance meeting, everything had changed. She'd met the man to whom she would give herself, body, name, but never soul. The soul, however, proved useless in marriage. It was the one piece a woman retained that offered no protection or shelter from the hell of those unions.

She should have known. The lone white scar along the horse's shoulder should have alerted her to the truth of the viscount's character. Or rather, lack thereof.

How very different one man should treat his mount than another.

Martha's gaze crept over the easel, over to the kitchens and Mr. Graham Malin's small quarters. She didn't want to trust him or his motives, because she'd been burned enough by her own folly and life to see how ultimately every person failed you.

Martha sucked in a shuddery breath and forced herself to resume her sketch. Yes, all the signs had been there. But she'd ignored them. And there could be no undoing that. All she could do was focus on that which she could control in her and Frederick's present.

As Martha worked, the bandage she'd assembled with her left hand slipped and sagged. With a quiet curse, she tossed her charcoal down. Unwinding the scrap stained with remnants of both blood and charcoal, Martha attempted to draw the fabric tighter.

To no avail.

Removing it altogether, she quit her art station and made for the kitchens to replace the bandage.

Go gather what you need and be on your way…

After all, Mr. Malin's quarters were just off the kitchens, separated only by a small oak door. At this hour, their new servant was likely sleeping. Even if he wasn't, he'd not be so bold as to leave his quarters.

Why did all those truths send a wave of disappointment through her?

Because you are a damned fool. Because you are lonely. Because you've never seen a man who was not your father treat Frederick with the kindness and patience Graham Malin did.

She strained her ears, searching for some hint of sound from the long vacant servant's quarters. The faintest scratching slipped into the quiet, so faint she struggled to bring clarity to it through the hum of the nighttime silence and the ice pinging against the windowpane.

If she were being completely honest with herself, at least in this moment… she'd been lonely. Oh, she had Frederick, a gift she didn't deserve and for which she'd be eternally grateful. But there had been… no adults with whom to speak, or share her worries or thoughts, or anything. Her discourse in the stables earlier that day about her son's regard for horses had been all that she'd shared with… anyone since her family's scandal had come to light.

That was why, moments later, when Martha entered the kitchens to tend her injury, she secretly hoped that Mr. Graham Malin might be awake and join her.

AS A BOY AND THEN a young man at university, Graham had always struggled to put words onto a page. It wasn't because he didn't understand words or possess a vast vocabulary. He did. There had, however, always been something about him trying to order his thoughts so he might properly assemble them on a page that had always eluded him.

It had almost been as if his mind were… hopping, while he sat there, a young student trying to keep each idea still so he could capture it.

His father had towered over Graham's desk, refusing to move until Graham mastered his studies. When that had failed, Graham's tutors had bloodied his knuckles more times than he could recall. Those assaults on his hands had lasted only as long as it had taken his mother to learn of that treatment and sack the tutors.

It had all been to no avail. None of it had worked. The words had been trapped there, filled with a restlessness that countermanded all those efforts his father had made to make Graham a "proper student" like his brothers.

This time, while he was seated at the small oak table in his temporary quarters, the empty page before him had nothing to do with that struggle and everything to do with the woman he'd been tasked with watching after and reporting on.

Before, she'd been an assignment.

Now, she was a person. A mother. A woman tormented by people without a shred of her strength or spirit. One rightfully wary of him, but who, despite those reservations, had still allowed him to remain on.

And he felt like a bloody bastard for it.

He straightened as he caught the faintest tread of footsteps in the kitchen, the delicate steps he'd come to recognize as hers.

The irony was not lost on him. He, Lord Sheldon Graham Malin Whitworth, who wagered too much, drank even more, and bedded scandalous beauties, and who'd long believed himself past feeling *anything*, suddenly felt a modicum of guilt.

And at a time when he acted on behalf of the king and Crown. Any other agent would have entered this household and carefully disengaged any feelings for the people involved.

Graham scrubbed a hand down his face. Mayhap the Brethren had been wise to reject him at the onset. Whoever had looked over his file and made that decision had surely seen the same failings within him that his father had. Ultimately, Graham failed. That had been the true state of his existence. Nor was that just a self-pitying sentiment. It was grounded in the reality that had been his existence.

Of course you should fail to secure a post in the Home Office, Sheldon. There is no further help I can offer you.

She continued flitting about the kitchens.

Bloody hell. Enough. She's a woman you've known for not even a day and your assignment at that. You're a damned agent for the Crown, man. Act like it.

Graham let his hand fall to the nicked surface of the tabletop. Firming his jaw, he forced himself to write.

Miss Martha Donaldson, "Marti" to family, is in dire financial straits. The widow's cottage, stables, and connected buildings are all reflective of her economic struggles. Her mounts have been sold off but for one, older mare. The lack of feed and the condition of hay are also indicative of her depleted funds. The cottage is also in a sad state of neglect.

Graham paused and reread the statement for his superior.

It was completely accurate. Methodical.

And it was a coolly emotionless account of the two people who dwelled here. It conveyed nothing of Martha's wary green-blue gaze or her pride. Or her son's desperate need for companionship.

And he wasn't supposed to care. About any of it. About them. Martha Donaldson and her son represented the means to an end, so that Graham might then move on to his next and more antic-ipated assignment. After all, any task would be more anticipated than looking after the Donaldson pair.

With that reminder, Graham made himself finish the meticulous accounting, including the piece that mattered most for this assign-ment and information his superior required immediately.

I've reasons to suspect Miss Donaldson is at risk. In addition to the uni-versal dislike and cruelty she is subjected to from the local people of High Town, Miss Donaldson was followed by two unknown subjects.

It was why Graham was needed here in High Town. The usual frustration with his assignment, however, did not come this time.

He folded the note. Mindful of the woman who still moved about in the kitchens, Graham reached for the silver wax seal, careful to not strike the cylindrical tray as he sprinkled puce pow-der upon the Brethren's mark. When he'd finished, he stuffed the note inside his satchel.

Stretching, he rolled the tense muscles in his shoulders.

All the while, his body remained attuned to Martha Donaldson, separated from him by only that slight oak panel. The woman who was his assignment and nothing more. That was what he reminded himself as he came to his feet and walked over to the door. It's what he told himself again as he opened it.

Seated at the modest kitchen table, with a scrap of linen fabric clenched between her teeth, Martha stared back, a delicate blush staining her cheeks. She would be the first of many widows of his acquaintance who'd ever managed one. "Huhlo," she mouthed around that piece.

"Hello." Of course, his former lovers and mistresses would not have brushed their own hair, let alone bandaged any injury. He alternately marveled at Martha Donaldson's strength and loathed the world where she had no one to rely upon except herself. Wholly unaware of his thoughts—she'd no doubt blister his ears for them—Martha gave all her attention back to that torn strip.

"May I—?" The gentlemanly request died as, with a frown, Graham took in the wound he'd failed to note earlier. An injury she'd said nothing about. "You were hurt," he said quietly, joining her at the table.

"If's fine," she said, the fabric still tucked between her teeth as she continued to wind it around her left palm. A palm stained with the remnants of blood and… and charcoal.

Ignoring her assurance, Graham sank to a knee beside her bench. "May I?" he asked, already reaching for her hand, but making no move to collect her stained fingers. Wanting her to grant that touch. Refusing to force her. She was a woman who desperately sought control of her own world, and he'd allow her that where he could.

Martha held her injured hand close a moment and then, in a remarkable show of trust, laid her palm in his.

Graham inspected the heavy gray dusting upon it, the black inking the beds of her jagged nails, her fingers also caked with…? He lifted his head.

"Charcoal," she murmured, having followed that wondering.

"Ahh, you are an artist, then." He knew that much about her. It had been a detail, more an afterthought, within her file.

"An artist," she echoed in a quiet murmur. She contemplated that for a moment. "I… I never thought of it in those terms."

"What other terms are there to think of it in?" Curiosity drew the question from him.

"Well…" She fiddled with the strip of fabric now stained black. "I've always loved sketching. I have since I was just a girl who'd discovered my late mother's charcoal." She pointed to the wall beyond his shoulder, and Graham followed the gesture to an ambiguous mural along the right side of the doorway to the main living quarters. He squinted, attempting to make sense of the amorphous shapes there in faded greens and blues.

Martha took mercy. "It's a tree."

"And a bird?" he hazarded.

"A flying squirrel." She gave a playful toss of her head. "I'll have you know, they are a thing. I read of them. They aren't like bats or birds, but rather, they glide between the trees."

Her hand momentarily forgotten, he stared up, entranced by the teasing glimmer in her eyes. This was who she should be. This lighthearted imp with mischief in her eyes and a smile on her lips. This was likely who she had been before… whatever event had required intervention from the Brethren. Her smile slipped, and he was besieged with an urge to call that levity forth once more.

He forced his gaze away from her lush, crimson lips. "I take it that was your first masterpiece?"

Just like that, he restored them to their earlier ease.

Martha grinned, displaying slightly crooked front teeth and a dimpled cheek that held him enthralled all the more. She pointed to the artwork below the window. "My second."

They shared another smile.

"My mother died when I was a babe," she went on as he returned to studying her injured palm. "But my father saw that I always had some form of canvas for sketching. Even if it was… the walls." She paused, and he found himself wanting her to continue. Wanting to know details about the mysterious woman who lived in a for-gotten corner of Luton. *For his report on her. It was only about his report…* That assurance echoed in his mind, pinging around there as the lie it was. "But," she went on, her voice reflective, "I never considered myself an artist."

Graham continued to hold her hand, her fingers warm in his own. "And why not?"

She snorted. "Artists are paid for their efforts. Men who have their work hanging in museums. There's hardly a place for a woman from Luton skilled with paints and charcoals."

"Hardly." He scoffed. "You've never heard of Fede Galizia."

Martha went wide-eyed. "*Who?*"

"She was a Renaissance artist."

Dropping her chin atop her uninjured hand, she shook her head. "I've only ever heard of da Vinci and Michelangelo."

How many times had he ridden by the Royal Academy and not

given art so much as a thought? Martha deserved to be there, in London, surrounded by those artistic pieces to observe and study. "Tell me about her," she urged.

"She was the daughter of an artist in Milan. Her father raised her to believe that she too could and should be an artist. By twelve, she was already accomplished enough to earn mention by renowned Italian artists."

Martha's entire body remained motionless as she stared on, enrapt. Had anyone ever looked at him that way? Had he ever *given* anyone reason to look at him that way? It was dangerously heady for a man who'd long since ceased to feel the effects of fine spirits and hedonistic pleasures. That a look from a woman should stir… this… whatever this was inside. It compelled him to continue. "Her work survives to this day, no less valuable or revered for her gender."

"How do you know this?" she breathed.

His neck went hot, and he coughed into his hand. "I fear the truth will only humble me. I saw one of her portraits. *Judith with the Head of Holofernes*. It was a painting of a woman holding a head in her hand." To his tutor's horror, Graham had been endlessly fascinated and learned everything there was about that piece. "Gory, graphic, horrific stuff."

Her crimson brows drew together, the familiar suspicion darkening her eyes. "No… how does a *stable master* come to know so much about female artists?"

Graham silently cursed himself to the devil. "I wasn't always a stable master."

She peered at him. "You weren't?"

He'd been so focused on encouraging her own work and maintaining that slightly adoring glimmer in her eyes, that he'd made a careless misstep. He flashed a wry grin. "I served on the staff for a nobleman whose entire household was filled with those pieces," he said, not missing a beat, "and I was so fortunate as to have the mistress of the household care for me when I remained"—a disappointment, a failure—"invisible to so many."

She stared wistfully back. "And you gave all that up?" she murmured, searching his face. "You traded all those opportunities and experiences away with the hope—"

"For more," he finished. "Yes."

"I understand that," she said softly, glancing down at her hands. "For a long time, creating my sketches, even knowing the world would never see them, was enough... for me. Somewhere along the way, it all... changed."

She sought employment. Only, she didn't speak of her skills in terms of her need for work.

"There's this feeling I have..." She scrunched up her brow, searching and then finding. "I don't know how to describe it. This... feeling that can only come in creating something from nothing." The wonderment in her husky tones as she spoke so lovingly of her craft was no mere afterthought or detail in a Home Office file. Hers was a tangible joy that lit her eyes—and scared the hell out of him for the unknown feelings it stirred. She didn't speak of money or security, but rather, some intangible thing.

"Joy?" he ventured.

She shook her head. "No. It is... different. It's equal parts wonder, and frustration, and exhilaration, all wrapped together. Have you... ever felt anything like that?" she asked hesitantly.

He sank back over his heels. "Have I...?" Did he feel that sense of wonder for anything? Had he ever? Society and his family would have readily supplied an answer for her that gave a nod to Graham's years as a rogue and the illicit pleasures and passions he'd pursued. And they would have all been wrong. For he had felt that way about something. "I feel that way when I care for horses." Or he had. Before his father had ordered him from the stables and barred the stable master from allowing Graham to assist him.

Disquieted, he shoved to his feet.

"Yes, you should retire. The morn comes..." Her words faded as he stalked over to the shallow wood trough set into the top of a cabinet.

Graham grabbed the nearest pot and dipped it into the trough. Filling it halfway, he carried it to the table and set it down. "May I?" he asked, reaching for her hand.

She wet her lips and then nodded once.

Graham dipped her stained, injured palm into the cool water.

"What are you doing?" she asked, glancing between him and her hand.

"Come now, Miss Donaldson. Surely you've come across Hippocrates' treatment of injuries."

"I haven't." A curl fell over her eye, and with his spare hand, Graham brushed it back, tucking that silken tress behind the shell of her ear.

"There are those who believe cleaning a wound will help to prevent infection from setting in," he explained, dipping one of the white linens into the water and gently washing the charcoal from around the injury first and then the remainder of her hand.

They settled into a companionable silence, with Graham washing and then wrapping her cleaned hand. While he did, he felt her eyes taking in his every movement.

"Martha," she said softly, and he stopped mid-wrap. The long, graceful column of her throat moved. "You should call me Martha."

His gaze wandered unwittingly to the mouth that had captivated him from the moment she'd entered the White Stag Inn.

Her lips parted, and she tilted her head back. Graham froze, transfixed by her. By this moment. Martha's lashes fluttered closed. *Kiss her. She is offering that gift. Take it when you desperately want it.*

Graham moved closer to her lips, so close the hint of plum that lingered on her breath filled his senses, filled him with a taste of sweet fruit. Of her.

He'd had numerous lovers, including inventive widows with the lush bodies of fertility goddesses. What was this enigmatic pull Martha Donaldson had over him? He swallowed hard, warring with himself. Fighting what he wished to take. Needing her to end this connection and send him away, as she should. "I should go."

"Why?" she whispered. Nothing more than a single syllable that spoke of her desire for him to remain.

"Because I want to kiss you," he said, his admission hoarse with restraint. "And I shouldn't," he said regretfully. If they'd met somewhere else, as different people, brought together for different reasons… He forced himself to step around her.

He'd made it halfway across the kitchens when her husky tones sounded behind him, tinged with hesitancy.

"What if I want you to?"

CHAPTER 9

WHAT IF I WANT YOU TO?

Martha's heart hammered.

As a girl, Martha had wondered, even dreamed about, what her first kiss would be like.

Until she was a young woman newly married to Viscount Waters and had been subjected to her first kiss.

From that moment on, Martha had long abhorred any form of intimacy. While her children had pined over their absent father when he was in London, missing the ruthless cad whose evil they hadn't known, Martha had secretly rejoiced over his absence. With the viscount gone, she'd been spared from him "claiming his husbandly rights," as he'd reminded her during their every encounter.

Through all the unpleasantness she'd known in his arms, there had been something particularly distasteful in his kisses—sloppy, wet, stinking of garlic and spirits. She used to turn her head in a bid to escape that act whenever her husband paid a visit to Luton.

When he died, she'd vowed to never again subject herself to the distaste of one of those embraces.

In this moment, alone in the kitchens with Graham, there had been a piercing heat that radiated from his gaze, that singular focus she'd learned to run from when she'd seen it in Lord Waters' eyes.

And in this sliver of time, she *wanted* Graham Malin to kiss her.

Because something in the searing intensity of his eyes, coupled with the restraint he'd shown, had told her that Graham Malin's kiss would never be like Lord Waters'. That Graham Malin would not take, as if her lips or any part of her body were his due, but rather, as if they were a gift that he'd cherish.

It was madness, that faith she had. Utter madness. But then, everything about Graham's arrival in High Town and presence here defied any sort of reason.

And yet—he made no move to face her.

As time stretched on, and with it the thick, deafening silence, embarrassment stole away the excited little fluttering in her belly.

Mortification brought her toes curling hard into the arches of her feet. My God, what he must think of her. The wanton widow all of High Town took her for. Perhaps she was precisely what they accused her of being. "Forgive me," she said, hurrying to gather up her medical supplies to give herself anything to do, all the while praying for the floor to open and devour her whole. "I should not have asked you to… to…" *Kiss me.* She could not get the words out. "That was inappropriate on my part. You are a man in my employ, and I've surely scandalized you by—" She gasped as he turned swiftly around.

Graham was across the room in three long strides. Cupping her gently by the nape, he angled her head and covered her mouth with his.

Martha stilled, and then the scissors slipped from her fingers, the noisy clatter as they hit the surface of the table muted by the beat of her own heart.

This kiss was nothing like… any kiss she'd ever known from her husband. Ever.

It was an explosion of heat and sensation that seared her from the inside, his lips hard and masterful, but with a gentleness that stood in impossibly beautiful contradiction.

Martha crept her fingers up his chest, a hard wall of contoured muscle, and she clung to his shirtfront, giving herself over to his kiss. Taking that gift he now gave.

He tasted of peppermint, unadulteratedly pure and crisp and heady. Martha angled her mouth to better receive each slant of his mouth, meeting each stroke of his lips in return.

"I… never knew," she rasped between each kiss, "that it could feel like this."

He groaned into her mouth, the slightest, most delicious hum of a vibration that brought her lips apart, and Graham slipped his tongue past them.

Martha's legs went out from under her, but Graham was there. He caught her by the waist, guiding her to the edge of the table, never breaking that kiss, exploring her.

Nay, they explored each other. There was no demand. There was no one person taking what another didn't wish to give. It was a union of two mouths by two who wanted all of each other.

His mouth left hers, and she bit her lip to keep from crying out at the abrupt loss, but he was only shifting his attentions lower, to her neck, caressing with the tip of his tongue the place where her pulse beat wildly.

Martha moaned, a low, wanton sound she didn't recognize for what it signified and from the place where it came.

Graham lightly nipped at her sensitive flesh. He suckled, teasing at the skin. His cheeks, faintly coarse from the day's growth upon them, brushed her chin and earned a faint, husky laugh.

He paused in his ministrations and glanced up at her through thick lashes. Desire poured from those sapphire depths.

"It tickles," she breathed, stroking her fingers along the angular planes of his harshly beautiful face. And before she did something maddening, such as allow reality to intrude upon this, Martha stretched up and kissed him.

Graham's muscles went taut under her, and then he was claiming her mouth again, scooping his hands under her buttocks and bringing her close. As if he sought to meld them, bodies and souls, joining them as one, in an act Martha had only despised.

But she knew, the same way she had about the magic that Graham's kiss would be, that lying beneath him would wield a beauty and wonder she'd never known.

That I want to experience…

It was a realization she'd not had—that she'd not allowed herself to have—until now. Martha yearned to be a woman capable of feeling desire and passion. And as Graham searched his hands over her, caressing the curves of her hips and the swell of her buttocks, Martha reveled in the warmth that tripped through her body, spreading like a slow-burning fire that consumed all it touched.

It was a conflagration she'd gladly turn herself over to.

GRAHAM HAD KISSED A NUMBER of women.

Each of those kisses had been a casual act that had meant nothing, a basic one that had been a precursor to sex with women who'd been as experienced as he was in the art of lovemaking.

And none of those kisses had been… like this, and none of the women had been like the one in his arms now.

Despite her title of widow, there was a tentativeness coupled with innocence that contradicted her eager response. The initial hesitancy in her kiss, however, had dissolved as she returned his kiss with utter abandon, free of all restraints.

It was not enough…

Graham caressed his lips over the skin exposed along the trim of her modest décolletage.

Martha whimpered softly and tangled her fingers in his hair, clenching and unclenching, holding him close.

"The moment you entered that inn, I was captivated," he breathed against her chest, straightening to take her mouth again.

"I… w-was angry," she panted between kisses.

"You were magnificent in your fury." She'd been a warrior woman prepared to burn the town down, in a display he'd never before witnessed from any lady.

Graham guided her down, and she melted upon the table, so trusting.

Offering herself to him.

He hovered above her, braced on his elbows. His breath came hard and fast.

Oh, God. Please do not let this be the moment to develop a damned conscience. She yearned for this as much as he did.

Uncertainty flashed in Martha's expression, and she stared at him through eyes hazed with desire. "Wh-what is it?"

His gut clenched. All he needed to do was draw her gown and undergarments down to expose that luxuriant cream-white skin. The hint of plum that lingered on her breath filled his senses, filled him with a taste of sweet fruit. Of her. Beckoning.

Graham moved closer to her lips.

Oh, and Whitworth? I was ordered to give you one more instruction about your assignment: Do not go seducing the young woman.

Bloody hell.

Graham squeezed his eyes shut and reluctantly drew himself away from everything he wanted. Lord Helling's orders pounded at his head, and he placed several much-needed steps between him and Martha. "I should not have done that," he said, his voice rough with unsated desire.

Martha lay sprawled for the span of several heartbeats before hastily shoving up onto her elbows. "Of course," she said quickly. Her cheeks still flushed with the hint of unsated desire, she scrambled to her feet. Her hands shaking, Martha adjusted her garments, tugging her gown back into place.

Smoothing her skirts.

Straightening her hair.

All the while, she avoided his gaze like he was that serpent-headed devil Medusa who'd freeze her with a single look. "I'm sorry," she said on a rush. "I should not have…"

He closed the space between them and touched a finger to her lips. He'd not have her apology. "I am the one who owes you an apology," he murmured, stroking the pad of his thumb along her cheek. "I should not have kissed you." Graham tipped her chin up, angling her gaze to his, so their eyes met. "Yet, I have no regrets. I'm not any sort of gentleman that I would regret any of what we shared." With every ounce of restraint in him, Graham released her.

Collecting the strips of fabric that, at some point, had fallen to the floor, he tidied up the kitchen table.

"I can do that." She made a hasty grab for those items.

"I have it."

When he'd finished, Graham made to leave.

"Graham?" she said, taking ownership of the name he preferred and none had ever used. Wrapped in her low, husky tones, none would ever be able to command that name the same way she did. He made himself face her. "Thank you"—her cheeks pinkened— "for caring for my hand."

"You needn't thank me." *Leave.* He'd blurred too many lines between them. In this instant, he stood before her with weakened defenses that challenged the vow he'd made to the Brethren and his superior before he'd gone off on this assignment. Nonetheless, he remained rooted to the floor, needing to say one more piece.

"Martha… It… doesn't have to be one or the other. It's possible for your art to be both: something you find joy in and something you do as a craft." He held her gaze. "That you are a woman should not prevent you from seeing yourself as the artist you are."

"You've not even seen my work," she gently pointed out.

"No," he agreed. He'd like to. He'd like to see what manner of moments and memories she memorialized upon a page. "But anyone who feels as passionate as you do about your work deserves to be recognized for that love and commitment."

Her lips parted, and a little sigh slipped out. "Thank you," she whispered.

Before he did something like return, take her in his arms, and resume kissing her as he'd done moments ago, Graham left.

CHAPTER 10

$\mathcal{S}$HE'D KISSED HIM.

And in the light of a new day, there should be a modicum of shame and shock that she'd done something as scandalous as kiss a man who, until the day before, had been a stranger.

Martha, however, couldn't muster even a false showing.

Their embrace had been... pure wonderment. The magic that young women read of in Gothic tales.

"You're no innocent miss anymore, either," she muttered to herself. Dusting the back of her arm over her damp brow, Martha dunked her mud-stained cloak into the heated water. *Scrub. Dunk. Rinse. Repeat.* Martha went through the familiar motions. If she wanted to... to... make love or kiss a man, she should be able to.

Only, this hungering wasn't for simply that experience with any nameless figure, but rather, with the man who'd cared for her injured hand and spoken so comfortably with her about her love of art.

Martha peeked over the same wood trough Graham had fetched water from last evening and searched for him on the snow-covered grounds.

The early morn sun had begun to warm the frosted glass, sending moisture dripping down, blurring the glass. She ducked and turned her head in an attempt to better see.

Her heart did a little leap as she caught sight of him.

Scrub. Dunk. Rinse. Repeat.

Except, laundry forgotten, she watched Graham at work.

Devoid of a coat, Graham moved through the stable yard with his sleeves pushed up as though it was the heart of summer and not the dead of winter. His muscles, laden as he was with the two bales of hay he carried, strained the fabric of his lawn shirt. How effortlessly he made a task that would have taken her three times as long.

Her fingers still burned from the feel of those muscles under her hands, the rigidness and strength of sculpted biceps and a flat stomach, both marks of a man who worked with his bare hands.

Unlike her lazy husband, who'd worked at... nothing. The entire lazy lot of nobles, of which Graham bore not the remotest hint.

He was direct and forthright and—

He glanced up, and their gazes collided.

Martha froze like the doe she'd once painted at the river's bed. Oh, bloody hell. She resisted the urge to groan at being caught staring after him like some giggling village girl. How was one supposed to be after the embrace they'd shared not even twelve hours ago? *Be casual*... Martha inclined her head in greeting.

Graham's lips eased up into a slow smile that briefly halted her heart's beating. He winked once.

"It isn't laundry day."

She gasped, and her cloak landed with a thump in the murky water. It splashed her eyes, and she blinked back the sting. "Frederick," she greeted lamely, facing her son.

Did she imagine the suspicion in his eyes? "Yes. Who else would it be?" he asked as though she were dicked in the nob.

No, she'd not imagined his suspicion. She lifted her cloak and wrung out the excess water and soap. "No one," she said, forcing herself to speak in smooth, measured tones. "Who else would I greet, silly boy?"

His brow puckered. "That's what *I* said."

Martha tamped down a sigh. So much for evenly collected. Alas, Frederick had been correct yesterday. She was rot at prevaricating. "What were you staring at?" he asked, going up on tiptoe to look around her shoulder.

Martha darted and weaved her body, mimicking his movements in a bid to obstruct his vision. "No one." Bloody hell. "Nothing," she squeaked, following Frederick's stare.

Gone. She whipped her gaze around the stable yard. Why, she

might as well have imagined him. Graham was nowhere in sight.

"What are you looking at now?"

"The snow," she automatically responded, proud at the ease with which that falsehood had slipped out. Martha deposited her cloak into another pot, settling it to soak in the clean water. When in blazes had her son begun asking so many questions?

"You hate doing laundry. Why are you doing it twice this week?"

And yet another question. *Scrub. Dunk. Rinse. Repeat.* Alas, laundry would always be a far safer topic of discussion with her son than… well, nearly anything else pertaining to their lives. "Because this is one of my only cloaks." Because the other was coming undone at the seams. Reaching behind her, she ruffled Frederick's hair. "Because it requires laundering given our carelessness this week." The days of her possessing multiple cloaks of fine quality had come and gone.

"I wasn't careless," he said with a bluntness only a child could manage. "You're the one who fell."

She stopped mid-movement. Frederick's small trousers in her fingers sent water dripping all over the floor. He'd become increasingly belligerent. The resentment that had simmered in his eyes since his father's death, and grandfather's imprisonment, had boiled over into his speech. "Very well. You're the more careful one. How do I explain these, then?" she asked, lifting the small brown trousers soaking in the trough.

Frederick blushed furiously. "I told you, I was playing—"

"At the river," she interrupted, dropping the garment back into the water with her cloak. "I know what you told me." Martha gave him a stern look. "When we're playing at the river, we're to exercise more care." She tweaked his nose, softening the rebuke.

"We don't play anything." He tightened his mouth and swatted away her touch. "We used to," her son added. "Now, all we do is work."

That sad and all-too-accurate observation stirred a familiar wave of motherly guilt. This wasn't how life was to have been. Her marriage was to have provided her the time and resources and energies to be, at the very least, a mother to her children, and not even that had come from her union with Waters. "It will get better," she promised.

He scoffed, and that absolute lack of faith hit her square in the chest.

"I heard you awake late last evening."

Just like that, she had the tables flipped on her by a small boy. He'd heard her? Oh, good God. "What?"

"As in 'not sleeping.' Were you working on another sketch to submit?"

She leaped on that offering. "I was." His eyes narrowed, confirming he knew more. "For a bit," she modified. "But then I changed the bandages on my hand." She paused, giving all her attention to dunking his trousers once more. "And Mr. Malin helped." Martha peeked out of the corner of her eye, searching for some kind of response.

"He helped change your bandages?"

Except, even with his question, Martha could not make out anything of what he was thinking or feeling.

Scrub. Dunk. Rinse. "He did."

"Hmph."

Hmph?

Frowning, she paused mid-dunk. "What?"

Frederick lifted his spindly shoulders in a half shrug. "Just seems I was right about hiring Mr. Malin, and you were wrong. It doesn't seem like he's such a bad man, after all."

"I never said he was." There was a difference between questioning a person's character and being guarded. Leaving the freshly laundered garments to soak, Martha went over and collected the tattered muslin cloak that hung by the door. "I simply said we should be cautious because…" *As cautious as to kiss him wildly?* a voice jeered at the back of her mind.

She forced it back.

Her son shoved past her and grabbed his coat. "I know why we have to be cautious," he said evenly. "I don't need you to remind me." With that, he shrugged into the garment. "We have work to see to."

Work.

Yes, they did. Every day. Day in and day out, there were tasks for them to see to. Her son had grown up… overnight. Nay, he'd been forced to. Their circumstances had thrust him into a new role where he was neither child nor man, but something trapped in between. Tears smarted behind her eyes, and blinking them back, she made a show of clasping the once elegant garment.

"Mother?"

There it was again. *Mother. I want to be Mama again. I want to go back to simpler times when I was Mama to not just one child but two little girls and a smaller boy, all joyous… all here. With me.* Nay, not here. She'd take them all far away from this place if she could. "Y-yes?" she asked, her voice shaking. She discreetly wiped the back of her hand over her eyes, lest he see those tears for further proof of her weakness, and turned.

Frederick lingered, looking like he wanted to say more. When he spoke, there was a tentativeness to his voice. "I… heard you laughing," he admitted, and this time, there was a shocking absence of anger. "Last night, in the kitchens with Mr. Malin."

"I… I…" She didn't know what to say to that.

"And I"—he studied the tips of his shoes—"liked it. I haven't heard you laugh in a long time. I'll see you in the stables," he muttered. With that, he shrugged into his coat and let himself outside.

Martha followed his little form through the foggy, iced pane. She wiped her palm over it, dissolving some of the sheen. He sprinted with more enthusiasm than she'd ever remembered to the stables and then, wrestling with the heavy door, let himself inside.

As he disappeared from view, her heart clenched.

Frederick was correct: Martha had *not* laughed or smiled. Not really. When one lost two daughters, had her father carted off to prison, and had only a small boy whose life and safety all fell to her, there were few reasons to smile. But even before that, even when there had been a normality to her existence, with her family intact, sadness and regrets had made it impossible to be the young woman she'd once been. A woman who'd smiled and chased rainbows and believed in happily ever afters.

The death of her own happiness was something she had come to terms with long ago. She owned that decision to marry the viscount, and any misery she had was her own.

The heartache that would never go away had nothing to do with her and everything to do with Iris and Creda. And Frederick.

In longer than she could remember, *Frederick* had not smiled. He'd not laughed. And she wanted that for him. She didn't want him to be the cynical little shadow of a child she no longer recognized.

And what was more… she didn't know how to restore him to the boy he'd once been.

Rubbing her hands across her eyes once more, she wiped away the remnants of her tears.

With a sigh, she set out for the stables.

WORKING IN STABLES HAD ALWAYS provided Graham a distraction from life.

When he was tending those stalls, everything fell away—his failings, his father's disapproval. All of it.

Until now.

Now, he was riddled with thoughts of her. Just as he'd been since last evening. Nor were those thoughts solely about their shared embrace, but rather… her.

"You're a damned fool," he muttered. Removing the hay from Scoundrel's now empty stall, Graham carried the aged bedding and dropped it just outside… when the door opened.

Martha's son heaved all his weight into closing the door behind him. "Hullo, Mr. Malin." The boy cleared his throat. "I've come to work."

Graham wiped the sweat from his brow and studied the owner of that announcement. Frederick lingered in the middle of the stables. There was a determined set to his narrow shoulders that was contradicted by the hesitancy in the words that had come more as a statement.

Whereas yesterday he'd dreaded the boy's presence, now there was less a foreignness to his being here and more of an ease. "Grab a shovel," he said by way of greeting.

Quickly, as if he feared Graham might send him on his way, Frederick grabbed the rusted instrument and scurried over. "Now, the first order of business in overseeing a stable is the horses need to be fed, stalls mucked out, and then the horses groomed," Graham elucidated. By the disorderly state of the stables and grounds, not much of any order had been followed by the Donaldsons. It was as if the boy had flitted from task to task without ever successfully accomplishing one. "That is the schedule that a stable master sets and follows. I'll start—"

The door opened once more, dousing the stables in the sun's light and illuminating the crimson-headed beauty who stood there. The morning rays played off the bright hues of her hair. Graham froze. He'd never given much thought to the color red. It had been just that... a color. With Martha Donaldson at the threshold, broom in hand like some kind of Spartan warrior woman, he appreciated for the first time those burnt-scarlet tones—dusted with copper and strawberry hues and countless others he couldn't identify or name—that held him spellbound.

And he, Graham, worthless rogue, rotted scoundrel, had the breath knocked out of him by the mere glimpse of the determined warrioress standing there.

"You'll what?" Frederick prodded, giving him a slight nudge.

"Hmm?" he murmured as Martha shut the door behind her and started toward Guda's stall.

"You saaaaaaid, 'I'll start...' *What* will you start?" the boy asked, jolting Graham back.

I'll learn to draw proper air into my lungs and speak again. "I'll see to Scoundrel's and Guda's stalls. I want you to begin cleaning out the empty stalls." From the corner of his eye, he caught Martha sweeping the clean bedding away from Guda's stall door.

Frederick followed his stare. "We both work together at the chores," he said in hushed tones, misunderstanding the reason for Graham's silence.

It was the first time in his life that Graham had witnessed any woman mucking out a stable, and in that moment, he was fair certain he lost a bit of his rogue's heart to the young widow so in command of this space. And yet... she deserved more. Her cloak indicated she'd once been a woman who'd enjoyed greater comforts and privilege and now tended this stable because she had to. Graham squeezed the boy's shoulder. "Set the wheelbarrow outside Guda's stall and then go clean the empty stalls of the hay and straw there."

The little boy nodded and rushed off.

Collecting his rake, Graham started over to Martha. "Good morning, Martha."

"Mr...." She paused. "Graham."

Graham. She wrapped that one syllable in her soft, husky timbre, a seductive song composed of nothing more than his name. Desire bolted through him.

And because of nothing more than the sound of her voice. *Good God, I'm a depraved bastard.*

Frederick dragged the wheelbarrow in front of the door and then rushed off.

When he'd gone, Graham entered the empty stall.

"What are you...?" Her words trailed off as he scooped the physical droppings from the straw bed and deposited them just outside the stall door. "You don't have to... I can do that..."

He paused and swiped his forearm across his damp brow. "I've known you just one day, and I suspect you can do anything, Martha." His pretty words weren't meant to seduce, but instead, they came from a place of truth.

Martha's lips parted, and there was a softening to her usually guarded eyes that sent terror running through him. Graham jerked his focus back to the task, tossing the mount's soiled bedding out and shoving the clean bedding against the wall.

Martha set aside her broom and collected a rake. And proceeded to work... alongside him.

His mother embroidered. His mistresses, as a habit, had shopped. If the lives of any of the ladies of the *ton* had been dependent upon them mucking out a stable, they'd have promptly asked directions to the hereafter.

He was filled with equal parts admiration for her strength and frustration that this was her lot. And fury. There was that, too. For the unknown member of the Brethren who was supposedly concerned for the young mother's fate and didn't know the lady was mucking out horse shite and donning ripped muslin cloaks.

Graham stepped in front of Martha.

With her plaited hair flopping over her shoulder, she stared quizzically up at him.

"I can do this, Martha," he murmured. "This is why you've hired me."

"It is too much for any one person to do," she said matter-of-factly, returning to her task. She heaved another batch of clean straw past him. "You'll not be here long."

No, he wouldn't. Odd that such a reminder should leave him strangely bereft. He'd known her just a day, but even with that logic, the sentiment lingered. Graham settled a hand on her arm, staying her. "You shouldn't have to do this." Someone had failed her. Many had. The husband whose name the Home Office hadn't divulged. The Brethren.

"But I have to," she said simply. Martha must have seen something in his eyes, because she frowned. "And I don't mind it. Really," she insisted. She fiddled with the handle of her fork. "I…" She hesitated. "I once voluntarily joined the servants to help." A little laugh escaped her, sad and colored with her husky tones and beautiful for it all at the same time. A damp curl fell over her brow, and Martha brushed it back. It sprang forward, determinedly stubborn, and this time, she let it lay forgotten against her cheek. "What person chooses to muck out a stable when she doesn't have to?" she whispered. "And yet, I did," she said, her smile fading, her gaze growing wistful. "I did, because I enjoyed it." As she spoke, her voice grew more and more animated, like one who'd recalled a lost joy. "I loved the smells of this place, and the quiet of it all, and the company of the animals. These great creatures, just appreciative of your presence, ask for so little and offer so much."

A memory tripped forward, shoved for so long to the back of his mind, it had remained dormant until now.

"What does he think? That he's a bloody stable boy? For the love of God, he is a duke's son, Caroline."

Seated outside his father's office, his legs drawn close to his chest, Graham listened to the familiar fight on the other side of that door panel.

"He enjoys it, Samuel. There is nothing wrong with him looking after the horses…"

"No, there is everything wrong with it. There is everything wrong with him. He isn't natural."

Martha must have registered his silence, for she abruptly stopped. A pretty blush blazed across her cheeks, washing over the delicate smattering of freckles. "Forgive me. I'm sure that doesn't make sense."

"No," he said quietly, taking that errant curl, the strand like silk in his fingers. "I understand that in every way," he murmured, placing it gently behind the soft shell of her ear. "I have…" He paused, his gaze shifting beyond the top of her head. "I had two brothers. My father had expectations and hopes that we'd be accomplished scholars. They were. And I?" He grinned wryly. "I was not."

"I don't believe that," she said with a confidence he didn't deserve. But then, just as he didn't know her beyond the words in her file and his one day here, she knew nothing about him.

"I wasn't." He acknowledged his failings, hating that he'd shatter whatever illusions she'd allowed herself of him. "Any lessons I received never made sense. I couldn't bring them into any real clarity. My mind…" He struggled to find the words to explain how crippling it had been to order his thoughts and found himself prevented from doing so by that very same failing.

"Why can't you finish a sentence, Sheldon?" his father entreated. "You are a duke's son. Own your words like you are one."

Whereas that pressure had been applied to him by his father, brothers, and too many tutors and professors to remember, Martha did not urge him on with his telling. Instead, she waited. In the end, he proved… unwilling? Unable? Mayhap a bit of both, to share the deficiencies of his mind. "Horses always made sense," he settled for. "In ways that books never did." *Or would.*

Martha leaned against the wall and scraped her rake along the floor. "Hmm."

The vague utterance revealed nothing. Was it a recrimination? Disgust? Was it the same distaste his own father had for Graham over the years? At her scrutiny, he resisted the urge to yank at his collar. Instead, he resumed working alongside her.

"My father was rubbish at keeping the accounts and ledgers," she said suddenly, unexpectedly. Pausing, she leaned over the head of her rake. "He hated it." She laughed softly, her heart-shaped features a study in nostalgia. "I hated it more."

"What makes me believe you oversaw those tasks anyway?" he murmured.

"I did." That was the kind of daughter she would have been, because that was the manner of woman she was—one unafraid and unashamed to work or take on onerous tasks that would have made most grown men balk. "I despised it all. Adding up the expenses, resolving the columns. It was tedious. I toiled over it. It took me endless hours to force myself to finish the task." How free she was as she spoke. There was an absolute lack of artifice in both her words and demeanor. Unlike the coquettes he'd seduced and bedded who'd been practiced with their every word and look. "Sometimes," Martha went on, "I'd sit until the candle burned down and the sun came up, finishing our accounts. Because, if one

makes a mistake with ledgers, it matters. An error cannot be transformed into anything other than an error."

"Unlike your artwork."

Her eyes lit, and she pointed her rake at him. Graham took an
automatic step away from the rusty combs. "Precisely," she said,
planting it back on the stable floor. "Numbers *should* make sense.
They are certain and add up to mean something definitive. But to
me, they don't." Gripping the handle of her rake with one hand,
she more safely gesticulated with the other as she spoke. "Yet, hand
me a blank page with nothing upon it, and I can see structures and
faces and images that belong there."

Something went through him. "That is what stables are like for
me," he said softly. "This is a world I understand." He glanced
around. "And in here, surrounded by these loyal creatures, it doesn't
matter what a man's station is. What rank or title he was born with.
Here, there is only a sense of accomplishment that comes in looking after the stalls and seeing the completion of one's efforts." At
work in his family's stables, Graham hadn't been a duke's son. He
hadn't been a familial disappointment, or the man who'd failed
more times than he'd succeeded at anything.

Martha drifted closer, erasing the space between them. "I understand that," she murmured.

I understand that… Those three words filled his chest with the
most inexplicable lightness. He hadn't sorted through just why
he'd preferred this work—until now.

They shared a look, and in that instant, a bond was forged,
kindled from a shared appreciation and understanding. And something more.

"My own father thought I was mad because I enjoyed being in
the stables."

Martha frowned. "There is no explaining where a person finds
their pleasures. Nor should there be. It should be enough that you
found joy in that task. You shouldn't have had to explain that love
or been sneered at. I want my own ch—" She stared back with
stricken eyes and shook her head.

Graham furrowed his brow.

"My child," she finished, her voice threadbare. "I want my child
to find and celebrate happiness wherever and whenever he might
find it."

He'd been a rogue and a scoundrel so long that he'd developed an appreciation for the texture of a woman's skin, for the feel of a woman in his arms. Only, now he was captivated, in ways that made a mockery of all that past rakish admiration, by a young mother's devotion to her child. "My mother has always been of a like opinion," he finally admitted, absently raking the clean hay against the wall. "In the end, my father, however, always had his desires obeyed."

Martha drew in a shuddery breath. "That is something I understand at every level and in every way." As she quietly resumed raking the corner of the stall, Graham gripped his own rake hard.

The details surrounding her marriage are irrelevant, Whitworth.

"Mr. Donaldson?" he asked, even with his superior's order blaring loudly in his mind.

"Mr. Donaldson was my father." She slowed her back-and-forth strokes of the rake and then stopped altogether. "Mr. Barrett was my husband."

It was a name she loathed so much she'd ceased to go by it.

"I'm finished," Frederick called out from another stall, and Graham silently cursed the interruption.

"Splendid." Martha beamed. "Run ahead and brush down Guda." She stared on as the little boy sprinted off, until the door had closed and she and Graham were again left alone. Her smile dipped, and silent as the grave, she returned to her work.

I don't want to feel anything for this family. I don't want to feel pity or pain or regret or anything. All those emotions went against every lesson and code of not only the Brethren, but also what he had learned about self-preservation. To allow oneself to feel only brought a person pain. He'd had enough of that sentiment that he'd never subject himself to all that went with it.

"And Mr. Barrett was a disapproving father?"

"Mr. Barrett was a self-absorbed father," she clarified tightly. "He didn't *see* Frederick, and when he did, he was only interested in him as Frederick's presence could benefit his needs or wants. 'Get me this, Frederick. Get me that. Get him gone…'"

What would it have been like for a woman to be married to a man such as that? "He did not help, then, around the stables?" he asked, even as he already knew.

A laugh gurgled up from Martha's throat. "He couldn't have

identified a mucking rake if someone had held it to his nose."

So… how did a woman who enjoyed the simple pleasures to be found in the stables come to be married to a man such as… that?

"My father trusted it was the best match for me," she explained. "And I trusted my father. And it was the last time I freely trusted anybody." Martha looked to him, and for the span of a heartbeat, her piercing gaze on him, he thought she knew. He thought she knew that his being here was no chance meeting and that even now she was calling him out for the impostor he was. Then some of the tension went out of her. She smiled. "You have been the first I've allowed myself to trust." She laughed quietly. "I didn't believe you were a stable master, but rather, a man with dishonorable intentions towards me."

Guilt stabbed at him.

"I've finished," Frederick announced as he drew the door open and let Guda into one of the empty stalls.

This time, with the boy tying up the mount, Graham gave thanks for the intrusion.

"Here," Martha called out, and her son trotted over. She handed off her rake. "I have to finish the laundry. Help Mr. Malin." She went to drop a kiss on his cheek, but the boy angled his head away, and her lips merely grazed the air.

Yes, her leaving at that moment was safer. With her revelations here, and the evidence of how she'd lived, she'd left him at sea.

"What should I do?" Frederick asked when they were alone.

"Guda requires fresh hay."

The boy scrunched his mouth up tightly. "She already has straw. I filled it yesterday."

"There's a difference between straw and hay."

Setting aside thoughts of Martha and instead focusing on the safe, familiar topic he'd learned at the hands of his family's stable master, Graham explained, "Hay is for feed, straw is for bedding." Setting his rake down alongside the trough, Graham dropped to his haunches. "Here," he said, and Frederick joined him. "Straw and hay both begin as a field crop." He held up a stalk, and Martha's son took the piece, studying it. "Hay is the entire harvested plant and used as animal feed. Timothy, rye, alfalfa, wheat oats, are all intended for consumption." Graham turned over another stalk for the boy's inspection. "Straw is the stalk after the grain or seeds have been harvested. There's little nutritive value for a horse there. See how dried out it is?" he asked, gathering straw from the floor. He crushed it in his hand. "We want to change Guda's bedding daily. It gives her a warm, clean bed to rest on. It protects her joints and legs."

"How do you know all this?" Frederick whispered, awe underlying the question.

"I had... a good instructor."

Mr. McNair, the groom who'd served Graham's mother's family and then shifted over to the Duke of Sutton's stables when the couple had married. In some ways, he'd been more of a father than Graham's own. Old Mr. McNair, who'd died too young and been replaced by another who'd been of a like opinion to Graham's father about a duke's son being underfoot. Graham hadn't allowed himself to think of McNair in more years than he could remember. Uncomfortable with the emotion that memory brought, he came to his feet. He fetched his rake and resumed his earlier work. "You should—"

Then his ears caught it.

The faintest of sniffles.

Oh, bloody hell. His palms went moist, and coward that he was, Graham continued raking, hoping he'd been wrong. Hoping that hint of sound belonged to the hay scraping the floor. Or Guda's whinny. Or—

Sniff-sniff.

Bloody hell. There it was again.

He forced himself to turn. Frederick stood precisely where he'd left him. Silent. Somber.

Even when life had been the most miserable for him, Graham had never been either of those. He'd been unruly. Wild. Garrulous. But he'd never been quieted by his tutors or his stern duke of a father. His brothers, though they'd exercised some restraint, had also not been the subdued, colorless heirs and spares that one would expect from most ducal sons.

This boy, Frederick, and his demeanor, and everything about him, were alien to him. "What is it?" he asked, setting his fork down.

Martha's son clenched and unclenched a little fist around the handle of his shovel.

All the while, Graham remained silent, allowing the boy the time he needed.

Frederick slashed his spare hand through the air. "I don't know how to care for any of this. That's why it's a mess. It's why I don't know the order to do things or how to properly care for a horse. Or any of it. Not like you." As if deflated, the boy's shoulders slumped.

Oh, bloody hell. I'm supposed to say something here…

Had Graham been presented with a woman in a diaphanous gown, or actress just finished with a performance, he would have known precisely what to say.

But the person before him… was a child, and the extent of Graham's experience with children was… nonexistent, reserved for the time when he had been one years ago.

"Frederick?" The boy picked his head up slowly, meeting Graham's gaze. "You've done a wonderful job here. The upkeep of a household is great for anybody." Let alone a boy and his young mother.

"I didn't help before," he said, his voice threadbare. "My mother did it all. We had servants. My father never…" Frederick's thin lips flattened, and a hatred better suited to a man twenty years his senior radiated from the depths of his brown eyes.

His father.

That mystery figure that Graham's own superior hadn't named. For what reason? Who had the Brethren sought to protect? Given the deliberate omission, Graham wasn't intended to know, and the boy's lingering statement should go without exploring. "Your father never…?" he prodded, the gentle urging coming not because of his assignment, but rather, because of a selfish, inexplicable need to know about Martha Donaldson and the husband whose name she refused to claim.

"He never came round. And when he did, he never helped," Frederick spat, his tone pitching more and more to the stable rafters as he spoke, the words pouring out of him. "He expected the servants to wait on him. He expected my mother to wait on him like she was a servant…" And then the fight seemed to go out of him. "And she did. And I let her. We all let her. We didn't help her. She did… *everything*." Frederick's voice dissolved into a barely there whisper. "Everything."

The revelations ripped a hole in a heart Graham belatedly discovered he was in possession of. Martha Donaldson was a woman
just twenty-eight years of age. An age when the ladies of the peerage were enjoying the luxuries permitted them as young women
recently married: greater freedoms, idle time to partake in frivolous
pursuits, and, given his own parents' marriage, whatever pursuits
the wife wished. Only, Martha's life had been one of strife and
suffering, and it ate at him. And because of that, Graham couldn't
find any suitable words for the child before him. For none of them
would take away the misery he and his mother had known.

Frederick cleared his throat. "Yes, well, anyway. Mother would
say I shouldn't speak of those things with you because you're a
stranger, but I trust you."

The lash of guilt landed another blow. It shouldn't. Graham
would remain on, carry out his responsibilities for the Brethren,
and then part ways as Martha and Frederick both expected, with
neither the wiser about just what had brought him into their lives.
Telling himself that, reminding himself of that, didn't ease the
pangs of his conscience. "Your secrets are safe," he vowed.

"I know," Frederick said automatically, and the blade of guilt
found another mark.

For with that, he'd succeeded beyond his wildest expectations
in his assignment: After just a day, he'd wheedled his way into a
mother and son's life and earned their trust.

*Consciences are a dangerous thing, Whitworth. Never forget that right
or wrong doesn't matter in the work you'll do. All that matters is your
assignment.*

"But the reason I told you"—Frederick scrunched his mouth
up—"what I did about my mother was because I want to help her
now. She's an artist. She's very good, you know. And she should be
doing that like she used to, and I should be caring for the stables.
But I don't know how." Graham opened his mouth to speak, but
the little boy spoke on in a rush. "I know you won't be here long.
We don't have the funds to employ you. But as long as you are,
I thought since you know so much about horses and stables, you
can teach me everything you know." There was such admiration
and awe in Frederick's tones that Graham again found himself at
sea.

Nothing he'd done had earned the awe or appreciation of…

anyone. His mother loved him, but none had seen Graham Whitworth as being in possession of any skills of worth. Hell, even the Home Office had passed him over at first. "I'd be honored to," he said, his voice slightly hoarse.

Frederick's lower lip quivered so faintly that had he not been studying the boy so closely, Graham would have missed it. And in that instant, as regret tugged at him, he wished he hadn't been looking. Because the last thing he needed, the last thing he could afford, was to care about or worry after a little boy with anger simmering under the surface.

"Frederick, look at me," he said. When Martha's son met his gaze, he spoke. "Everything you do here on the farm is valuable and a help to your mother. One task isn't more important than the other. You've done wonderfully in the role you have." When it should have been the rotted Mr. Barrett who'd not only seen to the upkeep of the farm, but who should have seen it settled in his death. "And I promise, anything you want to learn, anything I can teach you"—*while I'm here*—"I will."

The boy brightened. "Thank you, Mr. Malin."

As Graham and Frederick Donaldson went back to ordering the stables, Graham, who'd lamented his assignment, now found himself dreading the day he left Martha and her son.

CHAPTER 11

Since she'd been forced to send away her family's handful of servants, all to preserve funds, Martha had mourned the time she no longer had to sketch. It had been one more aspect of her life that had changed. Instead of creating her artwork during the day as she'd done as a *viscountess*, she'd instead had to wait for the late night, when all the day's chores were completed and Frederick was abed. Except, by the time the house was still, exhaustion set it, so that even the pleasure of creating lost out to her body's need for sleep.

Now, with the addition of Graham, an all-purpose servant, she at last had that coveted gift—and could not bring herself to focus on her artwork.

The bread recently removed from the ovens and now cooling on the counter, Martha stared out the window. Graham and Frederick were escorting Guda from the stables, drawing her to the middle of the stable yard. As the unlikely pair talked, Graham tied the mount with a quick-release knot.

With him focused on that task, Martha freely observed him at work.

Had she truly doubted that he sought work as a stable master? After his first day on her family's property, she'd conceded he possessed a greater skill and mastery around the farm than any of the servants previously employed by her father.

Martha had been wrong about so very much.

So much so that, after her husband's death and father's imprisonment, she'd been mired in self-doubt, questioning her judgment and each decision she made or did not make. Because of that, she had very nearly sent Graham Malin away.

And that would have proved another mistake.

Graham had been here with them for nearly ten days now.

And each morning, Martha awoke dreading the day, fearing that each would be the day when he thanked her for the temporary shelter and went off to find paying work. As he should. With his skill and capabilities, his talents were entirely wasted on the Don-aldson farm.

When he did leave, this place would be, for the first time since her father had been carted off to prison by Mr. Nathaniel Archer, Lord Exeter, put to rights.

But for how long?

Martha glanced around her kitchens. The bread was baked for the day, the laundry done, and this room and all the others were neatly ordered, while the grounds and stables had also been per-fectly tended.

They wouldn't remain that way, however. They couldn't. Not with only her and Frederick here seeing to the tasks that the pow-erfully built Graham Malin completed in less than half the time.

Your tidy cottage and property are not the real reason you'll miss him, though, a voice taunted in her head.

Unbidden, Martha looked out the window.

Side by side, Graham and Frederick worked together grooming Guda.

She stared, riveted on an exchange that did not involve her, and yet, at the same time, had everything to do with her.

Graham said something to her son and stepped aside.

With a masterful touch that hadn't been there eleven days before, Frederick collected the mount's left foreleg and, using a metal pick, he pried out the dirt and debris lodged there.

As he worked, Graham spoke, and Martha stood at the window, hanging on the ease of that exchange. Taking in all of it. The way her son's shoulders came back in a proud carriage. The flush of happy color on his cheeks.

Martha longed to know what words of praise were passed on. She ached to know just what compliments Graham bestowed on a boy who'd never even known those simplest of gifts from his own father. Tears stung her eyes, and this time, in the solitude of her own kitchens, with Graham and her son none the wiser, she let them fall. This was the relationship she'd longed for her children to know with their father.

While Martha's own father had been endlessly devoted and proud of her to a fault, he'd not imparted lessons that would have seen her grow, the way Graham now did with Frederick. Instead, her father had placed her upon a pedestal, and the inevitable fate for anyone on such a high platform was the eventual fall.

As if he felt her eyes on him, Frederick glanced her way. He waved and then returned all his focus to the man he looked upon with an idolatry that scared the everlasting hell out of her. That same man now doffed his hat like he was a gentleman and bowed his head like she was a respectable widow and not the bigamist she was.

It is because he doesn't know. It is because you haven't told him.

No doubt, if he knew the truth, he'd have never even sought the post.

Gathering the bottom of her apron, Martha swiped the remnants of tears from her cheeks.

This game of pretend, this world of make-believe where Frederick spent his days with a man who saw his value and respected him and cared for him, would not last. It couldn't.

He would leave upon his discovery of her past—because eventually it would come to light, just as it had for the people of High Town—or he would move on to secure a true position as a nobleman's stable master.

"And then what?" she whispered into the silence.

What would it be like for Frederick when Graham one day left? He'd been an unsmiling, somber child. He'd only just begun to find his voice and let go of his anger, because of the questions he had for Graham. But what happened when he lost all of that?

Do not think of it… Do not think of it…

Graham's leaving was a decision beyond her control. Martha would have no say. Just as she hadn't had a say in so much of her life these past years.

The pragmatic reminder playing in her head did nothing to ease the tightness in her chest that came at the prospect of him leaving.

Do not be a fool. Martha caught the inside of her cheek. "You were pathetically weak before." In every way. She'd not be that emotional, helpless figure again. She might have been lied to and publicly humiliated, but she had survived the scandal. She drew in a breath, taking strength in the reminder of what she'd overcome. When Graham left, she and Frederick would be fine. They always were.

We are not fine.

Frederick's charge had reverberated around this very room when he'd hurled that pronouncement.

How was it she'd failed to realize just how much she abhorred silence? Because before, she'd known only three chattering children and a garrulous father. As such, she'd not properly appreciated the sounds of other human voices until most of them had been taken from her.

Compelled forward, Martha gathered her cloak and quickly shrugged into it.

Letting herself outside, she glanced around the back gardens. The empty back gardens.

She frowned.

Nothing.

Or rather, no one.

A wind pulled at the slight gape in her cloak, and drawing it back into place, she wandered out. The snow crunched noisily under her boots as she walked.

"Frederick?" she called out. "Graham?" Her voice, however, carried on the winter still. Squinting in the bright afternoon light, Martha raised a hand to her brow, shielding the glare as she searched.

For the first time in the more than a week since Graham had been here, a shiver of apprehension dusted her spine. "Frederick?" she shouted, franticness adding a high pitch to her voice. Letting her arms fall to her sides, Martha sprinted off.

Then something collided with her chest.

She gasped, staggering back under the unexpected affront and the shocking cold of it.

Martha stared down at the snow on her chest. In stunned disbelief, she touched the ice-flaked remnants. Why… why… she'd been hit with… a snowball.

No sooner had that thought registered than another ball hit her square in the shoulder.

The perfect strike was met with a pair of laughs, a deep rumbling one and the other lighter, belonging to a child.

Martha swiveled her gaze and found the offenders. She narrowed her eyes.

Both males were smug and entirely too pleased with themselves. Martha shook out her skirts. "I take it you've overseen the—"

Graham tossed another snowball. This one hit her lower belly and knocked the remainder of that perfunctory question from her lips. Martha gasped. "You… You…" His grin deepened. And then, slowly, he winked. "…hit me," she brought herself to finish.

"With a snowball," Frederick piped in with a child's glee.

Martha bent down and gathered snow, packing it into a tight ball. When she straightened, she registered the brief surprise in her son's eyes before she charged ahead and launched that missile.

Frederick's rich, snorting laugh filled the grounds as her expertly aimed snowball knocked Graham's old hat from his head.

Graham widened his eyes. "You have deadly accurate aim, madam."

With a pleased little smirk, Martha tossed her head. "I—" She jumped out of the way as another snowball was launched, but it landed a square hit upon her midsection.

And this time, it came from the unlikeliest of the pair.

Frederick stared back with mischief glimmering in his brown eyes.

"Not another step, Mr. Malin," Martha warned, holding up an index finger, staying any interference from the stable master hovering close to her son.

His palms held up in mock surrender, Graham backed slowly away from Frederick.

"Mr. Malin!" her son exclaimed, taking a step closer to the retreating man. And all the levity briefly lifted as she stared across the stable yard at them. They were so perfect together that one might have imagined a different life for Frederick. One might imagine a life where he'd had a father like Graham and—

Her son's smile dipped. "Mother?" he ventured.

"Traitor," she called. She dropped to her haunches once more, assembled another snowball, and raced forward.

Laughter shaking his little frame and pealing around the glen, her son took off running. "Truce. Truce," he cried playfully, his words leaving little puffs of white in the early afternoon air.

Martha stopped abruptly, and Frederick continued on for several strides before glancing back and finding her rooted to the cobble walkway. "Truce," she agreed and then surged forward with the Donaldson snowball battle cry.

Her frosty missile hit him square in the back, ice and snow fragments spattering upon the wool garment.

Her triumph was short-lived.

Graham gathered up another snowball.

With a breathless laugh, Martha gathered her skirts, and bolted back toward the cottage.

"Never tell me you're admitting defeat," he called after her, and despite the ache of the winter cold stealing the air from her lungs, her chest shook with a breathless laughter that felt so very good. So wonderful. She'd not remembered what it had been like to frolic in the snow and run about for no purpose other than joy and pleasure.

You'll never catch me, Mama.

Martha stumbled as Creda's bell-like giggles pinged around her mind, so tangible they seemed to linger in the High Town air. Her heart squeezing, Martha stopped, her back presented to Graham and Frederick.

A wave of desolation and grief battered at her, its immense pull threatening to drag her under.

She stared blankly down the remainder of the cobbled path, at the dry stalks where flowers had grown that summer. Deadened flowers that at one time had been picked lovingly and handed over.

Oh, God…

Absently noting Graham's vague query behind her, Martha ripped her gaze from the gardens and forced it downward to stare at the ice and snow upon her wool skirts.

Her throat moved painfully from the emotion stuck there. She hadn't been hit with a snowball or thrown one since before her father had gone, back when her daughters were here. In their absence, she'd not allowed herself those pleasures. Because where was the fairness in that? Where was the rightness in a mother moving on and finding any happiness after her family had been torn asunder by mistakes she had made? And yet, how easily she'd allowed herself to just… forget. To play snow games with Graham Malin and her son.

"Mother?" Frederick was saying.

She forced herself back around. "I've work to see to," she said, fighting to steady her voice. Fighting to not think of those two little girls she'd sell her soul ten times to Sunday for. But hadn't she already? Hadn't she when she'd sent them away to preserve their reputations and save them from the mire that Martha had made of their existence?

"I have work to see to, Frederick," she said again, her voice flat to her own ears. "As does Mr. Malin," she added for the man responsible for her momentary lapse, in guilt, in focus.

Her son's face fell.

Even with the distance between them, Martha detected Graham's thick, black lashes sweeping down, obscuring his piercing gaze.

Frederick let the snowball in his hand drop to the ground, where it broke apart noiselessly. Jerking his head forward, he dashed off, retrieving his previously abandoned shovel.

Martha caught the inside of her cheek, wanting to call out to him. Wanting to redo the moment so it didn't end with Frederick's usual sadness. Wanting to be everything she should be, not just for him, but for all her children.

Instead, as he let himself into the stables, closing the door behind him, she was presented once again with the reminders of all her own failings where her children were concerned. Unable to protect them. Unable to see them all simultaneously happy. Unable to feed them.

While I play. While I engage in a child's games, the same ones I had with not only Frederick but Creda and—

There was a faint whirring in her ears.

Splat.

Martha jerked in startled disbelief.

Her mouth moved, no words coming out as she stared at her snow-covered cloak. "I said we are done here, Mr.—*oomph.*" Another snowball killed the question, this one grazing the top of her hood, sending it falling back so that snow landed in her eyes. Sputtering, she blinked the blurred remnants back. "It is time we both return to our work," she gritted.

She gasped and, this time, ducked out of the way in time as Graham sent another missile flying. It hit the wood panel, exploding behind her. Martha straightened. "That is *quite* enough."

Apparently, he was of a dissenting opinion. She jumped out of the way just as Graham hurled another snowball at her. What in blazes was he *doing*?

"Have you gone mad?"

CHAPTER 12

THE CHARGE OF MADNESS WAS not a foreign one, as it had been aimed at Graham many times before.

As a boy of ten, he'd listened in on his parents' late-night conversation in which his father had spoken with the duchess about his fears that Graham was not right in the head. That had been the first time he'd heard the word *madness* voiced aloud to describe him.

The moment had frozen him outside His Grace's bedchamber doors. He'd been riddled with the terror that came with that nervous query from a duke who admitted weakness to none, coupled with Graham's own worries for having possessed a like fear.

In this instant, with Martha snapping her skirts free of the snow residue clinging to them, a different type of madness held him in its grip.

"What are you doing, Mr. Malin?" she demanded. Her voice dissolved into a little squeak as he stalked over.

"Mr. Malin?" he countered. "I hardly think given our embrace that—"

She slapped a finger to her lips. "Hush," she ordered.

With furious steps, Graham lengthened his stride. Martha staggered away from his approach, and her back knocked against the door, rattling the oak panel.

Graham expected her to turn on her heel and disappear inside.

He should have known better where the stubborn minx was concerned.

Placing her hands on her hips, Martha met him the remaining distance and braced her legs in a wide, battle-ready stance. "I already indicated I have work to see to."

"In case it has escaped your notice, madam, you are always working."

The winter air had stained Martha's cheeks with bright red splotches. "I assure you," she said in crisp tones that the queen herself couldn't manage, "I know precisely how I spend my time."

Tending to the laundry. Cooking. Caring for the grounds and stables. She did more work than any man ought, let alone a young widow on her own. And his fury only burned all the deeper at the Brethren for failing to see her cared for. Graham, however, focused on the easiest source of his ire—the woman who stood before him.

Graham folded his arms at his chest. "I trust you've also noted how much time your son spends working." It was not a question.

Her cheeks fired all the more red. That effectively silenced the minx. For a moment. "How dare you? I don't need you informing me on how my son spends his time, Mr.—"

"Someone should," he shot back. He'd been that boy, stealing moments of pleasure where he could, escaping the reality that was his existence. Only to have his father crush those all-too-fleeting pleasures.

If looks could burn, she'd have cleared the whole of High Town of its ice and snow-covered grounds. Martha shot a glance past his shoulder to the stables Frederick had rushed into, and when she trained those green-blue eyes back on Graham, she dropped her voice to a low whisper. "I know precisely how Frederick spends his days."

He spends his days doing nothing of value, Caroline. He needs to be more serious like his brothers… Not everything is about his pleasure…

Graham narrowed his eyes. "If you know that, then you wouldn't begrudge him a few stolen minutes of fun in the snow."

Her features crumpled.

Oh, bloody hell. He'd preferred her snapping and hissing… to this.

He'd never known what to do with a woman's tears. Even as he'd known his past lovers had employed them like methodical warfare meant to secure a bauble or sympathy or something that had been all too easy to give to make it stop.

This, however… was different.

Then, as quick as that weakening had come, it fled. Martha closed the last bit of distance between them with quick steps, and stopping a handbreadth away, she angled her head up and met his gaze squarely. "Yes. We do work all the time, but it's because we have to. I have to. This farm, you saw what it was like when you arrived. What do you believe it will be like when you leave?"

Graham's gut clenched. When he left, her only hope for salvation would lay with the nameless member of the Brethren doing right by her. And Martha Donaldson wouldn't be his business any longer. Graham's stomach muscles twisted all the tighter. But before he left, he'd have her realize she needed to allow moments of joy for her son, and herself.

"There is nothing wrong with finding happiness in life."

She jerked like he'd struck her and fluttered a hand to her breast, where melted snow had turned the fabric a shade darker. "I would never begrudge my son that," she whispered.

"No. Not intentionally. But you would intentionally withhold those sentiments from yourself." Graham brushed his knuckles down her cheek in a fleeting caress. "You are the example Frederick sees, Martha. He—" The stable doors creaked open, announcing the little boy's presence. Graham let his arm fall to his side.

Frederick ducked his head and, with a bucket held in his arms, loped off toward the river. Graham waited until the child had gone, and when he and Martha were alone once more, he continued speaking. "Frederick takes his understanding of how he should live his life and that which is right or wrong from you. And in your unwillingness to exist for anything other than your work, he believes that is all that matters. And it's not."

She hugged herself in a lonely embrace that belied the fire in her gaze. "You don't—"

"Know anything about it?" he gently interrupted. "No. I don't know about whatever secrets you carry." Only the ones that the Home Office had provided him. "I do not know what has made you so sullen and somber, but Frederick deserves more."

Whatever Martha was about to say was lost as a short cry echoed in the distance before cutting out altogether.

As one, Graham's and Martha's gazes went in the direction of that shout, and they sprang into action.

"Frederick," she rasped, and collecting her skirts, Martha took off flying.

Graham was already racing ahead, his longer strides surpassing her smaller ones. His chest pounded with panic. It pulsed in his ears, the frenetic rhythm of his heartbeat deafening as he tunneled all his energies, all his focus ahead.

Cool logic. Do not go rushing headlong into any battle unprepared.

That lesson doled out by his mentor reverberated in his memory, but Graham let it go ignored.

Frederick.

He tore through the copse and then skidded to a stop at the sight that met him.

Two children—nay, the boys were too old to be children, mayhap near sixteen or seventeen years—had Frederick between them. Both went white-faced at Graham's appearance.

The taller, bulkier of the pair had an arm about the child's waist and a hand over his mouth. The other, a gangly, thin lad with oily skin and pimpled cheeks, held a boot in his hand, the tip of a knife damningly pressed against the sole.

Graham narrowed his eyes, taking in Frederick's one bare foot.

Around his assailant's palm, horror, fear, and embarrassment all seeped from Frederick's eyes. And then, he dipped his gaze to the ground.

My God, the boy is… ashamed.

As one who'd felt the keen burn of that sentiment, he recognized it in another.

It sent a new wave of rage and fury burning through his veins. "Release him," he seethed, and when the bullies didn't immediately act, Graham, in one fluid motion, removed the pistol tucked in his boot and aimed it at the pair. "Now." He wrapped that whispered word with an edge of steel, leveling it as the threat it was.

The bastard holding Martha's son immediately dropped the boy.

Frederick crumpled to the ground, landing at the feet of the oily skinned, thinner boy. "Who are you?" Graham asked evenly, and when neither boy answered, he brought the hammer of his pistol back.

In their rush to speak, the two bullies' words spilled over each other's.

"Phinneas Tanner."

"Dudley Holbrooke. We weren't doing any—"

Graham leveled his gun at Dudley Holbrooke, and the dark-haired, gangly young man with pimpled cheeks promptly wet himself. A dark stain spread on the placard of his breeches, even as his cheeks splotched with color.

The painfully thin bully dropped Frederick's tattered boot, and it fell with a thump beside Martha's son.

Just then, Martha came charging through the brush and jolted to a stop.

From the corner of his eye, Graham caught her wide-eyed stare taking stock of the scene around her. Her gaze lingered for a moment on Graham's pistol. "What is going on here?" she demanded of the two bullies.

"I'm fine," Frederick mumbled, his cheeks red. "I fell," he said unconvincingly.

She ignored his empty assurances, continuing forward until she earned such a dark glare from her son that she staggered to a stop beside him and hovered, uncertain.

"I said I'm fine," her son repeated more insistently, peeking up at the boys behind him.

Graham waved his weapon at the pair of bullies. "Get out." The command hadn't even fully left his lips before the young men went scrambling off.

As soon as they'd gone, Martha dropped to a knee beside Frederick. "Are-are you all right?" she asked, running her hands frantically over his little frame. "D-did they hurt you?" Her voice was breathless, her chest heaving from her exertions.

Frederick gave her hands a hard shove. "I told you I'm fine."

"Don't lie to me, Frederick," she pleaded. "Surely you don't truly expect me to believe Dudley and Phinneas, who haven't helped a villager in all of High Town, were good enough to help you." She grabbed his shoe and held it aloft. "My God, they removed and cut up your boot."

Frederick lashed out once more, smacking the ripped shoe from her fingers, and a gasp tore from her as the boot landed with a thump. "I don't care what you believe," he shouted, and several birds took flight overhead, rattling the crisp, errant leaves that had clung to the barren branches. He stood over her and shouted at the top of her head. "All of this is because of you. All of it." Frederick balled his hands into little fists at his sides. "You're the reason people hate us. You're the reason why it's so miserable here. You're the reason our family has been cut in half."

Martha simply took each one of the hateful charges as if they were her due. Kneeling on the snow-covered ground, she gathered up the boot and clutched it to her chest, maintaining a deathlike grip.

Through the volatile exchange, Graham hovered, an interloper at a fight that moved far beyond a boy's hurt pride at being caught and then challenged by his mother.

Martha glanced to Graham, her usually direct eyes now refusing to meet his own. "This is neither the time nor the place for this discussion."

"Because of Mr. Malin?" the boy charged, unrelenting in his fury. "What? Are you worried because he doesn't know? Or because of what happens when he finally knows the whole bloody truth?"

She jerked and then righted herself with the aplomb only a mother could manage. "Watch your language."

"My language?" Frederick laughed, a jaded, ugly sound empty of mirth. "Do you *really* think whatever bloody words I use matter?"

"Frederick," Graham said quietly. "That's not the way a gentleman speaks to a lady."

The boy showed more courage than the pair two times his age. He lifted his chin mutinously. "But I'm not a gentleman, and she isn't a lady. And when you know the truth about her, you're going to feel the same way as all the others." Ripping the boot from her hand, Frederick went running, crashing through the brush. Dried out twigs and branches cracked, signaling the path he'd gone, until silence stretched around the copse.

Martha sank back on the ground, sitting there as casually as if it were a summer day and she'd stolen herself several deserved lazy moments.

Still hovering, Graham returned his pistol to his boot, and then to give his fingers something to do, he doffed his hat and beat the article against his thigh.

For the first time in the whole of his roguish life, he found himself without a single damned word for a young woman.

"I suspected for some time, you know," she murmured softly,

directing the admission to the imprint Frederick's boot had left on the ground. Martha trailed a fingertip along the outline. "It was easier to pretend that he was simply being clumsy than admit that he was being bullied for sins that didn't belong to him…" Her words trailed off.

Those sins that her son had alluded to had likely been the reason she'd earned the concern of some member of the Brethren.

Do not let a person's pain matter… Do not let a person's pain matter…

It should not. Not personally. She was an assignment, and a previously unwanted one at that.

As such, Graham should make as hasty a retreat as Frederick had.

Instead, he found his legs carrying him over to her side. Graham sank down to his haunches.

She looked up with surprise lighting her pretty green-blue eyes. "They've been bullying him." She voiced the truth aloud, and then her eyes slid shut. "And I knew. Deep down, and not even that deep. I knew because…" Martha shook her head.

Graham rested a hand on hers, stilling the distracted trail her fingers made. "Because…" he murmured, urging her to have it said, because he knew she needed to say aloud whatever misery consumed her and the angry boy who'd dashed off.

Martha finally lifted her gaze to his. "I knew because I'd found myself bullied enough times to recognize that it was happening to my own son."

A pressure weighted in his chest. He'd come upon her on the Birch Path, facedown in the mud. How many other times had she and Frederick found themselves so, with no one about to protect them? To defend them? And what would happen when he was gone? Would she be once more forgotten by the Home Office? "The people of this small village combined cannot add up to your and Frederick's worth," he said quietly. A woman who worked as she did without complaint and the son who toiled alongside her.

A small, sad laugh spilled from her. "You say that, but you don't know me. Not really."

"I know enough to know I'm right." And all of that understanding had come not from her file, but from their every exchange.

Martha fiddled with her skirts. "I married a man I had no place marrying. He was… a viscount."

Graham rocked back on his heels. "A nobleman?" he repeated

dumbly. Of anything she might have said about her past or her marriage or secrets, that had been the least expected.

She nodded once. "A viscount."

His mind raced. Martha Donaldson was... a viscountess, the wife of a nobleman. And likely that nobleman was a man Graham knew or had passed in some ballroom or club. This was her connection to the Brethren, then. And coward that he was, Graham didn't want to know the bastard's name. He didn't want to know the name of the one who'd given her children and known her laugh and who'd failed her in every way...

A restless energy thrummed to life, and Martha stood and wandered off to the shore of the slightly frozen river.

He'd been strictly advised to allow Martha Donaldson her secrets. His superiors did not want him prying into her past. Graham, however, had never done what was expected of him... by anyone. He started over to where she remained motionless next to an ancient, gnarled oak tree. The hem of her skirts kissed the edge of the ice.

At his approach, the long, graceful column of Martha's neck angled ever so slightly.

Graham stopped beside her, standing shoulder to shoulder with her, staring out.

And once more... he waited, allowing Martha her time and more, allowing her the choice to share what she would with him.

Wind gusted along the shore, tugging at her cloak, and some of the errant brown leaves that had fought the winter's pull at last ripped from the branches overhead and fluttered forlornly onto the ice.

"He was a stranger to High Town," she said softly, at last breaking the quiet around them. Her voice carried on another gust of wind. "No one had ever seen him before."

While she spoke of that nameless, faceless *him*, Graham tried to imagine a younger, more innocent Martha, untouched by life's ugliness. Who would she have been in those days? Bright-eyed, no doubt. Brimming with the same husky, unrestrained laughter that had left her lips as she'd chased him around the gardens. "Was it... love at first sight?" Some foreign sentiment, something green and insidious that felt very much like jealousy, ran through him. Which was preposterous. Him... jealous about this woman he'd known little more than a week, or *any* woman for that matter.

The irrational sentiments were shattered. "With him?" Martha snorted. "Hardly. I was just sixteen." She'd been all but a child. Nay, she had been a child. "He was more than thirty years older, without a sliver of charm in his rotund frame."

The air hissed between his teeth. "Thirty years?" My God, the man could have been her father. "And yet, you married him," he said, a statement that she answered like it was a question.

"And yet, I married him." Her voice was distant. "My father thought it would be best."

Graham's jaw tightened. "Best for whom?" he asked rhetorically, unable to keep the distaste from creeping into his voice. Ultimately, what fathers of all stations sought—rank, privilege, or pride—outweighed all.

"Ah, but he represented an escape from"—she gestured to the tree-covered landscape—"all of this."

But for the handful of pieces she'd shared, he knew nothing about the man, but that was enough for him to despise the man with a loathing that burned. "Your father was the reason you married that viscount." Who was this letch who'd marry a child? Had it been a member of the Home Office? Is that why they were so determined to see her looked after?

Frowning, Martha skimmed her fingers along a nook in one of the branches. "I wanted…" She fiddled with a crisp brown leaf that dangled forlornly from the tree.

When it became apparent she didn't intend to add anything more to that, he drifted closer. "What did you want?" he quietly urged, wanting to know about her past and who she was. And this time, he didn't attempt to force the lie upon himself that the need came only from his assignment.

Martha looped her arms around the branch and reclined a bit, her gaze fixed on the cheerful blue sky exposed by the leafless trees. "I wanted to see London. I wanted to attend lectures and visit museums. The theater." Her eyes lit for a world he'd largely despised.

"Have you ever been?" she asked abruptly, knocking him off-kilter.

Or mayhap he'd already been dangerously upended when she'd tossed her first snowball.

"To London," she clarified. "Have you ever been to London?"

He'd lived there more than he had at any of his family's country properties, and never once had he appreciated the metropolis for anything other than the den of sin he'd taken it as. He cleared his throat. "I... have," he said lamely, wanting to add nothing more, because anything he added at this point would be a lie. All the while, he knew Martha Donaldson would never be content with simply that.

"You have?" She exhaled those two syllables. "What is it like?" she asked, taking a step closer to him.

"What is it like?" he echoed, glancing distractedly about. A small, odd pile of stones snagged his notice. To give his hands something to do, he retrieved the flat rocks. "The air is thick with fog and dirt." Graham tossed one of the rocks across the ice, and it skidded across the surface before eventually falling into the part of the river that was not yet frozen.

"That is it?" she asked, incredulity and disappointment rolled together. Martha placed herself in front of Graham just as he made to launch another stone.

Let lying come as easy to you as responding to your name, Whitworth.

"It is crowded. The streets are brimming with people and conveyances. And noisy," he added. "It is that, too. Nor have I visited any museums." But he had the theater. Never, however, for reasons he could or would admit to this woman—that he'd been watching a mistress or lover perform. Those reasons now left him with an unexpected niggling of shame.

Martha sighed and stepped aside so he might complete his throw. "Yes, well, that is how those of our station live," she said after his rock had landed with a plunk in the river. "We see the dirt and the noise and the crowds, while the places of beauty that exist within those worlds belong to others."

Guilt. It had a taste and a feel and the power to consume.

Of all the damned times to develop a conscience, it would be when you're conducting official work for the Crown.

Martha held her hand out, and he stared at her callused palm a moment before turning over several stones. She tossed one at a distant hole in the ice, and the rock disappeared below the surface. "All those places and experiences I'd only read of in books but dreamed of seeing for myself at last seemed... real. A place I could go and see for myself and be part of. I wanted to sketch in Hyde Park." She peeked around, as if she feared some interloper might overhear her and judge that a silly longing. "I've read of the Serpentine and the queen's gardens and imagined what it would be to paint those visions." With that, she'd opened yet another window, offering him another glimpse into who she'd been… mayhap who she still was—a woman who sought a life away from this place. And it was an escape he understood. Because it was one he had craved since he'd been a boy faced with a disappointed father and unable to be more or do better—at anything.

The bright glimmer in her eyes died. "I sold my soul for the promise of all that." Martha let the rocks in her hand fall, and they rained down around her feet with a staccato clunking. "My father believed the viscount represented my path to that dream. But ultimately, it was my decision, and I live with that." Her gaze moved beyond his shoulder. "No one forced me."

"You were a child, Martha," he said gently, willing her to see that. "You were a child." He fought to keep the hatred stinging his veins from spilling out into his words. "Your father should have taken you to London." Except, that was a slip on his part. It was an admission that he was aware of the funds the missing Mr. Donaldson had been in possession of at some point. Martha, however, gave no indication that she'd heard or recognized that tell. He took her by the arm and gave a light squeeze. "And then your husband should have, too. He should have provided you the world you dreamed of."

An image flickered forward of a moment that didn't exist, nor would ever: Martha sitting alongside Hyde Park and sketching the grounds, Graham at her side, observing her while she worked and tossing stones, Frederick at his other side.

"He wasn't," she whispered, slashing through the jarring tableau in his mind.

He wasn't?

Martha wet her lips. "My husband."

Graham shook his head. "I don't understand."

Martha's features contorted into a mask of such grief and horror that it briefly robbed him of breath. "I was married to a man who was married to another woman…" She drew in a breath, stirring another one of those little clouds of white from the cold, and then through the fabric of her cloak, Martha rubbed at her arms. "At the same time. Except, I came second." Her lips twisted in a macabre rendition of a smile. "The *second* Viscountess Waters."

He knew what she was saying. All the words were there. Only this time, the jumbled thoughts in his head were not a product of his madness or dull wits, but rather, the implications of what she revealed. The murder of the lecherous Viscount Waters had rocked Polite Society. Graham hadn't bothered with the tawdry details that had riveted the *ton*. Now he wished he had kept on with the gossip for altogether different reasons: that nobleman had been Martha's husband.

"I'm a bigamist," she whispered, misunderstanding the reason for his silence. Martha bit down on her lower lip. "Not intentionally, of course. I would have never... Had I known, I wouldn't have..." She stopped her ramblings, and studied the ground intently. "But I didn't know. My father murdered him," she whispered.

"He...?"

Martha slowly lifted her gaze; shame brimming in their depths. "He murdered him for making me a bigamist and my childr... son a bastard." This was where he was to say something. Good. Waters deserved the fiery fate he was surely enduring in Satan's inferno. Nor was he gentleman enough to coat that ruthless glee. He opened his mouth to say as much; to tell her that the bastard had deserved to die...and painfully.

He was too slow.

Martha hastily averted her gaze. "Now you know, Graham. I... should go find Frederick."

As she rushed off, Graham remained motionless, staring after her until she'd gone from sight.

He scrubbed his hands over his face. *Bloody hell.*

This first assignment was supposed to be simple—no doubt the reason they'd given it to him. He was to have reported on Martha Donaldson's circumstances.

He'd believed himself an unfeeling rogue who cared about nothing more than his own pleasures, only to discover here, between the broken and hurting pair, that he was capable of feeling. And he despised it. He preferred a world where he felt nothing, compared to this stabbing agony at Martha's and Frederick's suffering.

And, something told him, that when he left this place, he would never be the same again.

CHAPTER 13

S HE'D TOLD HIM.

In a moment of weakness, she had revealed *everything* to Graham Malin.

Nay, not everything. Not Creda or Iris, but rather, all the shame that had led to her sending her daughters away.

Seated on the floor, alongside the hearth, with her legs drawn close to her chest and her sketch pad forgotten beside her, Martha stared into the wildly dancing flames.

Or, mayhap confiding in Graham had not had anything to do with a moment of weakness or Frederick's urging.

"Mayhap it had nothing to do with either," she whispered into the quiet. Mayhap it had come from at last having another person to speak to. Had there ever truly been anyone she'd talked to about anything that mattered?

She had been so young when her mother died that Martha carried no memories of her. Martha's father had been loving and devoted, but he'd placed her upon a pedestal, a figure to be cherished like a prized heirloom left behind by his beloved wife. Never had they discussed her hopes or dreams, or anything aside from the day-to-day dealings of their property. It was why he'd sought a noble match for her, one that would raise her pedestal all the more.

All the while never considering what Martha had wanted or why she'd agreed to that match.

Because she'd not told him. Because she hadn't known how to talk to him.

Martha rubbed her chin back and forth over the coarse fabric of her wool skirts and stared off to the doors that led to the kitchens and beyond, to Graham's rooms. How to make sense of this inexplicable ability to speak to him, a man she'd known less than two weeks? A man whom she'd not seen since her confession.

The front door burst open, and heart racing, she looked up.

Glowering at her, Frederick kicked the door closed with the heel of his boot. "You told him, didn't you?" Fury spilled out from his expressive brown eyes.

Martha came scrambling to her feet. "I don't... What...?"

Her son charged forward. "Mr. Malin." His voice climbed. "Who do you *think* I'm speaking about? He's gone."

The earth dipped, and Martha searched her fingers around the air before finding purchase on the back of the sofa. "What?" she repeated, gripping the high back. Her heart sank.

"Gone." Frederick began pacing, his little legs furiously pumping as he strode back and forth. "I woke up early to muck the stalls before he was there. And then I'd finished, and he'd never come, and so I went to his rooms—" Her son came to an abrupt stop. "Gone." The fight went out of his voice and eyes, until he was left vulnerable before her in ways he hadn't been since his father's death.

"Y-you are certain?" she asked, her voice hoarse.

He gave a jerky nod. "His horse is missing, too."

Martha slid into the nearest chair. Trying to think. Trying to process what her son had revealed. And unable to manage anything past that one truth: Graham had left.

Of course, it had been inevitable. He was never destined to remain on forever. He'd left, just as the previously loyal men and women who'd served their modest household had. But neither had Martha allowed herself to think of the day that Graham eventually would. And that day would have always included a parting. A word of goodbye and well-wishes expressed by each of them.

Something from a man who'd been more of a father to Frederick than the man who'd sired him. Something from the man who, one late night, had cared for her injury and then kissed her.

No.

She squeezed her eyes shut. By Frederick's account, Graham was gone, and as much as that announcement should have come as a matter of fact based on the inevitability of it all, an emptiness gnawed at her heart. Whether it denied reason or not, the truth remained: She cared about Graham Malin. And he was gone. *What did you expect? That you should reveal that he was employed—and not in a paid post—by the village bigamist, and he should be the one person who'd not condemn you for that?*

Martha bit her lower lip.

She had deluded herself with that dream.

Fool. Fool. Fool.

"Are you listening to me?" Frederick cried, giving her shoulder a shake.

Martha snapped to. "Yes," she said with a calm she did not feel. *How am I so composed?*

Her son thumped his fist on the back of the sofa. "Damn it, what happened when I left you?"

Unable to face her son, Martha gathered up her sketch pad and charcoal and stood. "I don't like your tone or language. Ask again."

Frederick stamped his foot. But this time when he spoke, he did so in more measured tones. "Mother, would you share what transpired between you and Mr. Malin upon my leaving?"

"We spoke..." she hedged.

Frederick's panic-laden groan trailed behind her. "You told him," he repeated, his voice cracking.

"You advised me to tell him." Placing her materials atop their place on the easel, she carefully arranged the items, lining up the charcoals.

That you are a woman should not prevent you from seeing yourself as the artist you are.

Martha blinked back the dust in her eyes and instead focused on the inane task before her, so she didn't have to confront the truth: Graham was gone. And her cottage was not unkempt, but rather, there was an altogether different reason for the sheen blurring her vision.

"And?" her son prodded from across the room.

Martha discreetly wiped the back of one hand over her eyes before facing her son. "And that is precisely what I did."

"I was angry," he cried, racing over. "You weren't supposed to really tell him."

"You were angry," she said softly. "But you were also correct.

That secret needed to be brought to light, and if it had not been me…" It would have been one of the nasty High Town villagers. The same men and women whom Graham had gone toe-to-toe with to defend her honor. That, however, had been before he'd known what had so earned Martha the disdain and disgust of all.

Including him.

Her throat closed up.

Odd that she'd known Graham less than any of the people in this entire miserable village, and yet, his defection landed worse than any of the vicious slaps doled out by her *husband*.

Through her own misery, Martha registered her son's absolute silence, and then her heart crumpled all over again. In her selfishness, she'd fixed almost exclusively on what Graham's departure meant to her. The sharpest, most intense of all the guilt filled her— maternal guilt. Thrusting aside her own feelings and hurt, Martha urged her son over. "Come here, Frederick." When he made no move to join her, she spoke in firmer tones. "I said 'come here'."

Her son hesitated, and then dragging his heels, he at last complied. Martha sank onto the bench near her easel, so she could look him in the eye.

Then promptly wished she hadn't.

For it was not pain or confusion reflected back.

Hatred sparked in those brown eyes that were the viscount's eyes, exuding that same antipathy. Mayhap it was Martha's lot to be despised by all. And surely there was some deficiency in her that merited it. But all those other detractors could go hang. This boy and the two girls she'd sent away were the only ones her heart beat for. "Frederick, Mr. Malin was only kind and generous and helpful. But, dear-heart, he was not going to stay forever." *But I wanted him to stay longer, too. I wanted to wake up knowing he was here with us.*

"You drove him away," he exhaled. "You drive everybody away. Father, Creda, and Iris. Even Grandfather is gone because of you."

Had he kicked Martha in the gut, his accusation couldn't have hurt more. It didn't matter that she'd made the decision to send Creda and Iris away so they might receive an education. It didn't matter that the choice had been hers. Frederick's words stung like vinegar on an open wound.

She was saved from trying to formulate any response by an unexpected knock at the door.

As one, she and Frederick looked toward the front of the room. Another heavy rap followed, and something she'd not seen in too long lit her son's features—hope and happiness. Those like sentiments sent her heart pounding into a double-time beat.

Frederick took off flying across the room, yanked the door open, and then deflated. "Oh," he said dumbly. He stepped back. "You." Martha's hopes sank along with his.

Squire Chernow barely spared the boy a glance. "Master Frederick," he offered, an obligatory greeting. "How—?"

Before the lanky leader of the village had gotten the remainder of that query out, Frederick darted around him and went off running.

"That one's become rude, Marti. A real problem there," the squire admonished, ripping off his gloves and letting himself in.

She knew he was rude, but hearing someone else disparage her son was an altogether different matter. "He is not, Squire Chernow. He is… direct."

"He's rude," the older man persisted, stuffing his gloves inside his jacket and advancing forward.

Oh, bloody hell. He intended this to be one of his lengthy visits. "I'm afraid I cannot—"

"Regardless, he's not the reason I've come," he cut into her curt dismissal. "The sole reason, that is," he amended.

Unease stirred, that all-too-familiar sentiment that had lain dormant for eleven days. How odd that she'd had protective walls up, along with her guard, these past years, only to let them all collapse around Graham… and because of him. Because of that false sense of security, she found herself in a place she had not been since her husband's death—knocked off her guard.

Sidestepping his approach, Martha made a measured trek for the chair closest to the door—and close enough to escape. She placed her father's beloved upholstered walnut chair between her and his former… friend. "Why don't you say whatever it is you've come to say?" And be gone. She bit her tongue to stifle that tart retort.

"I've heard the rumors about you, Marti, and I don't approve."

"The rumors?" she echoed. Society had somehow learned those sordid details more than six months ago.

His cheeks turned a florid shade of red. "This… this… servant you've hired." Graham. "You do not have the funds to pay him."

Not anymore. At one time, the Donaldsons had employed an entire staff. "I made you an offer, which you declined only to make yourself whore in the cottage I own to a stranger to High Town."

A haze of red fell over her vision, briefly blinding, and she tasted the fury, acerbic on her tongue. "Is your affront over the fact that I've"—she tensed her mouth and had to squeeze the words past her lips—"whored myself in this cottage, or that I've whored myself to a man other than you, Squire Chernow?"

His flush deepened. "You ungrateful girl. Since your shame has been brought to light, I've only done everything in my power to ease your way here. And you, Marti, have not been suitably appreciative."

It was on the tip of her tongue to tell him off, but then there was no doubt he would toss her and Frederick out.

And then where will you go?

He smirked, a man confident that he'd come out triumphant in this particular battle. "If you wish to remain here in this cottage, Marti, there are certain rules I would go over with you." And then, the owner of her home in every way, Squire Chernow motioned to her father's chair.

Martha struggled. The spirited, prideful woman whom she'd had to restrain wanted to order him out on his arse, the consequences be damned. Her gaze, however, went to the latest sketch that hung upon the easel, only partially completed—the outline of her son's visage alongside Graham's. The image of the child was a reminder that whatever she wanted or wished to say came second to that little person—the three of them—who depended on her.

With stiff, jerky movements, Martha sat.

Squire Chernow smiled. "Splendid." Withdrawing a page from inside his jacket, he unfolded the sheet and gave the creased page several slaps. "Now, let us begin."

GRAHAM PACED THE FLOOR OF Lord Edward's office.

He'd arrived at the Brethren's Leeds field offices nearly three hours ago, but there was still no hint of his superior.

Bloody, bloody hell.

He glanced at the clock.

Again.

At this hour, Frederick would have already risen and seen to gathering Martha's water. She would be awake.

It would be only a matter of time before they discovered Graham was missing.

At the faint click of the door handle being pressed, he abruptly stopped and faced the entrance.

Lord Edward strolled in.

Strolled. As if walking through damned Hyde Park or a damned ballroom.

Graham's ire threatened to spill over. "You're late," he snapped as the other man pushed the door closed behind him. "That's a violation of Code Three. Being late sees men and women killed and missions compromised." A very likely possibility when an ever-suspicious Martha rose to discover him gone.

Instead of any hint of remorse, Lord Edward, a file in hand, continued over to the brass-bound mahogany decanter box. "Sit, sit," the commanding officer urged, waving Graham to the pair of chairs in front of his desk. "A drink?"

"I don't need a goddamn drink," he said restlessly. "I've been gone four hours now." Two and a half more than he'd anticipated.

"It's your half day at the Donaldsons'," Lord Edward noted. The clink of crystal touching crystal and the quiet stream of spirits had always had a calming effect—until now.

"She'll notice my absence." And it would undo any trust he'd built with her. Trust that had all been constructed of a lie.

Nay, not all of it. She would not, however, see it that way. That was, were she to ever discover it. Which she would not.

Three days. There were just Three days left...

An odd pressure squeezed off his airflow.

Snifter in hand, Lord Edward turned a frown on him. "She shouldn't," he said flatly. "Stable masters go unnoticed."

He flushed. "I'm the only damned servant in her employ, unless Miss Donaldson is a lackwit"—which she decidedly was not—"she'd notice."

His superior's lips turned down farther at the corners as he slid into his seat. And then in a display meant to demonstrate his absolute control, Lord Edward reclined in that thronelike chair and waited, sipping his damned drink.

Suppressing a growl, Graham yanked the chair out, scraping the legs along the hardwood floor, and seated himself.

Even with that, Lord Edward took several slow sips. "Now," he said, setting his glass aside and reaching for the folder. "Your report on Miss Donaldson?"

Reaching inside his jacket, Graham withdrew the notes he'd kept and shoved them across the immaculate surface of the desk. The pages touched the edge of the brandy that remained forgotten.

The older man picked up the pages and skimmed the meticulous notes. His expression deadpan, his gaze revealing nothing, he continued to read.

How bloody casual the other man was… about everything surrounding Martha. From his tardiness to this appointment, to the speed of his steps, to the stop at his liquor cabinet, and now that almost bored skimming.

Fury pumped through him.

"She is in dire straits," he said icily, wanting some damned reaction from the man.

"I see that."

And still nothing in that acknowledgment. "They'll be dealt with now. Finish out the assignment you've been given, and by that point, a plan will be set." With an air of finality, Lord Edward opened his black leather diary and began to write furiously.

Graham waited, the *click-click-click* of the quill striking the page grating, until his patience snapped. "That is it?"

His superior paused, his gaze still trained on his page, and then resumed writing. "What else is there to say? You've done your work."

"And I don't even know the outcome that awaits the young woman?"

This time, Lord Edward did look up, his hard gaze leveled square on Graham's face. "Ah, but it isn't the role of an agent to know those details. Your role was to report on her circumstances." He lifted the stack of Graham's notes. "Which you've done. And now Miss Donaldson and her son will be passed on to the next agent."

That was it.

Of course that was it.

That was the perfunctory, methodical flow of an assignment—

no one person became too involved. Each agent's interest was not to extend too deep or too far beyond the specifics of a mission. "What will become of them?"

"Does it matter to you?" the other man shot back.

The answer expected of him was *no*. Among the many rules and lessons ingrained in him had been to never let one's subject close—it was a means of self-preservation.

"You're hesitant to answer," Lord Edward noted. Picking up his snifter, he took a drink.

"Because I know the answer expected of me. An agent gathers information but doesn't care how the outcome might affect the figures being investigated." He repeated the words by rote.

"And yet, you do."

As it was a statement, Graham let it remain as such.

Lord Edward continued sipping his drink, contemplating Graham. "There's been… debate among past and present members of the Brethren on… just how much we as an organization should 'care' about the men, women, and children involved in investigations. Nathaniel Archer, the Earl of Exeter upon his retirement, sought to set a new system of governance in place where mercy is shown to victims caught up in our work, or discovered through it."

"Martha Donaldson," Graham said, the reason for his assignment at last clear.

His superior nodded. "Miss Donaldson," he repeated. "There were those in the ranks who took umbrage at the changes implemented by his lordship. The man who replaced Exeter as Sovereign, and those he appointed to roles of power decided the policies Exeter set into place before he'd left were ones that showed weakness. They reimplemented the oldest codes of the Brethren." *Never reveal a weakness or vulnerability.* "The policies were reversed…"

"And Miss Donaldson and her son were abandoned," he murmured.

Lord Edward lifted his head. "Precisely."

She'd gone from a woman who'd lived a comfortable existence with her son and father, to a bigamist, her entire world fodder for village gossips and her struggles forgotten by the Brethren. Bitterness sat on his tongue like acid. Graham sat back in his seat. "And here I believed the Brethren was a branch within the Home

Office that honorably served and protected all members under the Crown." What a lot of rot. The organization and those within it were as self-serving as any other gentlemen.

"There has been an internal struggle for power that has seen a rapid changeover of leadership," Lord Edward expounded. "It's why many were asked out of retirement." It was why Lord Edward now found himself in the position of the Sovereign.

Graham considered those revelations. "Why are you telling me this?" he asked cautiously. When, as a rule, leadership was to reveal little and say even less.

"Because I suspect you are one of those men who, once trained as a member, would 'care' about the fate of those deserving of the Brethren's support."

And with that, Graham was knocked off-kilter.

"I went through the files of rejected candidates and studied past candidates for consideration. They say one can tell much about a person by the way they treat their horses." A faint grin turned Lord Edward's lips. "I'm one who happens to ascribe to that truth. As such, I'd be alarmed had you continued to express a disinterest in Miss Donaldson and an eagerness to forget her and move on to your next post."

"So this… All of it has been a test," Graham said slowly as understanding dawned.

Lord Edward touched a fingertip to his temple. "Everything is always a test. As for Miss Donaldson, based on your findings, we'll see that she secures employment."

All his muscles tensed. "*That* is what you're suggesting?" Graham asked, incredulity and disgust all wrapped around that question. "In addition to caring for her child and running a household, you believe adding additional work to her existence is helping her?" That was what they'd reduce her to?

"What do you propose, Whitworth?"

He searched his mind. "I…don't know." She deserved more. So much more. *There's this feeling I have… I don't know how to describe it. This… feeling that can only come in creating something from nothing. It's equal parts wonder, and frustration, and exhilaration, all wrapped together.* "The young woman has artistic talents," Graham said into the quiet. "If I may suggest that work be found that allows her to use those abilities."

If he had to leave, that was one small deserved gift he'd leave her with.

Picking up his pen, Lord Edward jotted something in his book. "I've noted it."

Panic filled him. The end was closing in. It couldn't simply just... end. Not like this. "I'd like to petition for more time." The request was pulled from him before he could call it back. And if he were honest with himself, he didn't want to call it back.

Lord Edward again set his pen down and clasped his hands on the desk. "Go on."

"Martha and her son are being persecuted by the villagers. At one of our first meetings, I discovered her knocked down by someone. Her son was nearly harmed yesterday."

Lord Edward's brows came together. "Were either injured?"

"They did not sustain physical wounds." The pain Martha and her son knew went far deeper.

"You identified the assailants?"

"Two of Frederick Donaldson's. I've reason to believe the young men who attacked her son were different than the lady's attackers." At Lord Edward's probing look, Graham explained, "I identified and measured the tracks made by all. The tracks of whoever was following Martha were larger, and there were two of them."

"And you suspect there is something more at play than small-minded villagers taunting a woman accused of bigamy?"

How casual the other man was. "I don't have any proof of such," he reluctantly conceded. "But neither can I say definitively that she is not being threatened for other reasons."

"Who might wish her ill?"

"Mayhap her late husband's legitimate family." It, of course, made the most sense. "Perhaps the man's legitimate son."

Lord Edward leaned forward. The slight shifting of his slender frame sent the leather to groaning. "How do you know about the young woman's past?"

"She confided in me." On a lie. She believed Graham was something other than he was, someone other than he was, and trusted him.

Frowning, his superior reclined in his seat once more. "Unless you have proof, I suggest you kill that empty supposition. The late viscount's 'legitimate' family is, in fact, linked by marriage now to

Nathaniel Archer."

An incessant muscle ticked at the corner of Graham's eye. "I've no proof."

"Then you have no reason to stay," Lord Edward said, finality in that statement. "And as you're concerned Miss Donaldson will be suspicious of your absence, I suggest you make your return."

Graham remained seated for a moment, wanting to battle the older man on the point, wanting to insist he allow Graham to remain on at the Donaldson farm. What grounds could he provide, however? "My lord," he said stiffly and climbed to his feet.

A short while later, Graham quit the offices of the Brethren and rode hard for Martha's properties. Riding had always managed to clear his head. Not this time. Now, his mind clamored with thoughts of Martha and her son and his concluding time with them. She deserved a goodbye, and it was, of course, easy enough to give her a false reason. All he needed to do was tell her he'd secured a paid post as a stable master and be gone.

Graham conceded the accuracy in Lord Edward's statement: There was *no* reason for Graham to remain behind with Martha and Frederick.

Aside from one dangerous, undeniable one—he wanted to.

Around noon, Graham arrived at the path leading to Martha's cottage. Dismounting, he collected the reins and guided the sweaty mount on to the stables.

The moment he opened the doors, he blinked to adjust his eyes to the dark space and immediately found Frederick. The little boy sat on a hay bale in the middle of the stables, twisting Graham's John Bull hat.

"Mr. Malin," Frederick whispered, and then jumping to his feet, he came flying across the barn. He launched himself at Graham, knocking him slightly back.

"Oomph," he grunted, automatically righting him and the little child. His arms came up reflexively about Martha's son in a light, foreign embrace. The duchess had always been free with her affections. Graham's father, however, would have sooner lopped off limbs than use them to display warmth and be perceived as weak.

"Frederick," he greeted, his voice slightly hoarse.

I'm going to miss not only Martha, but her son, too.

Bloody hell. It had been just eleven days since he'd known them.

He wasn't supposed to care.

Frederick's little frame stiffened, and then he hurried out of Graham's arms. Clearing his throat, he stuck a hand out.

Graham eyed it for a moment and then took those little fingers in the boy's surprisingly strong handshake. "I th-thought you left," Frederick said, a faint tremble to his words serving as an unneeded reminder that, for this display, he was still just a child. Frederick's stricken eyes went to the hat he still clenched in his other hand. "Or-or did you only come back for your hat?"

"No, that isn't why I'm here," he said, swiftly reassuring.

"But your things were gone." The boy looked to the bag Graham held.

He followed his stare. "I had… business I needed to see to."

Frederick grinned, the smile dimpling his left cheek. Just like his mother. "But you're back. For good."

Oh, God. Pain continued scissoring away at his heart. Calling forth the indolent mask he'd crafted early on, he offered a smile. For he was here for another three days. He'd deal later with the reality of never again seeing Martha or this child before him. Now? Graham did a sweep, filled with an inexorable hungering to see her.

Then he registered the sudden darkening of Frederick's features. "What is it?"

Frederick scuffed the tip of a frayed boot along the dirt floor. "I may have shouted at my mother," he whispered.

"You… may have?" Graham asked guardedly.

With a sigh, Frederick stuffed his hands in his pockets and rocked back and forth. All the while, he avoided Graham's eyes. "She told me that she told you about… about"—he stole a peep at Graham—"being a bigamist. And I… We thought you left because of it. I blamed her."

Graham swiped a hand over his face. "Oh, Frederick."

"It is her fault, though. You wouldn't be wrong—"

"It's not her fault." He went to a knee and touched the boy's nose. "Look at me?"

The boy immediately complied.

"It's not her fault. Your mother… was wronged. Lied to. And hurt because of it. Men have a responsibility to be honorable, truthful at all times." He winced, stumbling over that. "And respectful to women," he finished. "Your mother deserved that from the viscount, and she deserves that from you. Because that is the way a real man should be. Do you understand what I'm saying?"

"That I should be kind to my mother," he mumbled.

"No, I am saying you should be respectful to all women." He winked. "But especially your mother." Gathering up his bag, he looked around. "Where is she?"

"I left her inside." His cheeks went red, and as he spoke, Graham struggled to hear the whispery-soft remainder of his words. "With Squire Chernow."

"Who in blazes is Squire Chernow?"

"He's the man who bought our cottage. He used to be friends with Grandfather. He was going to have Mother sketch his manor, but he keeps telling her that her work isn't any good. But I… I don't like how he looks at her. He stands close to her, and I probably shouldn't have left, but I was angry."

Graham narrowed his eyes and forced a calm he didn't feel. "Run along and rub down Scoundrel, will you? I'm going to visit your mother."

The boy nodded, and they fell into step, exiting the stables.

Graham continued on, his large strides eating the remainder of the distance to the cottage, and with every footfall, a red-hot bloodlust pumped into his veins.

CHAPTER 14

MARTHA STARED DOWN AT THE lengthy list compiled by Squire Chernow and his wife.

Rules of decorum, propriety, and expectations.

"Number thirty-six, I trust is clear," he was saying. His reading spectacles perched on the bridge of his nose, he studied the sheet.

"No impolite visitors," she drawled. "You may trust that I'd never *voluntarily* keep company with any impolite guests." Whether he heard that veiled rebuke, he gave no indication.

"And the last item, Miss Donaldson," he went on as if she hadn't spoken, like a tutor doling out uninventive lessons to a student.

Martha turned to the final sheet. *You'll not keep company with any man as long as you reside in High Town.* Of course, that was what this was really about. "I have a stable master, Squire Chernow," she said tightly.

"A man whom you do not pay for his… services."

Heat splotched her cheeks. She'd not even dignify that accusation with a response.

"I'll not have you taking up with another in my property, madam," he said, thumping his pages onto the table next to him.

With that presumption and gall, the veneer of civility she'd forced around this man lifted. "Let us be clear, you'll not have me taking up with a man other than you," she shot back. "That is what this is about." She came to her feet. All these years—with the viscount, even her father, and now this man—she'd tiptoed around how she felt or softened how she spoke.

"How dare you?" he said.

Graham had been the first man… nay, person, she'd shared freely of her feelings and thoughts, and in that, she'd set herself free. This man might own her cottage, but she needn't fall down weak before him. "I dare because it is true," she said. "What would Mrs. Chernow say should she learn of your advances?"

His eyes bulged behind his glasses, and he lunged for her.

Martha easily sidestepped the balding squire, keeping her chair between them.

Squire Chernow smirked and, with methodical movements, removed his spectacles and tucked them in his jacket. "She'll know what I tell her… That the High Town Whore offered herself to me in exchange for living on rent-free. A shameful offer which I, of course, declined."

And the world *would* believe him. Because ultimately, no one ever trusted the word of a woman. When a woman rebuffed a man's advances, those cads would take what they wanted anyway and leave a woman with nothing more than a blackened name and sullied soul.

"I'm not agreeing to these items," she said flatly, holding out the sheet. "How many of your widowed tenants have you put such terms to?"

He scoffed. "That is entirely different. You are a young woman, on your own, already with a reputation as a whore. You sully the village by simply being here. And I've been magnanimous enough just letting you rent from me."

"Yes, how kind," she shot back, her voice dripping with conde-scension. And *this* from a man who'd been her father's friend. But then, her father, even with all his *lessons* on 'paying attention to how a man treated his animals', he hadn't followed his own advice, and proven rubbish at judging a person's character. His approval of Viscount Waters was testament enough of that. Martha folded those sheets and handed them over. "I'll not agree to any of them. And I'll certainly not send away Mr. Malin." She and Frederick would find another cottage to rent and begin again.

On the heel of that was a swift panic at the sheer impossibility of finding a new home. There was no money. There was—

Squire Chernow pounced.

She gasped as he caught her by the arm.

"I don't take kindly to those who threaten me, Marti," he scolded, giving her arm a squeeze. Martha wrenched at it, but the older man demonstrated a surprising display of strength. "Now, I've been nothing but fair. I've been patient. Waiting for you to come round. But I'll not sit about anymore while you freely give to some bloody servant what you've been withholding from me."

"Release me," she ordered, hating the warble in the demand. Her heart pounded hard in her chest as she tried to pull out of his reach, but he retained his hold, drawing her closer.

"If you'd rather put on a show of offended sensibilities," he whispered against her ear, "I will play the game, kitten." He roved a hand along her hip, just as another man had before. This touch was so different from Graham's.

Graham, who'd left her and Frederick. She squeezed her lashes shut.

He brought her around to face him, and there was nothing paternal in the roving hands that moved punishingly along her waist and then higher. He cupped her right breast, and an animalistic groan filtered from his lips. Eyes closed, he lowered his head.

Martha brought her knee up, and he shifted, rendering her blow ineffectual.

"So we *are* still playing this game, then, kitten," he rasped. "Splendid."

The door burst open, and her heart soared.

"Graham," she whispered. Only, this was Graham as she'd never seen him. Not even at the riverside with a pistol leveled on the town bullies. The threat of death glinted in his gaze. That gaze shifted briefly over to her, and he did an up-and-down sweep of her person, taking in her wrinkled skirts and touching on the strands that had pulled free from her braid. His eyes narrowed, a question there.

She nodded once. "I'm fine," she mouthed.

Gulping loudly, Squire Chernow released her, and Martha hurried away from him. "You've no—" Whatever brave response he'd found the courage to utter ended on a squeak.

Graham surged forward and caught the squire by the wrist, the same hand he'd had on Martha moments ago. With a vicious ferocity, Graham wrenched it up. "If you ever touch her, speak her name, or even look at her or her son, I will end you," he whispered.

Squire Chernow cried out, "Please. She wanted it. You are new to the village and do not know, but she is a whore."

Graham spun the older man around and buried his fist in his face. There was a sharp crack as cartilage gave way to that punishing fist. He continued to pummel the squire in a raw, violent display.

Martha clutched at her throat. "Graham," she called out, but he ignored the attempt to stay him.

The squire crumpled into a noisy, blubbering heap. Blood spurted from between his fingers. "My God, I'm d-dying," he rasped.

"Your damned nose is broken, you coward," Graham spat and then dragged the squire to his feet and hauled him over to the door. "Let this be the last time you threaten Miss Donaldson, or you can be sure I'll see you pay."

With that, he yanked the door open and tossed the squire out on his buttocks.

A moment later, Graham closed that panel, and a peculiar hum of silence rang in the room.

Her mind sought to muddle through the most important details. But she could settle on only one fact. "You're here," she whispered.

"I'm here." Graham stalked over and then stopped, as if afraid to touch her. "Did he hurt you?" he asked, his voice hoarse with something she'd never heard from this strong, unshakeable man: fear. *For me.*

And the horror of the squire's assault receded. "No, I…"

Graham collected her wrist, his grip tender where the squire's had been punishing. He dusted his knuckle over the imprint left by Squire Chernow's thumb, the crimson mark vivid upon her pale skin.

"I should have killed him," he whispered.

He cared that much… for her? "No. You shouldn't have, Graham." She'd not have any man's blood on Graham's hands. Not for her.

"Fine, then I should have thrashed him until he was senseless." Graham carried her wrist close to his mouth and placed his lips upon that mark.

Butterflies fluttered in her chest, a swarm set free by his caress. "I thought you'd left," she whispered as he continued to worship her wrist. She made herself say the rest. "Because of what I revealed."

He stopped the delicate back-and-forth caress, and as he let her arm down gently to her side, she wanted to cry out at the loss. To ask him to not stop.

"You think I would leave because of that?" he murmured, tucking her loose curls behind her ears. "Is your opinion of me so low?"

"Never you." Her opinion was low… of herself. Martha studied the tips of her boots intently, but Graham gently, determinedly guided her gaze up.

The raw intensity in those piercing sapphire eyes sucked the breath from her lungs.

"I could never… would never blame you for the crimes of some bounder like Waters. Or any man, Martha. What he did to you? And your son? Those were testaments to his character, or rather, lack of. Not yours."

Her lower lip trembled, and she caught it between her teeth. "Thank—" He glared the words of gratitude from her lips. "I've never had anyone who has come to my defense." She glanced beyond his shoulder to the place where Viscount Waters had first sat when he'd visited, a guest. "Never my husband." She grimaced. "He was free with his fists. My father even saw him strike me, but… never intervened. He didn't know what to do, and so? He looked the other way."

A tortured groan reverberated around the room.

It took her a moment to realize it belonged to another.

Graham's face was a mask carved in agony and fury.

In that instant, she fell in love with him. This man who was a stranger nearly two weeks ago, who was as free with his smiles and guidance for a boy and his support of her, and also who had restraint.

Martha drifted closer to him. "But you defended me, Graham," she said softly, laying her palms against his chest. His heart hammered wildly under her fingers, and she savored that steady beat. "When anyone else before you has said I wasn't worthy, you've helped me see otherwise, and I will be eternally grateful for that gift."

His throat muscles moved, and she leaned up on tiptoe, wanting to know the beauty of his touch again. Needing to claim another moment in his arms because of her want and need for this man.

Graham dipped his head, and then, his mouth moving as if in silent prayer, he backed away from her.

The door burst open, and this time, Frederick came pouring through the entrance. "He's returned! Oh," he blurted, looking at Graham. "You know, then."

Martha coughed into her hand. "Yes. I... know." What else was she to say in that instant?

Graham started over to her son. "Why don't we go muck out the remainder of the stalls?"

He might as well have handed her son the moon and stars. Frederick grinned, a slightly gap-toothed smile. The pair took their leave, with Graham pausing in the doorway to cast her one last look.

As soon as he'd shut the door behind them, she gathered her sketch pad and charcoal. And this time, she allowed herself to create. She let her fingers dance over the pages as the errant laughter, the cherished sound of her son's laughter, drifted in from the stable yard.

Until she'd finished.

Graham's visage stared back. Graham as he'd been when he'd come upon her in the copse, an honorable man whose intentions she'd feared. Who'd sought little and offered everything.

And yet... she frowned as the unwanted thoughts she'd not allowed herself to consider slipped forward.

Where had Graham gone this morning? Of course, it had been his half day, and he'd every right to leave. But he'd taken his belongings. How did one account for that peculiarity?

As she set to work sketching another piece, she could not rid herself of the unwanted niggling that deep down she didn't want to know the reason.

CHAPTER 15

HIS KNUCKLES CRACKED AND BLOODIED from his earlier thrashing of Squire Chernow, Graham should have been in some pain. Instead, the materials he'd set upon the kitchen table to tend his injuries sat forgotten as he replayed that moment in his mind.

That old, vile lecher, with his wandering hands and vile words about Martha dripping from his thin lips.

And now ten hours after he'd thrown the bastard out on his arse, all Graham felt was the same palpable rage he had had when he'd entered the cottage. It burned through him now as intensely as it had when he'd come upon that bastard.

And he wanted to beat him bloody and senseless all over again.

But this tumult that raged inside was not solely for the lecher, but rather, for what the incident meant. He'd leave, and Martha would be on her own. There'd be no one to challenge the bounders who made her indecent offers. Nay, more than that. Graham wanted to be the one who challenged them. Who defended her honor, as she deserved.

Graham stiffened, feeling her presence before he heard her. As if he'd conjured her from his need to see her and talk to her.

Hovering in the doorway, Martha rapped lightly on the door-jamb. "May I… join you?"

He shoved to his feet. "Of course."

"When you do you that, Graham, you make me feel like we're playing at lord and lady," she teased, shoving the sleeves of her night wrapper up to her elbows.

"You are a lady." And by nature of his birth, he was a lord. He had to force himself to meet her eyes, lest she look close enough and see all the lies between them.

"Because I was almost a viscountess? Hardly. You heard Squire Chernow. I'm a whore." She spoke so casually.

He balled his hands. "Don't say that."

"But I am. An accidental one," she said, lifting a finger at his nose. "But a whore all the same. Sit." Martha assessed his medical supplies.

"You're wrong," he said, ignoring her urging.

"And you are arrogant in your convictions."

"I'm right in them," he said flatly. "You're not a whore, because you were wronged. You were a woman who trusted and was betrayed in the cruelest way. You are a woman who emerged from that stronger, unbroken by life. That"—he matched her earlier movement, lifting a finger close to her freckled nose—"makes you more worthy than any woman I've ever known."

Her eyes went soft, those aquamarine pools beckoning, and he was so very content to lose himself in their depths. "Here," Martha murmured, sliding onto the bench. She patted the spot beside her. "Sit," she repeated.

"I have it," he assured, but she frowned, taking his palm in hers anyway.

"Oh, hush," she chided. "It is only fair." She smiled up at him. "You, after all, cared for me." She cradled his injured hand with such tenderness, and yet, there was a realness to her grip. Her skin was callused and rough from her work, and different from that of the pampered, privileged ladies who'd have never managed to survive as Martha had. Dragging the bowl over, she gently dipped his hand into the warmed water. "It is important to see that wounds are cleaned."

"An interesting bit of knowledge you have there, Miss Donaldson."

When she glanced up, there was a twinkle in her eyes. "I had a very skilled instructor."

"Did you?" he teased in return.

"Oh, yes," she said with a forced solemnity. She lowered her voice to a whisper. "If a bit arrogant."

"Arrogant, was he?" he drawled, tickling her side until he'd pulled a squeal of laughter from her.

Then the mirth died in her eyes, and he wanted to bring it back. Wanted to see her as she'd been moments ago and throwing snowballs days earlier, with her gaze filled with joy and levity. "Thank you."

"You don't have to thank me," he said quietly, not pretending to misunderstand. "Not for that."

"I do. No one has defended me. And if you hadn't been there…" The squire would have raped her.

The metallic tinge of fear filled his mouth. For what would happen to her when he was gone? The Brethren would now see her watched over, but she would still be a woman on her own, prey for any scoundrel who believed a woman was his for the taking, whether she wished it or not.

She smiled again. "But you were there." Martha must have seen something in his eyes. "What?"

He shook his head. *Just say the damned words.* In the end, she proved more intuitive than he was brave.

"You're leaving."

Graham hesitated a moment and then nodded once. "I've secured a position as stable master."

She wet her lips. "I… see." Silently, Martha resumed caring for his bruised knuckles.

What exactly did she see? He needed to know when he couldn't see anything with any real clarity anymore. Not since he'd come here.

"When do you leave?" She directed the question to the bowl of water. Squeezing the excess water out of the cloth, she took his hand from the bowl and wiped away the crusted remnants of blood.

"Three… two days," he amended. He was nearly out of time with her and Frederick.

"Is that where you went this morning?"

He managed a nod. For his visit with Lord Edward had yielded an end to this post and the eventual beginning of another.

This time, she didn't say anything. Dropping the damp cloth, she reached for a clean scrap and proceeded to dry his fingers. "It is… odd," she murmured as she wiped the water from him. "I feel like I know so much about you, and I'll… miss y-you." Her voice broke, cracking free another piece of his heart. She drew a breath in through her teeth, and a sheen of tears filled her eyes. Martha brushed the back of her arm over them, wiping at the drops.

"Martha," he whispered, reaching for her. This was killing him, shredding the rest of his heart.

She quickly stood and stepped away from him, and he mourned the loss. She'd retreated. It was a strategy of self-preservation he well knew, but had somehow managed to forget around this woman.

"Do not worry about us, please." A pained half laugh spilled from her lips. "And to think nearly two weeks ago, I didn't want you anywhere near my property." Her voice faded to a barely there whisper. "And now I can't imagine you not being here." The life seemed to drain from her, and she slid onto the bench beside him once more. "I've always been rubbish at goodbyes. I hate them so very much." She wiped at her nose, and Graham fished out a kerchief, handing it over.

Martha plucked it from his fingers and lightly blew into it. "The only person I was always happy to see leave was my husband. Each day he went, I gave thanks to the Lord and prayed he'd never return."

And if Viscount Waters hadn't already been dead, Graham would have gladly murdered the bastard with his bare hands and then happily sent his rotted soul on to hell where he was even now burning.

"But aside from him, I've just always hated goodbyes. There is a permanency to them."

And there was a permanency to this one. When he was gone from this place, he'd never again see her. Their only link would be the one through the Home Office, which she was unaware of, one that he wouldn't have a reason or right to press for further information.

Martha fiddled with the fabric in her hands, crumpling the white linen into a little ball and then straightening it.

He froze. The embroidered initials of his name, threaded in sapphire, disappeared and reappeared in a damning kaleidoscope. *SGMW. SGMW.*

Martha set the kerchief down and curled her fingers on her lap.

Swiftly retrieving the rumpled, damning cloth, he stuffed it into his jacket front and spun on the bench so they sat side by side in a like repose.

"I don't remember anything about my mother. The only memory I still have of her is the day I said goodbye. I remember standing at her bedside and thinking, if I just left, I wouldn't have to say goodbye. I was angry with my father, blaming him for making me say goodbye, believing that was why she left... and so I never said that word to anyone in parting again. I fared them well and gave them my best, but never my goodbye."

"I hate the word, too," he said softly, startled by the truth of that. He'd not allowed himself to think on it. "They were the last words I spoke to my brother."

Where had that revelation came from? He shared nothing about Lawrence with anybody.

Martha twined her fingers with his, interlocking their digits in a joining that eased some of the pain that would always be there. "I spoke them in jest. I taunted him. We were always competing, and we were racing that day. I allowed him to believe he was winning." Because that was what his family had always expected. That Graham would finish last. "And then I surged ahead. I looked over my shoulder and shouted goodbye. Lawrence urged his horse into a reckless gallop, and the mount came up lame. Threw him."

He pressed his eyes closed. His and Heath's screams had rolled together, deafening, as Lawrence had lain there, eternally silent, his neck bent at an impossible angle.

Martha rested her head against his shoulder, and he took the support she proffered. "It wasn't your fault."

"It was, though," he said simply. He knew that now. "My father never forgave me, and with good reason."

"There was nothing to forgive. It was an accident. A horrible twist of fate that saw him fall."

He shook his head before remembering she wasn't looking at him. "It was me being reckless, attempting to prove my worth."

"I married a man because I sought a life outside of High Town. Do you hold me to blame for my circumstances?"

He blanched. "Of course not." His neck went hot as her meaning became clear.

Martha tapped the tip of his nose. "And yet, you'd hold yourself responsible for a chance accident."

"It's not at all the same."

"No," she countered, shaking her head. "It is not exactly the same, but neither did you or I intend for the outcomes we met that day."

All these years, he'd spent hating himself. Unable to look at himself without seeing his brother's death reflected back in his visage. Only to have this woman, not very long ago, a stranger, hold forth an absolution. Her words of forgiveness washed over him.

"Martha, I…"

When he paused, she peered up at him. "Yes?"

I want to remain with you. He wasn't ready to leave. Not yet. He needed more time with her. And Frederick.

"I will miss you," he said quietly, bringing her hand to his mouth. He pressed a light kiss against the inseam of her wrist. "And I'll miss Frederick."

Her lower lip quivered. "I'll… We will miss you, too. I'd… ask you something before you go."

"Anything," he vowed.

Martha wet her lips. "Will you make love to me?"

MARTHA'S HEART POUNDED.

Where had that query come from?

Nay, Martha knew precisely where it had come from—a place of longing and desire and need to know Graham Malin and the pleasure he'd helped prove she was capable of.

Rather, where had she found the courage to form that utterance?

"Martha." Her name was an entreaty. "I cannot…"

"Because you are leaving?" She lifted her chin and dared him with her gaze to speak the truth. "Or because you don't want me."

"Of course I want you. I've never wanted anyone more."

Catching his uninjured hand, Martha drew it to her breast. "Then make love to me," she said softly.

His long fingers curled around that small swell, so perfect it fit in his palm, and as he caressed her, delicate with his touch, tender, heat sparked low in her belly. "I never knew a man could be gentle," she confessed, closing her eyes and giving herself over to the sensation of that gentle kneading. Through the fabric of her gown, he tweaked the erect nipple, sending another wave of warmth spiraling through her. "I want to learn everything else I don't know, Graham. And I want you to be the one to teach me."

With a groan, he covered her mouth with his.

This was nothing like the first gentle meeting of their mouths that had been slow and explorative. This kiss, this joining, was all raw heat and desire. Martha parted her lips, allowing him entry, and they tangled with their tongues. Theirs was a duel, and she met every stroke of that flesh.

Never breaking contact with her lips, Graham scooped her up by the knees and started across the kitchens for his rooms.

The moment he'd closed the door behind them, he turned the lock and carried her over to the bed.

Kneeling on the lumpy mattress, they frantically divested each other of their clothes. Martha shoved his jacket off and reached for his lawn shirt. He shrugged out of the articles, and they fell in a heap at the bottom of the bed. Her wrapper joined them.

Next, he was drawing her night shift over her head, so that Martha knelt bare before him.

Her chest rose and fell hard as he stopped. His gaze lingered on her, and for the first time since she'd put her request to him, uncertainty crept in.

You are hideous. You should be grateful I give you any attention, you crimson cow.

She hugged her arms to her chest in a bid to shield herself from his focus as, unwanted, the viscount's hateful charges whispered forward, kindling all her own self-doubts.

"Do not," he whispered, staying her hand, and she reluctantly let her limbs fall uselessly at her sides, exposing herself to him once more. With a reverence in his touch, he cradled her right breast, weighing it like he measured spun silk. "You are so beautiful."

She bit her lower lip, his touch as seducing as his words. And while he continued to caress and worship that skin, her head fell back, and she gave herself over to simply feeling and surrendering all she was to him and these feelings and this moment.

Graham captured the swollen, sensitive tip between his lips and suckled.

Martha whimpered, her hips undulating of their own volition with each pull and tug of his mouth. And then he was moving his attention to the previously neglected tip, laving it, tasting her.

She tangled her fingers in his silken hair, holding him close. "Please, don't stop," she panted. "Promise you'll not stop."

"Never," he vowed against her skin, and while he continued to worship her breast, he slipped a hand between her legs.

Martha bit her lower lip to keep from crying out as he palmed her. Then his fingers found the nub shielded by her curls. He teased her in an erotic game that was both torture and rapture combined. Sweat beaded on her brow as she thrust into his touch. Needing more. Wanting more.

"Please," she begged, and it was as though he knew for what she entreated, no more words needed, when she herself didn't know.

Graham slipped a finger inside her sodden channel, and she hissed, clenching her legs around his hand. Riding it. Her body was climbing higher, carried higher by him and his every stroke.

It wasn't enough.

Then he was gone, and her body went cold.

But he was shoving his trousers down, kicking them aside so that he knelt before her naked.

Martha stilled, her breath catching in her chest.

He was... all masculine perfection, his body cut of sinewy muscles, a light matting of black curls upon his chest.

Martha stroked her fingers along his chest, and he groaned. A thrill of female pride moved through her. Emboldened by her own power over this man, she continued to stroke him. She trailed her palms down his flat, muscled belly and lower to the hard, long length jutting out proudly from a whorl of black curls.

"You are magnificent," she whispered. She'd spent her adult life hating the male form, finding it repulsive and vile, only to have Graham's muscled physique available for her exploration and pleasure and finding the beauty in it.

Nay, it was just him. There was no man like him.

And he would be leaving.

Sadness stabbed at her heart.

Do not... do not let that in...

"What is it?" he asked hoarsely when she'd stilled her fingers.

She'd steal this moment from him and hold on to it forever. "I've never known a man like you, Graham Malin," she whispered and then leaned up, taking his mouth in a kiss.

Graham caught her under her buttocks and drew her close. The heat of his body rippled from him, burning in its intensity.

He guided her down. The mattress creaked with the shift of their weight as Graham lay between her thighs, cradling her between his elbows.

She felt him at her entrance. The head of his shaft slipped inside, and her body, wet for him, slicked the way, and there was no pain. Only splendor. Only bliss. Only them.

Lowering his head to her breast once more, he teased that sensitized tip, and the dueling sensations sent her body into a frenzy as she lifted her hips, needing him. All of him.

He plunged deep, and she opened her mouth, letting out a silent scream of ecstasy. Then he withdrew, and she gripped him tight around the back, clinging to him. "Please," she begged. Not knowing what she begged for, only knowing he could ease the ache that throbbed at her center. He was thrusting, moving within her, his strokes slow torture, luxuriant, toying with her sanity. And Martha matched each lunge, lifting her hips, their bodies in perfect harmony with each other.

The tense, almost painful set of his face, a study in concentration and hunger, sent her desire climbing. She caressed a palm down his cheek. "Faster," she urged, and as he increased his rhythm, Martha met his thrusts.

Each stroke of him inside brought her higher and higher to some unfamiliar place she'd never been, a precipice that beckoned.

"Come for me, love," he urged, the hoarse whisper tickling the shell of her ear.

"I want… I want…" she panted, her body tensing as he thrust, touching her to the quick.

And Martha shattered.

She screamed. His mouth, however, was already there, on hers, swallowing the animalistic sound as it ripped from her throat. Wave after wave of white, searing ecstasy pulled her under, the waves of her release crashing over her, and she let herself drown in simply feeling.

Graham buried his head in her neck and, with a muffled shout, surrendered himself to that like oblivion. He drew out. His hot speed spurted onto her belly, and then catching himself on his elbows, he collapsed over her.

A small, contented smile toyed with her lips as she burrowed against him. "That was magic."

He caressed his lips at her temple. "It was." Leaning over, he rescued his jacket and fished out a kerchief. With a tenderness that brought tears to her eyes, he cleaned his seed first from her belly and then himself. The thoughtfulness of that, his restraint, and his ministrations were tenderness she'd never once known from the man who'd sired her three children.

"What is this, love?" he whispered, catching one of her tears.

Love. When spoken in those husky tones, she could believe that endearment was more than a throwaway word. "I'm just happy," she said, snuggling against him. And where there was usually guilt without any hint of joy, now she let herself feel those emotions without shame. "I haven't been happy in so long." As soon as the admission left her, guilt found its home in her chest. Because there was Frederick, but there was also pain.

Rolling onto his back, Graham brought Martha atop him. She lay sprawled there, her hair a cascade about them and her ear pressed against his chest.

Closing her eyes, she listened to the steady beat of his heart.

"I've never been happy like this. Not truly."

That quiet confession came partially muffled by the tilt of her head. Propping her chin on the light whorl of curls, Martha searched Graham's face. There was a somberness to him. And it highlighted all the ways in which this man was still a mystery to her, and she desperately longed to know all those parts and pieces of him. "Surely you've been happy at some point. Because of someone… family… a love?"

"Oh, I've had moments of happiness. My father despises me, but my mother has been only ever more adoring than I deserve."

She snorted. "That is rubbish. You've no doubt been a devoted, dutiful son."

A twinkle lit his eye, giving him a boyish look. "Dutiful would have been the last word ascribed to me." She stared at him wistfully, trying to imagine the boy he had been. One sneaking off to care for horses.

Martha wriggled herself higher until their noses touched. "Either way, dutiful, devoted, or not, you were always deserving of her love, Graham." She cupped his face between her hands, the faint stubble tickling her palms. "Just as you were deserving of your father's." He made a sound of protest, and she gripped his face lightly, silencing him. "A parent loves unconditionally. Or they should. And that you do not feel that love? That is a failing not on you, but on him."

THAT IS A FAILING NOT *on you, but on him.*

Those words echoed in Graham's mind, spoken by Martha with such surety. Spoken with the convictions of one who believed them, when Graham had only ever seen his own flaws as the reason for his relationship with his father.

The duke's inability to care for Graham had come long before the day of that fateful race. It stretched far back, to a time when Graham had still sought his father's approval and believed winning it was possible. Until he'd overheard that late-night discussion about the possibility of Graham's madness and acknowledged the truth—his father, no matter what Graham accomplished or achieved, would never love him, because of the flaws inherent in his mind, beyond anything he could ever control.

Graham leaned up and took her mouth in a kiss. When he drew back, her thick crimson lashes fluttered. "What was that for?"

"You asked what makes me happy. You do." And it was true. For a brief moment, built on both a dream and a delusion, he thought of leaving his position with the Brethren and living here on the fringe of Luton. Just the three of them—a family.

She swatted at him. "That does not count as one of your items. Before me, Graham. What brought you happiness before?"

He considered his answer for a moment. There had been countless evenings spent with lovers. Those exchanges, however, had been functional in a purpose. The women, his relationships with them, had been… tedious. There'd never been talks of… of… anything of import. "I've found peace working in stables," he finally said, rubbing a palm over her back in a counterclockwise circle. "There is a sense of right that I always find there, but I've never had this…" He paused that massage. "Absolute joy," he finally said. He locked his gaze with hers. "Until you."

Her breath caught. "Have you ever been in love?"

"No." His answer was instantaneous. "There have been… lovers." But no woman had ever held his heart. His mind shied away from that thought.

"I've been in love," she confided. Jealousy darkened his vision, and he hated the bastard unseen. Despised him for having known that gift. Martha lifted three fingers. "Three times."

Graham puzzled his brow.

A mischievous smile danced on her lips. "Well," she began. "Frederick," she murmured. "I hated my husband. I feared him, but the moment the midwife placed my boy in my arms, I was filled with this overwhelming love. He kept me from becoming the empty, broken shell of a woman I would have been had I never had him."

"And... the others?"

She wouldn't meet his gaze.

It was the most telltale of the signals to mark a person's unease. But in this case, with Martha in his arms, he felt that disquiet in the way her toes curled against his legs and the tightening of her calves. As if it took all the energy and muscles within her being to keep her secrets in.

"I have two daughters," she blurted.

He stilled.

"Creda and Iris." And then she spoke on a rush. "Twin girls. So very clever. Far more talented artistically than I could ever dare dream and with freckled cheeks and matching gap-toothed smiles and—" Tears filled her eyes, and she lowered her head back to his chest.

His mind raced. There hadn't just been Frederick. But also two girls. How much of her was still a secret? And how he wanted to have all her secrets peeled away so he knew everything there was to know about the brave woman before him. "What happened to them?" he asked gruffly.

She drew in a shuddery breath. "I sent them away."

He drew back. "You sent them away?" he echoed.

She frowned, drawing back slightly. "To preserve their reputations, Graham. I sent them away to protect them."

"For how long?"

Martha said nothing.

Then it dawned. "Forever." She'd sent away her two children and had no intention of ever again seeing them. "And they'll remain... wherever it is you've sent them."

"To be protected. You can't understand. No man can."

"Perhaps I cannot," he shot back, aching for her and the two girls she'd described, children who needed her. Those young girls would only ever be better women for growing up with Martha as their mother. If they had her near. "But how is their living away from their mother and brother protecting them?"

Martha struggled to a sitting position. "I'll not be lectured. Not on this." Swinging her legs over the side of the bed, she reached for the sheet and wrapped it about herself.

"I'm not lecturing you, Martha," he said in the tones he used for the most fractious mounts. "I'm trying to understand."

A sound of frustration escaped her. "Come, Graham, you aren't naïve," she said tightly. "You've seen how Frederick and I are treated for our circumstances. So do not pretend no hurt will come to them, the bastard daughters of a bigamist." Martha started to rise, but Graham caught her, keeping her close. He didn't want her to leave. Not like this.

"Don't you see, Martha? Keeping your girls in hiding will not change who they are or the circumstances surrounding their births. They'll come to believe there is something wrong with them. That your sending them away was… is because of a defect in who they are."

She recoiled. "No. I didn't… That isn't…" And then she went limp, losing her hold on the sheet. It fluttered around her in a whispery heap. "Oh, God. In all my considering about Creda and Iris leaving, with all the tears I've silently cried into my pillow, I've never considered… that." Tears filled her eyes and rolled down her cheeks.

The evidence of her despair ripped him apart inside. He wanted to take away the pain she'd known and make it his own. He wanted to shield her from any further hurt.

On a damned lie… She doesn't even know who you really are.

Fighting off that taunting voice, Graham rested his hands on her shoulders, and she started, staring at him like she'd never before seen him.

"They belong with you, Martha," he murmured, placing a lingering kiss against her temple.

"Perhaps," she whispered. "But what if they shouldn't? What if they are better away from me?"

He guided her around and tipped her chin up. "Impossible, Martha. Any person is just better for being near you." As he lay back down and drew her into the crook of his shoulder, they lay there, no further words spoken, each taking the warmth and comfort the other offered.

What am I going to do without her?

CHAPTER 16

$\mathcal{A}$T SOME POINT AFTER SHE'D fallen asleep in Graham's arms, he'd carried her to her rooms and left her there, covered.

When she awoke the following morning, there was a note. Working on the laundry even now, that note seemed to burn a hole in her stained, damp apron pocket.

I'll return.

That was it.

Two words. An assurance that he would return. But when she'd rolled over and found it resting on the empty pillow beside her, there had been a buoyancy in her chest at what he might say.

What? Did you expect poetry and pretty words?

Scrub. Dunk. Rinse. Repeat.

Did you think he'd write how much you have come to mean and profess an inability to leave you or Frederick?

Of course, after such a short time, none of that would have held true. *I just wish it did…* Despite the cold of the winter's day and the wind ramming at the stone walls of her cottage, the blaring heat of the kitchen stoves had moisture beading at her brow. As she saw to the laundry, she remembered last evening, the moments after they'd made love.

She'd confided in him about Creda and Iris. The need to protect her daughters, however, to keep their identities secret and the scandal around them buried, should have kept her silent, but she'd yearned to tell him all.

And in so speaking, she'd let them live again in this place they'd called home.

Last night, his disappointment had stung.

In the light of a new day, she weighed what he'd said about her as a mother and her little fractured family.

Don't you see, Martha? Keeping your girls in hiding will not change who they are or the circumstances surrounding their births. They'll come to believe there is something wrong with them. That your sending them away was... is because of a defect in who they are.

The point Graham had raised niggled around her mind and could not be unheard or go unthought.

If her girls grew to hate her, the pain of that would gut her. But for them to resent her and hate her for selfishly choosing to keep them close would leave her broken.

Martha paused and stared down at the suds that concealed the laundry.

Was it simply fear that had allowed her to live without her daughters? Had it been strictly fear of how the world would treat them? Or a worry of how they would view Martha as a woman?

An errant bit of sweat trickled down her cheek, and dunking the trousers in her hands, she wiped the moisture away with the side of her elbow.

The kitchen door opened, and she looked up from her task. "Good—"

"Mr. Malin is gone," Frederick stated without preamble, and rather than the fear that had riddled his features yesterday, now there was just curiosity. Frederick stalked over to the hook where his jacket hung, and going on tiptoes, he tugged it free.

"Yes, I know." And in just a couple of short days, he'd be gone altogether.

And it felt like the cruelest of lies she'd ever perpetrated against her son. Even greater than the truth of who and what his father had been. Very soon, Graham would leave, and Frederick would find himself as devastated as he'd been yesterday.

God help her for the pathetic mother she was. She could not tell him. Not yet. Soon. She'd not ruin the last couple of days of his happiness.

Frederick skipped over, joining her at the trough. "Where did he go?"

"I don't know. He did not say, just that he'd return."

Scrub. Dunk. Rinse. Repeat.

Frederick shrugged into his jacket. "I'll gather more water for you."

"I have enough. Go for a ride. Guda needs the exercise."

He froze. His eyes formed round circles in his face. When was the last time she had encouraged her son to simply take the pleasure he could from life? Graham had shown her that. It was a gift he'd leave behind.

She winked. "Go, before I change my mind."

With a wide grin, her son bolted for the door. "Goodbye!"

As soon as he'd slammed it shut behind him, her smile fell.

Goodbye.

That hated word hung there, cruelly echoing in her son's innocent tones. For there would be a goodbye. One that she desperately didn't want to make.

"You might always ask him to stay," she said aloud, wringing the excess water from Graham's trousers. "After all, you never asked." The only thing she had asked him to do was leave. And there was so much she and Frederick would have missed.

As soon as the selfish thought slid in, she shoved it away. From the moment she'd come upon him in the stables with Frederick that first day, she'd come to appreciate just how much Graham respected horses. He was one who belonged in a stable, and to keep him here, offering nothing, would be the height of selfishness.

No, there would be some other woman someday for him. A woman who was not mired in scandal the way Martha was and who'd rightfully earn Graham's heart. And she would be so very lucky for it.

Until Martha drew her last breath, she would wish it could have been her.

How different life would have been if eleven years ago, it hadn't been the viscount her father had let into their household, but Graham. Her heart twisted. Those dreams, however, weren't for women like Martha Donaldson. Martha shook out the garment and carried it over to the hearth where the other damp articles now hung, drying.

A distant knock sounded at the front door that offered only one certainty about her visitor—it was not Graham. Graham no longer knocked. He entered the household as if he'd lived here the whole of his life, and in a wonderful way, it felt like he had.

Aside from him, no good visitor had ever rapped on this door. *Rap-rap-rap-rap.*

At that slightly impatient staccato, Martha wiped her wet hands down the front of her apron and reached the door just as the person on the other side knocked again.

Martha drew the panel open and stopped.

Of all the figures she'd thought she might find there—Squire Chernow, his angry wife there to shame Martha for whatever tale her husband had told—she'd not expected… this.

An officious little fellow, two inches shorter than Martha, with a shock of white hair and wearing a crimson liveried uniform with gold epaulets upon padded shoulders, had not been it.

"May I help you?" she greeted hesitantly.

"I'm looking for a Miss Martha Donaldson," he said impatiently in a nasally crisp King's English.

Martha partially closed the door, taking away the full view she'd previously allowed the man. Another man of an elevated station had come here on behalf of the Crown nearly two years ago. He'd left with her father and false promises to Martha about the security of her and her children. The warning bells rang out loud, signaling danger. "What do you want with her?"

Despite the height disparity between them, the little fellow managed to look down his long nose at her. "You're her."

"I'll not ask you again," she said tightly.

"I've come to discuss a matter of business with you. May I come in?"

Something in his tones indicated he had no intention of leaving. "What kind of business?" she demanded, gripping the edge of the door, her nails leaving marks upon the wood.

"It involves the Duke of Sutton."

A duke?

Relief swept through her, and a giddy laugh spilled from her lips. "I'm afraid I cannot help you. I've certainly no ducal connections." Which wasn't untrue. Martha made to shut the door.

The stranger stuck a hand out, preventing her from closing the door. "But… but… I have it on authority you do."

"And you have it on my authority that I don't," she said impatiently, giving the door a shove.

He pushed back. "You have a son," he exclaimed.

Rage coursed through her. She yanked the door open so quickly, the stranger stumbled forward and promptly fell, landing facedown on his gold buttons. "Do not ever threaten my son," she whispered. "Ever."

Scrambling to his feet, the small man went white-faced. "I'd never threaten a child." He straightened his jacket. "I've come to provide assistance to you and your son."

That knocked her aback. "What? Why would you…?" None of this—his presence here, his words, his assurances, any of it—made sense. "Who are you?" She settled for the most basic query.

"My name is Mr. Neville Barclay. I serve as the man-of-affairs for His Grace, the esteemed Duke of Sutton. May I sit?"

Unlike Squire Chernow, who'd commandeered a seat before she'd granted him permission, this man… this… Mr. Neville Barclay remained standing, waiting. And she wasn't the same woman she'd been years ago, trustful of the motives of unexpected visitors. "What do you want with me?"

"We understand that the duke's son Lord Sheldon Whitworth has been"—a shade of red to match his jacket splotched the man's cheeks—"*staying here.*"

"I'm afraid His Grace will have to look elsewhere. I've no connections to the nobility." Not anymore. They'd all been severed by death or dishonor. "Now, if you'll excuse me?" She started for the door.

"His name is Lord Sheldon Whitworth," he spoke on a rush. "His mount is a black stallion named Scoundrel."

She stumbled, catching the door handle to keep from falling. Her heart stopped and then resumed a slow, sickening thud. "I beg your pardon?" she asked, her voice coming as if from a distance.

"His name is Lord Sheldon Whitworth." The gentleman's name was unfamiliar. "His mount is Scoundrel. He…" The buzzing in her ears grew. The man's mouth moved, but she couldn't bring any clarity to what he said or asked. All she heard was a whirring of confused noise through which one piece made any sense. *His mount is a black stallion named Scoundrel. Scoundrel…*

It's just a horse's name. It means nothing. But it could mean everything…

"Perhaps we might sit and talk for a moment?" Mr. Barclay was saying with a gentleness she'd not have expected from such an officious man.

This time, instead of ordering him gone, Martha let her legs carry her to the nearest chair, and she collapsed onto the edge.

"I don't know a Sheldon Whitworth." She spoke before he could again. Because as long as she filled the silences, nothing bad could come. Whatever secrets he possessed that she didn't want to know would remain buried. "I do not know the duke. I've never heard either of those names."

"His father has received word that he is here, however. Black hair."

Black hair. Her stomach muscles clenched. "That could be any-one."

"With a mount named Scoundrel?" he asked in such painstaking tones that she bit her lip. "I've been employed by His Grace for nearly twenty years. The duke and his son have long had a rela-tionship that is…" He coughed into his fist. Yes, no family cared to have their enmity bandied about, and certainly not ducal families. "Fraught with… tension," he settled for.

My father despises me, but my mother has been only ever more adoring than I deserve.

Nausea broiled in her belly. "I'm not certain what any of this has to do with me. I don't know anyone by those names." *But you know… Deep down, you know…*

"The duchess was in the midst of hosting a house party when her son disappeared."

"A house party," she echoed dumbly, knowing she sounded like a lackwit. But what Mr. Barclay spoke of was as foreign to her as Martha visiting the moon. Dukes and house parties.

"Correct." The servant beamed like she was the cleverest of stu-dents. "He is… That is… His Grace is determined to keep his son from scandal. And if you are"—if he turned any redder, his blush was going to set him afire—"keeping company with Lord Shel-don, His Grace is prepared to offer you a generous compensation to… to… stop." Mr. Barclay withdrew and handed over a sheet of folded velum.

With numb fingers, she accepted the ivory page and stared at the blood-red seal of a falcon atop a crown, its wings spread over three shields. She angled her head. Or was it a hawk, mayhap? Yes, she rather thought it was a hawk.

A half-mad giggle swelled in her throat, choking her with the inanity of what she debated in her mind. Sliding her jagged nail under the seal, she broke it and read.

One thousand pounds.

There it was. The sum a duke would pay to keep his son from dallying with a woman outside his station. *But I'm not that woman, and Graham isn't that man.*

Lying... You are lying to yourself...

"I am so sorry, Miss Donaldson." And oddly, by the aching quality of that apology, she believed him.

Martha neatly folded the page. "I don't know this man, the duke's son. The only person who lives here with me and my son is our stable master."

The servant sat up straighter. "A stable master, you say? What is his name, Miss Donaldson?"

Tell him. Tell him that your Graham Malin is different than his Lord Sheldon Whitworth and send him away. So why could she not bring forth that admission?

My father had expectations and hopes that we'd be accomplished scholars. They were. And I? I was not.

Crushing the page in her hands, Martha dug her fingers against her temples and rubbed hard, willing his voice and those tellings gone.

Horses always made sense. In ways that books never did.

"Graham Malin," she whispered. "His name is Graham Malin."

Avoiding her eyes, Mr. Barclay removed the smudge-free spectacles from his long nose and, collecting a kerchief, wiped the glass lenses, his silence telling.

Her gaze locked on that scrap of fabric. And the hum in her ears grew like the swarm of bees that Frederick had knocked free of their hive three summers ago. "Miss Donaldson?" Mr. Barclay's concerned query came from a distance.

No.

Jumping up, Martha went running to the kitchens. Already knowing. She'd known the moment he'd said the name Scoundrel. And yet—

She staggered to a stop at the trough, catching the edge of it.

Reaching into the dirty, soapy water, she withdrew article after sopping article. Tossing them. They landed in a noisy heap around her, splattering the floor, soaking her garments, dampening her hair. Until her fingers at last collided with the small piece of linen.

She drew the item out and stared at the kerchief Graham had so tenderly cleaned her with last night. A lifetime ago.

SGMW.

Sheldon Graham Malin Whitworth.

No.

WHEN HE'D RISEN THAT MORNING, Graham had resolved to put as much of Martha's life here to rights before he went.

Graham adjusted his naval satchel on his shoulder and started down the narrow graveled path to Martha's cottage.

As he did, he acknowledged the truth he'd known… It wouldn't be enough. When he took his leave, neither she, nor Frederick, nor the daughters she'd mentioned would ever be forgotten by him. He wouldn't allow it.

His rank within the Brethren would afford him the opportunity to see that she didn't again fall forgotten by some shift in power at the Home Office.

It was the smallest of consolations, and yet, also the most important. His feelings and regret at losing her were secondary to Martha's well-being.

He reached the front door, and as he let himself inside, the first thing he registered… was the silence.

But for the crack and hiss of the fire blazing in the hearth, only empty quiet greeted him.

Unease tripped along his spine.

Slowly setting the bag down so it landed silently at his feet, Graham withdrew his pistol, doing a search… and finding her at the fireplace.

The tension left him.

"Martha," he greeted, striding over. And stopped. It was Martha, but not as he'd come to know her these past days. Seated, her arms layered to the sides of her chair, she stared at him with empty, hardened eyes. "What is—?"

Then he noted that which had escaped him until now.

His belongings packed and resting at her feet.

His heart sank in his chest and then knocked fast against his rib cage.

"Good afternoon, Graham." Her lips curved up in an icy smile that raised gooseflesh on his arms. "Or should I call you Lord Whitworth?"

Oh, God. The earth dipped. Moved. Swayed, and somehow, he remained standing. "I don't…"

She arched a red brow. "I'm sorry, do you expect a curtsy? You must forgive me. I'm unfamiliar with the rules of how to address a duke's son."

She knew. Somehow, she'd gathered the truth of his identity. His stomach pitched like the first time he'd set foot on a naval ship. And he was at sea as he'd been then, a lad of eighteen, fighting to keep in the contents of his stomach.

Then, finally, whatever mastery of control she'd managed snapped.

"Do you have nothing to say?" she cried, exploding to her feet.

"I can explain," he said hoarsely. Except, he couldn't. Not truly. More lies. He could offer her nothing but more lies.

"Can you?" she demanded, her strident voice pitched and ricocheting through his heart. "Can you… please?" That last word was a whisper, an entreaty.

Graham settled his hands on her arms and rubbed lightly, trying to will her to see the truths that had existed between them. "Nearly everything I told you, Martha, has been in truth. About my love of horses and my relationship with my father and my brothers. All of it." He'd shared pieces of his life with her that he'd never before shared with anyone. Or would again.

A frantic little giggle spilled from her lips. "Do you expect me to be honored? Or trust you?"

He briefly closed his eyes. "No." He had no right to the former and no reason to expect the latter.

"You are no stable master. You never have been."

"No."

"And you weren't here 'looking for work'?"

How to explain that? "No," he said carefully. Did she pepper him with those questions to hammer home for herself the mistruths he'd given her?

Martha stifled a sob with her fist and began to pace. "I knew. Of course I knew, and I ignored those instincts yet again. Strangers don't come here, and you…" She paused so quickly, her skirts whipped angrily about, slashing the air. She looked at him with such derision and hate that it ripped a hole through his chest. "You with your fine speech and fancy ways and fine horseflesh. I knew." Martha wrapped her arms tightly around her middle. "I knew," she repeated on an agonized whisper. "You spoke of Renaissance artists."

He stretched a hand out imploringly, taking her fingers, those same fingers that had a short while ago run along his back and explored all of him. "All those stories… they are true," he said, fumbling for words. "The only part I withheld is that I am, in fact, a duke's third son."

"Lies," she hissed, yanking free of his touch, recoiling like she was repulsed by him.

Everything ached—his heart, his head, his soul. All of him. *Make it right. Say something to make it right.* But there was nothing to say. She'd see only the betrayal, which it was. "Yet again, I'm the fool for letting you in. What was it, Graham?" She stopped abruptly, her gaze stricken. "Lord Whitworth."

"Graham, my name is Graham," he begged, wanting to hear it from her lips, the only one to speak that preferred name.

"Were you a bored nobleman escaping your mother's house party? How very terrible for you. Was she perhaps trying to play matchmaker between you and some respectable miss who'd never do for a rakish lord like yourself?"

Heat splotched his cheeks at how unerringly on the mark she was. And yet, completely off target at the same time.

Martha's eyes rounded. "That is it?" she whispered. "I'm correct."

"You are not…" He dragged a hand through his hair. What could he tell her? That he was here at the request of the Home Office? That she'd been an assignment. In that, she'd view his role here as work and their every interaction together as fabricated to break down her defenses.

The fight faded from her eyes. "Will you not say anything?" she whispered.

"I am so sorry, Martha," he said, his voice rasping. "I never meant to hurt you, and these past days together have been—"

"Not another word," she said tiredly, sinking into her seat. "I don't want any more of your lies." All the fight seemed to drain from her, and she rocked back and forth like a wounded creature nursing its suffering. He took a step closer, wanting to take that pain from her. Only, he'd caused that misery and had lost the right to hold her.

"I hated my husband because he beat me and raped me."

A tortured groan lodged painfully in his chest, trapped there, deepening the ache.

"I hated him for lying to me and making me a whore and my children bastards." She lifted her gaze, and the agony there sucked the air from his lungs. "But what you did, Grah… What you did," she amended, "was so much worse. Because I"—his heart froze— "c-cared about you." She stumbled over the word he'd ached to hear, even if it was in loss. "I cared about you and shared parts of my body and soul that I never allowed any man, not even my husband." A single tear rolled down her cheek. Met by another, and another. "You are just like him: a bored nobleman playing with the stupid villager."

Oh, God. Had she grabbed the fireplace poker and rammed it through his chest, it couldn't have hurt more. But he was deserving of her mistrust and hate. All of it. It didn't matter what had brought him into her life. What mattered was the lies on which he'd based her trust in him.

Graham sank to a knee beside her chair. "I—"

She looked at him with such loathing, a pressing agony shook his soul. "Get out."

Get out.

It was done. Over.

An ending that had been inevitable, and not for the reasons he'd expected, but ones foisted on him.

He nodded. "Of course, Martha."

"You've no right to my name," she commanded, a queen on her chair, dealing with her unwanted subject. "Oh, and, Lord Whitworth?" Reaching into the pocket of her apron, she hurled a note that danced in the air between them. "You can tell your father I'd rather forage for food and feed my son with honor than take his monies."

His father.

Ice stung his veins. The duke had discovered Graham's where-abouts. And would have, of course, taken umbrage at Graham being here with her. But this? Martha's hurt and sense of betrayal didn't belong to Graham's father. They belonged to him. "I'll leave," he said quietly, coming to his feet. "But before I do, I'll have you know I love—"

She blanched. "Go," she rasped. When he didn't move quickly enough, she screamed, "Go."

Collecting his belongings, he spun on his heel.

The door burst open.

"Mr. Malin!" Frederick cried excitedly. Then he took in Graham, the bag in his hand, and Martha. "What is happening?"

"Not now, Frederick," Martha said in the gentle motherly tones she always reserved for the boy.

"I asked what is going on?" he cried.

"I have to go," Graham explained, moving closer.

"Do not speak to my son," Martha ordered, storming over.

"Why? What is happening?" Frederick glanced frantically back and forth between them.

Martha, however, was right in this. Graham had no place to speak for her about this, about them, with Frederick. That had never been his right. He bowed his head. "Frederick."

With the boy's shouts and Martha's sobs echoing behind him, Graham left.

CHAPTER 17

CHRISTMAS WAS NEARLY HERE.

It had also always been one of her favorite times of the year because it had been her children's favorite.

All her children had equally adored the holiday season. And once upon a lifetime ago, Martha had loved it, too.

Now, there was little love. And certainly no joy. As a mother, however, she still tried.

Hovering outside her son's rooms, Martha fiddled with the clasp at her wool cloak.

Her son lay on his bed, his back to her, staring out the window. In the week since Graham had gone, it had become an all-too-familiar position. For both of them.

Martha scratched at the doorjamb.

"What?" he snapped.

"It's beginning to snow again." Martha glanced at the little flakes coming down. "I thought we might go outside."

"Don't you have laundry to do?"

She did… It was that hated time of week, and not even a month ago, she would have been hard at work in that familiar *dunk-scrub-rinse-repeat* pattern.

I trust you've also noted how much time your son spends working.

There is nothing wrong with finding happiness in life.

You would intentionally withhold those sentiments from yourself. You are the example Frederick sees, Martha.

Martha balled her hands, hating that even with everything Graham had done wrong, he'd been right in that important lesson for her and her son. "I do. But the laundry can wait," she said instead.

"Maybe your chores can, but I have to muck out the stables." This time, Frederick flipped over and glared at her. "After all, there isn't anyone around but me to see to them."

It was yet another clear reference to the man who'd changed both their lives. They now peppered every exchange between Martha and her son. Despite Graham leaving, however, Martha had been unable to shatter the boy's illusion of him. And so she'd lain down on the sword and sacrificed herself to the memory of a man who didn't exist so that her son could believe that there were men who were honorable and good. Frederick was never going to have seen her as good or worthy, anyway. At least let him believe there were respectful, hardworking men who were kind to horses and children and widows.

Knowing that did not diminish the palpable hatred Frederick had for her.

Nonetheless, she tried again. "I also thought I could tell you the story behind the tradition—"

"I don't need to hear it. I've heard it for years." He rolled onto his belly in a dismissive manner and grabbed one of the remaining books that hadn't been sold off or taken by the Crown.

He'd always loved talking about the grandmother he had never known and who'd left behind the odd custom that her husband, Frederick's grandfather, had carried on during the Christmastide. Martha made another attempt. "Very well, we don't have to talk of it. We can go and do it."

He paused in his reading. "Do what?"

"Cut down a tree and decorate it."

"Why would I want to do that?"

"Because you've always loved to," she said evenly.

"There was a lot I used to love." The up and down he gave her along with the blatant meaning of his words cut to the quick. "Do you know who'd probably like to join you?" Frederick didn't give her a chance to answer. "Creda and Iris." He tapped the back of his hand to the middle of his forehead. "Oh, that's right. You sent them away. Well, if you're looking for someone who cares about your silly traditions, go find them."

Forcing a smile to her lips, all the while feeling and fearing every muscle in her face would crack and shatter, Martha nodded and took herself off.

She kept that smile on as she gathered up the saw resting at the door and walked out into the snow and continued walking.

Once the cottage had faded from sight, she ran and continued running, pushing her legs farther and farther. She wanted to run and never stop, until she reached a point where pain ceased to be and there was only a blissful emptiness.

Reaching the heavily wooded copse, Martha stumbled and staggered and then fell to her knees. Her lungs raw from her exertions, she tossed her head back and screamed into the winter sky. Dropping the saw, she covered her face and screamed and screamed, until her throat was ragged and her screams became noiseless.

Collapsing back on her haunches, she stared overhead at the whorl of tiny flakes drifting down, the gray-white sky peeking out through the barren branches overhead.

For a brief, brief time, she'd been happy again. She'd smiled, and Frederick had smiled, and they'd felt like a family. Until they weren't. Until Graham had left. Nay, not Graham.

"Lord Sheldon Whitworth," she whispered into the quiet.

The pompous name didn't suit a man unafraid to work with his hands, mucking out stables and rubbing down horses.

Why should he have done those things? Why would a duke's son have wanted to, or have the skills to rival any servant overseeing those onerous tasks?

Nearly everything I told you, Martha, has been in truth. About my love of horses and my relationship with my father and my brothers. All of it.

Not for the first time, the seeds of doubt grew, rich and fertile, in a mind that wanted to believe his being here hadn't been just another ruse carried out by a bored nobleman. For Lord Waters had played at the country husband, but in all the years of that hated false union, he'd never lifted a hand to help her. Only to hurt her. Nay, he'd not have sullied his hands with work meant for servants. So how, then, to explain Graham… Lord Whitworth?

None of it made sense. Not any of it.

Didn't it, though? a taunting voice of reason mocked.

"You are p-pathetic," she said, her teeth chattering in the cold. She'd guessed all too correctly the reason Graham had been there. His duke and duchess papa and mama had been attempting to maneuver him into a marriage with some entirely, appropriately innocent, ladylike bride. A match he'd wanted no part of, and in a bold act meant to turn his nose up at their intentions and exert his own control, he'd gone off and found the most unsuitable, most inappropriate woman that that noble pair would never approve of.

She wanted to see that which wasn't there and never would be—honor and genuine caring from the man who'd stolen her heart.

Giving her head a shake, Martha shoved herself upright. "It is done," she said firmly. All of it. No good could come from that. It was time to move on… no matter how lonely that would be.

She collected her saw and started on the path to the evergreens, bypassing the older, taller ones for the small ones she could manage on her own.

She walked onward, the tranquility of the winter snow and the silent landscape filling her with a slight calm. Not peace. There would never be that. There would be…

Martha slowed her steps.

With a frown, she stared at the large, fresh footprints upon the snow.

A chill that had nothing to do with the frost hanging in the air tingled at her nape. Clutching her saw closer, she did a sweep.

You're being silly. You are being irrational. It was simply that she'd had Graham here and had allowed herself to rely upon him.

All lies.

She'd failed to heed those instincts before. Each time she had, she'd fallen or faltered.

A faint whirring hissed through the copse.

Martha gasped and fell to her knees.

The arrow vibrated overhead, then thrummed, shaking back and forth in a tree trunk.

Crumpled on the ground, Martha stared up with horror. *It would have hit me.*

Terror pounding at her breast and her mouth dry with fear, she unclasped her cloak, and with painstakingly slow movements, she divested herself of the garment and crept out from under it. Leaving it behind.

All the while, she braced for the next arrow. Or attack.

That didn't come.

Just silence.

She trusted silence as little as she trusted strangers.

And then it came, the faint crack of dry branches giving way under the heels of heavy footfalls.

Oh, God.

Frederick.

Fear sprang her into motion, and she crawled through the brush. Keeping low. Squirming on her belly, she wound a reverse path through the forest, and then started back towards her cottage. Each sound she left in her wake, deafeningly loud in the still.

Somewhere up ahead, a twig snapped.

Her heart climbed into her throat, and Martha stopped alongside a rotted-out tree. Fear kept her momentarily frozen as she waited.

And waited.

There they were… again.

The steps drew closer, closer. And stopped.

He was there. Close. Just beyond her hiding space. Above it? Was he even now toying with her?

Fear turned her mouth dry. *Frederick.* He was alone. Everything in her said to take flight; to race back to the cottage and her son. Only the thin sliver of logic she held onto, reminded her that she would do no good to her son, dead.

Martha clenched her eyes shut and fought to keep absolutely still. All the while, the winter cold battered at her body, the snow melting on her face, freezing her skin.

Please. Please. Please.

And then there was silence.

Now.

Martha jumped off and took off sprinting. She ran so fast, her lungs burned, aching from the cold and exertions. And with every stride, she called forth her son's face. Creda and Iris. Even Graham slipped forward. Graham, who'd urged her to bring her daughters back.

For this?

To be hunted and tormented by the people of High Town.

This would be the fate that awaited them. Preyed on by villagers for their bastardy. No, they were safer away from Martha. They all were. Frederick deserved more.

Her pulse hammering in her ears, Martha quickened her strides.

Her children. She needed to see them again. Frederick…her daughters. *Please do not let anything happen to them.*

Keeping your girls in hiding will not change who they are or the circumstances surrounding their births. They'll come to believe there is something wrong with them. That your sending them away was… is because of a defect in who they are.

Martha sprinted so fast her lungs burned, and through the panic, she found a soothing calm in just remembering his voice. His words.

She broke through the clearing and found her way down the same path she'd run, following the broken branches. Only, there were no other tracks. Only her own. Martha staggered to a stop. "What?" she whispered. It…didn't make any sense.

There were…no tracks.

Martha reached the tree where the arrow had struck, she tugged at it, wrestling it free. She studied the arrow a moment before resuming her march. And then slowed her steps.

A deer, a matching arrow stuck in its chest, lay with a crimson stain upon its fawn fur, the blood spilled onto the snow around it.

A deer. Of course. Someone had been hunting a deer. Not her.

Coupled with relief was sadness for the fallen creature.

"You're going mad out here," she whispered to herself. Imagining monsters in High Town.

Nonetheless, Martha moved with quickened steps, relief swamping her as her cottage appeared over the slight rise. Then she broke into a full sprint, stumbling, her skirts dragging through the snow.

And then she stopped.

A slow tremble shook her body, greater than any cold. Her teeth chattering, she drifted closer to the front door.

Bigamist.

The crude letters, charred into the old oak panel, stared back jeeringly.

Punctuated by… an arrow through the B.

She'd been wrong yet again.

Frederick.

Bile climbed up her throat. Her son was in there alone.

Clutching at the handle, Martha tossed the door open. "Frederick?" she cried, shoving the panel closed with the heel of her boot. "Frederick?" she begged, stumbling around the cottage; tripping over her sodden skirts. "Fred—?"

"Mother?"

That small, child's voice slashed through the panic.

She spun.

He hovered at the kitchen; a worried gaze on her.

With a sob, she launched herself across the room at him, and yanked him into her embrace. "You are safe," she whispered. "You are safe." It was a mantra she repeated over and over, to both of them. For the both of them.

"Of course I am," he said gruffly, but she clung to him, refusing to relinquish his small but sturdy body.

And yet, as she held her son, she acknowledged the truth…she was, in fact, being hunted.

But by who?

CHAPTER 18

GRAHAM SAT AT A FAMILIAR table in a familiar place in London—Forbidden Pleasures.

It was one of the most scandalous hells in England, where whores could be had for any price and men of the peerage lost and won fortunes with the mere turn of a card.

As one of Society's most notorious rogues, this was where anyone expected to find him.

And that was why he was there now.

When you return to London, play your usual part. You're a rake. Act it.

With that order from his superior officer, he'd done precisely what was required of him. Oh, it had been all too easy not to return to his family's house party. After his father's interference, the duke could go to the devil. And so, with that, when most of the peerage had abandoned London for the holiday season, Graham remained with the small number of other dissolute, wicked lords with reputations to rival his own.

Graham stared into the amber contents of his snifter.

How empty all of this was. How meaningless. The gaming tables. The whores. The drinking. All of it.

Graham swirled his brandy in a circle, studying the smooth circle. The rub of it was, he'd always known his existence had been largely without purpose. He'd learned it early on as a duke's son who'd not received the attention his brothers, the ducal heir and spare, had. His reason for being, the same as all third or fourth or any other number thereafter sons, had been this amorphous, ambiguous question that neither Society nor his own family could answer.

It's why he'd wished to join the navy. Only to find himself relegated to a post that protected him as the third ducal son, a man spared by tragedy and useless in that endeavor.

Again, he'd tried after that. Swallowing his pride, he'd sought a post at the Home Office, humbling himself by asking his father to coordinate an interview on his behalf.

He'd sought to build meaning into who he was and what he offered the world.

That was why he'd chafed at the first assignment given to him, to play the role of servant to a widow and her son.

What irony that the short time he'd spent with a widow and her son should prove the most significant, meaningful part of his whole life thus far.

Graham tossed back a long swallow and welcomed the path it burned down his throat.

God, how he missed her. Missing her was a physical ache that was with him until he managed to sleep and then was first to greet him when he awoke the next morn. And he missed her son. He, Graham Whitworth, rake beyond redemption, should find himself mourning the loss of a young child who, not long ago, had been just a stranger.

He glanced around at the company he kept now… again… the company he'd always kept. The thirty like dissolute lords and gentlemen who didn't have anything of true value and so stayed here.

Surrounded by strangers and acquaintances, and in some cases, friends, yet managing to be alone at the same time.

From the corner of his eye, he caught the approach of a red-headed beauty. She moved with a seductive sway to her hips that sent her scanty satin skirts clinging to her lush thighs.

A damned redhead. A bloody ginger-haired beauty should be the one to approach him this day.

He tamped down the need to laugh at the irony and hilarity of it all.

"Hello, my lord," she purred. Snaking her arms around him, she captured Graham in a makeshift embrace.

He stiffened.

"You are in need of company, my lord," the beauty purred against his ear. She flicked her tongue out, toying with that shell. The faint hint of musk on her mingled with the heavy rosewater she'd used, and it stung Graham's nostrils.

Any other time, he would have taken her. He would have allowed her to lead him off to her rooms and lost himself inside her until the mindless sex brought release and temporary oblivion. But her hair didn't have the burnt hues of rust and a summer's sunset wrapped with sunrise. Her smile was false and not the dimpled one that belonged to another.

Forcing a lazy grin, Graham neatly disentangled her vinelike hold on him and freed himself. "Afraid another time, love. I—" From across the room, he caught the approach of a figure striding purposefully through the crowd, on a direct path toward Graham.

At least two decades older than most of the other patrons presently in attendance, he stood out among them.

Lord Edward Helling stopped at Graham's table. With a slight disapproving frown, he took in the whore at Graham's side.

His superior didn't wait until she'd sashayed off before speaking. "I'm here at your father's request."

He stiffened. "My father?" he repeated in measured tones.

Waving off a servant, Lord Edward pulled out his own chair and, uninvited, claimed himself a seat. "Both your parents have appealed to me to see if I might convince you to return for the holidays."

Graham took another drink. "That is a definitive no," he said, setting his glass down with a *thunk*.

"Very well." Lord Edward tugged his gloves off, beat the brown leather articles together. "Your father's... interference with a certain... lady was unrelated." Unrelated to Graham's work with the Home Office. That had been the question he'd demanded answers to.

"Of course it was," he said bitterly. His ducal father could and would ferret out secrets with the skill of any man who served in the Home Office.

"He didn't approve of the lady," Lord Edward murmured, his lips barely moving. "That was the reason."

Didn't approve? How could anyone not admire and approve of a woman of Martha's convictions and strength and courage? God, he despised his father and all of Polite Society. "He can go hang," he said through tight lips.

"Your father and familial attention, however, is not the whole reason I am here." Graham stilled. "I have word on your assignment."

This was a business meeting, then. So where was the excitement that should come with official Crown business? Where was the anticipation he'd felt the last time he'd met with Lord Edward?

Lord Edward slid a note across the table. It was addressed in his father's hand, with the seal belonging to the Duke of Sutton, and yet, as he broke that crimson seal and read... The contents were entirely related to other matters. It was a forgery to facilitate the secrecy and maintain some justification of why the two would be meeting. As Lord Edward was godfather to Graham's brother, Society would be content with the illusion. Invariably, they never looked closer and saw any more than what was on the surface.

Graham sat a little straighter.

The bulleted details were not about his next case.

Martha.

He locked on that name. Hers.

"Your... instincts proved correct."

"My instincts," he echoed, entirely fixed on the letter.

"Regarding your suspicions about her well-being." Lord Edward picked up the empty glass and poured himself a drink.

Graham's heart slowed and then took off at a gallop. *Restraint. Always restraint.* He frantically scanned the note.

"With care," Lord Edward warned, and Graham slowed his movements. Except, with that cryptic warning quietly delivered in the middle of a damned gaming hell, Graham was one step from madness.

Lord Edward lifted his snifter and spoke, shielding his mouth. "We have reason to believe there might be some threat to the lady's safety."

Panic threatened to swarm him. Oh, God. "Has she been hurt?" he asked hoarsely. *I should have been there. I should have been with her.* He had no right to her, of course. No right to watch after her or her son.

"Drink," the other man said through the humming in Graham's ears. There could be no mistaking his superior's statement as anything more than a command for Graham to gather control of his emotions.

Graham made himself lift his glass, sip, swallow, and then repeated the movement several times.

"Someone shared her secret around High Town, and now Lord Exeter received a missive informing him that they know his wife's secret." His wife's secret was also… Martha's.

The air hissed from between his teeth. Someone threatened to expose her past. For what purpose? The answer of the immediate suspects—Waters' legitimate family—no longer made sense. They would have been set on maintaining the façade of respectability. "Their contention is with Exeter."

"But Miss Donaldson could also be at risk. We're removing her from Luton," Lord Edward was saying. "Keeping her in London so she is close."

That penetrated the haze. "What?" he blurted.

She would be here… in London. Close to him, but also close to all the places she'd longed to be. As soon as that thought slid in, reality came following swiftly on its heels.

"Her threat isn't greater being here… near Exeter's family?"

"I suspect if there is, in fact, a threat, she is at greater risk alone in the countryside. London is largely empty for the holiday season. The gossip will be less. Our hope is that we secure her and her situation soon, while the *ton* is away at their country properties. And after that…"

"After that?" he prodded.

Lord Edward shrugged. "We will secure work for the lady. Those details are still being worked through."

That was to be her fate still. Work.

"She has… agreed to come to London, then?" This place she'd always wanted to see.

I wanted to sketch in Hyde Park. I've read of the Serpentine and the queen's gardens and imagined what it would be to paint those visions.

Lord Edward shook his head, but Graham saw the hesitation. "Neither is she, however, at this point aware that she may be in any peril. I've an agent who has been scouring High Town and all of Luton in the event there is any threat."

"And… if she comes to London?" he asked in even tones. She'd be near him, and yet, they would still be divided by his betrayal and her hatred of him. "Who will be assigned to her?"

"There is first the matter of securing her agreement."

"But if she agrees?" he asked impatiently, wanting the damned name. Needing to know which bloody member of the Brethren would be close to her when Graham wanted it to be him and only him. And despite every code of loyalty to his fellow members that he'd sworn, Graham wanted to bloody with his bare hands the one who ultimately found himself close to her and her son.

"That is actually the reason I'm here," Lord Edward murmured. "There is some concern, given the organization's failure to fulfill the promises made to her, that Miss Donaldson might be reluctant to trust us."

"As she should," he said coolly. Martha and her children had been betrayed by everyone who should have loved and cared for them. *And I failed her, too.* In lying to her and keeping that lie alive—she'd been correct in her charge—Graham was no different.

"I do not disagree with you. Several members and I have discussed the lady's circumstances. We've decided based on your familiarity with the boy and widow and, more importantly, their familiarity with you, it would be wisest to have you speak with her."

"You think I can convince her?"

"We have hope that you can."

I never said goodbye to anyone in parting again. I fared them well and gave them my best, but never my goodbye.

His superior might be skilled, but he was delusional if he believed that Graham could help. "Impossible."

"I hope not. You'll be accompanied by another. He is waiting for you now."

They took Graham's role in this as a certainty. "She has no wish to see me."

"That's neither here nor there," Lord Edward said crisply, drawing on his gloves. "Fix whatever hurt feelings you left and convince her that this is in the best interest for both her and her child. At which point, you will be assigned as her guard." The older man finished off his drink and then climbed to his feet and started across the room.

Graham stared after him for a moment. His pulse thudded sickeningly, with both dread and an excitement he had no right feeling.

If Martha agreed to come to London, he would be the one with her.

Again.

For the first time since she'd tossed him out, his belongings neatly packed, the agony lifted. With a calm he didn't feel, Graham followed behind Lord Edward. They didn't again speak until they'd gathered their cloaks and waited beside Lord Edward's carriage.

And all earlier joy was replaced by logic. "She'll not agree to this." Any of it.

"I believe she will."

The other man spoke with a confidence that could come only from age, and there was a naïveté that dismissed Martha's hurt sense of betrayal.

Lord Edward tossed an arm around him. "Despite being duped by you"—Graham gritted his teeth. True though that might be, Graham had been acting on behalf of the Crown—"and her hurt feelings," the other man went on, "she will ultimately agree to accompany us because of her son."

Yes, she'd given everything to her three children. She might hate him and resist the idea of joining Graham in London, or having anything at all to do with him, but where Frederick, Creda, and Iris were all concerned, she'd put them before even her own hurts.

It would be the hollowest of victories.

And yet, as Graham and Lord Exeter, another of his superiors, set off for High Town soon after, that hollowest of victories also brought with it something else—hope.

CHAPTER 19

Martha no longer slept.

She hadn't since she'd been hunted in the copse and had her door burned with that hated, hateful word.

Each night, she lay abed with her fingers in reach of Papa's gun, alternating her stare between the door and the window.

Waiting with a sick anticipation for when someone launched another attack upon her or her household. Or worse, her son. Until sheer exhaustion overtook her and brought her eyes shut for a brief rest that was never easy.

As she lay there in the dead of night, she'd come to appreciate how the sounds of a quiet house and the elements outside conjured monsters.

The unexplainable settling of hardwood floors that, after forty years, should be without those errant creaks and groans. Or the scrape of a branch against a lead windowpane that set an imagination to believing fingers were tapping. Waiting for the break of the glass and the unimaginable that would come after.

Never once had she worried while Graham was here.

There'd been a peace and sense of safety that she'd never truly known.

All the while, with that trust in him, she'd failed to see that he was the one she should have been worried about. He, the greatest of thieves, for he'd stolen her foolish heart, and all on a lie.

Was he even now courting the lady from whom he'd been running? Perhaps he'd returned to his ducal family for their house party, and he and the handpicked lady had discovered together that they were truly a match for each other. Like some blasted romantic novel she'd once favored, back when she'd believed a woman could know that gift and had dreamed of it for herself.

Rolling onto her back, Martha stared overhead at the cracked plaster ceiling in desperate need of new paint. The small fire in her hearth cast a soft light upon it, holding her transfixed.

Martha closed her left eye, and that faulty portion of the ceiling drifted out of focus. She alternated, opening her left and closing her right, and there it was again, the five-inch imperfection.

If one just closed an eye, it disappeared, and one was able to believe the illusion. Forget the flaws. Forget him.

As if taunting her for even daring to think that a possibility, the naval bag in the corner drew her focus.

She should have tossed it behind him that day. And yet, through the tears and her son's shouts, she'd failed to realize that sack had been left behind. She'd dragged it to her room and left it there.

Abandoning all hope of sleep, Martha swung her legs over the side of her bed and stood. She shivered at the cold that touched her bare feet. Hurrying to the bag, Martha dropped to a knee beside it.

That day, his father's man-of-affairs had come when Graham had been off—for what purpose? Martha reached inside the bag… and then froze as her fingers collided with cool leather.

Her heart shifting strangely in her chest, she drew out the small pair of black boots. For Frederick.

Tears stuck in her throat, and she forced herself to swallow around that emotion. That was what he'd been doing, then. She reached in once more, drawing out another pair. Larger, designed for a woman. For her.

Rap.

The pair slipped from her hands, landing with a sickeningly loud thump. Her heart knocked against her breast as she angled her head toward the frosted windowpane.

Rap.

Oh, God. There it was again.

Her body broke out in a sweat, and rushing back to the bed, she retrieved her gun. *You're being foolish. You hear the same sounds every evening, and every evening it is fine. The sun still rises on the morn and then goes down at the same early evening hour.*

Gathering up her wrapper, she hurriedly donned the garment, and sidestepping the loose floorboards, Martha tiptoed over to her son's rooms.

Peeking inside, she found his little frame burrowed under his threadbare blanket. She searched the small space and then brought his door shut.

Rap.

No good had ever come from any visitor to this household, and a visitor late at night could only portend peril. Holding her gun out, Martha made herself move toward the intermittent knocking.

Before her courage deserted her, she yanked the door open, her gun pointed—and her mind went black. It had been more than a year since she'd seen him. The moon played off his silver-streaked temples. He was darkly clad, with a somber set to his features. Martha might as well have drawn him back from that dark day.

"Miss Donaldson," he greeted.

"You," she said flatly.

"May I—?"

She straightened her arm, leveling her gun at the middle of his chest. "Get out."

"I need to speak to you."

Speak to her? "Do you think me mad? Or just foolish, as I was when we last met," she spat. "I said go. There is nothing I have to say to you." And no reason he should be here… unless… An idea slipped in, and her gaze went over to the damning marks burned into her door. He followed her stare. "It's you," she breathed, and he shifted all his focus back to Martha. "You want to harm me." How many times would she be the fool?

"I have no intentions of harming you," he murmured in the calming baritone she'd been a fool to believe.

Martha gnashed her teeth. "Liar."

He reached for the front of his cloak, and she moved her gun back and forth in warning. Lord Exeter went motionless.

"Why… why… you seek to silence me." It all made sense. Her mind whirred with the realization. She'd been fine left alone to live as long as no one knew she existed. "You want to be sure your wife isn't touched by the scandal of my being alive."

His brow dipped. "Have you come to any harm?"

"Don't pretend you don't know," she sneered. "Or that you've ever cared." No one did. Not about her and her son. Every last man was a self-serving opportunist. They didn't care about anyone other than themselves and their wants.

"You're wrong, Miss Donaldson. My intentions have only ever been to help you."

"Is this helping me?" she rasped, pointing her weapon at the damning letters emblazoned upon her door. Struggling for a semblance of calm, she steadied her arm. "For a brief time, I believed you intended to help." When he'd come and offered to send her daughters to a school where they could live untouched and unsullied. "No more. Now, go."

He remained in the doorway, as immobile as a damned mountain. "If you want me to leave—"

"I do."

"But not until you hear me out. I have reason to believe, based on information I've come by and now because of what you've confirmed"—he flicked his gaze to the scarred door—"that you might be in danger. As well as your son."

It's a trap...

"It is not a trap," he said softly.

"I didn't speak." That retort emerged sharp to her own ears.

"No, but I know what you're thinking, Miss Donaldson. Please. A moment, and if after you hear me out, you ask me to leave, I will."

Martha's fingers tightened around the handle of her pistol as she battled with everything inside that said to send him on his way. Because, Lord forgive her for being weak when her son deserved strong, she could not bring herself to move the hammer back— even if this man intended to end her. Swallowing a sob, she let her arm fall. She backed away as he entered and closed the door behind him.

"We failed you," he said quietly, unexpectedly. But then, he was a master at treachery.

"Never tell me? You didn't know that all my father's monies had to be forfeited for his crimes? Or that my cottage was purchased out from under me? Or my name bandied about?"

"None of it. Until now."

Martha scoffed. "I'd be a fool to believe that."

"Yes. And even with that, it is true." He pulled off his black leather gloves, a midnight shade to match his cloak and hair, and he was the devil. She'd known it the first time he'd come upon her son and begun peppering him with questions about Martha's father. "After the case involving your father, I retired."

It was an enticing dream where one no longer had to struggle and was able to simply enjoy the fruits of his labors. "Congratulations," she said crisply.

A smile grazed his lips. "Thank you, but I was explaining why you experienced a change in your circumstances. Following my retirement, the gentleman who replaced me—"

"Decided a bigamist from High Town was undeserving of supports and the promises made me?" she interrupted.

He inclined his head. "Actually, yes. That is precisely what was decided."

That honesty knocked her off-balance. If he sought to wheedle his way past her resentments and suspicion, he'd not acknowledge that or any other mistake.

"What is known is that your secrets have come to light. That violation was not made by me, or any… connected to me." His wife or his wife's family.

How odd to be taking assurances from a man married to the woman who'd also been the rightful wife of Martha's… husband.

"You have every reason to doubt my word and motives."

"I do."

"But there is a real concern your secret will be soon circulated… more widely."

It had been inevitable. At first, Martha had deluded herself with the tantalizing dream that a widow in High Town could remain just that. Until the secret had been unveiled by some unknown foe—very possibly the man before her now—and she'd accepted that all the world might as well, and would, eventually know. But… "In London?"

"Among Polite Society," he elucidated.

"Who amongst the *ton* would do that?"

"That is the question we've only just begun to try to find an answer to."

"Either way, why should anyone wish to harm me for it?"

He clasped his hands behind him. "And has someone? Wished

you harm?"

Martha searched his face for a hint of falsity. But there was nothing there. Not even concern. He might as well have been wearing a mask. "You saw the door. There was an arrow in it. And also…"

He nodded once.

"A matching arrow nearly struck me when I was outside."

The graveness of his expression was more terrifying than had he uttered a response. With a shaky sigh, Martha wandered over to the hearth. She rested her gun atop the mantel and then caught the stone edge in her hands, staring into the dancing flames. "What do you want?"

"To see you safe."

"And what does that mean exactly?" she asked impatiently, facing him once more. "You made a similar promise, and then you failed."

He bowed his head. "It was my belief that if your secret was kept, that would be enough. That you could live a life of obscurity amongst the town where you grew up. And I trusted, given the promise I received, that your funds would be left intact."

"Wrong. Wrong. And wrong." On every score.

Then, shock of all shocks, Lord Exeter blushed. "The mistake lay in not having someone specifically assigned to remain here with you. There should have been an agent reporting back on your well-being and affairs."

"Spying on me," she said bluntly.

"That would have ensured that your circumstances were discovered when they deteriorated." He waved his hand. "Either way, I've since learned from the mistakes I made surrounding you, and I'm asking that you allow me to rectify them. For the benefit of your son and daughters."

Just like that, he came out a victor over her determination to send him on his way. Martha closed her eyes. "What do you want?"

"For you to come to London," he said automatically. "This time, you'll have a guard assigned to you until we ferret out just who disseminated your secrets and ensure you are safe."

How simple he made it all sound. "And… after that?"

"Then I'd like to provide you funds—"

"I don't want your pity," she cut him off. "And I'll not take money like a beggar."

"Then we will find you some form of employment, so you can have security for your family." His answer came so automatically, he'd clearly anticipated her rejection of the offer he'd made.

Security. It hung there, a mere word dangling in the air, a promise, an ideal that had seemed unattainable. She was likely mad for trusting him yet again. What choice did she have at this point? The decision was ultimately about her children. "Very well. I'll join you."

"We'll leave tonight. Before we do, I'd discuss your arrangement with you and the gentleman assigned to you and Frederick."

"Arrangement?"

There they were… the bells of warning. Tinkling at the back of her mind like the old church on Sunday.

Lord Exeter went to the door and drew the panel open.

A figure stepped inside. Tall, a black fine wool cloak about his person, an elegant Oxonian hat atop his head.

Martha shook her head. It wasn't him.

He just… *looked* like Graham. The dark strands, however, were shorter. There was none of the usual growth on his cheeks at this hour. His eyes… She could not make out the color with the space separating them. She was seeing him everywhere.

Nay, she was simply seeing him because she'd thought of him so often.

"Hello, Miss Donaldson."

But it was his voice. God help her. Martha's eyes slid closed. That slightly husky, melodic baritone could melt the damned winter snow with the heat of it that now washed over her.

"What game are you playing?" Martha whispered. Angling away from Graham, she stalked over to Lord Exeter.

"There is no game, Miss Donaldson. Lord Whitworth is a member of the Home Office." Had he shoved her in the chest and knocked her on her buttocks, she couldn't have been more upended by that revelation.

"What?" She directed that faint question at Graham… Lord Whitworth. Whatever his bloody name was. All the while he'd been living here, he'd been working for the Home Office?

It was never a game, then. It was a lie… But it wasn't a bored nobleman toying with you.

Martha shoved aside the pathetic defense of what he'd done.

"I was to report on your circumstances, Miss Donaldson," he said coolly. Nay, matter-of-factly, and the indifference stung all the more.

Miss Donaldson. Not Martha. Just formality existed between them.

"Lord Whitworth has been assigned to watching over you in London until your case is resolved."

She whipped her gaze between both men. "Him? You expect…? Surely…" Martha shook her head. The Fates must be laughing uproariously at even the idea of it. "Absolutely not."

"May I speak to Miss Donaldson?" Graham asked quietly. "Alone."

IN ALL HIS THOUGHTS OF Martha, Graham had wondered after her, had mourned the lost bond they'd shared, and wished for more time with her. Never, however, had he believed he'd see her again. As such, he had no words prepared, nothing well-thought-out, for a time when they did one day meet again.

And that moment was now.

After Lord Exeter left, Martha stood there, stiff. She eyed Graham warily.

By a code of the Brethren, he should keep her off-balance. Prevaricate with words to further upend. That was, as his mentor had explained, the path to most victories.

But Martha Donaldson was not most women… and he didn't want to lie to her. Not anymore.

Graham clasped his hands behind him. "I did not want to come." She winced.

"Not this time," he clarified. "This time, I wanted to be here." With a wistful smile, he took in the modest cottage that had felt more like home than the almost-palace he'd spent most of his life in. His grin faded. "I wanted to see you." And Frederick. Graham withheld that name. As mistrustful as she was, Martha would believe his mention of her son was nothing more than a ploy to weaken her defenses. "But the first time," he murmured, drifting over, and she didn't retreat. It was the smallest of victories, but powerful in the hope it fueled. He made himself stop with several paces between them, wanting her to close the divide between them, unwilling to force his presence on her. "I wanted nothing to do with you or your son, Martha," he said with a blunt, raw honesty that he'd wished to speak with her from the start. "Or this assignment."

"And yet, you came anyway."

He tried—and failed—to make out what she was thinking or feeling from that statement. Regret? Resentment? Hate?

"I came because I had no choice," he said flatly. "When I spoke to you about wanting to have a life with purpose, it was in truth. This, however, represented that purpose. My work for the Home Office. Except, I was newly hired to my post. You were my first assignment. Even so… I fought it. I wanted something meaningful and craved something more." He began to pace. He hadn't known what he'd searched for forever. Until her. She had been the "more." He just hadn't realized… couldn't have realized that there was a woman like her… or a child like Frederick. "It was supposed to be a fortnight, and then I would be gone. An information-gathering mission that yielded nothing… until it did." Graham stopped and held her stare. "It yielded you and Frederick."

"Why are you telling me this?" she whispered, clutching at the neckline of her night wrapper. That same garment he'd freed her of a week earlier when they'd made love, and he'd learned there was, in fact, love and emotion in what had previously been only a physical ritual.

"I'm telling you this so you know that I care about you and your son. If you wish for someone to replace me in my current role, because of our past, that agent will serve as a capable guard. But I would lay down my life to protect both of you, not because of any assignment, but because I love you."

She gasped.

Graham's mind stalled and then resumed movement with a rush of nothing but jumbled confusion.

He didn't love anyone. He didn't even like himself. He'd missed Martha. He enjoyed being with her. He'd missed their every talk and working alongside her in the stables. He…

Loved her.

He had from the moment she'd faced down a room of lesser people who'd taunted her and called them out for the bastards they were.

"I love you," he repeated quietly, letting himself say it again. She'd cared for him when she'd thought him something other than he was—a servant. Yet again, she'd proven different than most any other woman, having preferred Graham when he'd been a mere stable master, even as every other lady of his acquaintance had sought a connection with him because he was a duke's son.

The air came to life with an energy that crackled and sizzled between them.

"Oh, Gra—" She cut off, his name hanging there as a question mark. "I don't even know what to call you anymore," she whispered.

"Graham. That is my name, Martha. It is the name I prefer." And the only one he wished to hear from her lips.

Martha linked her fingers and stared at the charcoal-stained digits.

I've never even seen her work… Not the art she's created now… I know she loves it… And there was so much more he wished to know about her. Everything. He wanted to know everything about her and what brought her joy and to be the one to bring her that happiness.

"I don't know what to say," she confessed.

Say you love me, too.

But neither did she hurl his profession in his face, and her eyes no longer sparked with hatred, and he took hope from that.

"I… understand why you were here and appreciate that you came to look after Frederick and me." At last, she lifted her head, meeting his gaze. "But there can't be anything between us. Not truly."

Why not? Why couldn't there be?

It took all he was to keep from asking those questions. She was coming to London with him. It was there in the softening at the corners of her previously tight lips. That was enough. It would have to be—for now. "I didn't tell you because I expect you to return those feelings." But he wished it. "I did so that you know that my reason for being here was a lie, but everything else was true. And as long as I'm with you and Frederick, you will be safe."

Martha drifted over to the hearth and stared into the flames. Thirteen ticks of the old longcase clock passed before she spoke.

"Very well." She turned. "But when it is determined Frederick and I are safe, I'll return to my life… and you yours."

He inclined his head.

Graham went to the door and allowed Lord Exeter to enter.

"I've agreed," Martha said after Graham closed the door behind the older gentleman.

"You and your son will reside with Lord Whitworth," Lord Exeter said, as if there had been no break in their previous discourse. "London is largely quiet for the holiday season, with most lords and ladies visiting their country properties. To protect your reputation, you're advised to remain inside until it is all…" Sorted out.

Martha folded her arms at her middle. "I'm to be a prisoner, then?" God, she was magnificent, unafraid to go toe-to-toe with any man.

"The more you venture out, the more likely your reputation is at risk."

"And if the lady is discovered with me?" She'd be ruined.

"The assumption will, of course, be that she is your mistress."

Fury snapped through Graham. The other man spoke of Martha's reputation as a throwaway concern.

"I see no other way to explain how or why a rake would keep company with a young woman, other than the reason given," Lord Exeter explained.

A muscle leaped in Graham's jaw. "How easily you speak of her ruin."

Martha balled her hands. "It is fine…"

"It is not fine," he gritted out, whipping around to face her. She still did not see her worth. "You deserve to be treated respectfully and honorably, and your living alone with me threatens both."

She gave him a sad smile. "Oh, Graham. My reputation was ruined long ago." Martha gave all her attention to Lord Exeter. "I'll come. Frederick and I, we'll join you."

With a last little peek in Graham's direction, she hurried to her room.

As he waited in silence alongside Lord Exeter, Graham considered Martha… and a future with her. She insisted there could never be anything more, but while she lived with him, he had two missions: one to see that she and her family were safe, and two, to show her he was worthy of her and that it was safe to love.

CHAPTER 20

¶IN THE DAYS THAT FOLLOWED, Martha's life wasn't her life.

It was a surreal daydream, and most times she felt as though she watched it from afar. Staring from the outside at a pretend world that she'd somehow become physically part of.

Now, Martha was curled on a window seat that overlooked an outdoor garden below. With a slick coating of ice upon the snow-covered terrace, Graham's gardens had the look of some mythical ice palace, resplendent with a tall, three-tiered fountain. The water pouring down had frozen, adding to the sense of majesty of this place.

His was a home grander than any she had ever, or would ever again, set foot in. Graham would one day share this palace with some rightful lady born to his station. And Martha despised the tableau that unfolded in her mind even as she knew she had no place in it.

Laughter pealed around the room with thirty-foot ceilings as her son raced across the floor in his stockinged feet. "Mama, look!" Frederick cried out, having slid back and forth across the gleaming mahogany floors so many times she'd lost count. "That was my farthest yet. I went… one, two, three"—as he counted, he stepped on each plank he'd crossed—"six."

"Very nearly seven," she said with a smile. Her chest was light in unfamiliar ways, having known only the weight of stress and fear and pressure before.

"Yes, yes, you are right," he replied, puffing his chest out, proud.

His eyes lit. "I'll try again!"

As Frederick rushed back to his makeshift starting point, Martha laughed, the feeling so freeing and healing, and she wanted to know this peace for—

She stopped.

He hadn't said *Mother*. Or *you*. But rather, he'd used that beloved affectionate term by which he'd once always referred to her—Mama. Happiness exploded in her heart.

"Are you watching?" he called out, and she blinked back through the glassy veil of tears.

"I am," she managed past the tears stuck in her throat, not wanting to shatter this moment with his questions.

"One, two…" Frederick took off racing before he'd finished his usual three count and slid. "Awww," he groaned.

"That was even closer to seven," she consoled.

He propped his hands on his hips and did a turn, glaring at the marquetry side tables and massive console with its red marble top. The pieces were finer and more costly than any of the items that had been carted off from her family's property. "There's too much furniture here. He's got tables and chairs and sofas."

Her lips twitched. "It is a parlor, Freddie."

"It is a nuisance," he muttered. "How is a boy expected to slide past more than six panels when one has to watch for these little tables? And furthermore, how many more tables does a person need? He has…" As he counted, Frederick raced around the room. "One… two… three… four… fi—what would one call this?" he asked, stopping beside a hardwood, marble inset piece.

"I believe it is a two-tiered stand," a voice drawled from the doorway.

She swung her gaze, finding the owner of that deep baritone, and her heart caught at the sight of him.

"Mr. Malin!" Frederick called out and sprinted over.

Chuckling, Graham caught her son to keep him from falling. "Graham," he instructed. "You may call me Graham now."

"Graham… I was racing and…" As her son prattled on, Martha freely observed Graham.

She'd resided in his household for four days, and in that time, despite his professions of love and a desire to be with her and near her, he'd stayed away. It was as she'd hoped and asked of him. And yet, when he'd complied, she'd been abjectly miserable… missing him.

Until now. Now, Martha looked her fill.

Everything about the man before her, attired in tan fall-front trousers and a tailcoat with black velvet trim and gold buttons, bespoke his wealth and level of influence. Even the midnight satin cravat loosely tied at his throat served as a reminder of the station divide between them.

And oh, how she wished he'd just been the stable master. Because then mayhap they could have had a life together. But this? He as he was? And she as she was? They could never be.

While Frederick continued talking, Graham looked over the top of the boy's head and winked, before returning all his attention to the small child demanding his focus.

All over again, she fell in love with him.

Whatever her son was saying made Graham widen his eyes. "I understand there is a problem with my furniture, madam?" he called out.

Feeling both pairs of eyes on her, Martha forced her features to reflect a calm she didn't feel. "Oh, indeed," she said with mock solemnity.

"The excess tables?" he put forward. His voice boomed and echoed off the high ceiling. She peered up at the cherubs dancing overhead in an art display that belonged in a museum.

"I was telling Mr.… Graham that he has too many of them."

"I believe the rule is five," Martha supplied.

"Is it?" Graham returned, capturing his chin in his hand in mock contemplation. "I was certain it was seven."

Martha inclined her head. "It was always five. However, even if it was seven, you've exceeded even that."

"The two-tiered stand," he murmured.

"Precisely."

They shared a smile.

Had she ever teased and been teased? Even as a girl? Except, Martha had never truly been just a girl. She'd been thrust into the role of replacement companion for her father, who'd happily and gladly passed on some of the essential roles of running their property to her early, early on.

"I've a solution to the great plank-race dilemma. Follow me."

Not waiting to see if they accompanied him, Graham spun on his heel.

Frederick instantly ran after him.

Martha lingered a moment.

I am weak around him… Nay, I am weak because of him…

Every instant they were together, she was in greater peril. Reluctantly, she set off after them.

She found Frederick and Graham waiting halfway down the hall. Arms clasped behind their backs, facing the left wall, they were a study in a matched pair.

It touched her to the quick, that display of them speaking so companionably they might as well have been father and son.

He'd entered her life on a lie and given her only falsehoods. As such, she shouldn't trust him. But how could one so effortless with a child be one to fear?

But then, mayhap that is why he poses such a danger to you.

Resolved to keep her defenses up, Martha brought her shoulders back and started for the pair. She stopped just beyond Frederick's shoulder and studied the painting that they now discussed.

"His name was Whistlejacket," Graham was saying of the chestnut memorialized upon the massive ten-foot canvas.

"Was he yours?"

"No. He belonged to the Marquess of Rockingham."

Frederick scratched at his nose. "He has a peculiar name. The horse, not the marquess."

"Whistlejacket was named after a cold remedy containing gin and treacle. He was magnificent. See the coloring…" Graham pointed to the canvas, moving his finger close, but not touching. "This flaxen mane and tail? Some believe they are the original coloring of the wild Arabian breed."

Frederick craned his head down, stretching his neck, to see the handful of paintings lining the hall. "They're all horses. I should think a nobleman would have portraits of crusty lords and ladies about."

Nearly everything I told you, Martha, has been in truth. About my love of horses and my relationship with my father and my brothers.

Just then, Graham looked up.

Martha schooled her features and hurried the remaining steps to join them.

"Mama, look. He has horse pictures."

"I see."

"That isn't what I wished to show you," Graham murmured, urging them on. He shortened his stride so Martha could keep pace.

"What is it?" Frederick pressed.

"You'll see."

They turned at the end of the hall and continued on to the lone doors in the hall, a pair of white, double panels. Simultaneously pressing both gold handles, Graham drew them wide.

Martha's breath caught.

"Oh, my stars in heaven," Frederick whispered, echoing her wonderment.

Six crystal chandeliers lined each end of the sweeping ballroom, Doric pillars strategically placed throughout to highlight the gilded archways inset with intricate floral paintings.

Dumbfounded by the splendor, Martha wandered off. Her boots fell silent on the white marble floor, and she took in the majesty of it.

She stopped at the center of the room. Tipping her head back, she gazed at the ceiling, painted in pale shades of blue interspersed with fluffy white clouds. A gold trellis, painted the whole perimeter of the mural, had been accentuated with flowers, the artist having created a masterful illusion of a summer's sky. "It is...breathtaking."

"Oh, that is not even the best of it," Graham called, his voice echoing.

Glancing over, her brow furrowed in question, she widened her eyes.

Propping his hip against one of the floor-to-ceiling columns, Graham wrestled off first one boot. He tossed it aside. Martha's brows shot to her hairline as the next followed.

Frederick giggled. "What are you—?"

Graham was already sprinting forward, then gliding in his stock-inged feet.

A laugh burst from her as she watched the slippery path he raced. She covered her mouth to stifle the mirth, but it bubbled out and echoed around the ballroom.

Frederick's applause blended with her laughter. "That must have been... one... two... three... well, at least ten floorboards in the other room."

Graham cupped his hands around his mouth. "Have a try," he encouraged, and while her son took time to get himself into a ready position, Graham looked to her.

The intimate look stretched into her soul and stole her breath. The same glance they'd shared over the top of Frederick's head, two people—nay, a man and woman—connecting with a shared love and regard for the little boy now rushing headlong toward Graham.

Martha rested her back against another of the massive columns and watched the pair of them, first measuring each other's sprints across the marble and then racing each other. Until time melted away, and there was just light and laughter and joy in this place… in her heart.

Panting and breathless, Graham glanced over, and even with the ten paces of marble flooring between them, she caught the boyish glint in his eyes, and she melted inside. "Never tell me you aren't one for racing, Miss Donaldson?"

"She's not," Frederick supplied before her. "She's a dancer."

"Frederick," she chided, her cheeks going hot.

"A dancer?" Graham echoed, so much curiosity in that query that her blush burned all the more.

"I'm not—"

"Oh, yes." Her son spoke over her. "She made us all learn to dance. Papa didn't know how to, so I always had to partner the girls." He stuck his tongue out in brotherly distaste.

"You don't like it?" Graham asked her son, giving Martha a brief look.

"No."

"You do not know what you're missing, then." Graham started forward in his stockinged feet and then stopped in front of her.

"What are you—?"

Graham stretched his arms out, sketching a bow. "May I have the honor of this dance, Madam Donaldson?"

She swatted at his sleeve. "You're making light."

Graham staggered back, an indignant hand to his chest. "I'd never do something as presumptuous as to make light of *dancing*." Placing his arms in a ready waltz position, he simply waited.

He, Lord Sheldon Graham Malin Whitworth, ducal son, who'd

had countless tutors and lessons and had likely been schooled by the finest French dancers.

"If you are worried after your toes, I've had numerous lessons," he shared. "My parents insisted upon it."

Of course they had. "That is… reassuring," she drawled.

More than that, he'd had the finest ladies as his dance partners. Graceful, delicate creatures who'd likely glided like swans and shared the same dance instructors as Graham. "I don't really formally dance. I've not had any lessons."

He grinned. "They are overrated," he said, not missing a beat. Graham waggled his fingers. "Well?"

Glancing about, she made one more desperate bid. "There's no music," she protested. *You want to take his hand, though. Before he's gone from your life, you ache to know his arms about you as you waltz around this mythical ballroom.*

"I'll sing," Frederick piped in.

"Thank you," she muttered.

"There you have it."

Martha emitted a little squeak as Graham caught her hand and tugged her along. "You're incorrigible," she said, faintly breathless… with laughter? Anticipation? Mayhap both.

"I told you as much myself," he said, guiding them to a stop in the middle of the dance floor. "See? Few lies. Very few of them." Graham looked over to Frederick and snapped once.

Her son cleared his throat and broke into a discordant rendition of "The Valiant Lady."

"It's of a brisk young lively lad
Came out of Gloucestershire,
And all his full intention was
To court a lady fair.
Her eyes they shone like morning dew,
Her hair was fair to see…"

Graham spread his arms wide again. "Music," he announced, a proud glimmer in his eyes.

With a sigh, Martha place her fingertips on his sleeve. "I'm not very good, you know."

"Do you enjoy it?"

She hesitated and then nodded.

He lowered his brow close to hers. "Then that is all that matters."

With that, he spun her around the ballroom, the crystals twinkling overhead like artificial starlight.

Martha closed her eyes and let herself feel... him and this moment, turning herself over to all of it. They moved in graceful time, and she went where he led as he guided her back and right, moving her through the steps.

Feeling his stare, Martha looked at him. "I forgot how much I missed dancing," she whispered. She'd forgotten how much she'd missed simply the joy of living.

He moved his lips close to her ear, and her body trembled. "May I tell a secret?" he tempted.

"Y-yes."

"I lied."

Martha tried to follow his words through the daze cast by this moment, and then his admission penetrated. "What?"

"To Frederick," he clarified. "I never enjoyed dancing." Graham swept her in a wide, looping circle. "Until now."

"Cried she 'Since I have found him,
And brought him safe to shore,
Our days we'll spend
In old England,
Never roam abroad no more!"

Frederick's song came to an end, and Graham continued twirling them through the empty ballroom, and then he stopped.

They stood there, locked in each other's arms still.

Graham was the first to break away, and she ached at the loss of his embrace. Slow-clapping, he saluted Martha. "Your mother was being modest. She could teach any of the instructors I suffered through." He turned the light applause on Frederick. "And you're a fine performer. Splendid. Capable enough to replace any orchestra."

Frederick laughed. "Do you know what else my mother would enjoy?"

"Frederick," she chided, rushing over to her son.

"Oh, fine," he mumbled. He flashed a devil's grin. "Do you know what I would enjoy? A visit to"—Martha pressed a palm over his mouth—"Hymph Parph."

She was shaking her head. "No, Gra—"

"Splendid idea."

"It's not," she insisted. Releasing her son, she rushed back to Graham. "Lord Exeter indicated it was best that I remain indoors until... until..." She could not bring herself to say it.

"Christmas is nearly here. Every last lord and lady of London has gone on to their country estates. The rogues and rakes and scoundrels who remain behind are all abed at this hour."

He spoke entirely too much as one who knew. "And I trust you speak from experience."

"Oh, out of an abundance of it." Graham winked, setting loose a wave of flutters in her belly.

"I said no."

"Mother!" Frederick cried.

"You don't want to?" Graham asked, his tones those of one who sought to understand.

If she told him she didn't wish to, he'd never force her. But it would also be a lie, and she the greatest hypocrite for expecting only truths from him. Martha caught her lower lip between her teeth. "It isn't that."

"What is it, then?" he murmured, stroking his knuckles along her jaw.

She shook her head. How to explain that she wanted that visit more than anything? But that she, as a mother, wasn't permitted to allow her wants and desires to come first. That other people's—her son's and daughters'—well-being came first.

"Mother?" Frederick asked haltingly.

Graham sighed. "Very well." At that easy capitulation, regret filled her. *You are a contrary creature, Martha Donaldson.* "We shall put it to a vote."

"A v-vote?" Martha sputtered. "That is preposterous."

"Those in favor of remaining behind?" he put forward. Martha shot her hand up. "And those all for going to visit Hyde Pa—" Frederick had his fingers in the air before Graham had finished the sentence. Graham added his. "It is decided."

A short while later, she, Graham, and Frederick were carriage-bound for Hyde Park.

And being honest with herself, she conceded that she was so very glad to have lost.

CHAPTER 21

GRAHAM HAD SNEAKED OFF MANY a Hyde Park riding path. As a young rake out of college, there'd been something wicked in meeting equally wicked ladies at those trysting spots. There, just beyond the view of respectable society's eye, but near enough that it had lent a forbiddenness to the exchanges.

Now, he used one of those paths for entirely different purposes… with a woman completely engrossed in something that was most certainly not him.

Martha sat with her knees close to her chest and a sketch pad upon them in a makeshift desk. Her fingers flew over the page with a once whole, now a nub of gray charcoal. Periodically, she glanced up from her work, looking at him and then out to where Frederick played in the snow, before resuming her sketch.

"May I see it now?" he murmured.

"Shh." She lifted a silencing finger and then used her hand to balance the book once more. "Not yet."

The winter wind gusted over the river, battering at her hood and whipping at strand after strand of crimson curls. And not once did she stop, not even to so much as brush those tresses away.

He'd never before witnessed someone so attuned to any task. As a man who'd found it a struggle to maintain focus in nearly every aspect of his life, he sat in awe of Martha's ability to shut the whole world out and tunnel into just that page before her.

Another wind stirred the branches around them; it set the corner of her page to flapping. Martha quickly caught it, pushing it back into place.

She glanced up briefly and offered a distracted smile. It was a new smile from her that crinkled the corners of her eyes and dimpled both cheeks. Of a sudden, Graham wished he had a jot of her skill so he could capture her as she was in this instant.

He returned that grin, but she'd already resumed sketching.

"Graham!" Out of breath, Frederick came crashing through the narrow pathway that led into the remote sanctuary. "Is it frozen?" Martha's boy motioned to the river. "Can I step on it? I want to walk the length."

With that, Frederick managed that which had previously appeared impossible. Martha quit attending her work. "It's not safe."

"I walk across the one at home."

"Because it is five feet at the deepest, and we know when it is or is not frozen," she said with finality.

"I can check if it is safe." Gathering up a handful of stones, Graham tossed one through the barren branches, testing the ice.

"That's h-hardly—" Martha's protestations ended on a gasp as Graham came to his feet and started a slow, exploratory walk across the river. "Graham," she called out, jumping up. "Come back here now."

Graham paused in his trek. She was worried about him. Doffing his hat, he executed a flawless bow. "Rest assured, I'm entirely too skilled in the art of ice skating to find myself injured."

Martha stormed over to the shore. "I'm *more* worried you are going to fall through and perish in a watery death."

"I would rescue you," Frederick promised, lifting his hands over his head in a show of solidarity.

Martha swatted at her son's arm, and as the pair debated Graham's march across the ice, he continued his measured walk. Leveling himself slowly to a knee, he pressed a gloved palm over the surface, testing the feel of it. When he returned moments later, Frederick rushed him.

"Well?"

He inclined his head. "The ice is strong." On the heel of that was the realization that he'd overstepped. Graham cared about Frederick, but the boy wasn't his child, and he answered to only one. *But I'd like for him to be mine…* "Of course, the decision is your mother's. Her judgment in this area is equally sound. Perhaps more."

A daring glimmer sparkled in Frederick's eyes, revealing a hint of who Graham suspected the boy would one day be as a man. He recognized that daring trait as something he himself had always had.

"Mother?" Frederick pressed.

Martha nodded hesitantly. "But slowly," she called after Frederick as he started on the same path Graham had taken.

Together, she and Graham watched from the shore as Frederick, arms stretched out to steady his balance, picked a path over the ice. Occasionally, he would propel forward, much as he had in the ballroom. Throughout, his laughter pealed around the empty grounds of Hyde Park.

"Forgive me if I interfered," Graham began. "It was not—"

"No." She stopped his apology. "I'm... I've just been so accustomed to making every decision and having no one around to share opinions on Frederick. Hmph," she said, following Frederick's careful path across the river. "Actually, I've never had that. My father was more a playmate than one who knew how to care for children. My husband..." A shadow fell over her eyes.

Graham captured her hand, raising it to his lips. He'd not have Waters' ghost haunt this place Martha had always longed to be. She stared at their connected fingers. "I've sought to protect Frederick so much that I sometimes fail to allow him to go off and simply be... a boy."

"You love him, Martha. And someday, that is what he'll remember most and see in that protectiveness."

They remained there, side by side, a long time, the wind brushing the fabric of their cloaks together. Martha leaned against his shoulder.

At last, after nearly an hour spent watching her sketch, captivated by those loose curls, Graham caught them and brushed them behind the shell of her ear. "Is it time for me to see it?"

Her eyes sparkled. "Not yet." Whipping around, she gathered up her sketch pad and returned to her previously vacated seat.

While she scraped her charcoal across the page, Graham followed Frederick... until he reached the opposite side of the river. The little boy lifted his arm and waved excitedly.

Graham returned that exuberant greeting.

This was the life Graham wanted—one with Martha and him together, as a family. *And why can't you?* Despite the lies with which he'd entered her life, there was happiness now. Surely that mattered, if not more, then enough?

"All right." Martha held her sketch pad facing toward her and close to her chest. "Close your eyes first."

Striding over, Graham reached for the book. "The unveiling?"

She nodded. "The unveiling." But still, she retained her hold on it.

Graham wiggled his fingers. "Well?"

"It is very rough. I'd have spent more time on—"

"Martha," he interrupted.

"Fine," she muttered and reluctantly relinquished her sketch pad. Graham turned the book over and stilled.

The figures upon the page were unmistakable. From the harsh angular planes of his face, to the fit of his coat and breeches, it was Graham as he'd been moments ago, his legs stretched before him as he gazed off at Frederick tossing snowballs at the trunk of a towering oak. There was a rawness to her artistic ability, as if she'd frozen time to allow herself the opportunity to capture every last detail, from the bend in a branch, to the sheen upon the ice, with nothing more than charcoal.

But there was someone missing. Her... He wanted all of them, plus the two gap-toothed redheaded girls she'd described, in that sketch.

"You don't like it. As I said, it is just a rough render—"

"No. No," he repeated. "It is perfect. You are... Your work, Martha, is magnificent."

She blushed. "The sketch is yours," she said softly. "As a thank-you."

Just like that, the moment was shattered and, with it, his patience. "I don't need... nay, I don't want your gratitude, Martha," he clipped out. "I want you. I want to be a family with you and Frederick and the girls."

"What are you saying?" she whispered.

"I'm saying I want to marry you." He grimaced. Bloody hell, how had he, once a rogue with every last word and endearment in an arsenal he'd employed to charm, found himself blundering any exchange with this woman? The only one who'd ever mattered.

"Nay, I'm *asking you* to marry me."

She closed her eyes. "Oh, Graham. I love you."

"Then that is enough."

An agonized laugh escaped her that set his teeth to gritting. "It's not that simple. You are a duke's son."

"The third born son, nor would it matter if I was the damned ducal heir."

"Not to you. But to your father—"

"Who can go hang."

"Who also offered me one thousand pounds to set you free," she reminded him, yanking her book from his hand. "Despite your insistence, his approval matters. As does your mother's."

"That is rubbish," he snapped. "I don't live my life for their approval anymore."

"Simply saying it doesn't make it true."

He blinked. What in blazes was she saying?

Martha drew in a shuddery breath. "But this isn't about your parents. This is about us living in two different worlds." She cupped his cheek. "You speak of wanting to live a life of purpose and about the guilt you still carry for your brother. All the while, you've failed to see…" She went silent.

What? What was it she believed he didn't see? Graham clenched his fists, waiting for her to speak, too proud to ask her.

"You are still in search of approval, Graham." Clasping his hand, she pressed the sketch pad to his chest. "Just as you taught me that I need to see my own worth, you need to see that in you." She drew her sketch pad back. "I'm a bigamist. My children are bastards, and we will all be scorned, and one day you will be because of it."

He glared at her. "But we'd be together."

"And what if you came to resent me? That I could not live with."

Graham worked his gaze over her face. "If you believe that, then you don't know me, Martha."

From across the river, a squeal of laughter went up, followed by Frederick's familiar laugh.

Furrowing her brow, Martha rushed to the shore and stumbled.

Graham caught her by the elbow, steadying her.

In the distance, Frederick gave chase to a girl, the pair only specks on the horizon as they darted about. Graham belatedly registered Martha moving farther and farther out into the open clearing. Until she stopped.

"Martha."

She pressed her fingertips to her lips. "I've not seen him play with another child since his sisters left." Tears welled in her eyes, and she stared on, watching Frederick and the golden-haired little imp, who just then tossed a perfect snowball, hitting him square in the chest.

The grounds resonated with the little boy's war cry as he raced after the spritely girl.

"Who is she?" Martha asked, doing a sweep for a missing nurse-maid.

"I don't—" A young couple strolled over the slight crest in the walking trail, the lord and lady a study in golden English perfection. The Duke of Huntly carried a small child easily in his left arm, his other looped through the duchess' arm at her side.

Graham's entire body tensed. His features turned to stone. A moment later, a husky, dark-haired gentleman came bounding over that same rise, chasing after a squealing boy and girl.

"They are so... happy," she whispered. "I didn't believe a noble family could be"—she glanced at Graham and then back to the heartwarming tableau—"like them. Affectionate and playing games and—I always wanted that for my own children."

"You should return, Martha," he said tightly. "Come." He motioned for her to accompany him, and when she made no move to join him, Graham reached for her hand. "I'll gather Frederick." But Martha was already pulling away, picking her away across the frozen Serpentine.

"Martha," he implored.

Then, just as another slightly silver gentleman and an auburn-haired woman reached that same rise, Martha jerked.

Christ.

"It is Lord Exeter," she said blankly. "And..."

The former Lady Waters.

ONE SUMMER NIGHT, WHEN MARTHA had been a girl, she'd spent an entire long summer day outside, sketching. Her skin had turned such a shade of red, and her body had become fevered. She'd been racked by chills that set her teeth to chattering, while simultaneously burning from a nauseating heat.

This moment, observing the real Lady Waters, a woman who'd been married to the same man Martha had, had the same effect.

Her teeth chattered.

This was the viscount's family.

All… One, two, three… Seven adults and so many little babes and children running about that in her numbed state, Martha could not focus to properly count.

But they were all there, of all ages, from babes, to young children Frederick's age, to the silver-haired Lord Exeter with a babe of his own in his arms, and all smiling.

My children have siblings within that mix of people I don't know aside from the earl.

The Earl of Exeter glanced across to where Martha stood. His cheeks went white.

With a sickening, horrifying slowness, each member of that happy party looked to where Martha stood on display.

I'm going to be ill.

Graham touched her shoulder.

"Please get him," she whispered.

He nodded, and then with long glides, slid the remainder of the length of the frozen river.

He went, no questions asked, at nothing more than her request, a hero, while Martha, coward that she was, turned so quickly that she stumbled and fell. Agony shot along her hip and radiated pain down the length of her leg.

She ignored the discomfort.

Struggling to stand, Martha concentrated on putting one foot in front of the other. All the while, her nape burned from the stares of Lord Waters' family. After an interminable trek, she reached the shore and continued her cowardly retreat to the copse.

The moment she stepped within the shield offered by the enormous oaks, Martha let her shoulders sag.

An arm snaked around her, knocking the sketch pad from her hands. She opened her mouth to scream.

The stranger shoved his palm over her lips, burying all hint of sound. Her pulse beat loud in her ears as she writhed and thrashed against the punishing hold.

"You haven't made this particularly task easy for me, Miss Donaldson," he muttered. "But you and your family all being present here has certainly been convenient."

Miss Donaldson. How…? Who…? All the questions tangled in her mind, muted by panic.

Terror battered at her as she scanned her eyes over the horizon, searching for Graham. Oh, God. Frederick was with him.

"You have been a very difficult young woman to get to in London, you know?" he muttered, dragging her quickly through the brush.

Martha wrenched her neck frantically and bucked against him, digging in with her heels to try to slow their retreat from the path.

"I've no desire to kill you, however, or even hurt you, if you cooperate."

Liar.

She jammed her heel against his leg, but her skirts dulled the strike.

He sighed. "And now you are going to make this difficult for me, I see. Very well." His fist collided with her temple.

An inky blackness crept over her vision, and then she knew nothing more.

THE FIRST THING MARTHA BECAME aware of was a pounding pressure in her temples.

She blinked and attempted to make sense of where she was.

And then it all came rushing back.

Hyde Park.

Her assailant.

The attack.

"You are awake. That is good. As I said, you do me no good dead and little good asleep."

Martha forced her eyes open and then promptly closed them. An agonized moan spilled from her throat.

The clink of crystal touching crystal was followed by the stream of liquid.

"Here," her assailant said, as if he handed over a glass of tea in one of his formal parlors. "Drink."

Martha attempted to open her eyes again and this time forced herself to not shut them.

The first detail she noted was the gleam of the Chippendale furniture, a peculiar detail to note after being knocked unconscious and dragged off.

"Here," the gentleman said again, holding the glass out. Somewhere in his fiftieth year, with a faintly receding hairline, he was noble-born. His rank spilled off his person. As such, he expected her to accept the glass and take a dutiful sip.

Shoving herself up, Martha swung her legs over the side of the leather button sofa and pointedly ignored his offer. "You must think me mad to take a drink from a man who's tried to kill me."

The gentleman perched his hip on the arm of the sofa. "Tried, Miss Donaldson? Rest assured, if we'd wanted you dead, the arrow that day would have found a mark in your chest and not lodged in that tree." He spoke with a smile, like it was the most natural thing in the world to snuff out a person's existence. "From my understanding, you made quite a ruckus crawling across the ground. Though I do commend you for being fearless enough to climb into a felled tree and remain there for one hour and seventeen minutes."

My God... he knows that?

The gentleman smiled. "I know everything."

Something else he'd said took root. *We.* He, or they, had driven her off into the middle of the woods and had been there all along. Waiting. And they could have ended her. But they didn't. Despite the tremor that racked her frame from the remembered threat, she found a calm in that. "Who are you?"

He set down the glass in his hands. "Lord Charles Fitzmorris."

"Your name means nothing."

He chuckled. "Not to you. To the Crown, the king, and the Home Office, it means a good deal."

Since she'd committed herself in marriage to Viscount Waters, Martha had allowed life to happen around her and impact her, but she'd never taken control. Not truly. She'd been dependent, first upon her father, then her husband, then Lord Exeter... even Graham. She'd not be toyed with by this man. "What do you intend to do?" *To me.*

She was not so very brave to bring herself to ask about his intentions for her fate.

"To put England to rights." That cryptic pronouncement was met by a knock at the door. "Enter," he called out, coming to his feet.

Martha's mind spun. What had he meant by that statement?

A brawny footman entered.

She'd bet her right arm for sketching that the man standing before them was no servant, but some thug who did this man's bidding.

Lord Fitzmorris stalked over to the mahogany campaign-style desk. Gathering a small stack of notes, he held them out. "See them delivered immediately, and when they arrive, show them all in."

After the servant rushed off, closing the door behind him, Martha took to unsteady feet. She swayed, blinking back the fog from the ache at the back of her head, and stormed over to his desk. "You still have not said what role I play in all this," she said.

Lord Fitzmorris picked up his glass. "As I said, I intend to put England to rights, but you, Miss Donaldson, you are going to help me."

CHAPTER 22

GRAHAM WAS GOING MAD.

Slowly.

This insanity had nothing to do with the defect that had kept him from focusing on his studies. Rather, it was an insidious poison rotting his mind and, with it, the reason and logic he normally prided himself on.

And yet, he could not turn himself over to the panic, because now it was not just himself he had to think of.

Now, there was also Martha's son—Frederick.

Following Martha's abduction, Graham sat here, useless, while members of the organization searched for some information about her fate. For some clue of who'd taken her. Of why they'd wanted her. Waiting for a note. For some word.

Waiting. Waiting. Waiting.

"Useless," he whispered, to hear himself speak, or the tortured sound of silence would further drag him down the path to madness.

Seated behind his mahogany desk, his elbows on the top, he stared blankly at the gleaming surface. The smooth shine reflected his haggard visage. He'd been charged with looking after Martha and her son, and he'd failed her. He'd failed… again. The other failings, however… his father's ill opinion of him, his brothers' mockery, none of it meant anything. Martha… she meant everything.

A piteous moan spilled from him.

Filled with a restiveness, he jumped up and began pacing.

There had to be some clue... something that he was missing. A person simply didn't vanish. Not in Hyde Park. Not in broad daylight.

Who was it? Who was it?

"The Barretts," he said quietly. They were the likeliest lot, and it made the most sense that they'd wish Martha to vanish.

Edmund Deering, the Marquess of Rutland, was known first and foremost for the blackness of his heart. One of the greatest scoundrels in London, he'd been rumored to keep a book with the names of his enemies.

Graham scrubbed a hand over his stubbled cheek.

Strolling arm in arm, smiles on their faces and children running about, the Barretts and their spouses—Rutland included—hadn't looked the part of killers. They'd looked like a loving family and nothing more. Such a display, however, meant nothing. Over the years, hadn't Graham himself become a master of pretense?

No respectable family wanted a scandal about, and there was no greater scandal than the one Viscount Waters had visited upon his family—both of them. Martha and her children posed a threat to that joyful tableau on full display at Hyde Park.

Only—Graham abruptly stopped—it did not make sense. He trained his gaze on the longcase clock, following the staccato hand as it ticked away the seconds. The obvious answer was too obvious. If Archer had wished for Martha to... disappear, he'd had countless opportunities in the time in which Waters' treachery had come to light. The same held true for his sons-in-law and stepson. They'd all had ample opportunity to see that the late viscount's sins remained dead and buried along with him.

There was only one certainty—whoever had manipulated them all to get her here. There was no other accounting for the perceived danger in High Town. No, whoever had taken her had a use for her that went behind silencing secrets.

A knock sounded at the door.

His heart jumped, and Graham was across the room in several strides. He yanked the panel open—

"Oh."

His butler cleared his throat. "Her Grace, the Duchess of Sutton."

His mother tugged off her gloves. Her garments impeccable and not a strand of golden hair out of place, she swept forward. "No need for an introduction, Brambly. Or…" She dropped her voice to a conspiratorial whisper in a teasing way that Graham's father had never managed. "Perhaps, with the time it's been since I've seen him, it would be beneficial." She winked.

A sparkle glimmering in his eyes, Brambly backed out, and closing the door, he left the pair alone.

Doing a small turn about the room, his mother at last stopped in the middle of the room, commanding the office with her vantage. "I'll give you a hint," she teased. "This is generally where you gesture to a chair or offer to ring for refreshments."

Refreshments with his mother. His world was… had fallen apart, and he was engaging in this farce.

Dissemble at all times. You cease to be the man you were once you serve the Brethren.

That lesson ringing inside his head, Graham forced himself to indicate the pair of chairs in front of the fire. "It is a pleasure as always, Mother."

She snorted. "If that were true, you'd not have left my house party." His mother seated herself. "I take it, however, you were… expecting another."

Hoping for another. He'd been hoping there'd been some word. Some visit from the Brethren. Alas, his mother had always been more insightful than had been helpful to the troublesome boy he'd been.

He sidestepped her observation. "Things are dire indeed if you've gone and abandoned your houseguests." The consummate hostess, she'd never do anything as rude as leave her guests.

She laughed softly. "Come, you know me enough to know I quite despise all duties of hostess. It is your father who loves it so."

"Yes, anything that pays homage to his status." Gathering the untouched-until-now drink he'd poured himself, Graham lifted it in a mock salute. He took a sip and set the snifter down.

"He respects the title and its history, Sheldon. But he's not just that man."

That severed the thin thread he had on his patience. "Is that why you're here? To speak to me about the man my father is or is not?" He leaned forward. "I know precisely the manner of man he is." One who'd berate his son for never being the one he'd wished he'd be. One who'd send his damned man-of-affairs to make a young widow alone in the country an offer of funds if she'd leave his ducal spare to the heir alone. Graham firmed his lips. He was the last man who should have been assigned to Martha.

If... *when* she was found, he'd first beg forgiveness, and then he'd try to convince her that he was not only worthy of her, but capable of protecting her and her family.

But his mother wished to hear none of that, or that her husband, Graham's father, could go to the devil.

"Return home, Mother. If you've hopes of peace this holiday season, or my making a match with Lady Emilia, you've wasted your time."

Ever calm in the face of all her children's squabbling, she sat back. "Oh, Graham, I'll not lie to you and say that you are completely incorrect. That this... anger between you and your father has torn me apart for the whole of my life. That I wish there could be peace between you and him... and Heath."

"I've no problems with Heath."

A soft smile creased her face. "None that you ever speak of. None that my two boys have ever addressed."

His body went taut. This was a discussion he didn't wish to have. Even if Martha weren't in peril, he still wouldn't want to have it, ever. "I accepted long ago that my relationship with His Grace is dead and my one with Heath is fractured. I came to peace with it."

"What is this really about, Sheldon?"

He stared at her. "I don't know what you're asking."

"Your father believed your leaving the house party was nothing more than a display of rebellion."

"Of course he did," he said bitterly. His father's opinion of him had always been low. "And what did you believe?" No doubt the same lowly thoughts.

"I thought it had something to do with the... young woman you went off to... visit."

Graham started.

His mother gave him a wry smile. "You've always seemed to have an opinion about the relationship I have with your father. We speak, Sheldon. About everything."

Which also meant... Fury whipped through him. "So you knew what he intended to do," he stated, the handful of words infused with bitterness.

She hesitated, and that was all he needed to know.

Of all the disappointments he'd felt toward his father, never had it stung or hurt quite like this. The directive to order Martha away had come from his mother. "If you've come in the hopes I'll accompany you for the remainder of your house party, I fear you are to be even more disappointed." The least of the reasons of which had to do with his bloody father's insulting proposition to Martha and all to do with her. *Oh, God.* Madness shredded his patience and mind all at the same time. He came to his feet. "You should go."

His mother studied him for a long moment, the same maternal trick she'd employed with her troublesome son whereby she could pull forth every secret he'd sought—and failed—to keep from her, until now. "You care for her."

"No," he said automatically. Care was a weak emotion that could never capture the depth of what he felt for Martha Donaldson.

"You love her," she breathed.

Yes, he loved her. He loved her strength and courage and resilience in the face of all the ugliness life had heaped upon her narrow shoulders. He loved that she fought at every turn for the happiness of her children. *And she is gone…*

Graham dragged his hands through his hair. "I've nothing to say."

"You've already said everything with your silence," she said gently. His mother gave her head a little shake, a woman putting together the final pieces of an at-last-solved riddle. "Of course, she was… is nothing like the usual ladies you keep company with." She wrinkled her nose. "Actresses and notoriously emotionless widows and not young mothers from the country—"

The door opened, and Frederick rushed in. "I heard—" The boy's face fell, and all hope was extinguished as he took in Graham's mother. "Oh."

Had a mythical winged and horned unicorn swept into the room, the duchess wouldn't have been more surprised. She blinked wildly. "Hullo," she at last blurted.

Frederick cleared his throat. "Hello."

Graham stepped in to perform introductions. "Frederick, allow me to introduce you to my mother, the Duchess of Sutton. Mother, Frederick Donaldson."

There was a softening to his mother's features as she quit her chair and drifted over to the boy. "Hello," she repeated as she fell to a knee beside him. "It is lovely to meet you."

Martha's son glanced past her shoulder, a search for reassurance that eased the nagging ache that had been there since Martha had disappeared. "She's not one of those pompous duchesses," he promised.

"Oh, not at all," his mother readily agreed. Her fingers came up to smooth the wrinkled lines of Frederick's coat. "Where's the fun in that?"

Frederick continued to eye her with a world-weariness. Graham recognized the look too well, the desire to flee a situation that threatened... or, in this case, felt threatening.

"Frederick, would you allow us a moment?"

Relief paraded over the boy's features. He dropped a quick bow. "Your Grace," he murmured and bolted off, closing the door behind him.

His mother remained kneeling for a moment, staring at the door. "No, she isn't the usual company you keep. And I find I prefer it," she said, coming to her feet and facing him.

"She is not my mistress," he said tightly. "Nor do I want her to be. If she'll have me..." *If she is found. Do not think that. Do not...* "I intend to marry her."

That statement ushered in a thick, charged tension that blanketed the room. "I... see," she said, equanimous. Wandering past him, she retrieved her gloves. With slow, precise movements, she drew on the white articles. "I believed you'd left the house party because of your father." Which he had, countless times before. "Your father believed it was to see one of your many mistresses." Which had also been true countless times before. "But now?" She cast a lingering glance at the door. "Now I realize it had nothing to do with either, but rather, the young woman."

With that, she started for the door.

When she reached the panel, she stopped. "Oh, and Sheldon? You said earlier you are at peace, but if that were the case, you wouldn't be bitter. You wouldn't be resentful. Come home. Let us all try again... your father, Heath, you, and if you can convince Miss Donaldson to marry you? Her and her family."

With that offering, his mother left.

Graham hadn't a moment to contemplate the unexpected olive branch before the door burst open.

"There's no word?"

Graham motioned to the leather winged chair opposite his desk that Frederick had occupied nearly nonstop since Martha had gone missing. The only moment he'd abandoned it had been when Graham had sent him to the kitchens for food, so he could allow himself a moment to indulge in panic. "There hasn't been." Nothing outside the missives that he'd sent and received from those in the Home Office searching for her whereabouts.

"Do you believe she's all right?"

Since the discovery of Martha's abandoned sketch pad and the trail of her footsteps alongside another, larger, male pair, that had been nearly the only utterance to fall from Frederick's lips.

And just like each time he'd asked before, Graham brought himself to utter his return phrase. "I do."

That assurance wasn't solely for the boy, however. It was as much for Graham himself. Because he had to believe that Martha was all right. That she'd not come to harm. For he'd know it if she wasn't. There would be an empty hole where his heart, in fact, was.

"I shouldn't have been so mean to her." Frederick buried his chin in his chest, his words slashing through Graham's self-absorbed musings. "I–I've been rotted."

"Shh," Graham soothed. "This is not the time for regrets. When she comes home, you can show her every day you love her." *And every day I will prove why we belong together… All of us.*

"But I was rotten to her. She wanted me to go cut down a tree with her…"

Graham puzzled his brow.

"It's a tradition for the holidays," the boy explained. "And I told her my sisters would probably like to do it and then blamed her for sending them away."

Oh, Frederick. The guilt the boy carried was greater than that of any man. Graham came round his desk. Capturing the other leather winged chair, he dragged it closer to Frederick's. Not so very long ago, he'd have run off in horror at the prospect of offering comfort to a child, a role so foreign before, but now familiar. One that felt… right in every way. "As children"—regardless of age—"we know precisely what will agitate our parents. Or hurt them… And we often act without thinking." Sometimes with thinking, too. "Your mother knows you love her."

"No, she doesn't," he whispered, his voice threadbare.

Did his own father and mother realize the same of Graham? Or had he, with his own angry and unwillingness to talk about how he'd felt through the years, contributed to building the barriers that left them wondering why he'd resented them? "She knows," he promised. "But everyone benefits from a reminder now and then. And when she is back, you'll tell her how you feel." *Just as I will…*

Frederick gave a shaky nod. "I will." His was an avowal.

"And when she returns, Frederick… there is something I'd ask you."

The boy stared at him with a question in his eyes.

"I'd like to marry your mother. I'd ask for permission to wed her, if she'll have me." Graham held that direct little gaze. "If you'll all have—*oomph.*" He staggered back as Frederick hurled himself against his chest, and then Graham righted the both of them.

"Yes," Frederick cried. "You can."

Graham wrapped his arms around the boy and held him, this child, with his spirit and strength and courage, who was so very much like his mother. Tears blurred his eyes and clogged his throat.

Frederick scrambled out of his arms, a bright blush on his cheeks. He picked at his collar. "Err… That is…" He added a layer of deepness to his voice. "As long as you promise to care for her and love her and make her happy and not hurt her."

"I will," he promised. If she let him. If they found her…

His stomach pitched, bile climbing his throat as the traitorous thought steeped in reality crept forward.

To keep Martha's son from seeing that real terror, Graham returned to his desk and focused on her file, while Frederick sat in a companionable silence.

In the time since she'd been gone, Graham had scoured the pages of her file from the Home Office. Looking for clues. Looking for the names of her enemies.

Her captor wouldn't be a villager from High Town. They'd not have traveled to London to hurt her here when they'd had all the opportunities under the High Town sun to see to the act in that miserable countryside.

So who… who…?

Martha had gone of her own volition to London, but some unknown foe had impelled her into that decision. It therefore only made sense that it was a member of the peerage.

And where in blazes were his goddamned superiors with information? It had been hours since he'd received a damned note from anyone.

There was a quick rapping at the door.

His butler entered. "Lords Edward Helling and Exeter," he announced as the two older gentlemen swept forward.

About bloody time.

Graham, however, fixed his gaze on just one in that pair. Exeter. Fury pumped through his veins. The man who'd promised Martha assistance, who'd promised to keep her secret, had failed her at every turn. "Frederick, will you return this"—he handed over Martha's sketch pad—"to your mother's rooms? See that the pages are straightened, so when she comes home she doesn't see her work wrinkled."

Frederick leaped up and grabbed the book. Cradling it close to his chest like Bluebeard's trove, he hurried off.

Calling forth every lesson on patience and timing and silence, Graham waited a few moments before asking, "Who has taken her?"

"I don't know," Exeter said.

"Why are you here, then?" Graham demanded.

"To see if you've uncovered any information about who might have abducted Miss Donaldson."

They were relying on him to have information about her whereabouts. Holding off on sharing his speculations, Graham briefly turned his ire on Lord Edward. "You *insisted* she was safer in London."

"And you insisted on bringing her to Hyde Park despite my warnings." The other man bowed his head. "We were both wrong."

Guilt needled, deserved and well placed. Nonetheless… "That is *it*? Simply… 'we were wrong'?" Lord Edward temporarily forgotten, Graham pointed a finger at the earl, now the husband of the late viscount's rightful wife. "You offered Miss Donaldson assurances, and you failed."

The gentleman's face contorted. "I know. I'm deserving of that blame."

"Bloody right you are." Only, the other man's ownership of guilt and Graham's charges against him did nothing… Neither brought her back. Even so, he fed that outrage. "You were content with her buried away in High Town, while you lived your fairy-tale life with your new wife and new babe."

The color leached from Lord Exeter's cheeks.

"You," Graham sneered, "promised her security and safety, but that wasn't really your concern, was it?"

"Whitworth," Lord Edward barked.

"Was it?" he thundered. Graham rushed across the room and grabbed Lord Exeter by his lapels, dragging the slightly shorter man closer to eye level.

"Unhand him," his mentor commanded.

"You told her one thing. Mayhap you made yourself feel better at the idea of leaving a young woman with three children unprotected and alone."

Lord Exeter's throat moved. "I saw her daughters admitted to a school where they'd be treated with kindness and where they might build a future."

A red curtain of rage descended over Graham's vision, briefly blinding him. "She was separated from her children, you bastard," he hissed. He ignored Lord Edward's continued commands that he stand down. "Tell me… would having your new son sent away be some consolation to you?"

Lord Exeter's eyes slid closed, and his body slumped.

"No… Do you know what I believe?" Graham answered for the earl. "Mayhap a small part of you was determined to protect Miss Donaldson. But a larger part was determined to keep your wife and her family's dirtiest secret from ever sullying your names or lives."

Met with only a damning, guilty silence, Graham let out a sound of disgust and released him.

Setting aside his personal loathing for the earl, Graham focused on Martha's disappearance. "Whomever is responsible for Martha's abduction is someone who lives amongst the *ton*."

Lord Edward snapped his brows together. "Go on."

Quickly striding back to his desk, Graham retrieved the file that contained the enumeration of threats Martha had faced these past months. "Had it been someone in High Town, they had ample opportunity to do her harm without the Brethren ever being the wiser." He sneered once more at Lord Exeter. "We had, after all, forgotten enough about the lady where they could have killed her and her family. By the time you people developed a conscience and recalled broken promises, she would have already been dead."

Lord Exeter caught his jaw, and his gaze grew thoughtful. "He's right," he said to Lord Edward.

Succeeding where he'd only ever failed should have been the greatest triumph. Now, there was no victory with Martha gone. "Here." Graham passed his notes to his superior. "Someone wanted to drive her to London… to scare her, to show she was in danger, but to stop just short of harming her. They were sending a message."

"Why…?" Lord Edward's question, as he read through the notes, was the same Graham had been asking himself since his return from Hyde Park.

"She serves some use to someone," Lord Exeter murmured.

"Who would stand to benefit from Miss Donaldson's secret staying a secret?" Lord Edward talked the puzzle through. "Exeter's family."

That uttering, a cold, emotionless pronouncement about the woman who owned every last corner of Graham's heart, sent his rage spiraling.

Graham tamped down his resentment for the man before him and focused on his mentor's contemplative musings. "Lord Exeter's family, which now includes the Barretts."

Lord Exeter turned a hard look on Graham. "Are you implying my family is responsible…?"

"I've considered it and already decided they aren't the suspects, for the same reason it couldn't have been a High Town villager. You or yours could have… made Martha Donaldson disappear long before this, and without anyone the wiser." Turning his shoulder dismissively, he looked to Lord Edward. "Ask your previous question in reverse."

"Who… would stand to benefit from Miss Donaldson's secret coming to light?" he asked slowly.

Precisely. "Someone wants something. And no doubt plans on extorting."

The faintest look passed between the older members of the Brethren. He narrowed his eyes. They knew something. "What is it?"

Lord Edward gave the slightest nod.

The earl fished a small scrap from inside his jacket and held it out.

His heart slowed and then resumed a frantic beat. He ripped the note from the older gentleman's fingers and read.

46 Cyrus Street

London

3 o'clock

"It is an address," he said flatly. There were no sentences. This note was also the closest he'd felt to Martha since she'd disappeared into that copse.

"We both received one," Lord Edward murmured.

"I'm going with you." When the earl made to protest, Graham leveled him with a silencing look. "I'm going with you," he repeated.

The requests for the two former members of the Brethren, however, confirmed one obvious fact: Someone wanted something from both men... and somehow, Martha was a pawn the unknown foe sought to use to get it.

A SHORT WHILE LATER, THE RIDE quick through the London streets emptied for the holidays, Graham, the Earl of Exeter, and Lord Edward brought their mounts to a stop before a red brick townhouse.

Registering his superiors' silence, Graham looked over. "What is it?"

Both men exchanged a glanced. "It is a former office of the Brethren," Lord Exeter finally said.

"It is where I was trained," Lord Edward clarified.

Graham narrowed his eyes once more. Which meant... whoever had taken Martha was someone within their ranks. Someone who served the Home Office might have harmed Martha.

Oh, God. He fought back the panic that lingered at the back of his mind, wanting to pull him under, nearly succeeding.

They passed their reins off to a pair of street urchins, and matching one another's long strides, Graham, Lord Exeter, and Lord Edward climbed the handful of steps.

Graham pounded on the front panel.

"Always remain in control," Lord Edward said from the corner of his mouth.

Surprisingly, the door was immediately opened by a bald butler with kind, rheumy eyes.

Lord Edward rocked back on his heels. "Oh, bloody hell," he muttered.

Unlike his counterpart who'd let loose that outburst, Lord Exeter, remained remarkably implacable.

"Edward. Nathaniel." The servant greeted him as if welcoming old friends. "Allow me to take your cloaks?"

"This isn't a social call," Lord Exeter said frostily. "We'll keep our cloaks."

So his superiors knew, if not what the purpose of the meeting was, then the identity of who'd summoned them. Questions raced through Graham's head as they followed the butler, who led them down a long corridor and stopped at the first door. The servant knocked twice.

"Enter, Trombley."

All the color bled from Lord Edward's face.

"Who…?" Graham mouthed, and Trombley glanced over his shoulder.

When he'd turned back, Lord Edward gave an imperceptible shake of his head.

The moment they entered the rooms, Graham did a sweep.

An older, slightly graying gentleman, came forward.

Lord Edward cursed. "It is you, Fitzmorris," he hissed.

The other man smiled. "Surely you didn't think another could orchestrate all this?" He spared Graham a brief, dismissive look before turning all his focus on the pair near in age to his own years. "I see you've brought your recent *recruit* with you." With that slight emphasis, Fitzmorris managed to make that title an insult. "That is… unexpected." Lord Fitzmorris smirked. "Though, with the way you've currently been running the organization, not at all a surprise."

That slur, however, rolled off Graham. He didn't give ten damns about this man or anyone's opinion about himself. Martha. She was the one that mattered now. As the assembled party spoke, Graham continued his search.

His heart sank.

She wasn't here.

"What do you want, Fitzmorris?" Lord Exeter was asking.

The tall, wiry Fitzmorris chuckled. "And impatient, Exeter? But then, your timing was never great. It's why you were captured. Please, please, why don't we all sit and focus on the business that brings us together?" None would ever dare confuse that as anything other than the command it was.

Lord Exeter was stiff, silent, and unmoving, the glacial glimmer in his containing the threat of death for the man orchestrating whatever play they now took part in.

When everyone sat in the circular arrangement of chairs at the center of the room, Lord Edward repeated, "What the hell is this, Fitzmorris?"

"You know one another," Graham noted, an outsider in some... intimate exchange he wasn't supposed to have been part of.

"He was a mentor," Lord Edward quietly supplied. Sadness sparked in his gaze. "He recruited and trained past members for"—the Brethren—"the Home Office," he neatly substituted.

"And I was, of course, the best at what I did." Fitzmorris grinned. "What I... *do*."

Lord Exeter leveled a black glare on him. "What you *did*," he reminded. "You no longer serve the Home Office."

All business for the Brethren could go hang. "I trust you are the one who has abducted Miss Donaldson?" Graham asked, tired of whatever game this man played.

Resting his folded hands on his flat belly, Fitzmorris reclined. "Very impressive... and as impatient as Helling. All in due time. You see, Miss Donaldson is directly connected to... Brethren business." Another time, that thinly veiled insult would have chafed. Martha, however, had helped Graham to see his own worth.

"Say whatever reason it is you have us all here and be done with it," Lord Exeter said on a silky warning.

"You've failed the organization, Exeter. As did Aubrey and Helling. All of you." Fitzmorris rested his fingertips on the arms of his Louis XIV chair and drummed, that off-beat tap a contradiction to the vein pulsing at the corner of the older man's right eye. "I trained you." He glanced between the older gentlemen. "Both of you. You knew the men we made agents. Driven, calculated, unimpaired by emotion."

"We failed countless men and women with that heartless approach," Lord Exeter said quietly.

"And we saved more lives than we lost with it," Fitzmorris snapped.

Planting his hands on his knees, the earl leaned forward. "Don't you speak to me about what was *lost*. I was one who lost."

"You paid that price because you were careless… and you're instilling weakness in our ranks."

"They are not 'our ranks,' Fitzmorris."

"Ah, but they are. A member of the Brethren remains one until he draws his last breath. That"—Fitzmorris stuck a finger up—"is a vow *I* uttered and believe, Helling. Unlike you. Unlike both of you."

"I believe we can rule with kindness," Lord Exeter commanded.

"You were weak, Nathaniel. You let love soften you, and because of it, you allowed it to weaken the Brethren. I should have been Sovereign."

A muscle leaped at the corner of the earl's mouth, but otherwise, he gave no response to Fitzmorris' rebuke.

"And Helling, you've gone and perpetuated that folly by hiring… men like"—Fitzmorris peeled his lip in a sneer—"Whitworth. And," he went on, glancing around the assembled group, "all of you have demonstrated further weakness by looking after a woman who, if her relationship to the Brethren is discovered, taints the organization and all we stand for."

Fury stung Graham's veins at hearing a ruthless bastard like this former agent disparage Martha. She had more worth than every man gathered in this room.

"We stand on the side of right and doing what is right," Exeter said coolly. "And I'll make no apologies for it."

"Do you truly believe showing softness and emotion is the right way, Exeter? Good God, man, at what point did I fail you?" Exeter gave his head a little shake. "Your need to see Miss Donaldson protected made you all so careless that you rushed her off from where she was most safe"—he shrugged—"if uncomfortable with the village gossips, headfirst into my clutches. Furthermore, had you not promised to see the woman settled, I wouldn't even now have use or need of her." Fire snapped in Fitzmorris' eyes. "Therefore, do not act as though you're right in how you've led."

"She's a pawn," Graham breathed. As he'd predicted. However, new to the organization, he'd not been aware of the internal strife that dwelled within the secret division. "Your dying faction of the Brethren used the protective nature of its new members against us."

"Precisely," Fitzmorris said with a snap of his fingers. "You'll see how easily I turn that softheartedness against you. How I use it"—he grinned coolly—"*her* as a weapon to exact that which I want." He gave Graham a long look of consideration. "Mayhap you are not so much the failure I've taken you for." All hint of pretend geniality died as he looked to Exeter. "We, the older ranking members, are retaking the organization. We're going to reshape it in the original image it was crafted."

"The hell you are," Lord Edward spat.

Lord Exeter, however, was a study in calm. He stretched an arm along the back of his chair. "Do you truly believe those of us who've set the Brethren on a more honorable path will ever relinquish it?"

"If you convince them it is in their best interest to do so. Enter," Fitzmorris called out.

The door opened and—

Graham shot to his feet.

Martha.

Oh, God. Relief swept through him, a tangible gift that blazed through him, lifting his heart and driving away the madness that had gripped him.

Her lower lip trembled. "Graham."

"Are you all right?" he demanded, stalking forward. Then his hands were on her, verifying for himself, searching for signs that she'd been in any way harmed, and if she had, he'd rip apart with his bare hands the man responsible.

"She is fine. I've already assured her that had I wished to harm her, she would have been dead by now."

They joined the circle of assembled guests.

"You've left me a way to address the situation within the

Brethren and the Crown. Miss Donaldson has just been a clever, beneficial bargaining tool."

Dread slithered around Graham's belly.

Fitzmorris reclined in his seat and hooked his ankle across his opposite knee. "There has been a faction, as you're aware, attempting to… restore a greater sense of control to the kingdom."

"They are acts to repress the people," Lord Edward said curtly. "You were never one to condone those restrictions."

"Because the times then did not merit it, but these times? They do. Among those, there is a faction that wishes to"—his nose shifted as if in distaste—"loosen the restrictions on the Marriage Act of 1753. The legislation is in… draft stages."

Martha sat upright. Graham gathered her fingers, cold and moist, and held tight.

"Ah, you're a clever one, Miss Donaldson," Fitzmorris praised. "The legislation, if it succeeds, will greatly facilitate clandestine marriages. Such as the one Miss Donaldson found herself in."

"Don't do this," Lord Exeter said quietly.

"Of course," Fitzmorris went on. "I could care less about such legislation… but there are some who do and would greatly love to use Miss Donaldson as their political rallying cry. Those who are desiring to put a death knell in that faulty legislation would benefit greatly from one who serves as a reminder that bigamy is a threat to our noble families."

"You bastard." Graham shoved back his chair. "You'd use her as your pawn."

Martha gave her head a small shake.

Fitzmorris nodded. "I would. I will. I want the organization restructured as it was. I want the previous codes reimplemented. And you can see that happen, Exeter. And if you don't?" He shrugged. "Then Miss Donaldson's past will be used to ensure that your wife's family bears the shame of that."

The former leader of the organization let that sit in silence.

Martha spoke first. "Do not answer that or agree to that." Resting her hands on her knees, she leaned forward. "This is why you've terrorized me? To see my past brought to light so I could be used by you? I'll no longer be used. If you wish to destroy me, then so bet it. But I'll not have my life and my circumstances used as a chess piece by you… or any man."

And God help him, Graham fell in love with Martha Donaldson all over again.

"Ah, but I don't really need your decision, Miss Donaldson. I need Lord Exeter's."

All eyes went to the earl.

His skin waxen, Lord Exeter sat motionless, a man with torment in his eyes. A man at war with himself, caught between what he knew was right and the family he sought to protect. "Lord Whitworth, you were correct," he said unexpectedly. Coming to his feet, he strode past Graham and to Martha's side.

She eyed him warily.

"Lord Whitworth accused me of failing you and not seeing that your secret was kept and your family safe," he murmured. "He accused me of putting my family first, preserving their reputations, and keeping the scandal from them. I love my family. I'd protect them at all costs."

"You bastard," Graham hissed.

The earl ignored him, his gaze remaining locked with Martha's before he finally turned to face Fitzmorris. "Share *our* scandal, Fitzmorris. We'll not be extorted or threatened by you. My family stands with Miss Donaldson's."

Tears filled Martha's eyes, and she pressed a hand to her mouth.

Lord Exeter bowed his head.

Fitzmorris' rushed forward, cheeks florid. "You'll fight me on control of the Brethren, Edward? I trained you."

"You're no longer the man you were," Helling said sadly.

"Whitworth," Fitzmorris tried, "y-you would let Miss Donaldson be destroyed?"

Graham flashed an icy smile. "Ah, Fitzmorris, for one who prides himself on his skillful reading of men and women, you've proven yourself a marked failure. Miss Donaldson? She cannot be destroyed."

With the other man's shouts following behind them, the three noblemen and Martha left.

CHAPTER 23

After Lord Fitzmorris' threat, Martha should be braced for her scandal to come to light.

It was inevitable.

Just as it had been inevitable that the people of High Town would find out, so too would the whole world eventually know.

Before, that realization had hung heavy over her head, like a sword about to fall and sever the too-fleeting joy she'd known.

Now… Martha had found peace in the secret for which she'd harbored guilt and shame when Graham had opened her eyes to the truth: She was not responsible for those crimes. They belonged squarely with the dastard who'd made her life a lie.

Her life, however, was more ordered now than it had… ever been. With the help of Lord Exeter and Lord Edward, Martha had received a cottage in Leeds, where she could begin again with her son.

And it wasn't enough.

Because she was ungrateful.

Because she was selfish.

Her son sat atop the black lacquer carriage, finer than any conveyance she'd ever sat within, chatting with the driver and laughing happily.

And Martha was nothing but miserable.

Because she missed Graham.

Missed him, even as he sat across from her now on the opposite bench of the same carriage that now escorted her home.

To her new home.

He was home. *Tell him that...*

Graham, however, remained engrossed in the file on his lap, the same folder he'd read for the past forty-five minutes and handful of seconds, while she sat there watching him, with nothing to say when words had always come easy for her with him.

Of course, then he'd wished to talk. Since they'd left Fitzmorris' office, Graham had... retreated in every way a person could retreat. She'd not seen him again until he'd helped her into his carriage loaded with her belongings and climbed in across from her. "I—"

"You needn't thank me, Martha," he interrupted, not even lifting his head. Studying. Reading.

And then scribbling something on that page with a small pencil. He turned another page.

"Will you..." *Talk to me. Say something. Look at me.* And she found the latter wasn't enough. Graham didn't look up. "Spend the holiday with your family?" she finished lamely.

This time, he did look up.

"F-Frederick mentioned your mother paid you a visit, that she asked you to come home for the holidays." To the house party and the flawless lady his family had handpicked for him.

"Did he... mention anything else about my mother's visit?"

"No." Martha balled her hands, thinking of the words that must have been uttered about her. She'd become a source of contention between Graham and the mother he'd spoken of so affectionately.

"I still haven't decided. There's always tension when I'm with my family." For the first time since they'd been at Hyde Park, before the world had turned upside down, Graham smiled. "They're a stubborn group." A stubborn group she wouldn't meet, the mother he'd spoken of so affectionately and the brother he'd once been both rival and friends with. Graham went back to his work.

Martha stared down at her lap. She had no right to ask anything of him. She had no right to bare her heart to him and offer that gift to him now, not when she'd rejected his offer in the past. But she needed to anyway. She needed him to know that she believed in them and wanted a life with him—if he wanted one with her— and she'd not resent him for turning her away now. "Graham," she blurted. "I..." The carriage hit a dip in the road, and she caught the bench to keep steady.

"We've arrived."

They were here.

Her new home.

Frederick and she...

Peeling back the curtain, Martha peered out. The frosted window blurred the view of it, and she pressed her palm against it until the warmth had melted the sheen... and then stared out.

She wanted to cry.

The white manor house, with its green door and a small frozen lake, was... perfect. It was... so blasted perfect. Except, it wasn't. Because he wouldn't be there. Martha swiped her hands over her eyes.

"You're crying," he observed with such tenderness underlying his words that she cried all the harder.

"I-I am," she croaked. "Because it is lovely. I-it really is. And I-I am going to s-sound most ungrateful when I-I have no right to ask you for anything more or a-anything at all," Martha managed between tears. She brushed at them in frustration. "I want to be with you." Through her misty vision, she met his gaze.

His throat moved. "Martha—"

"I-I know we're of a different station and I'm likely to only bring scandal to... to whomever is in my life, but... I love you, and... th-that is all."

A smile grazed the corners of his lips. He opened his mouth to speak.

"No, that is not at all!" she exploded, needing to say everything. She had concealed and carried everything these past years: her marriage, her children, her secrets. Graham had helped free her from the restraints she'd imposed upon herself. "I don't want to live here. I don't want to stay hidden from the world, Society's dirty secret." She pressed a hand to her breast. "I don't want my children to be hidden."

Graham leaned across, resting his head against hers. "I don't want your children to be hidden anymore, either."

"I kn-know that." Her voice quavered. "You were the one who opened my eyes to all that was wrong with sending them away." He had been outraged on behalf of Creda and Iris when she'd shared their existence with them. In that annoyance on her daughters' behalf, he'd been far braver than Martha had ever been. Life would be hard, and no doubt ugly oftentimes, for her children. "I want to face all of it, Graham... with you... because with y-you at my side, I can do anything and be anything... and—"

Graham kissed the remainder of that vow from her lips. It was an achingly beautiful kiss that asked for nothing, but gave all, warmth and tenderness. "Oh, Martha," he whispered against her mouth. "You always could do anything and be anything. It never had anything to do with me." He cupped her cheeks, wiping away the tears with the pads of his thumbs. "But I want to be there at your side, so you don't have to be 'everything'... alone. Please, ma—"

She hurled herself into his arms. "Yes," she sobbed.

"Marry me," he finished anyway. "Let me be a husband to you and a father to your children." Her body shook with the force of her tears. "And know that any struggle we face will ultimately be fine as long as we are at one another's side. Together."

A knock sounded on the carriage door.

Martha caught Graham's hand as he reached for the handle. "I don't want to live here... unless you're here with me."

His brow furrowed, and then understanding flashed in his eyes. "You think this is your home."

"Not unless I'm here with you." She looked out the window to where Frederick now played in the snow. "With us," she amended.

"This isn't the property purchased for you, Martha."

Martha angled her head. "It is not?"

His lips twitched. "It is not."

"What...?"

Wordlessly, he held out his folder.

She looked at it questioningly and then back to him. Martha opened the leather folder, and her heart did a little leap. "Mrs. Munroe's," she whispered. "It is their school."

"I thought we would stop here first, so you might decide whether you want Creda and Iris to remain behind, or whether you are ready for them to come home... with us."

He'd sought to rescue her daughters, two little girls he had never before met, and reunite their fractured family.

"I imposed," he said uneasily. "It was again not my place. Just as I should not have gone against your wishes regarding Hyde Par—*oomph.*"

Martha had dropped the folder and launched herself at Graham, knocking him into the side of the carriage. "I love you," she cried. She kissed him and willed all the emotion, all the love she carried for this man into that embrace.

Breathless, Graham was the first to end the kiss. "The other business," he murmured, rescuing the folio from the floor and handing over the officious scrap. "Will you marry me, Miss Martha Donaldson?"

Her hands trembling, Martha accepted the marriage certificate, the offering of his name and respectability, and a testament to his willingness to stand beside her through the scandal and anything that came.

She struggled to bring his beloved visage into focus through the tears. "I will marry you, Lord Sheldon Graham Malin Whitworth."

Another knock sounded at the carriage door. Graham held out his hand. "Shall we, Miss Donaldson?"

With a smile, Martha nodded.

Martha stared at that gloved palm and slipped her fingers into his.

Hand in hand, with Frederick skipping off ahead, Martha and Graham started for Mrs. Munroe's … and Creda and Iris… and the rest of their future—*together.*

THE END

OTHER BOOKS BY
CHRISTI CALDWELL

TO ENCHANT A WICKED DUKE
Book 13 in the "Heart of a Duke" Series by Christi Caldwell

A Devil in Disguise

Years ago, when Nick Tallings, the recent Duke of Huntly, watched his family destroyed at the hands of a merciless nobleman, he vowed revenge. But his efforts had been futile, as his enemy, Lord Rutland is without weakness.

Until now…

With his rival finally happily married, Nick is able to set his ruthless scheme into motion. His plot hinges upon Lord Rutland's innocent, empty-headed sister-in-law, Justina Barrett. Nick will ruin her, marry her, and then leave her brokenhearted.

A Lady Dreaming of Love

From the moment Justina Barrett makes her Come Out, she is labeled a Diamond. Even with her ruthless father determined to sell her off to the highest bidder, Justina never gives up on her hope for a good, honorable gentleman who values her wit more than her looks.

A Not-So-Chance Meeting

Nick's ploy to ensnare Justina falls neatly into place in the streets of London. With each carefully orchestrated encounter, he slips further and further inside the lady's heart, never anticipating that Justina, with her quick wit and strength, will break down his own defenses. As Nick's plans begins to unravel, he's left to determine which is more important—Justina's love or his vow for vengeance. But can Justina ever forgive the duke who deceived her?

ONE WINTER WITH A BARON
Book 12 in the "Heart of a Duke" Series by Christi Caldwell

A clever spinster:

Content with her spinster lifestyle, Miss Sybil Cunning wants to prove that a future as an unmarried woman is the only life for her. As a bluestocking who values hard, empirical data, Sybil needs help with her research. Nolan Pratt, Baron Webb, one of society's most scandalous rakes, is the perfect gentleman to help her. After all, he inspires fear in proper mothers and desire within their daughters.

A notorious rake:

Society may be aware of Nolan Pratt, Baron's Webb's wicked ways, but what he has carefully hidden is his miserable handling of his family's finances. When Sybil presents him the opportunity to earn much-needed funds, he can't refuse.

A winter to remember:

However, what begins as a business arrangement becomes something more and with every meeting, Sybil slips inside his heart. Can this clever woman look beneath the veneer of a coldhearted rake to see the man Nolan truly is?

TO REDEEM A RAKE
Book 11 in the "Heart of a Duke" Series by Christi Caldwell

He's spent years scandalizing society.
Now, this rake must change his ways.

Society's most infamous scoundrel, Daniel Winterbourne, the Earl of Montfort, has been promised a small fortune if he can relinquish his wayward, carousing lifestyle. And behaving means he must also help find a respectable companion for his youngest sister—someone who will guide her and whom she can emulate. However, Daniel knows no such woman. But when he encounters a childhood friend, Daniel believes she may just be the answer to all of his problems.

Having been secretly humiliated by an unscrupulous blackguard years earlier, Miss Daphne Smith dreams of finding work at Ladies of Hope, an institution that provides an education for disabled women. With her sordid past and a disfigured leg, few opportunities arise for a woman such as she. Knowing Daniel's history, she wishes to avoid him, but working for his sister is exactly the stepping stone she needs.

Their attraction intensifies as Daniel and Daphne grow closer, preparing his sister for the London Season. But Daniel must resist his desire for a woman tarnished by scandal while Daphne is reminded of the boy she once knew. Can society's most notorious rake redeem his reputation and become the man Daphne deserves?

TO WOO A WIDOW
Book 10 in the "Heart of a Duke" Series by Christi Caldwell

They see a brokenhearted widow.
She's far from shattered.

Lady Philippa Winston is never marrying again. After her late husband's cruelty that she kept so well hidden, she has no desire to search for love.

Years ago, Miles Brookfield, the Marquess of Guilford, made a frivolous vow he never thought would come to fruition—he promised to marry his mother's goddaughter if he was unwed by the age of thirty. Now, to his dismay, he's faced with honoring that pledge. But when he encounters the beautiful and intriguing Lady Philippa, Miles knows his true path in life. It's up to him to break down every belief Philippa carries about gentlemen, proving that not only is love real, but that he is the man deserving of her sheltered heart.

Will Philippa let down her guard and allow Miles to woo a widow in desperate need of his love?

The Lure Of A Rake
Book 9 in the "Heart of a Duke" Series by Christi Caldwell

A Lady Dreaming of Love

Lady Genevieve Farendale has a scandalous past. Jilted at the altar years earlier and exiled by her family, she's now returned to London to prove she can be a proper lady. Even though she's not given up on the hope of marrying for love, she's wary of trusting again. Then she meets Cedric Falcot, the Marquess of St. Albans whose seductive ways set her heart aflutter. But with her sordid history, Genevieve knows a rake can also easily destroy her.

An Unlikely Pairing

What begins as a chance encounter between Cedric and Genevieve becomes something more. As they continue to meet, passions stir. But with Genevieve's hope for true love, she fears Cedric will be unable to give up his wayward lifestyle. After all, Cedric has spent years protecting his heart, and keeping everyone out. Slowly, she chips away at all the walls he's built, but when he falters, Genevieve can't offer him redemption. Now, it's up to Cedric to prove to Genevieve that the love of a man is far more powerful than the lure of a rake.

To Trust A Rogue
Book 8 in the "Heart of a Duke" Series by Christi Caldwell

A rogue

Marcus, the Viscount Wessex has carefully crafted the image of rogue and charmer for Polite Society. Under that façade, however, dwells a man whose dreams were shattered almost eight years earlier by a young lady who captured his heart, pledged her love, and then left him, with nothing more than a curt note.

A widow

Eight years earlier, faced with no other choice, Mrs. Eleanor Collins, fled London and the only man she ever loved, Marcus, Viscount Wessex. She has now returned to serve as a companion for her elderly aunt with a daughter in tow. Even though they're next door neighbors, there is little reason for her to move in the same circles as Marcus, just in case, she vows to avoid him, for he reminds her of all she lost when she left.

Reunited

As their paths continue to cross, Marcus finds his desire for Eleanor just as strong, but he learned long ago she's not to be trusted. He will offer her a place in his bed, but not anything more. Only, Eleanor has no interest in this new, roguish man. The more time they spend together, the protective wall they've constructed to keep the other out, begin to break. With all the betrayals and secrets between them, Marcus has to open his heart again. And Eleanor must decide if it's ever safe to trust a rogue.

To Wed His Christmas Lady
Book 7 in the "Heart of a Duke" Series by Christi Caldwell

She's longing to be loved:

Lady Cara Falcot has only served one purpose to her loathsome father—to increase his power through a marriage to the future Duke of Billingsley. As such, she's built protective walls about her heart, and presents an icy facade to the world around her. Journeying home from her finishing school for the Christmas holidays, Cara's carriage is stranded during a winter storm. She's forced to tarry at a ramshackle inn, where she immediately antagonizes another patron—William.

He's avoiding his duty in favor of one last adventure:

William Hargrove, the Marquess of Grafton has wanted only one thing in life—to avoid the future match his parents would have him make to a cold, duke's daughter. He's returning home from a blissful eight years of traveling the world to see to his responsibilities. But when a winter storm interrupts his trip and lands him at a falling-down inn, he's forced to share company with a commanding Lady Cara who initially reminds him exactly of the woman he so desperately wants to avoid.

A Christmas snowstorm ushers in the spirit of the season:

At the holiday time, these two people who despise each other due to first perceptions are offered renewed beginnings and fresh starts. As this gruff stranger breaks down the walls she's built about herself, Cara has to determine whether she can truly open her heart to trusting that any man is capable of good and that she herself is capable of love. And William has to set aside all previous thoughts he's carried of the polished ladies like Cara, to be the man to show her that love.

THE HEART OF A SCOUNDREL
Book 6 in the "Heart of a Duke" Series by Christi Caldwell

Ruthless, wicked, and dark, the Marquess of Rutland rouses terror in the breast of ladies and nobleman alike. All Edmund wants in life is power. After he was publically humiliated by his one love Lady Margaret, he vowed vengeance, using Margaret's niece, as his pawn. Except, he's thwarted by another, more enticing target— Miss Phoebe Barrett.

Miss Phoebe Barrett knows precisely the shame she's been born to. Because her father is a shocking letch she's learned to form her own opinions on a person's worth. After a chance meeting with the Marquess of Rutland, she is captivated by the mysterious man. He, too, is a victim of society's scorn, but the more encounters she has with Edmund, the more she knows there is powerful depth and emotion to the jaded marquess.

The lady wreaks havoc on Edmund's plans for revenge and he finds he wants Phoebe, at all costs. As she's drawn into the darkness of his world, Phoebe risks being destroyed by Edmund's ruthlessness. And Phoebe who desires love at all costs, has to determine if she can ever truly trust the heart of a scoundrel.

TO LOVE A LORD

Book 5 in the "Heart of a Duke" Series by Christi Caldwell

All she wants is security:

The last place finishing school instructor Mrs. Jane Munroe belongs, is in polite Society. Vowing to never wed, she's been scuttled around from post to post. Now she finds herself in the Marquess of Waverly's household. She's never met a nobleman she liked, and when she meets the pompous, arrogant marquess, she remembers why. But soon, she discovers Gabriel is unlike any gentleman she's ever known.

All he wants is a companion for his sister:

What Gabriel finds himself with instead, is a fiery spirited, bespectacled woman who entices him at every corner and challenges his age-old vow to never trust his heart to a woman. But... there is something suspicious about his sister's companion. And he is determined to find out just what it is.

All they need is each other:

As Gabriel and Jane confront the truth of their feelings, the lies and secrets between them begin to unravel. And Jane is left to decide whether or not it is ever truly safe to love a lord.

LOVED BY A DUKE

Book 4 in the "Heart of a Duke" Series by Christi Caldwell

For ten years, Lady Daisy Meadows has been in love with Auric, the Duke of Crawford. Ever since his gallant rescue years earlier, Daisy knew she was destined to be his Duchess. Unfortunately, Auric sees her as his best friend's sister and nothing more. But perhaps, if she can manage to find the fabled heart of a duke pendant, she will win over the heart of her duke.

Auric, the Duke of Crawford enjoys Daisy's company. The last thing he is interested in however, is pursuing a romance with a woman he's known since she was in leading strings. This season, Daisy is turning up in the oddest places and he cannot help but notice that she is no longer a girl. But Auric wouldn't do something as foolhardy as to fall in love with Daisy. He couldn't. Not with the guilt he carries over his past sins… Not when he has no right to her heart…But perhaps, just perhaps, she can forgive the past and trust that he'd forever cherish her heart—but will she let him?

THE LOVE OF A ROGUE
Book 3 in the "Heart of a Duke" Series by Christi Caldwell

Lady Imogen Moore hasn't had an easy time of it since she made her Come Out. With her betrothed, a powerful duke breaking it off to wed her sister, she's become the *tons* favorite piece of gossip. Never again wanting to experience the pain of a broken heart, she's resolved to make a match with a polite, respectable gentleman. The last thing she wants is another reckless rogue.

Lord Alex Edgerton has a problem. His brother, tired of Alex's carousing has charged him with chaperoning their remaining, unwed sister about *ton* events. Shopping? No, thank you. Attending the theatre? He'd rather be at Forbidden Pleasures with a scantily clad beauty upon his lap. The task of *chaperone* becomes even more of a bother when his sister drags along her dearest friend, Lady Imogen to social functions. The last thing he wants in his life is a young, innocent English miss.

Except, as Alex and Imogen are thrown together, passions flare and Alex comes to find he not only wants Imogen in his bed, but also in his heart. Yet now he must convince Imogen to risk all, on the heart of a rogue.

MORE THAN A DUKE
Book 2 in the "Heart of a Duke" Series by Christi Caldwell

Polite Society doesn't take Lady Anne Adamson seriously. However, Anne isn't just another pretty young miss. When she discovers her father betrayed her mother's love and her family descended into poverty, Anne comes up with a plan to marry a respectable, powerful, and honorable gentleman—a man nothing like her philandering father.

Armed with the heart of a duke pendant, fabled to land the wearer a duke's heart, she decides to enlist the aid of the notorious Harry, 6th Earl of Stanhope. A scoundrel with a scandalous past, he is the last gentleman she'd ever wed...however, his reputation marks him the perfect man to school her in the art of seduction so she might ensnare the illustrious Duke of Crawford.

Harry, the Earl of Stanhope is a jaded, cynical rogue who lives for his own pleasures. Having been thrown over by the only woman he ever loved so she could wed a duke, he's not at all surprised when Lady Anne approaches him with her scheme to capture another duke's affection. He's come to appreciate that all women are in fact greedy, title-grasping, self-indulgent creatures. And with Anne's history of grating on his every last nerve, she is the last woman he'd ever agree to school in the art of seduction. Only his friendship with the lady's sister compels him to help.

What begins as a pretend courtship, born of lessons on seduction, becomes something more leaving Anne to decide if she can give her heart to a reckless rogue, and Harry must decide if he's willing to again trust in a lady's love.

FOR LOVE OF THE DUKE
First Full-Length Book in the "Heart of a Duke" Series
by Christi Caldwell

After the tragic death of his wife, Jasper, the 8th Duke of Bainbridge buried himself away in the dark cold walls of his home, Castle Blackwood. When he's coaxed out of his self-imposed exile to attend the amusements of the Frost Fair, his life is irrevocably changed by his fateful meeting with Lady Katherine Adamson.

With her tight brown ringlets and silly white-ruffled gowns, Lady Katherine Adamson has found her dance card empty for two Seasons. After her father's passing, Katherine learned the unreliability of men, and is determined to depend on no one, except herself. Until she meets Jasper...

In a desperate bid to avoid a match arranged by her family, Katherine makes the Duke of Bainbridge a shocking proposition—one that he accepts.

Only, as Katherine begins to love Jasper, she finds the arrangement agreed upon is not enough. And Jasper is left to decide if protecting his heart is more important than fighting for Katherine's love.

IN NEED OF A DUKE
A Prequel Novella to "The Heart of a Duke" Series
by Christi Caldwell

In Need of a Duke: (Author's Note: This is a prequel novella to "The Heart of a Duke" series by Christi Caldwell. It was originally available in "The Heart of a Duke" Collection and is now being published as an individual novella.

~★~

It features a new prologue and epilogue.

Years earlier, a gypsy woman passed to Lady Aldora Adamson and her friends a heart pendant that promised them each the heart of a duke.

Now, a young lady, with her family facing ruin and scandal, Lady Aldora doesn't have time for mythical stories about cheap baubles. She needs to save her sisters and brother by marrying a titled gentleman with wealth and power to his name. She sets her bespectacled sights upon the Marquess of St. James.

Turned out by his father after a tragic scandal, Lord Michael Knightly has grown into a powerful, but self-made man. With the whispers and stares that still follow him, he would rather be anywhere but London…

Until he meets Lady Aldora, a young woman who mistakes him for his brother, the Marquess of St. James. The connection between Aldora and Michael is immediate and as they come to know one another, Aldora's feelings for Michael war with her sisterly responsibilities. With her family's dire situation, a man of Michael's scandalous past will never do.

Ultimately, Aldora must choose between her responsibilities as a sister and her love for Michael.

ONCE A WALLFLOWER, AT LAST HIS LOVE
Book 6 in the Scandalous Seasons Series

Responsible, practical Miss Hermione Rogers, has been crafting stories as the notorious Mr. Michael Michaelmas and selling them for a meager wage to support her siblings. The only real way to ensure her family's ruinous debts are paid, however, is to marry. Tall, thin, and plain, she has no expectation of success. In London for her first Season she seizes the chance to write the tale of a brooding duke. In her research, she finds Sebastian Fitzhugh, the 5th Duke of Mallen, who unfortunately is perfectly affable, charming, and so nicely… configured… he takes her breath away. He lacks all the character traits she needs for her story, but alas, any duke will have to do.

Sebastian Fitzhugh, the 5th Duke of Mallen has been deceived so many times during the high-stakes game of courtship, he's lost faith in Society women. Yet, after a chance encounter with Hermione, he finds himself intrigued. Not a woman he'd normally consider beautiful, the young lady's practical bent, her forthright nature and her tendency to turn up in the oddest places has his interests... roused. He'd like to trust her, he'd like to do a whole lot more with her too, but should he?

A Marquess For Christmas
Book 5 in the Scandalous Seasons Series

Lady Patrina Tidemore gave up on the ridiculous notion of true love after having her heart shattered and her trust destroyed by a black-hearted cad. Used as a pawn in a game of revenge against her brother, Patrina returns to London from a failed elopement with a tattered reputation and little hope for a respectable match. The only peace she finds is in her solitude on the cold winter days at Hyde Park. And even that is yanked from her by two little hellions who just happen to have a devastatingly handsome, but coldly aloof father, the Marquess of Beaufort. Something about the lord stirs the dreams she'd once carried for an honorable gentleman's love.

Weston Aldridge, the 4th Marquess of Beaufort was deceived and betrayed by his late wife. In her faithlessness, he's come to view women as self-serving, indulgent creatures. Except, after a series of chance encounters with Patrina, he comes to appreciate how uniquely different she is than all women he's ever known.

At the Christmastide season, a time of hope and new beginnings, Patrina and Weston, unexpectedly learn true love in one another. However, as Patrina's scandalous past threatens their future and the happiness of his children, they are both left to determine if love is enough.

Always a Rogue, Forever Her Love
Book 4 in the Scandalous Seasons Series

Miss Juliet Marshville is spitting mad. With one guardian missing, and the other singularly uninterested in her fate, she is at the mercy of her wastrel brother who loses her beloved childhood home to a man known as Sin. Determined to reclaim control of Rosecliff Cottage and her own fate, Juliet arranges a meeting with the notorious rogue and demands the return of her property.

Jonathan Tidemore, 5th Earl of Sinclair, known to the *ton* as Sin, is exceptionally lucky in life and at the gaming tables. He has just one problem. Well…four, really. His incorrigible sisters have driven off yet another governess. This time, however, his mother demands he find an appropriate replacement.

When Miss Juliet Marshville boldly demands the return of her precious cottage, he takes advantage of his sudden good fortune and puts an offer to her; turn his sisters into proper English ladies, and he'll return Rosecliff Cottage to Juliet's possession.

Jonathan comes to appreciate Juliet's spirit, courage, and clever wit, and decides to claim the fiery beauty as his mistress. Juliet, however, will be mistress for no man. Nor could she ever love a man who callously stole her home in a game of cards. As Jonathan begins to see Juliet as more than a spirited beauty to warm his bed, he realizes she could be a lady he could love the rest of his life, if only he can convince the proud Juliet that he's worthy of her hand and heart.

Always Proper, Suddenly Scandalous
Book 3 in the Scandalous Seasons Series

Geoffrey Winters, Viscount Redbrooke was not always the hard, unrelenting lord driven by propriety. After a tragic mistake, he resolved to honor his responsibility to the Redbrooke line and live a life, free of scandal. Knowing his duty is to wed a proper, respectable English miss, he selects Lady Beatrice Dennington, daughter of the Duke of Somerset, the perfect woman for him. Until he meets Miss Abigail Stone...

To distance herself from a personal scandal, Abigail Stone flees America to visit her uncle, the Duke of Somerset. Determined to never trust a man again, she is helplessly intrigued by the hard, too-proper Geoffrey. With his strict appreciation for decorum and order, he is nothing like the man' she's always dreamed of.

Abigail is everything Geoffrey does not need. She upends his carefully ordered world at every encounter. As they begin to care for one another, Abigail carefully guards the secret that resulted in her journey to England.

Only, if Geoffrey learns the truth about Abigail, he must decide which he holds most dear: his place in Society or Abigail's place in his heart.

Never Courted, Suddenly Wed
Book 2 in the Scandalous Seasons Series

Christopher Ansley, Earl of Waxham, has constructed a perfect image for the *ton*—the ladies love him and his company is desired by all. Only two people know the truth about Waxham's secret. Unfortunately, one of them is Miss Sophie Winters.

Sophie Winters has known Christopher since she was in leading strings. As children, they delighted in tormenting each other. Now at two and twenty, she still has a tendency to find herself in scrapes, and her marital prospects are slim.

When his father threatens to expose his shame to the *ton*, unless he weds Sophie for her dowry, Christopher concocts a plan to remain a bachelor. What he didn't plan on was falling in love with the lively, impetuous Sophie. As secrets are exposed, will Christopher's love be enough when she discovers his role in his father's scheme?

Forever Betrothed, Never the Bride
Book 1 in the Scandalous Seasons Series

Hopeless romantic Lady Emmaline Fitzhugh is tired of sitting with the wallflowers, waiting for her betrothed to come to his senses and marry her. When Emmaline reads one too many reports of his scandalous liaisons in the gossip rags, she takes matters into her own hands.

War-torn veteran Lord Drake devotes himself to forgetting his days on the Peninsula through an endless round of meaningless associations. He no longer wants to feel anything, but Lady Emmaline is making it hard to maintain a state of numbness. With her zest for life, she awakens his passion and desire for love.

The one woman Drake has spent the better part of his life avoiding is now the only woman he needs, but he is no longer a man worthy of his Emmaline. It is up to her to show him the healing power of love.

A Season of Hope
A Danby Novella

Five years ago when her love, Marcus Wheatley, failed to return from fighting Napoleon's forces, Lady Olivia Foster buried her heart. Unable to betray Marcus's memory, Olivia has gone out of her way to run off prospective suitors. At three and twenty she considers herself firmly on the shelf. Her father, however, disagrees and accepts an offer for Olivia's hand in marriage. Yet it's Christmas, when anything can happen…

Olivia receives a well-timed summons from her grandfather, the Duke of Danby, and eagerly embraces the reprieve from her betrothal.

Only, when Olivia arrives at Danby Castle she realizes the Christmas season represents hope, second chances, and even miracles.

"WINNING A LADY'S HEART"
A Danby Novella

Author's Note: This is a novella that was originally available in A Summons From The Castle (The Regency Christmas Summons Collection). It is being published as an individual novella.

~★~

For Lady Alexandra, being the source of a cold, calculated wager is bad enough…but when it is waged by Nathaniel Michael Winters, 5th Earl of Pembroke, the man she's in love with, it results in a broken heart, the scandal of the season, and a summons from her grandfather – the Duke of Danby.

To escape Society's gossip, she hurries to her meeting with the duke, determined to put memories of the earl far behind. Except the duke has other plans for Alexandra…plans which include the 5th Earl of Pembroke!

TEMPTED BY A LADY'S SMILE
Book 4 in the "Lords of Honor" Series

Richard Jonas has loved but one woman—a woman who belongs to his brother. Refusing to suffer any longer, he evades his family in order to barricade his heart from unrequited love. While attending a friend's summer party, Richard's approach to love is changed after sharing a passionate and life-altering kiss with a vibrant and mysterious woman. Believing he was incapable of loving again, Richard finds himself tempted by a young lady determined to marry his best friend.

Gemma Reed has not been treated kindly by the *ton*. Often disregarded for her appearance and interests unlike those of a proper lady, Gemma heads to house party to win the heart of Lord Westfield, the man she's loved for years. But her plan is set off course by the tempting and intriguing, Richard Jonas.

A chance meeting creates a new path for Richard and Gemma to forage—but can two people, scorned and shunned by those they've loved from afar, let down their guards to find true happiness?

"RESCUED BY A LADY'S LOVE"
Book 3 in the "Lords of Honor" Series

Destitute and determined to finally be free of any man's shackles, Lily Benedict sets out to salvage her honor. With no choice but to commit a crime that will save her from her past, she enters the home of the recluse, Derek Winters, the new Duke of Blackthorne. But entering the "Beast of Blackthorne's" lair proves more threatening than she ever imagined.

With half a face and a mangled leg, Derek—once rugged and charming—only exists within the confines of his home. Shunned by society, Derek is leery of the hauntingly beautiful Lily Benedict. As time passes, she slips past his defenses, reminding him how to live again. But when Lily's sordid past comes back, threatening her life, it's up to Derek to find the strength to become the hero he once was. Can they overcome the darkness of their sins to find a life of love and redemption?

CAPTIVATED BY A LADY'S CHARM
Book 2 in the "Lords of Honor" Series

In need of a wife…

Christian Villiers, the Marquess of St. Cyr, despises the role he's been cast into as fortune hunter but requires the funds to keep his marquisate solvent. Yet, the sins of his past cloud his future, preventing him from seeing beyond his fateful actions at the Battle of Toulouse. For he knows inevitably it will catch up with him, and everyone will remember his actions on the battlefield that cost so many so much—particularly his best friend.

In want of a husband…

Lady Prudence Tidemore's life is plagued by familial scandals, which makes her own marital prospects rather grim. Surely there is one gentleman of the ton who can look past her family and see just her and all she has to offer?

When Prudence runs into Christian on a London street, the charming, roguish gentleman immediately captures her attention. But then a chance meeting becomes a waltz, and now…

A Perfect Match…

All she must do is convince Christian to forget the cold requirements he has for his future marchioness. But the demons in his past prevent him from turning himself over to love. One thing is certain—Prudence wants the marquess and is determined to have him in her life, now and forever. It's just a matter of convincing Christian he wants the same.

SEDUCED BY A LADY'S HEART
Book 1 in the "Lords of Honor" Series

You met Lieutenant Lucien Jones in "Forever Betrothed, Never the Bride" when he was a broken soldier returned from fighting Boney's forces. This is his story of triumph and happily-ever-after!

~★~

Lieutenant Lucien Jones, son of a viscount, returned from war, to find his wife and child dead. Blaming his father for the commission that sent him off to fight Boney's forces, he was content to languish at London Hospital… until offered employment on the Marquess of Drake's staff. Through his position, Lucien found purpose in life and is content to keep his past buried.

Lady Eloise Yardley has loved Lucien since they were children. Having long ago given up on the dream of him, she married another. Years later, she is a young, lonely widow who does not fit in with the ton. When Lucien's family enlists her aid to reunite father and son, she leaps at the opportunity to not only aid her former friend, but to also escape London.

Lucien doesn't know what scheme Eloise has concocted, but

knowing her as he does, when she pays a visit to his employer, he knows she's up to something. The last thing he wants is the temptation that this new, older, mature Eloise presents; a tantalizing reminder of happier times and peace.

Yet Eloise is determined to win Lucien's love once and for all... if only Lucien can set aside the pain of his past and risk all on a lady's heart.

ONLY FOR THEIR LOVE
Book 3 in the "The Theodosia Sword" Series

Miss Carol Cresswall bore witness to her parents' loveless union and is determined to avoid that same miserable fate. Her mother has altogether different plans—plans that include a match between Carol and Lord Gregory Renshaw. Despite his wealth and power, Carol has no interest in marrying a pompous man who goes out of his way to ignore her. Now, with their families coming together for the Christmastide season it's her mother's last-ditch effort to get them together. And Carol plans to avoid Gregory at all costs.

Lord Gregory Renshaw has no intentions of falling prey to his mother's schemes to marry him off to a proper debutante she's picked out. Over the years, he has carefully sidestepped all endeavors to be matched with any of the grasping ladies.

But a sudden Christmastide Scandal has the potential show Carol and Gregory that they've spent years running from the one thing they've always needed.

Only For Her Honor
Book 2 in the "The Theodosia Sword" Series

A wounded soldier:

When Captain Lucas Rayne returned from fighting Boney's forces, he was a shell of a man. A recluse who doesn't leave his family's estate, he's content to shut himself away. Until he meets Eve...

A woman alone in the world:

Eve Ormond spent most of her life following the drum alongside her late father. When his shameful actions bring death and pain to English soldiers, Eve is forced back to England, an outcast. With no family or marital prospects she needs employment and finds it in Captain Lucas Rayne's home. A man whose life was ruined by her father, Eve has no place inside his household. With few options available, however, Eve takes the post. What she never anticipates is how with their every meeting, this honorable, hurting soldier slips inside her heart.

The Secrets Between Them:

The more time Lucas spends with Eve, he remembers what it is to be alive and he lets the walls protecting his heart down. When the secrets between them come to light will their love be enough? Or are they two destined for heartbreak?

Only For His Lady
Book 1 in the "The Theodosia Sword" Series

A curse. A sword. And the thief who stole her heart.

The Rayne family is trapped in a rut of bad luck. And now, it's up to Lady Theodosia Rayne to steal back the Theodosia sword, a gladius that was pilfered by the rival, loathed Renshaw family. Hopefully, recovering the stolen sword will break the cycle and reverse her family's fate.

Damian Renshaw, the Duke of Devlin, is feared by all—all, that is, except Lady Theodosia, the brazen spitfire who enters his home and wrestles an ancient relic from his wall. Intrigued by the vivacious woman, Devlin has no intentions of relinquishing the sword to her.

As Theodosia and Damian battle for ownership, passion ignites. Now, they are torn between their age-old feud and the fire that burns between them. Can two forbidden lovers find a way to make amends before their families' war tears them apart?

MY LADY OF DECEPTION
Book 1 in the "Brethren of the Lords" Series

This dark, sweeping Regency novel was previously only offered as part of the limited edition box sets: "From the Ballroom and Beyond", "Romancing the Rogue", and "Dark Deceptions". Now, available for the first time on its own, exclusively through Amazon is "My Lady of Deception".

~★~

Everybody has a secret. Some are more dangerous than others.

For Georgina Wilcox, only child of the notorious traitor known as "The Fox", there are too many secrets to count. However, after her interference results in great tragedy, she resolves to never help another... until she meets Adam Markham.

Lord Adam Markham is captured by The Fox. Imprisoned, Adam loses everything he holds dear. As his days in captivity grow, he finds himself fascinated by the young maid, Georgina, who cares for him.

When the carefully crafted lies she's built between them begin to crumble, Georgina realizes she will do anything to prove her love and loyalty to Adam—even it means at the expense of her own life.

NON-FICTION WORKS BY
CHRISTI CALDWELL

**Uninterrupted Joy: Memoir: My Journey through
Infertility, Pregnancy, and Special Needs**

The following journey was never intended for publication.
It was written from a mother, to her unborn child. The words
detailed her struggle through infertility and the joy of finally being
pregnant. A stunning revelation at her son's birth opened a world
of both fear and discovery. This is the story of one mother's love
and hope and…her quest for uninterrupted joy.

$\mathcal{B}$IOGRAPHY

Christi Caldwell is the bestselling author of historical romance novels set in the Regency era. Christi blames Judith McNaught's "Whitney, My Love," for luring her into the world of historical romance. While sitting in her graduate school apartment at the University of Connecticut, Christi decided to set aside her notes and try her hand at writing romance. She believes the most perfect heroes and heroines have imperfections and rather enjoys tormenting them before crafing a well-deserved happily ever after!

When Christi isn't writing the stories of flawed heroes and heroines, she can be found in her Southern Connecticut home chasing around her eight-year-old son, and caring for twin princesses-in-training!

Visit *www.christicaldwellauthor.com* to learn more about what Christi is working on, or join her on Facebook at Christi Caldwell Author, and Twitter *@ChristiCaldwell*